TAKEN BY THE ALPHA KING

ABIGAIL BARNETTE

ALSO BY ABIGAIL BARNETTE

Bad Boy, Good Man

Surrender

Where We Land

THE SOPHIE SCAIFE SERIES

The Stranger

The Boss

The Girlfriend

The Bride

The Ex

The Baby

The Sister

The Boyfriend

Sophie

THE BY-THE-NUMBERS SERIES

First Time (Penny's Story)

First Time (Ian's Story)

Second Chance (Penny's Story)

Second Chance (Ian's Story)

Baby Makes Three (Penny's Story)

Baby Makes Three (Ian's Story)

TAKEN
BY THE
ALPHA
KING

ABIGAIL BARNETTE

CHAPTER 1

February 15, 2017

I can't believe I did it.

Brushing my fingertips over the indentations of my words on the paper, I try to remember how I felt when I wrote them. Vague ideas like "exhilarated" and "terrified" come to me, but I can't experience that day again, no matter how hard I imagine.

It was the day my life completely changed. The day I invoked the right to leave our pack and live a mortal life for five years, instead of simply accepting the transformation and becoming a full werewolf.

The intercom chimed its gentle breakfast announcement and I put my old diary back in the bedside drawer, where it's awaited my return for the past five years. But I'm not the seventeen-year-old I was when I left. I'm a grown-up stranger in that girl's bedroom, with its soft pink canopy bed curtains and gleaming white furniture.

You just got home, I remind myself. *Give it time.*

I go to the vanity where I spent so many teenage hours practicing my eyeliner skills and contouring my face to

Kardashian perfection. Things were much simpler then, before I heard of the Right of Accord. I hurry through my makeup routine—I may have arrived in the middle of the night, but Vivianne Dixon expects her children to look "acceptable" to her standards no matter the circumstances —and dig through one of my wardrobe trunks for a silk floral peasant top and dark wash jeans.

My childhood home is an outdated "modern" mansion my parents had custom built in the late eighties, long before I was born. Our kind—*their kind,* until I make my final decision—live long enough to make a lot of bad style choices. Mother and father have already tucked into their breakfast in the stark white, oblong dining room. The black Lucite dining table is set with square white platters of more food than we'll eat, and mother looks up from taking a helping of mixed fruits from one of them. The cold blue light of the early morning filters down from the octagonal skylight and creates a halo of silver around her gray hair.

"Darling, I didn't expect to see you this morning. Hudson said you didn't arrive until nearly four." She doesn't rise from her seat, but waits for me to lean down so she can kiss the air beside my cheek. "That's an…interesting top."

"Thanks." I pretend she means it, and round the table to put an arm around my father's shoulder in a half-hug. By the time he swallows his toast and dabs his mouth with his napkin, I'm already back to my seat. I shake out my own linen napkin and smooth it over my lap. "I did get in late."

"Well, it's a long flight from London," father says, and it's probably all he'll have to say for the whole breakfast.

Mother will make up for it. "Other than the delay, how was your flight?"

"It was fine." I take a croissant and some fruit, my stomach still roiling from the salmon I ate on the plane. It had not agreed with me. "I slept most of the way."

"Good. Then you won't be too jet lagged for tonight."

"Mother—" I begin, but she doesn't look at me, concentrating on buttering half of an English muffin. If she doesn't look at me, she can pretend I haven't objected.

"Of course, if your flight had arrived on time, we would have been able to get you something suitable to wear." She glances up and briefly purses her lips. "No matter. I had Tara send over a few gowns. From before she gained all that weight."

I may have been gone for five years, but I've seen plenty of photos of my sister on Facebook. She's gone up a single dress-size, maybe.

Totally unacceptable for a daughter of Vivianne Dixon.

"Look, I just got in and the ball is a lot—"

"A lot of work?" Mother interrupts me. "Yes. It is. It's what makes it an obligation. And it's also the perfect opportunity to make a fresh debut to the pack. To show them that your little...walkabout, as it were, is finally over."

"I haven't—" I stop myself. I've been in my parents' presence for minutes and my mother has already started making me feel bonkers. I'm not about to start my first morning back with an argument.

"You haven't had time to unpack or do anything with your hair," she says, waving her hand.

I self-consciously touch my freshly straightened blonde locks.

"I've booked Jonathan for two hours with you today,"

she prattles on. "Not enough time to fix those highlights, but I'm sure he can make something out of all..."

My fists clench under the table as she gestures vaguely at my problem areas. Which, to her, is all of me.

"Listen..." I begin tentatively. It will do me no good to sound argumentative. "I know what a huge deal the ball is and how long everyone has prepared for it. I don't want to drag you all down and make you look bad."

"Nonsense, puppy," father says placidly, his eyes scanning his iPad the way he used to ignore us for the newspaper. "You could never make us look bad."

Mother chokes on her coffee and tries to pass it off as a gently teasing laugh. "Well. There was that one teensy little time."

The time I invoked my right to think for myself, to not accept the transformation as my fate. The time I dared put myself before the Dixon name.

"But that's all in the past. You're home now." Mother's smile is a warning. "And Ashton has been asking about you."

My stomach curdles in a way that has nothing to do with the first-class salmon. "Oh?"

"He's never given up on you," she goes on with a sigh. "Very romantic, if you ask me."

Or pathetic, if she asked me, but she didn't. I keep it to myself. There's nothing romantic about the idea of returning to my old life, my old fate, delayed by five years. I assumed that by rejecting the transformation, I effectively rejected Ashton Daniels.

"I thought he would have found a mate by now." *Hoped.* I hoped he had found a mate by now. But if he didn't...

"No. He's never renounced his claim on you, even after your little tantrum."

"It wasn't a tantrum, it was—" I stop myself, force another smile, and subdue my sigh of frustration. "I just hoped he would have moved on and found happiness, rather than waiting around for me."

"I suppose that's guilt you'll simply have to live with." Mother's words pointedly imply that my former fiancé isn't the only person I should feel badly about inconveniencing. "It's possible he's forgiven you."

"And it's possible he hasn't, and he'll mention that tonight, in front of everyone," Father adds helpfully.

Mother nods. "A bridge you'll need to cross when we come to it, Bailey. You publicly humiliated the poor man."

He was a poor boy, then, and at the time, I did feel terrible about invoking the right. But he had a choice. He could have invoked the right himself and come with me, if he really wanted to be together.

Thankfully, he didn't.

"And if he decides to humiliate me in return with a public rejection tonight, I can accept that." Besides, ending our engagement is the least he can do for both of us.

"He wouldn't dare," Mother reassures me. "The Fealty Rite is too important to risk making a scene."

Another warning. I'm not to fuck anything up for her, tonight. I already destroyed her carefully cultivated image in front of the pack.

Hudson, the thrall Mother and Father hired as our butler right before I left for London, enters, pushing a cart bearing two trays covered by silver domes.

It's a myth that werewolves can't touch silver.

Mother sits back as he places the plate in front of her and

lifts the lid. A human heart, glistening with congealed blood, rests on a bed of lettuce. Mother gasps in delight and softly claps her hands in appreciation. "Bravo, Hudson. I don't know where you keep finding these perfect little morsels."

"A trade secret, ma'am." He retrieves the other platter and sets it in front of father, lifting the dome to reveal a nearly identical meal. Father mutters a thank you, and both my parents take up their silverware and tuck in, traditional breakfasts forgotten.

It's a sight I've seen hundreds of times, before every religious ceremony and full moon over the course of my entire life. But after five years living among the humans, I view the organs a bit more personally.

As in, they were once people.

Either I hide my disgust well or my mother ignores it. She cuts a slice from the heart in front of her and nods toward my plate. "Well. Eat up. We have a busy day."

I choke my down croissant. My dread at the thought of the ball, of seeing Ashton again? Much harder to swallow.

CHAPTER 2

Toronto has no shortage of impressive houses, but Aconitum Hall is in a class of its own. Built long before the skyscrapers and urban planning, the city has crept up to the mansion's tower walls and tiered gardens, preserving it as a fairytale castle out of time. And since the very first stone was set into the foundation, it's been the traditional home of our pack leader.

It's Buckingham Palace but packed full of werewolves.

But it doesn't look much like the Queen's house. Aconitum Hall was built in early gothic revival style, which I know only from taking the tour more than once on school trips. It could easily be mistaken for a cathedral at first glance. There are spires on some of the conical tower roofs and a *ton* of gargoyles. Two of them leer down at us through the sunroof of the car as we pull beneath the porte cochere.

"First, we're received by the king. When everyone has arrived, dinner will be served," Mother repeats for me, as if I somehow forgot on the drive. "After that, dancing and socializing. Make sure you speak to at least one member of each family."

So they know our wayward daughter has fallen in line again. She doesn't need to explain that part.

The car pulls to a stop and a valet opens the back door. Mother and Father, who spent the ride in the seats across from me, get out first, before I, slightly carsick from the backwards facing ride, maneuver myself out. A regal red carpet is our path up the steps and into the blazing golden light of the massive foyer.

"Your wraps, ma'am, miss?" a valet asks as we enter. Mother and I hand over our furs and Father shrugs out of his smart wool coat, tucking the coat-check slip into the inside pocket of his tuxedo jacket. Though werewolves are more tolerant of the cold than humans, it's still January in Toronto, and the breeze from the open doors behind us raise gooseflesh on the nape of my neck.

Mother's stylist, Jonathan, has worked my ash blonde hair into a loose, romantic up do that looks tousled and free despite remaining entirely stationary no matter how much I might shake my head. A delicate halo of spun silver wire studded with winking white diamonds weaves through my soft curls, matching the crystal rhinestones clustered at the hem of my gray tulle overskirt. The gems rise and disperse liking fading constellations, and the silver silk layer beneath glows like the face of the moon.

It's not my dress, it's not how I would have worn my hair, and this is very much not a party I want to be at.

"Come along," Mother whispers with a tight smile, nudging me forward to join the line of partygoers waiting to be announced in the throne room.

My strappy silver heels are already digging into my feet. I can predict where the blisters will be tomorrow morning. That is, if I don't slip on the marble floor and split my head open.

"Aren't we going to wait for Tara and Clare?" I ask. In the past, we've all been together when my father has declared our allegiance to the pack.

The question discomfits my father; he looks as if he'll feel my forehead to make sure I'm not ill. "Tara and Clare are married, Bailey. They have their own families. They'll declare themselves with their mates."

"Oh, right." I know that they got married—missing their post-mating ceremony receptions had been one of the few sacrifices I deeply regretted making when I left—but I still can't quite get my head around my sisters being actual grown-ups.

Mother sees her opening and swoops in for the kill. "And next year, if the fates are willing, you'll do the same."

If the fates are willing. Whether or not *I'm* willing isn't her concern.

I don't address her remark. "I can't wait to see Tara and Clare. And finally meet their mates."

All I know about them is what I could learn from a few brief phone calls. My family wasn't supposed to be in contact with me while I was away in the mortal world, but my sisters and I have always been rule breakers. Tara's husband, Josh, went to school with us and now owns a social media company valued in the hundreds of millions. Clare's mate, Julian, is a partner at my father's firm, which Ashton hoped to be, back when he chose me for his future mate. I wonder if Father gave him a job as a consolation prize when I left.

I hear the drone of the majordomo announcing the names of the families as they enter the throne room, but we're not close enough that I can make them out. Everyone in the foyer is joyous and friendly. Mother and Father chat with the couple behind them and I cast my gaze down the line.

Five years, and so much has changed that I don't recognize any of the people around us.

When it's our turn, we pass between huge, black marble pillars and pause beneath the enormous glass and steel chandelier sculpted into an effigy of the moon in all her phases.

"Thomas Dixon the third, his mate, Vivianne Harcourt-Dixon, and his daughter, Bailey Dixon," the man's voice booms. He's a different majordomo than the man who previously held the position my entire life; yet another reminder that the world I walked away from has moved on in my absence.

As is the man standing on the dais.

I remember King Victor being a broad-shouldered sloucher with a well-groomed beard and a slight paunch, like an extra from *How to Train Your Dragon* dressed in an expensive suit.

The man we approach is not King Victor. This man, whoever he is, stands tall and straight. This man wears a tuxedo like the concept of tuxedos was invented because of him. I can't look away from the sharpness of his clean-shaven jawline or the intense gray of his eyes, which lock on mine. His black hair is short and parted at the side, and a hint of silver touches its strands.

Mother, head down, nudges me and I remember to curtsey, wobbling a little. I can't blame it all on being out of practice. The new king is so handsome he's knocked the wind out of me.

"Rise," the new king says, and his accent makes me

homesick for London. "Do you remain faithful to the pack?"

I keep my eyes downcast as the three of us answer the ritual question. "Yes, my king and my pack leader."

"And do you submit to the word of your king and pack leader?"

I can't help but glance up, and heat floods my face as I find he's looking at me while the three of us respond. When I tear my gaze quickly away, I still feel his willing me to meet it again. There's a confidence about him that has nothing to do with his position, an aura that fills the space between us and makes the air heavy as I breathe it into my lungs.

"Yes, my king and my pack leader," squeaks from my throat. I can barely catch my breath; I wonder how many people have passed out in front of him.

"Do you surrender your will for the good of the pack?"

That's the question that trapped my parents in their loveless, boring marriage. It's the question that will lead to becoming Ashton's mate.

The question that will mean my expulsion from the pack if I don't make my decision on the transformation, and soon. I can't invoke the right again. My time is up.

But to avoid the passive-aggressive wrath of my mother, I'm compelled to say, "Yes, my king and my pack leader."

The king motions my father forward, to the bottom of the dais steps. "As you would bleed for the pack, so would your pack shed the blood of your enemies." The ancient creed, which always sounded so ruthless to my younger ears, is like a low, sensual promise in the king's elegant voice. When he extends the royal signet ring for my father to kiss, I fixate on the veins on the back of the large, royal hand.

I remember to curtsey this time, and somehow stagger away, our family's tribute over. We move toward the doors to the grand ballroom, but whatever lies beyond them doesn't hold the same fascination as the man I just bowed before, the man to whom I ritually surrendered my will.

Did I imagine the way he seemed to focus solely on me as the three of us stood before him? Did he feel the charge crackling between us or did I invent it from a combination of nervousness and emotional confusion? I've never reacted so strongly to anyone at first sight. I can't even decide if it's a positive reaction or if he wildly intimidates me.

The majordomo calls the name of the next family entering the throne room, and I decide it's safe to take one last, quick look back at the king while his attention is on them. But the moment I turn my head, I'm caught.

The king is watching me walk away.

CHAPTER 3

While we eat, Mother, Tara, and Clare fill me in on the new king. My first assumption is the most obvious one: the old king died. But he has a son, and that son is not Nathan Frost, current ruler of the Toronto pack.

"Deposed," Mother explains, subtly inclining her head and lowering her voice. We won't be heard. Not over the clink of silverware, the laughing, and all the other gossip floating around. "He mated some ridiculously young thing, not much older than Clare, and installed her as queen. You can imagine how his children felt about that."

My sister, Clare, sits on my left. She's the most beautiful of all of us, more regal looking, even, than Mother.

It has been a point of who's-the-fairest-of-them-all contention in the past.

Clare's ruby pendant earrings swing as she leans in. "And imagine how his children felt when they were removed from the line of succession."

I take a sip of my wine. "I still don't understand how that leads to a random English guy coming in and taking over."

"Hush!" Mother warns sharply. "He is still your king."

Across the round table, my sister Tara doesn't bother to lower her voice. "There was a power vacuum and the Greater London pack stepped in."

Her mate, Josh, leans over and whispers something to her, and she is instantly subdued. I hate it. He seems like a nice enough guy, but he was brought up in the same society as every other man in this ballroom, and by the law of the pack they have the final say over the members of their families.

Except in one respect. My father's word wasn't as powerful as the Right of Accord.

My eyes widen and I glance at Mother. "Are we under occupation?"

"We *were* under occupation." Clare's husband, Julian, is as gorgeous as she is, with nearly identical honey blond hair. He has the same wry tone, as well. "Then everyone got over it."

"Not everyone," Clare whispers, nodding toward a table near ours, but I don't recognize any of the people seated at it. Our way of life doesn't allow me to overlook them; I memorize who is seated near whom, taking in every face.

"Oh, look," Mother announces suddenly as a thrall waiter approaches. "Dessert."

Tara shoots me an expression that promises we'll talk later.

And we do. After dinner becomes drinks and dancing, my sisters and I leave for the restroom and "get lost" along the way, stepping into a windowed alcove to talk, unencumbered by their mates.

"Look, Mother doesn't want to talk about it and Father

will never admit it, but Greater London *is* occupying the Toronto pack. King Victor made a huge mistake by taking his children out of the line of succession before securing a new heir."

"But why did the pack depose him? Because they didn't like who he married?" Such a thing is unheard of in modern times.

"Because he knew she had illegal dealings with the Manhattan pack," Tara explains. Of the two of my sisters, she looks the most like me, with the same ash blonde hair and easily readable face, which condemns our former pack leader. "And he covered them up."

"He lied to the council when confronted," Clare adds. "He lied to the pack."

"Wow. I guess I missed a lot while I was gone." My stomach is hollow. I've returned to the middle of a war. "Who were those people at the table you pointed out?"

Clare knows exactly what I'm referring to. "The Rogers family. Their daughter, Amber, was the queen who created this problem in the first place."

"Her family still thinks she has a claim. There's a rumor that King Nathaniel is in love with her and plans to bring her back to the pack," Tara whispers, an uncharacteristic volume choice but a smart one, when one is talking about one's supreme ruler. "You can imagine how nervous that makes the members of the council who *don't* want to see Frost removed from the throne."

It should make everyone in the castle tonight nervous. A deposed queen whose family hasn't been exiled is a danger; more so when she's the object of an invading conqueror's interest. It would only take a simple mating ceremony to neatly hand the Toronto pack over to Greater

London, with the support of one of the most powerful packs in North America.

We could lose everything.

And the commander of the opposing forces is walking down the strip of red carpet in the hall outside the ballroom. He's talking to someone, laughing as they move briskly in our direction.

My palms sweat. "Why don't we go back to the ballroom? I need a drink to handle all this."

"I don't blame you," Clare says, and to my relief she doesn't seem to have noticed the King headed our way.

I don't want him to walk past. I don't want to curtsey to him only to find he doesn't even notice our presence there. But I also don't want him to notice me. He already noticed me, and I nearly had an asthma attack. Now that I know he's a hostile in our pack, I don't want him to notice me, ever again.

I lead the way, my sisters trying to keep up behind me, and strike out on a direct course to the nearest catering bar. A tall, slender man turns as I approach, and he smiles as if he recognizes me.

It takes me a moment to recognize him.

"I think we'll go back to the table," Clare says, and before Tara can protest, she manhandles her off.

When I invoked the right five years ago, I did so not just to see what the human world had to offer. It was a potential escape from the mating claim my father had signed, sealing me to Ashton Daniels. Now, Ashton stands in front of me, nothing at all like the scrawny, awkward teenager I left behind. His smile grows—his teeth are perfect—and his blue eyes crinkle at the corners with genuine happiness to see me. His ginger complexion isn't as shockingly pale, his hair looks more like a rusty brown than the flame orange we all teased him about during our school days.

He puts his arms out—despite the black tie dress code, he's somehow gotten away with wearing navy blue, blowing the sartorial competition out of the water. I only realize that I'm gaping at him in what probably appears to be horror when his smile suddenly falters and fades. "You don't remember me."

His voice has changed, too. It's deeper, but he's still soft-spoken, and the effect is like warm honey. I stammer a little as I answer. "I—of course, I remember you." I burst into laughter and a smile I have to fake out of the sheer shock of the moment. Just to give myself a second to recover, I put out my arms, too.

He hugs me so tightly, I almost can't breathe; his arms are rock hard at my back. Leaning down close, he says softly, "I was so afraid you wouldn't come back."

Alarm bells go off in my mind. I step back from him and tilt my head, pretending to check my immovable hairdo to avoid looking him in the eye.

"You've been gone for five years," he says, suddenly pragmatic. "You might not feel the same way toward me that you did before you left."

How do you know what I felt for you? I almost snap.

My memory drifts back to the day he knocked on my bedroom door, startling me with his presence in my house, startling me more with the announcement that my father signed a mating pact. Ashton and I barely knew each other; though we were both educated at the private academy all children of the Toronto pack attend, we weren't friends. We barely spoke to each other before he approached my father.

To this day, I'm still not sure what Ashton truly sought

from our engagement. Maybe it was a rash decision made under the influence of a young, unrequited crush. He wanted a job from my father, so maybe Ashton thought a marriage would secure that position for him. Whatever the reason, I barely know this man standing in front of me, behaving like we're long-separated lovers.

My feelings for him haven't changed. Because they never existed in the first place.

"I thought you would have called off the mating pact by now," I say, praying "hope" doesn't replace a crucial word as I speak.

"Never." He shakes his head firmly and takes my hand, lacing our fingers together.

Somehow, in the five years that I've been gone, completely cut off from communication with the pack, I've been involved in a grand romance with my fiancé, a man I barely know.

"I appreciate that." What else is there to say? "My mother would be humiliated."

"I wouldn't do anything to embarrass your family. When they've already been through so much." He cuts himself off and his pained expression stops just short of a wince.

"It's all right," I reassure him. It's not all right; I don't like to be reminded that I'm a black sheep in a den of wolves. "I don't want to do anything to embarrass them, either."

And I realize too late, as he puts his arm around my waist, that he could take that as a declaration that I won't be breaking our engagement. That I will accept the transformation and stay with the pack for the rest of my life. I might as well have sworn fealty to *him*, with that remark.

He leads me toward the dance floor, saying, "Come. We never had a chance to make our debut properly."

I've been home fewer than twenty-four hours and I'm already right back to the world I left behind. All I did by leaving was delay the inevitable. I was a fool for thinking I would ever truly leave the pack.

My stomach roils as Ashton leads me onto the dance floor, where couples float and twirl to a waltz from a string quartet. I feel eyes on us from all the other pairs; he's handsome, he's suave, and he dances with such grace it extends to me. I tell myself that's why everyone is staring, why I see so many smug faces and tight-lipped whispers happening all around us.

But I'm not optimistic enough to believe it. They see Baily Dixon, who exploited an ancient rule to leave her pack. Who ran out on a mating pact, who rejected the transformation and in doing so made her family a subject of gossip and derision. They're all wondering what I'll do next to fuck up.

I want to vomit, and the twirling of the waltz doesn't help. I close my eyes and hold tightly to Ashton's shoulder, praying for the music to finish. Mercifully, it does, and we step apart to politely applaud the quartet.

I know an exit when I see one. I turn to Ashton to tell him I need to go out for some air, but before I can speak, I see the king striding toward me, his mouth bent in a mildly crooked smile.

He stops in front of us and inclines his head toward me. "Miss Dixon."

He knows my name. Not only that, but he doesn't even acknowledge Ashton standing beside me.

"Pack Leader," I whisper, curtseying.

I keep my eyes downcast and see his hand, with the

heavy royal signet ring, reaching for my own. He's the king. I let him take it and rise, praying my palm isn't as sweaty as I fear. The strings start up a tango.

He doesn't release my hand. "Will you honor me with a dance?"

CHAPTER 4

Nathaniel Frost, King of the Toronto pack, guides me smoothly from my fiancé's side. It's that easy for him to simply overwhelm me and render me helpless. It's dizzying, almost exhilarating, definitely terrifying.

"I haven't tangoed often," I manage to warn him as he pulls me far too close.

"It isn't my strong suit, either," he quips, though his feet prove he's lying as they somehow manage to avoid my clumsy ones. "Don't expect any dips or fancy footwork."

I snort; I can't help myself. "With all due respect, Your Majesty, that's about ninety percent of the tango."

"You're wrong," he informs me. "And while we're dancing, call me Nathan."

My mouth drops open. I quickly compose myself and try to shock my brain into remembering what, exactly, my body should be doing. *Step, step, step, close. Step, step, step, close.* Maybe all those dance lessons Mother forced us to take really were a practical choice. If Vivianne Dixon ever imagined that her daughter would be tangoing with the Pack Leader…

But this man isn't truly our King. He's a usurper. He's an enemy, and our bodies touch from ankle to chest. His intense gray eyes lock on mine as one of his large palms splays across my lower back. This is nothing like dancing with Ashton. I don't feel like Nathan is holding an imaginary version of me.

"You're the one who invoked the Right," he whispers.

I freeze, and he takes advantage of the moment to trap my foot with his own. To anyone watching, it's a stylized pause in the dance.

"What did you do in London?" he asks, moving one hand to my hip. I swear the heat from his palm burns through my dress. And yet, somehow, he still seems cold.

"I worked." The physical contact is unbearably distracting. Or maybe the conversation is distracting me from the physical contact and *that's* what I really want to focus on. Either way, it's interminable and I'm thankful that tangos aren't long.

"What kind of work?" *He's* not out of breath. *He's* not flushed and clammy. Somehow, only one of us is affected by the other's proximity and it's mortifying.

"Just office work. For an architectural firm." We move again, a cross-step that requires more concentration as I desperately try to recall those adolescent ballroom lessons. And I realize that's the point; he's picked this specific dance, which, despite his protesting, he's much better at than I am. He's trying to muddle my thoughts with his closeness.

I'm being interrogated via "Por una Cabeza."

Pretending I don't know his game, I add, "I wanted to

truly embrace the reality of being human. Were I to choose that path."

"And you did it without any support from pack members abroad?" He sounds more impressed than incredulous.

Is it a trick? Is he mocking me? I can only answer honestly. "I don't know any pack members abroad."

"Ah. Well. Now you do." His leg smoothly tangles with mine, and I have no choice but to lean into his body.

"You're not abroad. You're right here." I pull back but he leads me in a turn and stops my momentum suddenly.

His face is so close I see flashes of blue against the gray of his eyes like a ring of icicles around his pupils, but his tone is molten heat. "Yes, I am."

My knees almost give out.

The song finishes but he doesn't release me for a long moment. I'm not sure how I want the interaction to end, but just the fact that it *is* ending is a relief and a disappointment all at once.

No one has ever sent my emotions—and libido—spinning as out of control as he does with just a few words or a glance.

"It's been a true pleasure, Bailey," he says finally.

"Same, Nathan."

When a king tells one to call him by his first name, one should try it out at least once.

He grins. I've caught him off guard. Composing himself, he tells me, "Should you visit London in the future, call the royal office. There may be…opportunities to discuss."

And he just walks away like we had a totally normal interaction. He walks away and leaves me standing alone, under the sudden scrutiny of the entire ballroom.

———

The throne room is empty and cold, and I shiver in the darkness. It's not the temperature causing me to tremble; he's here with me, his hand on the nape of my neck. His grip is soft but strong, lightly possessive as he steers me toward the dais.

The King wants me. And I pledged that I would do anything for him.

The thin straps of my gown tear away like paper, leaving me bare before him. He's standing in front of me now, his eyes flashing silver, collecting up every faint trace of light, every stray glimmer from the unlit candelabras on the walls and lines of illumination leaking under the doors.

A predator's eyes that can see in the dark and take in every bit of me.

As *he'll* take every bit of me.

He doesn't need to take. I'll give all of myself, gladly. When he pulls me into his arms, I surrender control of my body over to him. His shirt is butter-soft, but it's still too much against my aching, oversensitive breasts. I need more than a feathery brush of fabric. I want his fingers, his mouth, I want him to reach up and pinch my nipples while I ride his cock.

"Please," I whisper as his lips tease my jaw.

"Grovel before your king," he commands, and I fall to the floor with a cry as pain shocks through my knees. He offers me no comfort. "I said 'grovel'."

He plants his shoe firmly on my shoulder and exerts steady pressure, until my burning skin meets the freezing marble. Then he strolls in a circle around me, every second of silence building my anticipation. What will he tell me to do next? What will he *make me* do next?

And when, oh please, when will he make me do it? I can't bear the wait, can't stand the way the stone warms as it leeches the heat from my body.

He kneels behind me and grips my hips, pulling them back, sliding my upper body along the floor with painful resistance. He grinds against me, still fully clothed, and I know my juices are smearing across the front of his trousers. He's so hard and so big, and I'm totally at his mercy. Only a zipper and his self-control stand between us.

He jerks a fistful of my hair and I let out a moan as he pulls my head back.

"Do you submit to my will?" he asks, his other hand cupping my hot, aching center from behind.

"For the good of the pack," I breathe.

"For your own good," he growls, and then he's biting my neck and I hear his zipper opening, his belt buckle clattering on the floor and it's going to happen, oh God it's happening, and he brushes against my aching core and—

My own cry of release wakes me, and I blink up through the darkness at the canopy over my bed. I kick off the blankets to free my sweaty body.

What the hell was that? And why did my brain have the nerve to wake me up?

Well, technically my pussy woke me up. I remember that happening only one other time in my life. And my brain probably had to snap me out of it this time, since I don't have any reference for how the rest of that dream would go.

I spent five years in the human world, but I have no idea if humans and werewolves can conceive together. It wasn't someone anyone talked about, especially in my family, where my sex talk was, "you don't have to worry about it until you have a mate, stop asking questions." Sure, there was sex ed at our high school, but that was all about the mechanics, and certainly no one addressed inter-species sex. As a result, my personal policy during those five years away was "take no chances."

Maybe I should have. I wouldn't be having horny dreams about our pack leader now.

Liar. I hate to admit it to myself, but I've never been so immediately and intensely attracted to anyone. Sure, there've been people I met and thought, "They're cute," but no one has made the air around me feel ticklish.

And of course, the first person to inspire that feeling just has to be the king *and* a political enemy to a majority of the pack. I don't even know how he seized the throne in the first place. Considering the fact that neither of my parents would even look at me in the car on the way home, I shouldn't ask more questions about it. At least, not from them.

I just danced with our new king, from a foreign court. After I disappeared for five years, to the home city of the pack that's currently taking over mine.

Tonight, Nathan Frost ruined my life.

CHAPTER 5

If there's anyone I *can* question relentlessly about the political nightmare of the past five years, it's my best friends. Hannah, Ryan, and I have been a matching set of three since kindergarten. We still are, even though Ryan and Hannah are mated now.

Despite having been apart for so long, going to their house is like all of us getting together after school. Sure, there was fully immature squeeing over each other when I arrived, but we quickly fell into our old ways, like I didn't break contact with them for five years.

Except for the "my best friends are in a mating bond" thing. "How did that happen, anyway?"

"It was him, or marriage to Dave Byron," Hannah says with a gagging noise.

I echo her disgust with, "Gross."

"Be nice," Ryan admonishes her. "It's not his fault his parents never told him no and gave him every damn thing he wanted."

Hannah ignores him. "Ever look at someone and just

know, deep in your soul, that they were an ugly baby? That's Dave Byron."

We're clustered around the huge island in their enormous kitchen. Hannah's copper curls glint gold under the sophisticated pendant lights hanging at asymmetrical lengths above us. Five years and a baby later, she still looks like a teenager, with her dewy pale skin and freckles. Her wardrobe is more sophisticated now—she used to show up for first period in her pajamas.

Ryan, however, has changed. When I left, he was a chubby, baby-faced Black kid with a penchant for blue lipstick and metal band t-shirts with illegible fonts on them. He grew up into a broad-shouldered dad-type who, yes, is wearing a band t-shirt, but who is also comfortable cooking dinner at a stove with twelve burners.

If they saw how people live outside the pack…

"So, it's a marriage of convenience, then? Just to dodge the Dave?" That's a little depressing. "You know, I always thought you were gay, Ryan. I just thought you were afraid to come out."

"Oh, I am," he answers without hesitation. "It's not just a marriage of convenience for Hannah. She's helping me out, too."

"And the fertility clinic helped us out, as well." Hannah picks up her half-empty beer bottle and tips the neck toward me.

"The gay dude and the asexual woman somehow had trouble conceiving," Ryan says with mock regret.

"Wow, I feel like an asshole for not knowing any of this," I admit.

"You're the one who invoked the Right of Accord and took off," Ryan reminds me.

"But you're back now, right?" Hannah's large brown eyes widen further in trepidation. "You're going to stay?"

"I…" Just by coming back, I'm implying that I'm going to transform and stay with the pack forever. What's the point of telling them about my doubts?

"You can't leave," Hannah says, a hard edge of anger creeping into her words. "Not again."

"You both said you were okay with it." When we found the Right of Accord referenced in a pack history book, we'd never heard of it. All three of us considered invoking it.

"I thought I was, but I'm stupid. I needed you when we were going through all of this, and I couldn't talk to you. They wouldn't give us any information about where you went or what you were doing," she goes on. "I missed you. Don't leave again."

My heart aches. "If I stay, I have to honor the mating pact. And I don't know if I can."

Ryan takes a pan off the heat and leans down to open the oven door. The smell of the steak under the broiler makes my stomach growl. They just went in a minute ago, but he's already removing them.

I don't mind. Transformation or no transformation, werewolves like our meat warm, not cooked.

"We made it work," Ryan says, like the situations are remotely similar.

Hannah has my back. "Uh, no. In our situation, neither of us thought the other one was going to be the traditional submissive little wife. That's what Ashton is going to want her to be."

"And I'll be miserable for the rest of my life." A lump rises in my throat. "But I'll be miserable without you two, and without Tara and Clare."

"I notice Vivianne and Thomas aren't on that list," Hannah says with a snort.

"First of all, they're the ones who set up the stupid mating pact in the first place. Second…they're not talking to me." I deflate a little. I don't know why I feel like I did something wrong; I didn't. The king asked me to dance. Was I supposed to refuse him?

"I heard about the ball. Sorry." Hannah winces.

"Why weren't you there?" It's more a lament than a question. "It was horrifying. Everyone just stared at me."

"If I had known you'd be there, we would have been. We pledged fealty at the morning council session," Hannah says. Ryan shoots a look to her.

"Ryan…are you a member of the council now?" This is interesting. And could work in my favor. It never hurts to have friends in high places.

He shakes his head. "No. Not yet. But I am in the running. Those of us on the shortlist were invited to morning session."

"It seemed more prestigious than the ball," Hannah says, and she's transparently talking bullshit.

I call her on it. "You didn't want to pay for a sitter."

"That too." She gestures to my empty bottle. "Another one?"

"Sure." When she gets up and goes to the refrigerator, I ask, "So, is it a secret?"

"Is what a secret?" she asks.

"Ryan being in the running for a seat on the council. You guys did a secret married couple eye communication thing." I point an accusing finger at Ryan.

"We just don't want to jinx it," Hannah explains. "It's hard to know who your friends are these days."

"Wait…" I sit up straight. "You guys don't know if you should trust *me*?"

"That's not it," Ryan says quickly. "It's just…a lot of stuff happened while you were gone. And you danced with the king last night—"

"Because he asked me to," I protest. "Hannah, would you turn down the pack leader if he asked you to dance? And keep in mind, the alternative is to keep talking to Ashton fucking Daniels."

"Your feelings are hurt," Hannah says, but she doesn't apologize for it.

"They are! I don't even know what's going on in the pack. I haven't talked to anyone for five years. I come back and there's all of this political scandal happening, and now my best friends are accusing me of being a spy or something." This is too much. I rise from my stool. "You know what, I'm gonna pass on dinner. Thanks, though. You have a lovely home."

"Don't be like that," Hannah huffs.

Ryan holds up a plate. "But it just got done."

I stop at the kitchen door. "Why do you even want me in your house if I'm so suspicious?"

"Because you're our friend, dummy." Ryan puts the plate on the island. "But you've been gone for five years. You're out of practice."

"Out of practice?"

"The pack is a different now. If we don't know who to trust, you don't, either. And one stray word…" Hannah's expression falls. "I'm not afraid you're going to run out and betray us. I'm afraid that until you've been here longer than a week, you might get yourself—or someone else—in trouble without even knowing you're doing it."

"You're right. I have no idea what's going on." I move

toward the island, dropping my purse from my shoulder. "Fine. All you really needed to do was say, 'don't tell anybody.' You know I can keep a secret."

"Yeah, but you also give away a lot of stuff by mistake," Ryan says.

And that's fair.

"Can you bring me up to speed on anything?" If they can't, I won't take it personally. I guess I really don't understand what's happening in the pack, if my very best friends are afraid to talk to me.

"Where should we start?" Hannah asks, with a huff that makes it clear the question is rhetorical.

"How about we start with the new king." I feel like a kid with a pathetic crush, but that's not why I'm asking about him. "Specifically, how he ended up becoming king in the first place."

"That's what a lot of people asked, when it happened." Ryan slides a plate toward me. I sheepishly take it; after the temper tantrum I just threw, I feel bad eating. But Ryan doesn't seem bothered. "You know about King Victor's new wife, the one who was dealing with the Manhattan pack, right?" I nod, and he goes on. "It looked like her plan was to wait out Victor—"

"Or kill him," Hannah interjects.

Ryan shakes his head, like they've argued over that take before. "Then, she would marry a member of the Manhattan pack and hand over Toronto."

"And be queen of both," Hannah adds. "She would have been queen of two of the largest packs in North America."

"She's got her eye on King Nathaniel, too," Ryan warns. "Her family needs to be exiled."

"Yeah, why hasn't she been, at least?" I ask.

"That's a part of the mystery," Hannah says with a sigh. "I personally think she owns someone on the council. They're the ones who voted against kicking her out."

"She's going to make a play for the king, that's for sure." Ryan brings over plates for Hannah and himself. "But she's not the reason he's here. That was another council decision."

"That was also bought?" I ask.

Hannah shakes her head and swallows a bite of risotto. "No, he's legitimately in the line of succession. He's Victor's father's second cousin. Something like that."

"If there was bribery involved," Ryan says, talking while chewing, just like when he was a disgusting teenage boy, "it probably wasn't much. Victor cut his sons out of the line of succession, so obviously there are some who think they deserve the throne more. And that's fair; Greater London has made a play for the Toronto pack before. But there's still a lot of suspicion about the whole family."

Hannah raises her beer as if in a toast. "Aren't you glad you came home in time for all this?"

"Oh, yeah. Definitely." I rub my forehead. "And it's great that apparently one dance with the guy puts me at odds with half the pack."

"I wouldn't say half," Ryan reassures me.

Hannah nods in agreement. "More like sixty-five percent."

We laugh, but dread settles like a rock in my stomach. Which isn't fair to the food, frankly; Ryan is an excellent cook.

"This is great," I say, wiping my mouth with my napkin. "Who would have thought the guy who ate nothing but tater tots all through high school would actually grow up to know his way around a kitchen?"

And though we laugh again, I want things to be the way they were before I left. I want to know that my friends have my back completely.

Instead, I feel more alone than ever.

CHAPTER 6

Since we didn't get a chance to talk much at the ball, Tara and Clare suggest we get together for lunch.

At a human restaurant.

I sat through salads and a main course and now I'm sipping my drink and trying not to ask my own sisters if their husbands know where they are.

"…and that's what they were talking about at the— Bailey!" Clare snaps, waving her hand in front of my face.

"Sorry. Too many mimosas." That's a lie. I'm not even tipsy after two of them. I try to focus on what she was telling me. Something about renovations on her master bathroom. "You were saying something about how they couldn't take a wall down?"

"Are you okay?" Tara asks me with genuine concern.

Do I admit to them that my head is all over the place after the ball? That I'm not sure where I belong in the pack? Because if my best friends don't trust me after that, there's no guarantee that my sisters will. Plus, their husbands don't seem like big fans of the new king.

And it's impossible to feel like my sisters' mates aren't an invisible presence at the table with us.

"I'm fine. I just…" I laugh and shrug. "I don't really get the renovations thing. Or the domestic stuff. It's not that I don't care. I just can't relate."

"Yet," Clare reminds me. "Have you gotten an event planner? Lupercalia is right around the corner."

"Um." I look between them. "I don't know—"

Clare waves me off. "Sorry. I'm jumping ahead. Mother's probably got every hour between then and now packed with preparations."

"Exactly." I'm relieved for the excuse to avoid potential talk about Ashton.

I don't want to be with him. I'm not as excited about me getting a mate as everyone around me is.

"Besides, she has a whole year," Tara says, swallowing some water. "They can't do the mating rite until after her first transformation, and Lupercalia is on the full moon this year."

"Get the party locked down now. The sooner the better," Clare presses on. "Mother and Father will be so relieved when everything is settled."

Since deflecting didn't work, I confront her head on. "Relieved how?"

She rolls her eyes like I'm a child. "You're not stupid, Bailey. You know that after the stunt you pulled invoking that loophole—"

"A right, not a loophole," I interrupt to correct her.

She doesn't pay attention. "—we're all hoping that Ashton can be a stabilizing influence for you."

"A stabilizing—" I begin, my fists clenching under the table.

"Are you coming to the full moon ceremony?" Tara asks, like it's at all possible to change the subject now.

"Um, yeah." My own sisters don't want to be seen in werewolf establishments with me; maybe Tara is asking because she wants to be forewarned. "I'd like to attend before my first transformation. If I'm not too much of an embarrassment to the family."

Tara and Clare share a look, before Clare says, "We're not embarrassed to be seen with you, if that's what you think."

"Really?" I look around the restaurant, where there is nary a werewolf in sight. "Then why aren't we at Minelli's? Or the Chophouse?"

"Because every time we go to the Chophouse, Clare orders something she doesn't like and then she complains about it through the whole meal," Tara says with a snort.

That's true, but it's not the reason.

Clare, at least, has the guts to be honest with me. "Bailey, you put our whole family in an incredibly awkward position at the ball. Ashton's father is powerful and well-respected in the pack, and he might view your actions as support for Frost's claim to the throne."

"How?" I scoff. "I just got back."

"You just got back from London," Tara argues.

This is absolutely ridiculous. "Would you guys stop acting like I'm part of an international spy ring? It was one dance! And you said he was in love with some lady named Amber."

"You had one dance. With the king," Clare reminds me, as if I need it.

"I didn't even know who he was until I went to the fucking ball!" I snap. "Are you actually worried about this? Or are you just parroting whatever your husbands want you to say?"

"That's not fair!" Tara makes her patented wounded face.

It might work on Mother, but it doesn't work on me. "What was I supposed to do? Tell him no? Tell our pack leader no, I don't want to dance?"

My sisters remain silent.

"Ashton was there. He could have said something. He could have stepped in," I point out.

"He has more to lose than you do." Clare frowns as if she's confused that I don't understand that automatically.

Which is bullshit, because I fully understand what she's saying: my supposed future mate shouldn't have to risk a damn thing for me, but I should risk everything for him.

They both stare at me in silence, and I realize in this moment that they're complete strangers to me. Whoever they were before I left, before they took mates and started the adult werewolf lives we're all required to live for the good of the pack, they are not those people anymore.

It's all my fears confirmed. I know that once I'm mated to Ashton, I'll be expected to support and agree with everything he might do or say. And these expectations won't be exclusively his; everyone around me, even my sisters who balked at that kind of behavior in the past, will believe that I'm not fulfilling my purpose in the pack if I don't fall in line and be the ideal mate.

"It's been great getting together," I say, summoning up my best impression of our mother's passive-aggression. "But I have to go."

I push my chair back and stand, and a crackle of energy pulls my attention to the restaurant's doors.

I feel him before I see him. It's unnerving. But I look toward the door knowing that Nathan Frost will be there. And when our eyes meet as he enters, it's clear that he feels my presence, too.

Five years ago, I would ask my sisters if that magnetism were real or if I'm just imagining it. But I can't do that now. I can't trust that they won't tell their mates on me.

The maître d' is leading Nathan in our direction. At least, the maître d' is *trying* to lead; Nathan is actually a step ahead. It's too late to avoid him. Our paths *will* cross.

I don't want to see my sisters' reactions, so it doesn't matter that I can't tear my gaze away from Nathan's. He doesn't try, and I know I'm not imagining this anymore. I can't walk away from the table because if I walk toward him, I don't know what I'll do. I might try to make conversation. Or throw myself at him. I'm not sure which would be more awkward.

My face grows warmer the nearer he gets. I swear I can feel my pulse in my eyeballs. But I can't look away. He gives me a nod and a tilted smile that one could uncharitably interpret as cocky, which is exactly what I decide to do. If I build him up to be an arrogant, vain usurper king in my mind, maybe I won't keep thinking about him.

For as much as I dismiss the incident at the ball as "just one dance" to everyone else, it occupies a stunning beachfront property in my head.

He doesn't say a word to me. He doesn't so much as hesitate as he passes, and I can't help but watch him until he disappears into a private room at the back.

"What's he doing here?" Tara asks, an edge of suspicion in her voice.

She can't possibly think that it's some kind of set up, or

that he knew I would be here. That would be absurd. Who would have told him? And why would he show up?

She thinks you *told him, dummy.*

Well, fuck that.

"Maybe he's meeting someone he doesn't want to be seen with," I say breezily, and head to the coat check.

I spend the ride home alternating between worry about what my sisters think of me and fear that I really hurt their feelings. Sure, Tara and Clare changed, but they're still my sisters. I need them in my corner because it's not like people are lining up to defend me.

We pull up to the gate and I hit the intercom. "Thank you. You can drop me off here."

I can definitely use some fresh air right now. I don't wait for the driver to hop out and open my door. Thralls are human and it seems cruel to make him leave the warmth of the car when he doesn't have my biological resistance to the cold.

Even though I haven't transformed yet, I'm still a were-wolf. I still have some of the perks.

I open the lesser-used pedestrian gate beside the giant, wrought iron monstrosity that covers the wide driveway, ducking under a canopy of ivy to enter the grounds. A crisp, unspoiled carpet of snow stretches across the lawn, and I balance against the brick fence to remove my shoes. Five years pretending to be human stifled my connection to nature, to the freedom of the fresh, cold air and the changing seasons. Humans view weather in general as a nuisance to be endured. Werewolves revel in it, despite how uptight we are about everything else.

With a whoop of joy, I rush across the lawn, crushing the ice-crusted snow beneath my feet. Every giddy, goofy leap I make, every twirl erases the tension of the day.

There's just no room for anger or dread or fear when my lungs are full of crisp, freezing oxygen and my feet are wet and chilled. I almost throw myself to the ground to make a snow angel, but then I spot the unfamiliar sports car parked in front of the house.

My stomach drops. It's not *that* unfamiliar. It's newer than the model he drove five years ago, but it's the same. It's a Porsche 911.

Ashton's favorite car.

CHAPTER 7

Mother is waiting for me the moment I step through the door. "Ashton is here," she hisses, reaching to fuss with my hair. I dodge her and she clucks in frustration. "What were you thinking, running around the lawn like a stray dog?"

"I was thinking how nice it is to be home." I blink innocently at her.

Her eyes narrow. "Is this all a game to you?" Before I can answer, she goes on. "After the stunt you pulled, leaving the pack and now whatever that display was at the ball, it's a miracle that anyone will still associate with us."

"Why wouldn't they—"

"Because they're afraid that what you did will spread!" Mother snaps, loud enough to be overheard, so she immediately lowers her voice again. "You were the first werewolf in a hundred years to reject the transformation and invoke the Right of Accord. Everyone was terrified that you'd opened the floodgates. People wouldn't speak to us because they were afraid of losing their young, too!"

It never occurred to me that by invoking the Right, I

might inspire other teenagers to take a break and consider their futures with the pack. I don't see how it's a bad thing, but I do see how my parents would interpret it that way.

She isn't done lecturing me. "You put your sisters' futures at stake, as well."

"They did all right for themselves," I say under my breath. I'm the youngest. They had already undergone the transformation and their mating pacts had been arranged. "And it's not my job to live their lives for them."

"It's your job to behave in the interests of the pack. Not in your own interests." Mother gets so close I can't really focus on her face, which is harder and colder than I've ever seen before. "You will go upstairs; you will clean up and make yourself presentable and you will come down here and receive your fiancé graciously."

I want to demand to know what fucking Jane Austen novel she stepped out of with her "receive your fiancé graciously" line but she's never hit any of us and I don't want to break her streak.

There's nothing I can say or do but nod silently and go upstairs.

I catch sight of myself in the mirror over my vanity. The hair is easily fixed by throwing it into a ponytail. My makeup is still fine, though my cheeks are flushed. I don't look nearly as terrible as Mother insisted I do.

But I change into a different pair of dark blue jeans; the pant legs of the ones I wore to the restaurant are soaked.

I'm expecting Mother to be waiting downstairs, but she's totally disappeared. I know where she'll have stashed my fiancé, though.

Ashton is in the sitting room. His back is to the double doors when I open one and step inside. He turns, his concerned frown easing into a blindingly white smile. "There she is."

He moves through the seating area, somehow graceful despite having to slip between the massive coffee table and one of the sofas. I take a few steps but let him come to me, because I'm not sure what he's expecting and it's easier to let him take the lead. He puts his arms out and hugs me, kissing the air beside my cheek.

"Sorry I kept you waiting," I say. *Even though it's not my fault because I had no clue you'd even be here.* Dropping in unannounced better not be a hallmark of our courtship. "I was at lunch with my sisters, and I just got back."

"Yes, I know." One eyebrow arches playfully. "I saw you."

I glance over at the giant picture window and spot my footprints leading a dizzying path up to the house.

"Yeah…" I don't have a good excuse for that. "I was—"

"It must be hard for you. Being your age and not yet truly a werewolf." He talks over me as he walks to the window. His tall, slender figure is like a streak of blue ink in his beautifully tailored jacket and trousers. The cold gray light outside can't diminish the warm copper in his hair. When he turns back to me, I'm struck by just how handsome he's become while I'm away. I noticed it at the ball, but now that we're alone, in better lighting and without our fancy formal clothes, it hits me that it's not like he's the worst thing that could ever happen to me. I'll look good on his arm, and if our kids got my complexion and his eyes…

What is wrong with me? Is this what happened to my sisters? One minute, a guy is condescendingly interrupting me, the next I'm like, *"oh well, better have his babies?"* If this is what a mating pact can do before it's even executed, I have no interest in what comes next.

Especially since my future mate apparently thinks I'm suffering some kind of deficiency. I try to sound as sweet and non-confrontational as possible. "I don't know what you mean."

"You haven't transformed yet." He states the obvious as if I need some kind of refresher. "At least, I assume you haven't."

"You were at our first ceremony," I remind him. "You know that I didn't transform."

"There are full moons in England." He lets the sentence hang between us and I can't decide if it's an accusation.

"There are," I confirm, all sugar. "But there wasn't a pack."

"Oh, there's a pack." He goes to the sofa and sits without me inviting him. Infuriatingly, it's him who gestures to *me* to sit down. In my own home.

I take a seat across the big coffee table from him, on the other sofa. I would rather chew my own foot off to escape a snare than get close to him. "Well, I'll have to take your word for it. I didn't have any contact with other were-wolves while I was there."

His expression totally changes to one of utter mortifica-tion. He puts a hand to his chest. "Oh no, Bailey. I hope you don't assume that I was accusing you of anything. I just wondered if you'd chosen to…try it out on your own."

"I wouldn't even know where to begin." The thralls oversee the magic that lets us control whether we shift our forms on the night of the full moon. I have no idea how to accomplish the change without the ceremony. "It sounds like that would be stupid and dangerous."

Still, his sad, apologetic eyes seem so sincere. "I would have thought it very brave."

I don't know how to respond to that, so I nod, and we sit in unbearable silence.

"I think we should clear the air, Bailey." His tone is gentle, oddly intimate. "People are talking about what happened at the ball."

And he wants to call off the mating pact. My shoulders sag with relief.

He mistakes the involuntary gesture for disappointment and rises to come sit by my side. It takes everything in me to not shift away when his thigh bumps mine, to not yank my hand away when he holds it.

"I don't care that people are talking about it." He reaches up and brushes a lock of my hair from my cheek.

Weirdly, I don't want to recoil anymore. Maybe a few days of everyone assigning ulterior motives to everything I've ever done have left me desperate for any shred of approval.

That's dangerous, because on paper, Ashton might be a dream guy. Rich, well-dressed, handsome, with a nice smile and polite manner. There's just that one tiny detail that bugs me: he basically bought me from my father without so much as a slight interest from me.

My wishes aren't integral to his life plan. They never have been, and I can't see that changing.

I pull my hand back slowly. "You're the only one who doesn't. According to my sisters, I've basically ruined your reputation."

"My reputation survived you jilting me." He smiles nervously. "That was a joke."

Joke or not, it stings. "It wasn't about you."

"No, of course not." He shakes his head. "I must admit,

when you first left, I did worry that you were trying to avoid becoming my mate. But that only lasted until the next full moon. I woke after a night of running and hunting and truly feeling like the werewolf I am, and my first thought was of you.

"No matter how cloistered they keep us, we know the human world is out there. And turning our backs on it forever, for something so different that we've never known… that's asking a lot of a seventeen-year-old."

Asking a seventeen-year-old to enter into an engagement with someone who will be their mate for life is a lot, too, but I don't point that out. Maybe he already knows that, and just doesn't care for the inconvenient reality of it.

"I just needed to be sure that this life is what I want." I'm still not sure, but things are moving so fast now. The full moon is in just a few days, and it's the last one before I have to make my final choice.

But coming back has made my choice for me, at least, in the eyes of the people around me.

"I didn't have anything to do with the Greater London pack," I blurt suddenly. Maybe I just need to say it to someone who'll believe me. Or who'll pretend to believe me. I'll take either.

"Of course, you didn't." It doesn't seem to have ever been a question in his mind, with the quickness of his answer. "Both you and them would have violated the Right of Accord if anyone had initiated contact."

I blink in surprise. "You know more about the Right than I thought."

"It was discussed at length after you invoked it," he explains. "Among the already transformed, of course. There was a panic that if it were taught in school, it could entice others to follow suit."

"Did it?" I hope it did. I hope at least one other young pack member exercised a modicum of control over their own life.

But Ashton shakes his head. "You're a cautionary tale, and an effective one. But I do wonder…"

He lowers his eyes as his voice trails off. I press him for the rest. "What do you wonder?"

He meets my gaze and a muscle twitches in his jaw. "I wonder if you're the only one of us who's ever been so unhappy that you had to leave."

"It wasn't unhappiness." Not entirely. And that's the truth. "I needed to see what's out there. Humans run the world. We live among them. I just needed to know why we're so separate."

Ashton takes my hand again and lifts it to his lips. He brushes a kiss across my knuckles and says, "because they don't understand who we are, what we are. Now that you've seen what their lives are like, is it what you truly want?"

Do I truly want a life where I get to pick my own mate? To decide when to have children or if I even want them? In a world where people are free to love whomever they choose, regardless of breeding potential?

"Within the pack, we have stability." He leans in just slightly, his eye contact becoming more intense. "You will never be without a home, without food. They don't protect each other out there. I know you've seen it."

"I have," I admit reluctantly. I saw the consequences of simple mistakes, the uncontrollable havoc wreaked on long chains of human lives. The human world, even with all its flaws, showed me freedom that I couldn't have as part of the pack. But I don't know what it actually means to be human; I always had the option of going home.

I was just a tourist.

Ashton's phone chimes and his fishes it from his jacket pocket with a mumbled apology. "I have to leave. A late dinner meeting. That's something you'll need to prepare for, in our marriage. I work a lot and I'm gone often. But I did come to give you this—"

He reaches into his jacket pocket again and produces a black velvet clamshell box. With very little ceremony, he opens it to reveal a dazzling, princess cut diamond set in a diamond-studded platinum band.

"I—" I close my gaping mouth. I can't think of anything to say.

"Do you like it?" He studies my face for the answer.

I nod. "Yes, I'm just stunned. It's beautiful."

It might as well be a pair of handcuffs, but it's beautiful. I take the box from him and slide the ring onto my finger.

"Now, after the full moon, we really do need to get planning underway," he says.

"Planning?"

"For the mating rite."

I still have one more full moon before I'm obliged to transform and decide my fate once and for all. This year, the moon of my decision takes place on Lupercalia, the festival during which mating pacts are finalized. I can't be mated to Ashton if I haven't gone through at least one transformation, and our marriage can only take place on the night of Lupercalia. We'll have to wait an entire year. My sentence has been suspended.

"We have a year to hammer out the details," I say with a laugh of relief.

A relief that's instantly sapped by his slight frown and, "We have a month." I open my mouth to argue, but he goes on. "Because the festival and the full moon coincide, the king has issued a dispensation. The mating rite can take place before the transformation ceremony."

The room spins and I blink. It's a shock that I'm not on the floor when everything rights itself again.

Ashton hasn't noticed. He's looking at his phone. I'm still frozen when he glances up to move in and kiss my cheek. "I have to go. I'll have my mother contact Vivianne. They can get the ball rolling on the arrangements."

I smile tightly against the panicky throw-up rising in my throat, and I nod and pray he'll leave the room before I yak everywhere. When he's safely out of the room, I grab one of mother's crystal bowls from the mantle and empty my stomach into it. Trembling, I sink to the carpet and wipe my mouth with the back of my hand, the diamond shining merrily on my finger.

A month. I have one month before I'm mated to Ashton forever.

CHAPTER 8

The full moon is a holy time for werewolves. Much in the way humans might dress nicely and congregate at a house of worship, a werewolf pack gathers for their own ceremonies together. For the Toronto pack, the place we gather is about an hour and a half northwest of Toronto. Long before Canada was New France, back in the days when our ancestors fled northern Europe in longboats, a pack inhabited a small village in the area, on what is now two-hundred acres of unspoiled land we can safely roam as the creatures we become every full moon.

The transformation ceremony takes place in the ancient circle of standing stones built over five centuries before Columbus could erroneously claim the first European steps onto the North American continent. The three stones bear tributes to the gods of our pack: Fenrir, the wolf who will devour Odin at Ragnarök, Lycaon, the cruel king punished by Zeus, and Lupa, she-wolf mother of Romulus and Remus. Once, the circle stood in a forest clearing. Now, it's protected in a tall, crescent-shaped building with a copper roof that retracts to allow the moonlight in and the smoke from the ceremonial fires to escape, and a retractable wall that opens to the night air.

I look down on the space, with its lit torches and pebbled paths, from the open upper level. The last time I was here, I stood trembling before Lycaon's monolith and rejected his curse, the price we pay for the power of Fenrir and the blessing of Lupa. Wrapped in my ceremonial robe, I called out the words that shamed my family and upset the community.

Now, I'm here to watch the ceremony for the second time in my life. Tonight, no young person is making the transformation for the first time. I wonder if that's on purpose. Maybe people are afraid that just seeing me here will inspire their children to make bad choices.

No one is thinking that. The only person thinking about you this much is you.

But that isn't entirely true. Mother and Father stay close, no matter where I go. Right now, they're engaged in conversation with another couple, but I know that if I so much as go to the bathroom, Mother will follow me. And when we arrived, Tara and Clare said hello but quickly distanced themselves.

I wish Ryan and Hannah were here. With a sick kid at home, they're bowing out of the transformation this full moon. Despite human beliefs and mythology, we can and do control whether or not we change forms. It's why I can be here and not be compelled to transform against my will, though after putting it off for five years, my skin is a bit uncomfortable, stifling, even, in the light of the full moon.

I turn away from the railing and take a deep breath, only to startle at the sudden appearance of a thrall bearing a tray of champagne flutes. With a grateful nod, I take a glass, and the human moves on.

In an unsavory part of our ancient past, thralls were criminals or prisoners of war enslaved by their captors. But they learned magic from our holy people, then became our holy people. Somewhere in the late Middle Ages, thralls learned a way to prevent us from changing at the full moon and offered us the secret in exchange for the untapped magic we emanate—and the protection of our teeth, claws, and fortunes. Now, they work their magic and keep our secrets for the promise of riches beyond any they could have hoped for in the human world. Born from families who kept the secrets of the pack since a time long forgotten, these descendants work tirelessly and live in luxury in homes built over the foundations of early longhouses.

Security. The concept had such a chokehold over anyone involved in the pack. Serve the pack and you'll be secure. Serve your mate and you'll be secure. They want us to believe we can't survive without each other.

I still haven't decided if that's true.

Ashton is here, somewhere. I've managed to duck him so far, and I'm hoping that will continue until the ceremony starts, but I *am* wearing the ring he gave me. Mother practically hyperventilated. We have an appointment with an appraiser on Monday. Is surviving on my own really worse than living like this?

The hairs on my arms stand up.

The king is here.

There's no use pretending that I don't feel his presence. I know he feels mine; even as the crowd parts and he greets people with handshakes and warm smiles, I sense the pull between us, his desire to seek me out, specifically.

When he gives into it, he doesn't bother to disguise the way he examines every part of me from the floor up, his gaze lingering over my hips and thighs. My brain lights up with images of his fingers sinking into my flesh and my knees threaten to buckle. My black wrap dress isn't overly modest, but it's not revealing, and I still feel like I'm exposed in front of him. His eyes rove over the tops of my breasts, up to meet my unwavering eye contact.

It's not strength that keeps me from looking away. It's fear. Not of him, but of my own attraction to him. He inclines his head, nostrils flaring subtly before he smirks and turns away.

Oh no. He can *smell* how attracted I am to him. My pheromones must be like pollen right now.

I couldn't be more embarrassed.

And he looked so pleased with himself. That made it so much worse.

I'm torn between disappointment and relief that once again, he hasn't spoken to me. How could he? We're in full view of the pack. *Or maybe you're stressed out and desperate about this mating pact situation and you're seeing something you want to see, not something that actually exists.*

I head to the bathroom, certain my face and neck are flushed. At least, my makeup hides the face part, but I sacrifice some of it to dab my forehead and cheeks with a cool paper towel. It's more effective and less bonkers than throwing myself into a snowbank outside.

I've just rejoined the crowd in the mezzanine when a thrall bearing the sigil of the king on his jacket approaches.

"From his majesty, King Nathaniel," the thrall says, and hands me a small black envelope.

Inside, a crisp card with strong, slanted script reads:

Ms. Dixon—

It has come to my attention that I've put you in an unfavor-

able situation. I would like to make it up to you. Come to dinner at the royal residence. Friday, eight o'clock.

Nathan

I swallow and read it a second time before stuffing it guiltily into my clutch. Scanning the crowd, I search for any sign that my sisters or Ashton or worst of all, my Mother, has seen the thrall passing notes to me like the king and I are in middle school. To my relief, the subtle flickering of the lights overheard, like a signal to a theater audience to take their seats, distracts everyone. They'll go down to a set of ritual dressing chambers first to change into ceremonial robes, then they'll take their place in the circle with the others.

With Nathan.

There are so many werewolves around, on the night of the full moon, and nobody has picked up on how hard my blood is pumping? How much fear and arousal I'm giving off? Fear that they'll know what I feel every time Nathan looks at me?

He wants to have dinner with me, presumably alone, at his home. That's not an invitation a king extends to just anybody. There has to be a reason. And I could feel that reason in the way he looked at me earlier.

I surrendered my will to him as my king and pack leader. How far does that vow extend? People didn't want me to dance with him; they definitely won't like it if I go to Aconitum Hall to dine with him. And judging from the way he looks at me, that's not all I'll be there for.

When I imagine that, what other people think and want doesn't matter. I know what I think and want.

I want Nathan.

"There you are."

My stomach plunges as Ashton stands beside me and

winds his arm around my waist. He leans in and sniffs my neck, and I will my body to sink through the floor.

"This is the last full moon I'll spend alone," he whispers against my hair.

If I try to speak, I might cry. I force myself to look up and smile at him.

He kisses my forehead. "I wish I would have found you here sooner, but now I have to go downstairs."

"It's okay," I squeak out. "Go on."

"I'll see you at brunch tomorrow," he reassures me, as if it's reassurance at all.

I'm dreading brunch with his parents almost as much as I'm dreading the marriage, itself. His father is stuffy and condescending, his mother cold and always quick with a covert insult or judgmental comment. They're going to be in my life for the rest of it, so I suppose I should get used to them.

Ashton takes my hand and lifts it to his lips with a wicked smile. "Remember to keep your eyes to yourself. I'm not that kind of werewolf."

He's teasing me about the nudity aspect of the ceremony. I know he'll interpret my flaming hot blush as being meant for him, but the only person I care to see tonight is Nathan. I laugh weakly and remember not to jerk my hand back as Ashton's grip lingers while he walks away from me. The mezzanine empties of all but a few stragglers, and I flag down a thrall carrying champagne. This time, I take two flutes.

I'm going to need them.

CHAPTER 9

The deep, hollow toll of a bell announces the midnight hour. In the round courtyard below, pack members file into the sacred circle. They wear ceremonial robes of silver silk, easy to remove once the transformation takes hold.

Humans imagine scenes in movies where werewolves scream in agony and tear out of their clothes, which I've never understood. We know when the full moon is. It doesn't take us by surprise. And we know how to dress for it.

Or undress. My breath freezes in my lungs as Nathan walks into the circle. He stops in front of the monolith to Lycaon and drops his robe.

I shamelessly look him over, the way he did to me, from his broad shoulders, down his chest dusted with dark hair that thins to a line on his shockingly sculpted abs. I wasn't expecting him to look as good as he does. I wasn't expecting that my mouth would water at the sight of his cock, that my thighs would clench together at the thought of how huge it must be hard.

I wish he could see me. I hope he feels me, smells me.

And I hope that the strange attraction between us is making him as crazed with need as I feel.

An acolyte—a thrall trained in our ceremonies and rituals—steps forward with a shallow silver bowl bearing a glistening human heart. It's required for the transformation; Lycaon himself was transformed into a wolf after he angered Zeus by feeding the God human flesh. Nathan grabs the heart with his bare hand and bites into it.

That's when he lifts his gaze and finds me, seconds before the transformation starts.

It begins with his eyes. They flash silver, then red. His face shifts, nose and jaw elongating into a muzzle. We don't turn into wolves. That's a myth. We turn into a creature that stands upright; body covered with short, silky hair from our clawed feet to our canine-like heads. The fur flows over every contour of Nathan's body and his spine curves, drawing him into a hunched posture. His ears elongate, pointing straight back, a shape humans would consider more elfin than dog-like, with tufts of fur accentuating the points. His arms grow longer, as well; in this predatory manifestation, a wide reach is an advantage.

In his animalistic form, he waits for the others but stares up at me. Like this, I'm vulnerable. Far too human. I would be no match for him, should he want me. And he does want me, but even this way, he has self-control, as well as some common sense. He knows he can't reach me, and so do I, but being the target of all that concentrated power and bestial drive is still heady and frightening.

The good kind of frightening. The kind that makes me wonder what could happen if I only push a little further.

The rest of the pack remove their robes as acolytes walk the circle offering bites of hearts, enough to go around. The communal nudity isn't arousing in the way

Nathan's was to me; it's just a fact of the transformation. They take their bites, change their shapes, and when a ring of fearsome werewolves stands in the circle, Nathan finally faces them. He throws back his head and releases an unearthly howl that reverberates through my entire body.

The rest of the pack joins Nathan in howling, the cries of not-quite wolf, not-quite human voices piercing the sky in a primeval prayer, and I run from the building. The valet thrall can see my urgency and hurries to retrieve my car—driving separately from my parents means I don't have to wait for them to return at dawn. I get into the driver's seat and peel off, trying to shake my own primal need to fulfill my true potential, to feel my body shift and change under the moonlight.

I've been putting it off, and now, with the howls of my pack ringing in my ears, I wish I made my decision tonight, that I joined them. The thought of waiting another month is agony, even if my transformation means shackling myself to Ashton Daniels for the rest of our lives.

I speed down the twisting private lane away from the ceremony site, trying desperately to control my breathing. I'm overcome with images of Nathan's broad back, the muscles rippling in his thighs, the veins bulging on his arms, his—

My blood is on fire. My skin is a prison. I want to rip my clothes open, bare my body to the night sky.

I want to howl.

The tires crunch on the gravel as I guide the car onto the shoulder. I slam the shifter into park and recline the seat, gripping the headrest in one hand and frantically yanking my skirt up. I slide my hand beneath my panties and gasp with relief as my fingers encounter my slippery, swollen clit.

I conjure up an impossible scenario. There I am, defenseless, vulnerable in my moment of reckless passion, when Nathan finds me. Not Nathan the polished, powerful king, but Nathan the fully transformed were-wolf, all hunger and exhilaration and lack of inhibition. And I'm caught, hand in my panties, the air thick with my scent, vulnerable and ready for him to take me.

I know there's no escape, even as I hit the door lock. He easily rips the door off its hinges, growling in frustration at the irritating delay. That's all I've done; delayed the inevitable.

I scramble backward into the passenger seat. It's a mistake; he's on me in a moment, his sleek body between my thighs. I can thrash all I want, but I'm pinned painfully over the center console, hips raised, and legs splayed wide. My dress disintegrates in his claws and he drags the scraps down my body as he lowers his head to my pussy and sniffs deeply.

His hot breath teases my clit and I want him to taste me, but instead he drags me from the car entirely, his grip strong around my calves. Somehow, I don't hit my head as my body crumples to the pavement and he drags me to the side of the road. The shoulder is muddy and broken and he pins me down in the slush, grit and salt from the dirty snow digging into my skin. The more I struggle, the filthier and wetter I get. He's setting between my legs, that huge cock ready to spear into me, his teeth sink into my throat and there's no escape—

I curl up from the seat, mouth open in a groan of relief of that doesn't make a sound. My thighs tremble and tense, and I come so hard my hand and my panties get soaked. The fantasy is so fresh and vivid in my mind, I'm surprised to find myself still dressed and safe behind the wheel of my car, though I'm panting and sweating. I grab some tissue from the glove compartment and clean up the mess on my hand, my thighs, and the leather seat between them.

How am I supposed to be with Nathan, alone, without climbing on him? I'm starting to hope I really am just hard up and imagining our attraction. I'm in a mating pact with someone. Fucking someone else is not allowed.

But I will never feel for Ashton the things I feel for Nathan. I can barely tolerate Ashton's touch, while I long for Nathan's. The idea of letting Ashton inside my body disgusts me, and I'm certain it's going to take more than duty to get me into our wedding bed. If Nathan were here, right now, I would beg him to fuck me. I wouldn't care how ridiculous the request sounded, given that we've barely spoken to each other. I would crawl on my hands and knees and beg.

That's dangerous, considering his invitation. Does he think I'll show up eager to please him, ready to do whatever he commands because he's the king? Because I would do anything he commanded, and more, and not because he's the king and has that power over me. I want to give myself to him totally. I want him to hold me down and wring every last ounce of strength from me with his hands and his tongue and his cock.

So, it's decided, then: I'm definitely not going to go to the royal residence. I'll have to send my regrets because I can't possibly behave.

When my heart rate is reasonably under control and my vision clears, I raise the seat again and put the car into drive. I'm not satiated. I'm not sure I ever can be, if I'm never going to know what it feels like to give Nathan Frost all of myself.

I wonder if he's out there in the forest right now, relieving his lust for me with some other member of the pack. With someone else's mate. Though I hate the thought of it now, it might be the only way I'll ever be able to be with him. Things happen at the full moon, or so I've heard, that aren't acceptable the rest of the month.

By the time I get home, the adrenaline has worn off. I shuffle up the wide staircase and into my room, where I barely get my shoes off before I collapse on the bed. But deeply instilled discipline dies hard, and Mother always stressed the importance of a nighttime skincare routine. By the time I get my face scrubbed clean and I've changed into my pajamas, I'm beyond exhausted. It will be a miracle if I can get up in time for brunch.

I've only been asleep for a few hours when I jerk awake to the sound of my Mother's outraged voice shouting, "What the *hell* is this?"

I rub my eyes.

Mother stands beside my bed, holding the note from Nathan.

CHAPTER 10

This can't be happening.

I sit up and yank the note from Mother's hand. "You went through my purse?"

"What do you think you're doing?" she hisses, disregarding my question. "You are in a mating pact. You can't see another man behind your fiancé's back!"

"I'm not seeing anyone. I'm sure you read it. It's an invitation to make up for—"

"It is an invitation to gossip. To scandal and ruin." She snatches the card back and rips it in half, then in half again before dropping the pieces to the carpet. "How long has this been going on?"

"How long has what been going on?" I almost argue that I've only been home for a few days, but then I remember that as far as everyone else in the pack is concerned, I could be a spy for Greater London. Maybe she thinks I was banging the king like a drum there, long before he seized the throne here.

Maybe she thinks I have something to do with him taking over the pack.

"You know exactly what I'm asking," Mother insists. "How long have you and the king been seeing each other?"

I press my fingertips to my temples. "Up until a week ago, I've been living with humans. Not werewolves, humans. I didn't even know Nathan was king until—"

"Nathan?" Her eyes narrow as she seizes on this new, unintentional evidence. "You didn't know *Nathan* was king?"

"I-it's his name," I stumble guiltily. "It's how he signed the note. If you didn't rip it up, you could check and see."

"He is the king!" she rages. "It doesn't matter how he signed it. You should think of him, speak of him, as if he's your king. And he should think of you as just another subject. He clearly does not."

She goes to my closet and throws open the doors, disappearing inside as she mutters about needing to buy me an appropriate wardrobe. I hear her pawing through my clothes in annoyance before she emerges with a black crepe top with pleated white sleeve cuffs and a prim peter-pan neckline. She jerks a pair of black tie-waist trousers off their hanger and throws the clothes onto the bed in disgust. "Get dressed. Your Father is waiting to speak to you downstairs."

She leaves and slams the door, and I immediately reach for my phone to check the time. It's ten o'clock, much later than I'm usually allowed to sleep, and the Daniels will be over for brunch at noon. I put as much hustle into getting ready as I reasonably can and still leave less time between then and now for Father to lecture me.

More likely, it will be Mother doing the lecturing while Father stands by, condemning me with glares of disappointment. And I'll shrink and feel small and apologize for things I can't control.

This isn't what you want. Pack your bags and go, right now. Take your car, live in it if you have to. I imagine getting behind the wheel and leaving everything behind.

Then I remember how I felt at the ceremony last night, how much I yearned to transform, and that fleeting moment of imagined freedom crashes down. I need to be with the pack. Not for security, but because it's my nature.

It's unfair that I have to trade away my future to belong.

I hear raised voices as I descend the stairs. They're coming from Father's study, and they're not voices I recognize immediately. The anger obscures the usually polite context in which I hear them, but it becomes crushingly clear as I approach the doors that Ashton is here early, as are his father and mother.

The argument goes silent as I enter, the eyes of my fiancé and two sets of furious parents falling on me, demanding answers to a thousand questions all once. If I can't deliver the right answers, right now, it will reflect badly on me. Unfortunately, I won't be able to give the right answers at all; they've already decided what I'm going to say and what my words will mean before I open my mouth.

Ashton's is the only face with any sympathy. He comes to me and takes my hands in his. "Darling. You must be so upset."

"Upset?" I look to Mother. Hasn't she told them all about the note yet?

"Being pursued so relentlessly by the king. He's abusing his power as pack leader. It's absolutely disgusting." He directs most of his statement to the room at large.

So, that's what the argument was about. *Whether or not I'm being courted by the king or stalked by him.*

Ashton's father, James Daniels, is like a middle-aged version of his son. A glimpse into the future of my marriage, and I guess it's not all bad. Thank goodness Ashton doesn't look like a constipated asshole when he talks to me, like James does. He asks, "What message did the king send you last night?"

Now, I'm double confused. I assumed Mother told them the contents of note. I open my mouth, considering how to not lie but also not reveal the entire truth. "It was an apology. For putting me under such scrutiny at the ball."

Ashton and his father exchange a charged glance. "And not an invitation to dinner?"

I cringe inwardly. Ashton asked the question as a defense of me, to his father. My fiancé expects me to back up his firm denial, but I can't and it's just going to make him look foolish.

I'm sure he'll *love* that, but there's nothing I can do to fix it, not with Mother and Father standing there, knowing full well what the note said. "He did invite me to dinner."

It's so quiet, the clock on the wall behind Father's desk ticks audibly.

"You're not going," Mother says firmly.

Ashton holds up his hand for quiet. His jaw visibly tightens. "Thomas, may we have the room, please?"

"Sweetheart," Mrs. Daniels wheedles. "Perhaps we should discuss this as a family. At ho—"

"Thank you, Mother," Ashton dismisses her tersely.

"Let's give these young people time to talk," Father says, holding an arm stiffly toward the open double doors, which he closes behind them as they file out, leaving Ashton and I to stand awkwardly in front of each other.

I don't know what to say. Worse, I don't know what he's going to say. I hope he's going to call off the pact.

Please, please let him call off the pact.

"You're not going," he says flatly.

The words knock the wind out of me. "Excuse me?"

"You're not going to dinner with him." He states it like fact, and that infuriates me.

I take a step back. And I realize this might be my salvation. If I defy him, give him a taste of what he can expect in our marriage…

"He is our king and our pack leader." I straighten in indignation. "Or didn't you listen to the words we just said when we were kneeling in front of him?"

"Kneeling in fron—" Ashton turns away, one hand flexing. That gives me a moment of pause. Will he strike me? And if so, will anyone care?

He whirls on me, his lips practically white with fury, and jabs the air in an explosion of anger. "*You* do not lecture *me* on loyalty!"

I take a step back. It's the last concession I'll make, I decide. He can walk right through me if he wants. I don't care. I'm not giving up any more ground, despite the stomps he takes toward me to punctuate his statements.

"You ran from the pact your father made with me." Stomp. "You ran from the pack entirely." Stomp. "You allowed a usurper to make a spectacle of you, and now you think I'll allow you to go to his home and have dinner with him? Alone?"

Ashton looms over me, but I don't quaver. I stare up in to his furious eyes, unblinking.

"I didn't run from you," I correct him. "And I didn't

run from the pack. I invoked an ancient right that hadn't been disclosed to us. It was your right, too!"

"And yet you didn't inform me of it," he seethes. "You waited until we stood in front of the Hierophant, and only then did you say anything about our right to leave to the pack."

That takes me aback. It never occurred to me that he might have wanted an out, as well. I denied him that. I suppose he has every right to be angry about it.

But not about whom I dance with or whom I see socially. Not when we aren't even mates yet.

"I'm sorry. I should have told everyone. But there's no going back now. And if I knew you would have wanted to—"

"I didn't want to!" He stalks away, running a hand through his hair in frustration, and turns back, one hand on his hip, his jacket pushed back. "Even if I had the choice, I would never have left. You shouldn't have left. And I'm tired of pretending I'm not embarrassed by what you did. From now on, there will be no more embarrassments. Do you understand?"

"Do you understand that you don't get to order me around?" I shoot back, braver now that he's across the room once more. "We have a mating pact, but we aren't mated. Not yet. And my pack leader has extended an invitation that's an honor, not a disgrace."

I hope it's a disgrace. One so bad, so awful that Ashton has no choice but to spare his family name and let this whole mating thing go.

"If it were any other king, or you were any other subject." Ashton curses, then lets out a deep, aggrieved sigh. "You're right. I can't stop you from going. But I also can't guarantee that I won't break our pact if you go. My father is a powerful man now, Bailey. He's on the council. Our family can't afford a liability. So, I would advise you to stop acting like one."

He strides to the doors and pauses, not looking back. "Make the smart choice, this time."

I sit, very still, on the brown leather sofa that my father has had since I was a child, and I listen to the raised voices in the hall.

I *am* going to Aconitum Hall.

I *am* going to see Nathan.

CHAPTER 11

The night of the ball, every light in Aconitum Hall was lit. Tonight, it's mostly dark. It's not as inviting; the towers loom sinister and medieval over the city, blotting out the sky rather than polluting it with added light.

I take a deep breath as I step out of my car. Mother and Father refused to let me take the driver and I'm not sure where one parks at a royal palace. My shoes crunch on the gravel of the small parking area beyond the front porte cochere. I head in that direction, my heart beating in an unfamiliar and worrying pattern. The door opens at the top of the steps, and I expect to see a thrall butler there. But it's Nathan.

Nathan just opened his front door. Like he's a person and not a king. I freeze in place. He does, too. It's a strange moment; before, the undeniable attraction between us was insulated by the presence of others and the etiquette demanded by our society. It felt like if only we were alone, nothing would hold him back. Now, it appears we are alone, and he's still restrained, despite the charge in the air that makes me want to run to him instead of walking the interminable pace required to appear normal.

"Ms. Dixon," he says as I climb the steps.

When I reach the top, I curtsey to him. "Bailey, Your Majesty—"

"No, no. Stand up." He chuckles ruefully. "Bailey, then. And you'll call me Nathan, agreed?"

I nod and give him a grateful smile, but if I open my mouth all my vital organs will leap out.

He's not wearing a bespoke tux or finely tailored suit now. At least he's wearing *something*; the last time I saw him, he was wearing considerably less than his current charcoal gray crewneck sweater and navy slacks. Remembering what's under them makes me feel a little faint.

"I think I'm overdressed," I say weakly, knowing for a fact that I am. My boat neck, beaded tulle illusion dress is more appropriate for a formal reception.

"Or perhaps, I'm underdressed," Nathan suggests. "You were expecting something more…official."

He's so close to me as we walk through the checkered entry hall. When he takes the staircase, I hesitate at the bottom. A momentary frown crosses his face. "The private residence is this way."

"Of course." What did I think, that we would occupy the state dining room, just the two of us? I've never been to the private residence, but I highly doubt he's just making it up as a ruse to get me upstairs and alone.

For one thing, we already seem really, really alone. I expected to see security or servants but the place is shockingly empty. And we're both still behaving like we don't know that we want to rip each other's clothes off right then and there.

"I apologize," Nathan begins, leading the way up the

wide staircase. "I thought I made it clear that this wasn't a formal visit, but a friendly one."

"Oh, I think it was clear enough." I have no idea why I said it and I want to crawl into a shell built entirely of mortification and just die in it. "I'm sorry, I—"

"You didn't come in a chauffeured car," he muses. "I know your parents have a driver. It's his night off?"

We reach a landing and I face him directly. "My parents didn't care for the idea of my coming here."

He's not surprised, but he half-heartedly feigns it, anyway. "I certainly hope it didn't create too much friction between you and…oh, what's his name? Your fiancé?"

"Ashton Daniels." I don't want to talk about him. I'm frankly annoyed that Nathan's brought him up. "And no, no friction. At least, nothing worth discussing?"

"Oh?" He sounds disappointed as we start up the next flight of stairs.

I keep my tone light. "We're not mated, yet. I still have a will of my own."

"So, I've heard," Nathan says.

Now it's my turn to say, "Oh?"

"Invoking the right of accord, when no one in your pack had done it for centuries? That's quite willful." His words hold an edge of teasing that I'm not sure I welcome.

"Maybe if anyone had been taught about it, if it hadn't been covered up for centuries, someone would have," I say, before I remember that Nathan is from a different pack. He had no control over what I was taught as a child. "What about Greater London? Has anyone invoked the right there?"

He nods slowly. "About thirty years ago."

"And was it a huge scandal?" I ask, then add, "If you were old enough to remember it."

"Don't try to flatter me," he mockingly scolds. We reach the top of the stairs, and he takes a right, then a left down another hallway, where we finally see security guards. They're thralls, and they wear the sign of the royal house. They open the towering double doors for us to enter.

The private residence is like a palace within a palace. The ceilings are so high, I feel like an undersized doll in a dollhouse. The furnishings would be at home in a dollhouse, too, all spindly antiques to match the early nineteenth century decor with its plasterwork like wedding cake frosting. The hall that stretches ahead of us has melon-pink walls and a black-and-white checkered floor, with two enormous chandeliers lighting our way. At the end of the hall, mahogany doors stand open, revealing a richly appointed sitting room. He leads me inside, where the furnishings are more modern and the blue-gray walls less aggressive.

"Please," he says, gesturing to the plush ivory sofa. "What may I get you to drink?"

The king is going to fix me, his subject, a drink? That's apparently what's happening, as he goes to a bar at the end of the room. I smooth my skirt and sit, blurting, "two fingers of vodka, neat?"

He blinks in surprise, but nods and sets about getting a glass and pouring. While he does, he picks up our conversation from before. "You left for five years. What did your fiancé have to say about that?"

I shrug. "At the time? Nothing. They swept me out of there before the ceremony was even over. I was on a plane to London before dawn."

"That must have been traumatic." He comes over and hands me a glass, but he doesn't sit beside me. Instead, he takes an armchair, leaning back comfortably with a high-ball glass of something amber-colored.

I'm not sure if I should downplay what the experience was like. It was definitely traumatic. After sitting in a bare office room, shivering in my ceremonial robe while Mother and Father screamed at me, I was whisked away home to collect as much as I could stuff into my luggage in thirty minutes. A change of clothes and I was on a private plane to an uncertain future.

Not even my sisters knew what happened to me. Not even my best friends.

Yet, I can blurt it all out to this stranger. "When I arrived in London, I didn't even have a place to stay. I went to a hotel and used the credit card Father gave me. A few days later, he wired me money and a promise that I would be taken care of, but at seventeen, with nothing but my passport and someone else's money, it was diffi-cult to get an apartment and get established. If the company that hired me hadn't taken a chance on me, I would have—"

My throat closes up with anxiety I never let myself feel in the moment. Did my father make good on his promise of regular wire transfers? He had. Did I find an apartment? Yes, after weeks of staying in that hotel, fearing they might kick me out at a moment's notice if my parents changed their minds and canceled the credit card.

It's so much more terrifying in retrospect. Maybe I just didn't have time then to really think about how precarious the position had been.

Nathan puts his drink on the coffee table and moves to sit beside me. "You're shaking."

"I'm sorry, I've never told anyone…" No. I cannot cry in front of our pack leader. Especially not over something I did to myself. I force a laugh and roll my eyes. "I faced the consequences of my actions. And I'm glad to be back."

"I'm pleased to hear it." He stands again, but this time he moves to the unlit fireplace. "I'm sure your fiancé is, as well?"

"I don't want to talk about Ashton." I can't believe the vehemence with which I reacted. I apologize immediately. "I'm so sorry, I don't know what that was about."

Nathan smiles, and it's definitely not the type of "friendly" he described this visit as being. "Will you allow me to make a guess?"

I nod, my mouth going dry as he sits beside me once more. He puts a hand on my knee and leans in close to my ear. My entire body shudders and flushes unbearably hot.

His breath stirs the wisps of hair that wouldn't stay in my hasty, loose bun. "You either feel that by being here with me, you're betraying him, or…"

The hand on my knee moves, only a little, just enough that the tips of his fingers are a centimeter from actually being between my thighs.

"You don't want to be with him."

I lean back so I can look Nathan in the eye. This close, it would take nothing at all for our lips to touch, for us to utterly devour each other. I wet my lips without meaning to and say, "Can't it be both?"

With a smirk, Nathan sits back. The sudden break in contact makes every millimeter of my skin cry out with want. But he can't hide that his reaction is similar. I can see his pulse ticking frantically below his jaw and note the way his lips part just slightly to take a breath.

Kiss me, I implore silently. *We both want you to.*

"And why do you feel like you're betraying him?" Nathan is enjoying this. Reveling in the unspoken need between us. "You're just here to have a cordial dinner at the pack leader's request."

You know why, I want to say, preferably while throwing myself on him.

Just then, a knock sounds at the door. Nathan rises and calls, "come in."

A thrall enters and bows. "Your Majesty, dinner is served."

"We'll be right there," Nathan says, dismissing the young man.

It's only taken a moment of separation, a slight distraction of Nathan's attention, and I feel like I can breathe again, think again. I stand and quickly throw back my drink, drawing on the smooth warmth blossoming in my chest for courage.

"Are you meeting with all your subjects this way?" I ask, pleased to see the mild shock that crosses his face at the question.

He recovers quickly. "Only those that intrigue me."

Not the answer I want, deep down in my heart. Despite the way it complicates things in my life, the tangible, yet unacknowledged attraction between us is one of the few truly exciting events happening in my life lately.

If he's got this same kind of thing going on with other werewolves, that *sucks*.

"I intrigue you? Because I invoked the right?"

He scoffs and gestures toward the door the thrall just exited. "Of course not. Why would that intrigue me?"

I move in his direction but falter when he adds, "After all, I invoked the right, as well."

CHAPTER 12

He follows that bombshell with, "I hope you like venison."

I stumble into the dining room, where a large table is set for two at one end.

"It's very fresh," he goes on. "I hunted it myself during the full moon."

I can't get past his earlier statement. "You did it?"

"Well, you know. The only things to do during the full moon are fuck, fight, or hunt." He pulls a chair out for me and I sit obediently, out of habit.

"I'm not talking about the deer!" I lean toward him as he sits and for some reason, I lower my voice like we're in danger of being overheard. "You invoked the Right of Accord? Your pack *has* a Right of Accord?"

He nods and lifts his hand to signal the staff for the first course. As the thralls place bowls of pale cream soup in front of us, Nathan elaborates. "All packs operate under the same law, given to us by Lycaon the Younger. Didn't they teach that in school?"

I shake my head. "I assumed pack law was just the law of our individual pack."

"Hmm." He considers for a moment. "Greater London teaches our children differently than Toronto does."

Our children. That's an interesting phrase. "Do you have children?"

"No. I've never had a mate." He unfolds his napkin and smooths it over his lap.

I do the same. "And does that have anything to do with invoking the right?"

He considers. "No. I don't think it did. And there were times I was glad to be free of those obligations."

The unfairness astounds me. As a male in the pack, he doesn't have to worry that life might pass him by. There will always be females lining up for a successful mate. And he will always have the choice to refuse a pact, whereas I'm pretty much stuck.

The soup is delicious. Cream, mushrooms, wild rice, and I detect a hint of leek. It's great soup and I'm probably going to throw it up from crying too hard at the unfairness of my life.

"It must be nice," I say, my hand trembling with rage as I lift another spoonful.

"What must?"

I swallow. "Being free from the obligations of family. I'm sure there are members of our pack who would rather concentrate on themselves and their own interests, rather than simply create fresh werewolves."

He laughs at that. "I'm sorry. It was your phrasing, not your concern. I'm beginning to sense that you aren't looking forward to Lupercalia?"

I might as well be honest. "I'm not. In fact, I'm not sure if I'm going to…"

I can't say it.

But then he says, "Go on," in his deep, commanding

voice and I want to say it. I want to tell him my most personal secret.

"I'm not sure if I'm going to transform."

There.

He frowns and sets his spoon down. Reaching for his water glass, he says, "You would leave the pack forever?"

When I think about it, it makes me sick. All alone again, but this time with no wire transfers or credit cards. Just fear and work and loneliness, unable to make meaningful connections with humans because I'm not one of them.

"I don't want to," I admit. "When I think about never seeing my sisters again, or my friends, my heart aches. But the thought of being with Ashton, having his children, living as his quiet, obedient—"

Nathan laughs again, and immediately apologizes. "I'm sorry. It's not funny. But I can't see you being quiet and obedient to any man."

"I'm glad you're so amused by my predicament." This is my life. Why can't anyone understand how trapped I feel?

"I'm not amused." He takes a sip of wine. "I'm interested to see how you're going to get out of this."

I just stare at him.

He shrugs and goes on. "You're not marrying Ashton Daniels."

"My parents, Ashton, and Aston's parents all disagree with you." I have to remind myself that I'm speaking to a king. There has to be a limit to what kind of sass I can throw around.

Maddeningly, all he says is, "Do you disagree with me?"

"There's a neat little piece of paper, a contract notarized

by the royal office, that disagrees with you." I take my own sip of wine, hoping he'll chalk my furiously hot face up to the alcohol we've imbibed.

"Not *my* royal office," he says off-hand. "And Victor was corrupt. Who knows how deep that corruption went? For all we know that mating pact might be nothing more than a piece of paper."

"I—" What is he suggesting? Is it something I should even hope for? "Do you mean it might not be valid?"

"I mean, nothing is set in stone. Until Lupercalia, of course." He nods toward my bowl. "You don't care for the soup?"

"It's delicious." I'm dizzied by the turn in conversation. "I'm just not used to eating so close to detonating bombshells."

His laugh is loud and tooth-grindingly arrogant, and I hate that it makes him hotter to me than he was before. If I want to be with a man who infantilizes me and finds me "intriguing," I might still be able to marry Ashton.

"Why am I here?" Before he can answer, I add, "It's not just because I intrigue you—"

"On the contrary, I find you quite—"

I keep on going. "—or to apologize for dancing with me. You're not stupid. You know that me being here is just making the scandal worse."

"And yet, here you are." He lifts his glass as if in a toast.

I nod slowly. "Here I am."

"Then you must not be worried about causing a scandal." He has me there and he knows it. "Or you know that defying your parents and your fiancé might work to your advantage."

"Okay. Fair." I narrow my eyes. "This isn't going how I expected."

"What did you expect?" Before I can answer, his voice takes on a darker tone that promises I'm not totally safe from the big, bad wolf in him. "Tell me the truth."

The truth is, I thought by now we'd have given in to whatever it is that sizzles the air around us. But I can't describe it that way. "Based on the way you look at me, I assumed I was here to leave with my virtue in tatters."

Worse. So much worse. Why did I choose those archaic words? It would have been better if I just said, *"I thought we'd fuck."*

He raises one eyebrow. "You have my word that you will leave tonight with your virtue intact."

Why is that so disappointing to me? And why doesn't it seem more disappointing to him?

Then he adds, "There will be other nights."

It's my turn to laugh. "Oh, will there be?"

He just nods and goes back to his soup.

Though I want to assert that he can't be so sure about that, he can. He has all the power here. He can command my presence every night, if he wants to. And he seems to know that as long as he does, I'll come running. Anything to make my fiancé potentially break the pact.

We eat in silence for while. The lack of talking should be uncomfortable, but my mind is reeling. There are paintings on the walls, portraits of past kings and queens of the pack, their legacies carrying on even into the new king's personal space.

It casts my predicament in a much different light. I'm worried about shaming my family, but at least I don't have to worry about ruining an entire pack.

"Why did you invoke the Right of Accord?" I ask him. "Your specific reasons. 'Because I could' isn't an answer."

"It's an answer. It's just not one you want." He isn't wrong, but he doesn't play coy. "A lifetime commitment to anything should be considered thoroughly, especially if one is indoctrinated to believe that commitment is desirable rather than having the consequences and responsibilities explained to them."

"Like joining a hetero-normative society that demands breeding at all costs?" I think about Hannah and Ryan and all they have to hide.

"That, and the reality that once you accept the transformation, your life is no longer your own. Most of us aren't prepared to live in a world outside of the pack. It's easy to tell our young that without us, they can't survive." He lifts his glass toward me again. "But you survived."

"Barely." But that isn't true. I certainly didn't have designer clothes or a mansion to go home to. There were no lavish dinners or garden parties. My father paid for everything, but I did have to learn to survive in a world where no one laundered my clothes or did my grocery shopping or drove me around. And while the humans I met in their world were perfectly capable of doing those things, no one bothered to teach them to us. We were promised a life where none of that would ever come up.

All sense of playfulness flees the room. Nathan stares intently into my eyes as he speaks. "You survived. And you saw how different things can be. For better or worse. The two of us…we know things none of these other werewolves know. Imagine how different life could be for our children."

"There's that 'our' again." I chuckle nervously. "Maybe

the rest of the pack isn't interested in co-parenting with their pack leader."

"I wasn't talking about their children. I was talking about our children."

I choke on my soup and frantically cover my mouth with my napkin.

He doesn't wait for me to finish being shocked. "I've decided to pursue you, Bailey. You would make an excellent queen and mate for me."

"I am engaged!" I cough out.

"And we've established that you don't want to be, so that's one challenge overcome."

And once again, I'm being steamrolled by a man who thinks he can just have me.

Meanwhile, my body is still shouting, *he can have you any time he wants!* But the chemistry between Nathan and I isn't enough for me to walk from one cage into another.

"Changes need to be made here if this pack is going to survive," Nathan tells me. "You and I are the only werewolves in the allied packs to invoke the right in a hundred years. Imagine what we could do together."

I have imagined what we could do together. Just not in the way he's proposing.

"That way, too."

Is he reading my mind?

He must see my panic, because he explains, "Your scent. Let's drop the pretense. I know you want me. And I want you."

What's it called when everything swells up and you can't breathe? Anaphylaxis?

That, but for my pussy.

"Think about what I've said." He switches smoothly

back into what sounds like a business conversation. "And the advantages I'm offering you."

"How romantic. Truly, the proposal every girl dreams of." I roll my eyes, and I don't know why, but I say, "I'll think about it."

"You'll agree," he says with a pleasant smile.

And that's it. That's the last we speak of it through a polite, if deeply weird, dinner. He asks me about my time in London, and tells me about his five years in Berlin, where he was exiled during his time away from the Greater London pack. We talk about the meal—the venison *is* delicious—and when it's over, he calls me a car and assures me that mine will be returned to my house before morning. He even shakes my hand at the door.

As we stand on the front steps of the mansion, he puts an arm around my waist and leans in to whisper in my ear. "Please don't take this chaste goodbye as an indication that I'm not interested; I am. But we have many nights ahead of us. I'm willing to wait."

He doesn't even try for a kiss. He's that's infuriatingly confident.

And I am so confused.

CHAPTER 13

The Dixon family motto could easily be, *"if it's uncomfortable, ignore it."*

My dinner with Nathan last week is currently causing my family maximum discomfort, and their unwillingness to speak to me about it is such a blessing, I practically beam on the ride to brunch and my fitting for my ceremonial dress.

Still, my heart and head are divided. While I desperately want to believe Nathan can get me out of this mating pact, it's not as simple as, *"I'm king, I can do what I want."* He'll face the wrath of the pack and a red tape nightmare. There's no way Ashton and his family will let someone walk all over them so blatantly.

And I don't know Nathan at all. There's no guarantee he means what he says. Maybe he's that magnetic and disarming with every woman he meets. There could be any number of potential mates in the pack that he's considering; there's no reason for me to believe otherwise, especially when rumors are swirling that he's in love with the former queen.

Still, if he's serious, dissolution of the mating pact could be tied up in council for months, even years. Ashton could just get tired of waiting and walk away. At the very least, it will postpone my sentence for a while.

For centuries, one particular family of thralls has been responsible for creating our ceremonial garb. They don't have a storefront; werewolves and humans alike need to be of a certain social station to know how to find R. F. Frobisher Tailoring and Dressmaking in their unmarked studio on Bloor Street West. Our driver lets us out in front of the building, and we make our way up to the eleventh floor. The elevator doors open on a crisp white lobby, where a receptionist greets us and directs us to a seating area currently occupied by my hopefully not-future-mother-in-law.

"Mrs. Daniels," I say politely, sitting beside my mother on the opposing white sofa.

Mrs. Daniels has a flute of champagne on the chic glass coffee table between us, but it appears untouched. She clutches her Launer bag by the handles so tightly that were she not wearing black leather gloves, her knuckles would no doubt be white. The corners of her harsh mouth are turned down and her flat, aristocratic face is pinched with fury at the sight of us.

"Vivianne," she says, nodding to my mother.

There's no greeting for me.

"The traffic was simply abysmal," Mother says, as if small talk will somehow break the ice around us. But this isn't ordinary social ice. This is the thick, unbreakable kind that shuts down nautical passage.

Mrs. Daniels blinks. "I wouldn't know. Our driver brought me."

She knows damn well that we have a chauffer, too, but

I love the way the remark lashes back at my mother. If anyone has the right to change the tone of the meeting, it's Mrs. Daniels, and she's not about to relinquish that control.

Before I can mentally gloat too much, I remember that I might be stuck at family dinners with her for the rest of my life. Maybe she'll stay mad forever and I'll never have to speak to her.

The doors to the studio open and a thin East Asian man dressed in all black calls "Daniels?"

Ashton's mother leads the way, but my stomach sinks at the realization that this reservation was made under my *married* name. As free and hopeful as my transgressive meeting with Nathan made me, I still have to play the role of Ashton's fiancé. I put on my peppiest smile and resolve to look every bit the excited mate-to-be. It might make my worst-case scenario future more tolerable if I can win Mrs. Daniels over now, instead of after-the-fact.

"I'm Stephen," the man who leads us down the stark white hall says. "You must be the bride?"

"That's me." As we walk, I sneak glimpses at a few of the open doors we pass. Bolts of fabric, drafting tables, a mundane conference room, it's all so normal. I don't know what I was expecting, but thralls fascinate me; a society living symbiotically with ours, as removed from the human world as we are, and still totally secret? It seems like it should have a little more panache, a little more mystery.

"You're going to be meeting with Melissa today," Stephen explains, pausing outside a set of frosted glass double doors. "She's one of our top designers."

Mrs. Daniels is taken aback. "We were supposed to be with Alexis."

"Sadly, Alexis has been called away on royal business," Stephen says, and he doesn't sound sad about it at all. "You'll be meeting with Melissa. As I said, she's one of our top designers."

His no-nonsense delivery shuts Mrs. Daniels's dropped jaw and I have to hold back a snort of laughter. Did Nathan do this on purpose? Maybe I'm giving him too much credit. Either way, it's pretty funny to see my mating pact once again meddled with by the very existences of the new pack leader.

Stephen opens the doors to a bright, sun-flooded studio with light polished wood floors and trim and tidy work-stations. A dressmaker's form on a short circular platform wears an intricately beaded ceremonial robe of dusky pink silk that freezes the breath in my lungs.

"Just as you remember?" a voice asks, and I turn to face the source, a dark-skinned woman with slicked-back white hair and dramatic smoky makeup, who looks like she should be costuming superheroes in a movie instead of making wedding gowns for werewolves.

I nod, my whole body numb as I turn back to the robe. I *do* remember it. At least, I remember something like it. Rough, unfinished pieces of it basted together the first time I came to try it on. That had been just a month before I invoked the Right of Accord, when my mating ceremony had been only a few full moons away.

I walk around the garment slowly, feeling dizzy and faint. How could I have forgotten? The business changed locations while I've been away, but somehow, being fitted for my own wedding dress slipped my mind. Maybe that isn't the right phrase; maybe it's more like a repressed memory. It was truly traumatic, standing there as my Mother and Mrs. Daniels debated whether the sash should tie in the front or at the side, whether the color washed me out.

All those feelings crash over me again. I've only delayed the trap laid for me by destiny.

Meanwhile, Mother gasps and coos over the beadwork, the sweeping angel sleeves and tall, structured collar, while Mrs. Daniels eyes Melissa coolly.

"Alexis has done a wonderful job with it," Mrs. Daniels says pointedly.

"It's truly an exquisite piece," Melissa agrees, not giving Mrs. Daniels anything to argue with. Then, Melissa turns to me. "But it was created with a much different bride in mind, I hear."

Before I can answer, Mrs. Daniels cuts in. "The same bride. It's the ceremony that's been delayed. My son isn't interested in paying for a new robe to match whatever new person this one has become."

"This one?" Mother's offense surprises me, considering she has much the same opinion of my leaving as Mrs. Daniels has.

"Shall we try it on?" Melissa suggests, and I nod, a pit in my stomach as she carefully undresses the mannequin and leads me to the curtained-off changing area.

The collar and shoulders of the robe are stiff, starched into unforgiving lines. Melissa frowns as she ties the sash. "You've gained some weight since the last time we measured you."

I try to hold the top closed over my cleavage. "Maybe we need to put a button or—"

"A button? On a ceremonial robe?" She shakes her head. "Let's not lead a fashion rebellion."

"I know we've done things a certain way for a long time, but it's not like buttons are a fad. We could probably adopt them and not risk the downfall of the pack," I say with a derisive snort I can't hold back.

"Your mate has to be able to take it off of you," she says.

It's all in a day's work for her, but talking about the actual act of mating as part of the ceremony makes me profoundly uncomfortable, especially since we're talking about Ashton being the guy doing the undressing. I try to laugh it off. "Look, I'm not going to claim my fiancé is the smartest guy ever, but I think he can handle buttons."

Melissa's expression falls, and suddenly I'm not sure we're having the same conversation. Her eyes dart toward the curtain, hardly a soundproof barrier between us and the women beyond it, and she lowers her voice. "Do you know what happens at the mating ceremony?"

I shake my head slightly; if I move it too much, the dizziness is going to come back.

She breathes in sharply then goes back to adjusting the neckline of the garment. "We have plenty of room to let this out, so it closes all the way. Nobody wants to see a bride spilling out of her robe on the way to the chamber."

That does nothing to make the dread go away. I zone out, staring at my own reflection in the mirror as Melissa tucks and pins and adjusts. I want nothing more than to rip the damn robe off and flee from the studio entirely, but the unspoken questions raised by this stranger's remarks will just follow me.

When I'm appropriately covered, Melissa takes me out to display her handiwork to Mother and Mrs. Daniels—both of whom remark how unfortunate it is that I've gone up a size, like I've got a fatal disease—and they approve the changes that need to be made. I'm little more than a hanger.

After I've changed into my normal clothes again and we're off to what promises to be a very awkward lunch with Mrs. Daniels, I pull my phone from my purse and text Tara.

You need to tell me everything about the mating ceremony.

The only thing I know about the ceremony is that the couples whose pacts are sealed at Lupercalia gather before Lupa's monolith to be anointed with blood from the day's sacrifices. Then, acolytes take them to the ancient chambers beneath the huge mound built by our ancestors. That's where the spectators' part is finished, and they all go off to enjoy the rest of the Lupercalia celebrations. Nobody has bothered to tell me what happens after I disappear down that torch-lit path to the mound.

Three little dots appear on my phone screen then vanish. They appear again, they vanish again, over and over as Mother complains to me about Mrs. Daniels's coldness and how horrible it will be to sit down to a meal with her. I pretend to listen but it doesn't matter. Mother will air her grievances to a blank wall, just so long as she can complain out loud.

Finally, Tara sends a return message. It just says:

I'll come over tonight.

That doesn't reassure me at all.

CHAPTER 14

I'm in my room when Tara arrives, and she chirps into the intercom that she's coming up. Even as kids, we never had to share our space with each other, but we're all in the same hall, which father referred to as "the girls' wing." Even though Tara and Clare have moved out, their bedrooms are still there, though they've been redecorated a bit to remove fairy lights and school trophies.

My door creaks open and I sit up on my bed, tossing aside my book. "Hey."

"Hey," she says, and sighs deeply, sliding her hands into the back pockets of her jeans and rocking on her heels.

"That bad, huh?" I try to laugh as I swing my legs over the side of the bed, but the mood in the room is somewhere between "right before you find out grandma died" and "the sex talk with your parents."

Not that I've experienced either; our grandparents are all still alive and probably have a good hundred years left, and Mother has probably never even said the word "sex" out loud.

"You can sit down," I say, rolling my eyes. "Stop acting like you're here to break bad news."

"I thought everything about your mating ceremony would be bad news," she counters, heading toward the bed. She doesn't sit down, but throws her whole body across the middle, pillowing her chin on her hands. "Especially after the whole dinner thing."

"The dinner thing was—" I stop myself. I don't know if she'll run off and tell Josh all the details. "Not as big a deal as everyone is making it out to be."

I wonder if I should tell her what is partially the truth: Nathan wanted to meet me because we both invoked the Right of Accord. But that's not why she's here, so I hold onto it as an excuse for later.

"Mother said you went to Frobisher's today, so I assume the mating pact is still…" she trails off, waiting for my confirmation.

"Unfortunately. So, I need you and everyone else to stop being cryptic about the ceremony. Because I'm starting to think I'm going to have to bite the head off a lizard or something." I force a little laugh.

Tara groans and sits up. "You know, they should tell us about it in school when we have the whole 'your changing body' talk."

That makes it sound a lot worse than lizard heads. "Did Mother tell you?"

"She did. She'll probably tell you, too, the night before the ceremony. But I would have appreciated some lead time, so I'll tell you now." As if we're still kids, she double checks to make sure the door is closed. "You know the part where all the couples go to the ceremonial chambers, right?"

"At the mound," I confirm with a nod. "Yeah."

She sits cross-legged, wriggling her toes in her painfully corny printed snowflake socks. "After the acolytes lead you and Ashton and the other—"

"No!" I wave my hands. "Depersonalize this, please."

"Okay, okay." She rolls her eyes. "After the acolytes lead all the couples into the mound, everybody gathers in this open part in the middle. I swear, the full moon lines up directly with the hole in the top. I don't know how they managed to engineer that so long ago, without telescopes or—"

"The ceremony."

"Excuse me, it's just really cool." She scowls at me before continuing. "There's another monolith to Lycaon in the center circle, and all the couples are anointed with blood from a basin at its feet. Then the brides are separated from the grooms and taken to the ceremonial chambers."

"There's more than one?" I imagined the inside of the ancient, earth-topped mound to be one big, open space.

"There's a bunch. They're not big. They're like…cells in a medieval monastery or something."

"I don't spend a lot of time in medieval monasteries," I remind her. "But do go on."

"Fine. They're like…" She pauses to think, then brightens. "They're about the size of the guest bathroom downstairs. There aren't any windows, but there's this iron grate thing overhead that lets the moonlight through. And there's a smaller grate in the door but it's so dark in there it's not like you can see out very well."

I'm claustrophobic just imagining it.

"Anyway, inside there's a post with manacles, and the acolytes lock you in those—"

What?

"Hold on. Manacles?" I clamp my hand over my wrist then repeat the motion with the opposite ones.

"Do you see why I'm telling you now, and not the night before? Imagined how freaked out I was," Tara says with a shudder. "But seriously, it sounds worse than it is. It's actually kind of…sexy."

"Our definitions of sexy differ," I say, trying not to betray how fully disgusted I am at the thought of it. "Or maybe getting chained up in a dirt hole is hotter when you're actually attracted to your mate."

She shakes her head firmly. "Trust me, I was *not* into Josh at the time, and it was still pretty hot. I don't know how to explain it, but once you're anointed and the moon is out, it's like the werewolf part takes over. You want to mate."

I can't imagine a primal urge strong enough to make me want to mate with Ashton.

"I have no idea what the guys are doing while this is going on," Tara confesses. "Nobody's ever mentioned it and Josh said it was private. If I was supposed to know, then I would know."

"Where have I heard that before?" I ask wryly.

She nods in commiseration. As kids, all of our questions about ceremonies or religion were answered with some variation on that theme.

"He's right, though," she says, as if it's completely natural for one's mate to give such a patronizing answer. "Anyway, whatever they do, the brides just wait in their cells until the grooms get back. They come into the cell and —don't freak out—they strip you and administer ceremonial lashes."

"Like at the festival?" That seems extremely silly. I will definitely not be able to keep from laughing if Ashton bursts into the chamber and starts hitting me with a rawhide strip, the way the thrall acolytes chase women around at the party. It's always so goofy, and it doesn't hurt. It's just a jokey tradition for good luck.

Tara can't look me in the eye now. "Not like at the festival. It's a real whip, and it really, really hurts. I felt so bad for Josh because he kept saying 'sorry' after every lash."

"No way." I push myself up from the bed and bolt across the room, as if I can escape the ceremony by getting further from my sister's description of it.

"Do you want me to keep talking, or have you heard enough?" Tara asks, genuine concern behind her words.

I don't want to hear anymore, but not knowing will only make whatever I imagine after worse than it probably actually is. "Fine."

She hesitates, but continues when I shoot her an icy glare. "After the whipping, he transforms and the two of you…mate."

"While he's a werewolf?" Maybe I've been around humans too long, but that sounds so disgusting to me. Plus, everyone else in there is doing it, too? "Do the acolytes like, watch or something? This is so gross!"

"Nobody watches. That I know of," she quickly revises. "But trust me, it's not as mortifying as it sounds. You really get swept up in the ceremony. You feel like you're a part of something. And when it starts… you want to be a part of it."

"They probably didn't anoint you. They just smeared drugs into your skin or something," I mutter as I pace in front of my window.

"Oh, stop. You wanted to know what it was like, and I told you," she reminds me. "But yeah, you do feel drugged, I guess."

"Great." I throw my hands up. "And then what? He carries you over the threshold of your new house and you get to the live the housewife dream? Stay home, raise the kids, do whatever the head of the household tells you because that's the way it's always done? Yeah, I'm going to pass on becoming a zombie in an apron."

"Thanks for letting me know what you think of my life." Tara gets up and goes to the door, and I immediately feel bad for offending her. Before I can say anything, she pauses to say, "You were a lot nicer before you left, you know that, right?"

My mouth falls open. "When I unquestioningly accepted everything we were told by the pack?"

"Oh, please!" She makes a wordless shout of exasperation. "If you ever, even once in your life, unquestioningly accepted everything we were told by the pack, you wouldn't have gone looking for the stupid Right of Accord in the first place!"

"I didn't go looking for it! I didn't know it existed!"

"That's bullshit! You were looking for a loophole and you found one. And now, you don't like that you can't have it both ways. You're furious that you can't just pick and choose what parts of pack law you want to follow." Her sneer of disgust cuts me deep. "If you don't want to be a part of the pack, fine. But don't pretend like you're better than the rest of us. Don't pass judgment on us because we know who we are."

She storms out and I let her go, because in my anger at the situation I'll say something she doesn't deserve. But once she's gone, there's nothing stopping me from imagining all those things she's told me, all those horrible things Ashton is going to do to me. The idea of sleeping with him was bad enough, but letting him whip me and fuck me while I'm tied up in some dank cell is beyond twisted.

But it might not be Ashton.

Maybe it shouldn't change my feeling on the ceremony, overall, but if I replace Ashton with Nathan in my mind, it does. No drugging required.

I was unfair to my sister. It's not like staying at home and being a mother is a bad thing. I just hate that it's not a choice, but an expectation. Tara didn't make our world, she's just a part of it the way all of us are.

I can't do this. I can't be that person for Ashton.

I grab my keys and shoes and run downstairs and out a service door before anyone can see me. There's only one person who can strike down this mating pact, and I need an answer from him tonight.

CHAPTER 15

I have no idea what I'm doing as I race to Aconitum Hall. I don't know if Nathan will be there or if I can even see him. But he's the king; it's not like I have his private cell phone number or anything.

Then maybe you shouldn't be driving over to his house unannounced. My rational mind has a point, but my panic brain overrides it. I'm not rushing over to his house to declare my love or beg him to be my boyfriend. He's the pack leader, I'm his subject, and I need help.

There's a gatehouse at the main entrance, staffed by a thrall who looks up from her book with a suspicious expression as I pull up. She reaches to her hip to flick the safety off the gun in her holster before she opens the window.

Outside of hunting, I've never seen an actual gun in person before. That makes me wish I had thought my actions through a little more before tearing over here.

"Name and purpose of visit." Her voice doesn't go up at the end at all. It's not a question, but a warning that I shouldn't be here without a damn good reason.

"Um, Bailey Dixon. For Nath—for His Majesty the King. On personal business." I wince. When I left the house, I was so confident that I could just show up and speak to Nathan. I didn't really count on hardcore security, but he *is* a king.

"Do you have an appointment." Same flat delivery, like it's not a question.

"No." I have a strong feeling I'm not getting in, but before the disappointment can wound me too deeply, something else takes over. That strange vibration that fills the air when Nathan and I are near each other. It's like I can feel him, which is absurd. He's in a frickin' castle surrounded by security. He probably wouldn't know if I was two rooms over in his palatial mansion.

"His Majesty the king—" The guard's beleaguered denial is interrupted by a tuneless series of chimes. She looks away from me, toward the phone on the desk, and doesn't take her eyes off me as she answers. She does close the window, but I can still read a few words on her lips. "Bailey" and "no appointment," are the two easiest to decipher, and I worry that someone is sending down reinforcements. Instead, she hangs up the phone, opens the window, and says, "go ahead," as the massive black gates slowly part.

The sudden reversal of the situation is unnerving. So is the fact that as I pull up the drive, to where I parked last time, that weird magnetic feeling just increases. Once again, he's at the door before I can even reach the steps to it. And just like before, I practically melt into a puddle at the sight of him.

It's obviously his night off from being the pack leader; he's wearing black silk pajama bottoms and a black wool robe.

I stop at the bottom of the steps and try to make a joke. "It looks like I'm overdressed again."

"You're dressed," he says, gesturing down at his pajamas. "It's not terribly difficult to outdo me at the moment. I try to have clothes on when I have company, but I wasn't expecting visitors."

He doesn't seem to be annoyed at my intrusion, but I'm still nervous. I don't know what to say, so I stand there and look up at him, crushed by the weight of the compelling force between us.

With a tender frown, he comes down to meet me. "Bailey…did something happen?"

"I'm sorry. I shouldn't have just shown up. I didn't mean—" I turn away, planning to get into my car and, I don't know. Drive away, abandon my life, and replay this mortifying moment over and over every night before I fall asleep, forever.

"Wait." It's a command, not a request. I turn back slowly to face him, my pulse like thunder shaking my whole body. He comes down to meet me; even barefoot, he towers over me. "You came here for a reason, and you're here now. Come inside. Please."

I nod, speechless in my despair. What am I supposed to tell him? That I came here unannounced to beg him for help? It seemed like a good plan at the time but now I just feel like a fool. I'm not even officially a member of the pack yet. Not until my transformation.

"All right," is all Nathan says as he puts his arm around my shoulders and leads me into the house. His touch electrifies me, and I'm grateful my jeans and over-sized sweatshirt don't reveal my skin, because all of it is covered in goose bumps. He doesn't ask any questions as he leads me up the stairs to the private residence and into the sitting room from before.

I'm on the couch with a drink in my hand—vodka neat, he remembered—before he asks again, "Did something happen?"

"Something…" I blow out a breath. "Something stupid. No reason for me to bother you at home. You're the pack leader and—"

"I'm your future mate."

The pressure of our strange attraction swells in me and I nearly burst into tears. "Please, don't say that. Don't get my hopes up when it might not happen."

"It's going to happen," he states, so sure of himself it's maddening.

"You didn't even ask me if that's what I want," I lash out at him. At the only person who's actually interested in getting me out of my mating pact.

He pours himself some scotch, barely looking at me as he asks, "Is it what you want?"

"I want the mating pact between Ashton Daniels and I dissolved. I want it dissolved or else—" Or else, what? I'll leave the pack forever? They can't force me to stay, but the thought of trying to live in the human world on my own, without my father's financial support, terrifies me.

"Never resort to ultimatums, Bailey," he says calmly. "It puts you in a weak position and ends a negotiation."

"It's not a negotiation. It's just…I can't be with him. The thought of the mating ceremony alone disgusts me." My face gets hot talking about it in front of him. I quickly add, "And I don't want to have to live with him and be the mate he wants me to be."

Tears roll down my cheeks and I swipe them away, but the words I don't want to say, the ones I haven't dared myself to even think, force their way out, pushed by my panic. "I'm afraid."

Now that I've acknowledged my fear, the full force of it grips me. Sheer terror, to my bones. Worse than the thought of leaving the pack, worse than the idea of sleeping on the street somewhere or starving to death. I would rather die than be forced into a mating with Ashton.

"Don't be," is all Nathan says. Again, so confident, when I'm an emotional wreck. He reaches into a side table drawer and produces some tissue for me to dry my sniffles away, but there's no other comfort, just his unfaltering belief.

And it's more reassuring than anything else he could have possibly done.

"You're not going to be mated to Ashton Daniels." He sits beside me and I'm acutely aware of his body heat through his thin pajama bottoms. "You're going to make a choice. Tonight. Are you leaving the pack, or are you staying to be my queen?"

My mouth dries up and I gulp down my drink. It doesn't help. "You're not going to give me time to think about it?"

He shakes his head and takes the empty glass from me to put it on the coffee table. "You've thought about whether or not you want me. You can't hide it from me, Bailey. Every moment that we're together, you're thinking about what it would be like. Not to rule over the pack at my side, but what it would feel like if I touched you…"

He leans into me, traces the line of my jaw with his fingertips, barely skimming my skin as they move lower, over my throat and to the collar my sweatshirt, and I can't help the noise of longing that I make.

He's not wrong. I have thought about it. I've thought about it *a lot*.

The wide collar of the shirt slips from my shoulder easily, and he leans to press his lips there. "What it would feel like if I tasted you."

Another small, mewling noise escapes me.

His hand is suddenly pushing my face up, forcing me to meet his gaze. "Haven't you?"

I swallow, my nerves and uncertainty mingling with the desperate pull I feel between us, and there's no use denying it. "Yes."

"I know you have." His crooked, self-satisfied smile only lasts a moment, fading into a hunger that shakes me to my core. "Because I have, too."

His mouth covers mine and I shudder at the modicum of relief his kiss provides me. My body throbs at the softness of his lips, the sweep of his tongue, the way he threads his fingers into my hair to tilt my head back, leaving me breathless and completely under his control. I grip his shoulders, bunch his cashmere robe in my fingers and kiss him back, hard, desperate to fulfill the pounding need between us.

My hands slip beneath the robe. I have to feel his skin, need to feel him against me. He shrugs the garment off and the motion takes me back to the night of the ceremony, the firelight on his broad shoulders, and I sink my nails into them the way I've ached to in my fantasies. He takes a sharp breath against my panting mouth and nips at my lower lip. It hurts. I love it.

Because the truth is, I don't want to just fuck him. I want us to destroy each other in our passion.

I lean back to pull my sweatshirt off, and he goes one step further, grabbing my bra and giving it a sharp, strong jerk. The straps cut into my flesh before they give way, utterly ruined. I'm in his arms again, reeling from the dizzying sensation of his hot skin flush against mine. Another crushing kiss and his mouth moves down my throat. With one huge hand splayed on the small of my back, he guides me down on the sofa cushions, covering me. I open my legs, wrapping them around his waist despite my jeans and shoes. The latter bump him, and he barely breaks his concentration as he reaches back to roughly pull them off.

I arch up as his sucking kisses move across my collarbones and chest, grind my pelvis against him in desperation. My panties are soaked, my pussy aching with need that only intensifies when his mouth closes over my nipple. He grazes me with his teeth and I shout, long past moaning. I don't care if every thrall in the mansion hears me. All I want is for Nathan to know how he affects me, how much I want him, how totally I'll surrender my will, my dignity, everything I have if he'll just take me right here and now.

Sparks of sensation race through my blood at every sweep of his tongue over my tightly drawn up flesh, and when he turns his attention to my other breast, I swear my cunt flutters the way it does when I come from touching myself. It's not enough to satisfy my craving for him.

"I smelled you," he groans against me. "The night of the full moon. I hunted for you. I knew you wouldn't be there, but I searched for you. Your scent was inescapable. Maddening. What were you doing?"

"Making myself come." The words are out before I can even consider how filthy they are. *Might as well double-down.* "Thinking of you."

He bites the underside of my breast, hard enough to hurt, not hard enough for me to object to it. "Tell me."

"I was in my car. I couldn't even make it home. I pulled over on the road and I didn't care who saw," I gasp as his kisses move down my belly. He grips the waistband of my jeans and opens the button and zipper, tugs the denim down my thighs and I moan, "I wanted you to find me. I wanted you to fuck me right there."

I help him maneuver my legs so he can pull my jeans completely off. My panties, however, get the same treatment as my bra. He lifts the sopping white cotton to his nose and inhales deeply and I almost sob under the onslaught of a desire so keen, it's painful.

"Your Majesty?"

With two words, everything comes crashing down.

"What?" Nathan snarls at the thrall who's entered the room.

I shriek and scrabble backward, but Nathan keeps me tucked out of view; I only hear the thrall's deep, calm voice. He's not afraid to have interrupted the king at such a crucial moment. "A call for you."

"Didn't I say to hold my fucking calls?" Nathan is furious, reaching down to retrieve my sweatshirt from the floor so I can cover myself. "Get out!"

"You instructed us to hold all but one call, Your Majesty." The thrall isn't afraid. I would be trembling if Nathan used that tone with me. But the servant merely adds, "This is that call," before leaving the room.

Nathan swears, and my hopes plummet. He sits back and scrubs a hand over his face. His cock is an intimidating ridge straining against the silk lounge pants and I can't help but stare at the length of it exposed above his waistband, deep, dusky red and visibly dripping pre-cum.

He laughs and I realize I've licked my lips uncon-
sciously. Taking my hand, he kisses my knuckles and says,
"I hope you understand how important this interruption
must be, if it takes me away from you right now. I would
much rather be inside you."

Would it be too pathetic to cry? Despite the interruption, I'm still desperate for him. But I nod and force a
smile, taking another obvious glance at his erection. "I can
tell."

He kisses me, but it's restrained. He must have iron
self-control. I'm not insecure enough to imagine that he
doesn't want me. In confirmation, he whispers against my
mouth, "Right now, I hate being the king."

"I hate it, too." But I sit back and reach for my jeans,
my hands shaking. We were so damn close. It's a shame
I'm going to die of horniness before I get a chance to
fuck him.

"You'll be fine on the drive home?" He doesn't mean
because of the small amount of alcohol I've imbibed.

I can't believe that after what we were just doing, I can
blush at anything he has to say. But here I am, red-faced
and giggly. "I can show myself out, okay?"

I stand and go to the door before I can beg him to let
me stay. My hand is on the knob when he says my name.

When I turn, he has my ruined panties in his hand.
"Think of me tonight. I'll be thinking of you."

He takes one last, appreciative sniff of my wetness and
tucks the scrap of cotton into his pocket.

CHAPTER 16

It's one dinner. Just one, I tell myself as I approach the restaurant doors.

But I don't actually know if it's the last time I'm going to have to sit across from Ashton and pretend that I'm going to be his willing little wifey. I have no doubt that Nathan is going to make good on his promise to nullify Ashton's claim to me. I just don't know when. Lupercalia is still two weeks away. Plus, I haven't heard from the king since the night we almost…

I try not to think about that as the maître d' leads me through the dimly lit main floor, to a round banquette of soft ivory leather. Ashton waits there, his coppery hair combed back and brushing the collar of his expensive suit jacket. He rises with a broad smile, takes my hands and kisses my cheek. "I almost gave up on you."

I wish you would. I physically bite my tongue to keep from saying it. "I'm sorry. I got turned around on the way here."

He frowns as we slide into our seats. "You drove yourself?"

"Mmhm," I affirm through my closed lip smile.

"You shouldn't have." His concern is infantilizing and infuriating.

"Why not?" I tilt my head and pick up the wine list that was left for us on the table. There's a reason I drove myself tonight: the car is a good excuse not to go home with him. After all, I can't just leave a Bentley in a parking garage overnight, even at a pack-owned establishment.

"Toronto is a dangerous city," he says, as if I didn't live in London for five years on my own.

"I know," I say, practically gritting my back teeth.

"Well, it doesn't matter. You won't drive yourself when we're married." He pauses as the waiter stops at our table and, without asking my preference at all, orders us a bottle of Pinot Grigio and an antipasto platter.

It annoys me so much that I can't help but tell him, "I don't care for olives," in my iciest tone.

"Oh?" He's completely nonchalant about it, the same way he was about the driving ban he just announced. "I'll note that for next time."

There won't be a next time. I want to shout it in his smug face. My only regret about this situation with Nathan is that I won't see Ashton's face when he learns that he's lost me.

Not that he's ever truly had me. Even if we did end up mates—and I *will* leave the pack before that can happen— he will never know me and he damned sure won't own me.

"Bailey," Ashton begins with an embarrassed little chuckle. "Please, don't think me jealous or possessive, but I must know what happened at Aconitum Hall, between you and the king."

For a moment, my heart stops. Every clink of silverware and whisper of conversation in the restaurant is deafening. It's just two rapid blinks before I realize he's talking about the dinner and not the part where I almost fucked Nathan on his couch.

"Now that I've said it out loud, it does sound jealous. But how could I be jealous if I didn't truly care about you?" His eyes widen and for a moment I actually feel bad for him. "Indulge me?"

"It was nothing," I reassure him. Because that night, it really wasn't. "It was about a strange coincidence. And he wanted to apologize about the ball. He didn't realize that dancing with me would be such a big deal."

Ashton seizes on the first part. "What coincidence?"

I wave a hand. "It's just weird. He invoked the Right of Accord when he was young and he'd never met anyone else who had."

This doesn't seem to minimize the event at all for Ashton. "He invoked the Right of Accord?"

"Yeah. Isn't it weird that he knew about it?" I force a laugh. "I found it accidentally because I'm a book nerd. I guess he must be, too."

"There are better hobbies than reading," Ashton observes. "I'm sure you'll find one."

My face flushes with anger. "I hope you don't expect that I'll just stop doing the things I like to do because we're married." I know it doesn't matter, because I won't be married to him, but it infuriates me that he would even think he had the right—

"Of course, I do." He's so chipper about it, I have a sudden urge to lunge across the table and stab him. "Not everything. But you're not going to have time to comb through dusty old history books at the library for hours and still have time to be a good mate to me."

"Have you considered how you're going to be a good mate to me?" I ask, propping my elbows on the table and resting my chin on the back of my stacked hands.

That makes him laugh. "Do you think I don't intend to provide for you?"

"That's not what I'm asking." I bat my eyelashes and feign innocence.

He's taken aback, judging by the way he shifts in his seat. "Well… Earlier this year, I bought a vacation home in Negril. That's in—"

"Jamaica. I know geography."

"Of course." He flashes me his dazzling smile. "There's the family yacht, and I've recently put my apartment on the market. I thought we could buy something nearer to your parents. I know you won't want to be far from them."

"I don't even like my parents," I blurt.

"I—"

"You don't actually know me." Now that the dam has broken, I can't hold back the flood of rage I'm feeling. "You don't know anything about me."

"I'd like to get to know you," he says, too baffled to shut me up.

"After we're mates, right? When you can rearrange all the little bits of me?"

"Of course not!"

I shake my head and keep my voice low and neutral so we don't cause a scene. Not here, at a restaurant owned by a pack member. It's too full of eyes and furry fucking ears. "If you knew me at all, you'd know I don't spend hours upon hours in libraries. I hate libraries. I hate reading. I've tried to do as little as possible since we left school."

"Noted, then," he tries to appease me.

But I don't stop there. "You would know that Negril is

the last place I would want to vacation because I sunburn through eighty SPF sunblock, and I *loathe* sand. And the thing that would make me happiest in my life? Would be staying as far away from my parents as possible."

"Negril is far away," he says, trying for a joke. When I don't laugh, he immediately changes his tone. "I'm not interested in a mate intent on arguing with me at every turn."

"Then break the fucking pact," I shoot back.

For a second, I wonder if he'll smack me right there in the middle of the restaurant. He certainly seems like he wants to. The fury on his face terrifies me to my core.

I square my shoulders and glare right back. "I don't want to be with you, Ashton. I don't want to be your mate."

His laugh is crueler than any words he could hurl at me. "What you want doesn't matter. It didn't matter when your father and I signed the pact, it doesn't matter now, and it will rarely matter in our future together. Do you understand?"

I say nothing. Knowing that there is no future between us is cold comfort when I'm faced with someone who won't acknowledge that I'm a person. I feel every moment of those miserable hypothetical years crushing the air from my lungs like the spikes of an iron maiden.

"We will be mated at Lupercalia," he says, his knuckles going white as he balls his hand to a fist on the table. "You will be a faithful, *obedient* mate to me. You will bear our children, you will raise them, and you'll have anything you desire, within reason. If you misbehave, however—"

"I'll be grounded? I'll lose my privileges?" I'm pushing him. I want him to yell. I want him to embarrass himself, the way he claimed I embarrassed him by dancing with

Nathan. I want to shout every single filthy thought I've had about Nathan, I want to make Ashton hear about all the places on my body Nathan put his hands and his mouth. Instead, I demand to know, "Why me? When you don't know me? When you know I don't want you?"

"Because I can have you." There's such mean triumph in his voice I'm glad the wine hasn't arrived because I'd cut his face up with the broken stem from a glass. "You were so beautiful. And you never looked at me. Not once."

"Then you should have known I wasn't interested!"

"I don't care if you're interested." He sits back, both palms flat on the tabletop. "I want you, and I can have you."

I shake my head vehemently. "No, you cannot."

"The laws of the pack say otherwise."

"I'll leave the pack." I expect him to get angrier. Maybe shout at me, or stalk out of the restaurant.

Instead, he scoffs. "You're not going anywhere. The pack practically owns this city. There isn't a train or a bus, certainly not a plane that leaves with you on it."

I laugh in his face. "That's preposterous."

"It's the truth. Whether or not you believe it." He leans back and folds his arms. "You really think you're going to escape."

The fact that he's thinking of it with the same vocabulary I am is chilling. He knows I feel trapped. He knows I *am* trapped, and he relishes my fear and despair.

"We have thralls everywhere. You won't make it out of Toronto before they drag you back." He nods toward the door. "Get in your car and try it. Try to drive to the airport. See if you're not stopped by the OPP on the road or detained by the RCMP at the boarding gate. If you're even able to purchase a ticket, once your father cuts you off."

"You're sick." Tears rise in my eyes and I try to blink them away because I know, deep down, that he'll love seeing them. "You're just trying to, what, prove to me that I should have paid more attention to you in high school?"

"At first, I truly thought I loved you. Unrequited love, but there was a way around that." He shrugs and doesn't even bother to look at me while he speaks. "Then you had the gall to do what you did, to reject me so publically. And I realized how much you owe me."

"You're a psychopath."

"Maybe," he concedes. "But I don't have anything to prove to you, Bailey. I'm going to win. And you're going to lose. That's all that really matters to me."

I push out of the banquette, heading straight for the door. Ashton calls after me, but he doesn't get up and follow. If he does, I'm mad enough to physically fight him, so I hope he just stays in his seat and eats all the damn olives himself.

When I get into my car, I start the engine and take a minute to calm my racing pulse and jittering nerves. *He's not going to win. He's not going to win. Nathan is fixing all of this,* I remind myself. I wish I had a number I could call or text Nathan at, just to be reassured that he's going to follow through on his promise.

He could be just as bad as Ashton, I remind myself.

But I know I'm wrong. Nothing could ever be as bad as being Ashton's mate.

I just have to hope that Nathan will do something, anything to stop this, and soon.

CHAPTER 17

Nathan doesn't contact me for a full week.

The preparations for my mating ceremony have hit crisis mode. Mother, Clare, and Tara fret over the morning-after celebration. Everything from the guest list to the centerpieces have to be perfectly correct to hopefully erase the stain of What I Did.

I try my best to participate, if only to keep up the pretense that I'll be marrying Ashton.

His threats haunt me. Nightmares of desperately trying to run from him, only to be dragged back to the pack kicking and screaming have me waking up in a cold sweat nightly. I'm constantly exhausted and on-edge, and people are noticing.

"The bags under your eyes," Mother says at dinner one night, making a quiet tutting noise in lieu of finishing the thought.

"I haven't been sleeping well." *Because of you, because of what Father agreed to. Because of the pack and the fact that I'm a prisoner.*

"Ma'am?" Hudson steps into the dining room,

followed by two thrall soldiers with the royal seal sewn onto their Kevlar vests.

Father throws down his napkin and gets to his feet. "Since when do we interrupt dinner with unannounced guests, Hudson?"

The butler nods apologetically, but doesn't make any excuses. What was he supposed to do? Deny entry to royal thralls?

Their presence in our home suddenly clicks in my mind, and all sound in the room is replaced by the rush of white noise in my spinning head. I know one of the thralls says, "His Majesty, King Nathaniel, commands your presence," but I'm not sure how I hear it when I'm on the verge of fainting under the onslaught of relief and nerves and the terror that somehow, something will go wrong. It's like I'm running toward my escape, just like in my dreams, and I'm so afraid I'll be pulled back.

Father turns to Mother. "Don't fret. I'm sure I'll be back before too late."

"All of you," the thrall says, pointing to Mother and I.

Mother rises from her chair. "Hudson, it's the driver's night off. Could you—"

"That won't be necessary, ma'am," the other thrall says ominously. "We'll provide transportation."

They let us get our coats, then march us out to a black van with tinted windows. They place us in a single row of seats in the middle and slam the door, and Mother turns to Father with fear in her eyes. "You haven't done anything…"

Father puts on his seatbelt, grunting with annoyance, but he doesn't answer her.

The ride to Aconitum Hall is interminable. No one says anything. Mother and Father don't bother with questions, either because they won't deign to speak to the thralls or they know the thralls won't give them any answers. But deep down, I know that this is it. It must be.

I'm not sure why Nathan chose to do it this way, with soldiers and after-dark van kidnapping, but this *has to be* the moment he frees me from the pact.

When we turn down a familiar street, I'm not so sure.

We pull up in front of Clare's house and the two thralls get out of the vehicle, locking the doors behind them. Just as quickly as they collected us, they march Clare and Julien out to sit in the row of seats behind us.

"What's happening?" Clare's eyes are wide and frightened and I feel guilty that I'm not immediately offering up what I know.

When we stop again for Tara and Josh to get into the very back seats, I begin to doubt that I know anything, at all. I expected something more along the lines of a letter or a phone call. Not…whatever this is.

All the lights at Aconitum House are ablaze, and there are more vans lined up, with more thrall soldiers escorting more werewolves toward the doors.

"It's a coup," Julien says quietly. "Greater London has taken over."

"Do you think so?" Father asks. He gazes out the window at a couple in evening clothes being marched up the steps.

"That's Barbara and Thom," Mother says. "They must have plucked them right out of the opera house."

Every second that ticks by, it seems less and less likely that I'm here for my salvation. By the time the thralls lead us up the steps and into the entrance hall, I'm sure I'm here for something so much worse.

It's surreal to walk past the stairway that leads up to

the private residence. I've been here, in this house, naked and splayed out on the king's sofa, and now I'm here as a prisoner. It's bizarre. And I don't like that all of the thralls around us are armed with guns. Visions of the Romanovs fill my head.

Nathan wouldn't have me killed, I think, and then a moment later, *why wouldn't he?* It's not like he loves me. I don't necessarily have any value; he wants to fuck me and thinks I'd be a good queen. That could probably be said of a lot of people in the pack.

Chairs are arranged in a semi-circle at the foot of the dais in the throne room. The thralls seat us in the front row, while more people fill in behind us. There are about five other families, but I don't see the Daniels.

This isn't about the mating pact.

This is something bad.

Then, beyond the doors, I hear Ashton's father demanding, "Why are we here? You can't just take us—" before a noise of wordless outrage as he and his wife are bodily pushed into the room. Ashton follows without resistance, and I turn my back before our eyes can meet. The sound of the throne room doors shutting behind us is so loud and final, I almost sob.

The same majordomo from the ball enters from a side door and announces, "His Majesty, King Nathaniel."

When Nathan enters, he doesn't look at me. I'm right in front of him, and he doesn't look at me. All I can hold onto is the inexplicable pull between us, but even that seems diminished somehow.

Nathan sits on the massive throne as we all rise from our seats and bow or curtsey. A bored wave of his hand indicates we may be seated again, and he waits until we are before he starts to speak.

"I assumed that when you all knelt before me and swore your fealty to me and to your pack, you did so in good faith."

My hopes plummet. What has my father, my entire family, done?

"I assumed that, like myself, you had nothing but reverence and respect for this pack, and a desire for its survival," he goes on. "That you wished to heal from the actions of your deposed tyrant king and become a stronger pack despite his treachery."

Father shifts in his seat beside me.

"Perhaps those assumptions were too optimistic." Nathan pauses and I swear I can count the breaths of every person in the room. They're all just as freaked out as we are.

"Julien Hart." Nathan says my brother-in-law's name like a death sentence. "Did you take a meeting with an ambassador from the Saint-Laurent council?"

My eyes widen as I look to my sister. Clare is just as shocked as I am, judging from the look on her face.

"I won't deny it." Julien lifts his chin, defiant. "There are no pack laws that forbid such meetings."

"No, there aren't," Nathan concedes. "But it troubles me that this meeting took place in the human world, away from the eyes of the pack. Your wife was at the meeting, as well, was she not?"

Clare shakes her head vehemently. "No, Your Majesty, I never—"

"My wife was at lunch with her sisters," Julien speaks over her.

The restaurant. That's why Nathan was there that day. He was spying. And my sisters didn't choose the restaurant because they were ashamed of me. They didn't mind letting me believe that, but they were there because their husbands were there. They just didn't tell me.

"Joshua Perdue, you arranged this meeting." Nathan isn't asking now. He's accusing.

And just like Julien, Joshua doesn't deny it. "I did. The ambassador is my cousin. We were having a friendly lunch."

"A friendly lunch," Nathan repeats back to him. "With an ambassador from the Saint-Laurent pack, your brother-in-law, your father-in-law, Stephen Daniels, Ashton Daniels, Jacob Wray…"

Nathan's voice fades into a muffled roar in my head as he lists the names of the men who are guilty of… well, I don't know. I was away from the pack too long to know much about current politics, but I *do* know that consorting with another pack, without the knowledge of the royal office, is very, very bad.

Punishable by some very, very bad things.

It's one word that snaps me back to attention. That word is "treason," aimed directly at my brother-in-law.

"Joshua Perdue, you have been found guilty of treason—"

"By whom?" Josh shouts.

Nathan doesn't answer him. He just pronounces the sentence. "All of your material assets are forfeit to the pack. You and your immediate family will be remanded into the custody of the royal guard and taken to a place of exile, where you will remain for no less than one century."

I've never been shot, but I know in my soul that it's less painful that the blow Nathan has just delivered. *My sister.* I've just come home, just gotten her back, and now Nathan is banishing her?

He sentences Julien and Clare to the same, and my

chest aches with agonizing pressure. *My sisters…gone.* We may live much longer than mortals, but a century is still an eternity to be parted from them.

Three families receive a reprieve from banishment but not from the loss of their bank accounts, their houses, their cars, their seats on the council. Another receives twenty-five years of banishment but retains their home and business. Nathan is ruthless in his edicts, ignoring the shouts of outrage from the condemned.

Nathan's skipped over Mother and Father, who glare up at him, their expressions without any emotion beyond hatred. Even now, in the face of total upheaval, they remain stone.

I must have some of that in me, because I don't cry, don't give my sisters tearful looks of goodbye or try to hold their hands as the guards lead them away. I don't look when I hear struggle behind me, which is quickly subdued. I don't want to know what's happening to anyone, because I can't even comprehend what's happening to me.

Ashton's parents are stripped of their wealth and banished for a century, just like my sisters and their husbands. Then, Nathan moves on. "Ashton Daniels."

A strange hope flares up in me. Maybe he'll be exiled. Maybe he'll be sent away and I'll never see him again. But then I remember that I'll likely be banished, too, and it's not the outcome I hoped for in this situation.

It startles me to realize that despite not really knowing Nathan and definitely not knowing where I fit into my pack, I don't want to be away from either of them. I truly did want to be queen, at his side. Maybe for vanity's sake, to prove that I'm better than everyone thinks I am. Maybe just because of the inexplicable draw we feel to each other.

But I was thinking that the worst thing that could possibly happen to me would be to marry Ashton.

This…

I can never forgive Nathan for this.

Then he says, "You are guilty of treason. All of your material assets are forfeit to the pack. And your mating pact to Bailey Dixon is void."

CHAPTER 18

I don't want to feel grateful or relieved that Nathan has freed me from my obligation to Ashton. I don't want to feel anything other than angry at the man who's sending my sisters away, ruining their lives, probably ruining my life, when he finally gets around to sentencing my father.

"Thomas Dixon." Nathan's tone takes on a strangely friendly note that I can't trust. "You have been found guilty of treason. But you came to my aid and proved a loyal ally during the earliest days of my reign. I wonder what I have done to lose your confidence."

"Your Majesty—" Father begins, but he doesn't seem to have anything else to say. He just shrugs his shoulders. "I've made an error in judgment. Please, don't punish my daughters for it."

"I'm not punishing your daughters for your wrongdoing," Nathan says, maddeningly reasonable. "They're being held accountable for their mates' crimes under pack law."

The other families have been taken away by the guards. Only Ashton, Mother, Father, and I remain.

Nathan rises and comes down from the dais. He surveys all of us in turn, and for the first time all evening, our eyes meet.

I hope he feels every ounce of hatred in my glare. I hope he feels all my violent thoughts like knives through his flesh. But it probably wouldn't matter; he seems incapable of understanding another person's pain. Otherwise, he wouldn't be causing me so much.

Did he ever promise you care? Devotion? I've been so foolish. No, I "intrigue" him. He's attracted to me. There's something strange in the air between us even as my heart has turned against him. But there hasn't been anything else. He doesn't owe me anything.

And my family has betrayed him.

"You've already lost two daughters," Nathan says, looking away from me, as if he has nothing to do with our family getting torn apart. "I would hate to see you separated from another. Your assets are forfeit to your daughter, Bailey Dixon. And you will sign a new mating pact for Bailey. With me."

Father looks to Mother, then to me, before he stammers, "W-what about banishment, Your Majesty?"

"Would you like to be banished?" Nathan asks coolly. "What about you, Mr. Daniels? Is that a punishment you believe you all deserve?"

None of them answer. If a feather drifted through the air and brushed up against the ceiling, we would hear it. And Nathan lets us sweat in that silence.

"I'm an outsider. It's not a secret," Nathan says, his piercing gray eyes fixing on my father. "But you, Thomas. You fought harder for me to assume this position than any council member. What could have changed, that you now think of me as a threat to your pack's independence?"

I think back to the night in the ballroom, the hushed conversations and whispers that Nathan had come to take the Toronto pack for Greater London. If Father believes that, he must have some reason.

"But would I seize my queen's throne?" Nathan asks. "Perhaps a marriage pact between your daughter and I will convince you that I am not here to claim Toronto on behalf of my former pack."

"Are you *fucking* kidding me?" Ashton bursts out, and Nathan is so shocked, Ashton is able to get in, "I lose my assets, my parents are banished, and Thomas Dixon becomes a member of the royal family?"

Guards move in, but Nathan raises his hand to stop them.

"I don't need to explain myself to you," Nathan reminds him. "But I'll forgive your disrespect this time. You're emotional. Criminals often are when they face the consequences of their actions."

What about the consequences my sisters are facing? I want to rage. *When they weren't the ones who did anything wrong?*

And why am I facing the consequences of something I didn't do? I haven't even been back for a full month. That's certainly not long enough to have been able to plot anything. I was entirely focused on not getting married to Ashton.

Well, I've certainly found my way out of that one.

Ashton hasn't grasped that, it seems. "You can't just take my mate."

"She isn't your mate," Nathan says calmly. "And she'll be mine at Lupercalia."

I hate the way my stupid, horny mind immediately flashes to the images I've fantasized about ever since the last time I saw Nathan; scenes of being chained up in the ceremonial chamber, Nathan's clawed hands holding my wrists, pinning me between the rough wooden post and his straining muscles.

This man just obliterated my life. I should be sick at the thought of being his mate. But that awful desire, the force I don't understand, has a stronger hold on me than my morality. And it frightens me.

Nathan turns and walks back up the dais. "The guards will see you out."

"We…can go home?" Mother asks, blinking in astonishment.

"No." Nathan sits on the throne. "You don't have homes anymore. They belong to the pack now. The council will decide what happens to them, but in the meantime, they're under guard while your belongings are searched and confiscated."

"Where are we supposed to go?" Father asks pathetically.

Nathan shrugs. "Quebec? I hear your son-in-law has family there."

All of our possessions are being confiscated. We don't have a place to sleep? I stand slowly and the room sways. My tennis shoes under my bed. My phone in my purse on my nightstand. The fucking *nightstand*. Everything is gone, in the blink of an eye, and if no one will take us in tonight, we'll suffer through the cold, alone.

"Come on, Bailey," Mother says gently. She's rarely maternal toward me, so I assume I must look as disoriented as I feel.

"No," Nathan says, the word echoing like a gavel. "I will take possession of Bailey immediately, while we await our mating ceremony."

Take possession of me? The arrogant, misogynistic

bastard. All of his bullshit about me making a choice, about how I'd be a good queen for him... all of this was going to happen, anyway. He knew all along.

He knew the night we almost...

I want to throw up. Had that been what the call was about? The one that interrupted the hottest night of my life? He'd been waiting for a call that would lead to the destruction of my entire family, and he'd gone right ahead and felt me up, anyway.

He would have gone farther, if not for that phone call.

Two guards approach me. I expect Nathan to stop them, but he just says, "Escort her to her rooms, please."

This can't be happening. I wonder what the guards will do if I try to run, but I should probably worry more about what I would do if I ran. Because there's nowhere I can go. Ashton's already made that clear.

We leave the throne room the way I entered, and they take me to the stairs I've walked up twice before. In the long pink entry hall of the private residence, the door to the sitting room is open. My stomach roils at the glimpse I get of the interior before the guards open a side door and lead me into a part of the house I've never seen.

The ceilings are taller here, and cathedral style, in contrast to any of the other rooms I've seen. Thick wooden beams held in place by heavy bolts cross high above our heads, and a huge stone fireplace dominates the space. There are chairs and a couch, a coffee table, and some other furniture, all of it in heavy, dark wood. It's beautiful, but a prison is still a prison, even if it looks like a minimalist interior designer built a Medieval Times restaurant.

"Hello, Ms. Dixon," a chipper voice says behind me, and I turn to see another thrall, this one thankfully unarmed—as far as I can tell—and dressed like a normal person. She's white, with a face that looks like what it feels like to get pinched, and peachy-blonde hair pulled back in a tight, low ponytail. "I'm Amanda. I'm here to help you in any way that I can."

"How the fuck do you think you're going to help me?" I blurt.

She blinks rapidly and throws her arm out toward a pointed arch doorway. "Your bedroom is this way."

We climb a stone spiral staircase, small, rectangular stained-glass windows following our path up. We're in one of the towers. I'm literally imprisoned in a tower.

At the top of the stairs, a half-circle bedroom decorated in the same modern-medieval style waits for me, complete with a huge bed with a wooden canopy, rose-colored curtains, and enough mattresses that it might actually be from the story about the princess and the pea. The thick ivory duvet matches the plush carpet and pillows in various shades of rose and gold take up easily half of the bed. There's another fireplace here, smaller than the one downstairs, and unlit.

A door on the room's lone flat wall stands open. "The bathroom and dressing room are through there, though there is, of course, a half-bath in your parlor," Amanda says.

"For whom? All the guests I'm going to have?" Maybe I shouldn't be taking my anger out on this poor thrall, but she's the only person here to lash out at. *Sorry about your luck, Amanda.* "Does *His Majesty* sleep here?"

"No, ma'am," Amanda answers without a hint of annoyance at me. "He sleeps in another tower."

Another tower. "You have got to be kidding me."

"His Majesty did say he intends to come to you later."

She sounds like she's trying to cheer me up. She's picked the wrong fucking tactic.

"I'm sure he does," is all I say in response. I can't take any more of this. "Amanda, can I be honest with you?"

"Of course, ma'am."

"My entire life was just ripped away from me. My family is destroyed. The one person I thought was on my side was using me and lying to me. I'm trapped here. And all I want," I say, my voice dropping to a deadly low I've never achieved before, "is a fucking cheeseburger and to be left the fuck alone."

"Cheeseburger," Amanda says, seizing on the only thing in her purview. "What would you like on—"

"Get out!" I shriek, and she curtseys and scurries down the stairs.

I stand there, frozen with shock. I dig my nails into my wrist, hard, because I have to wake up. I can wake up in London, to my alarm in my tiny little bedroom in the flat I share with three other humans. I won't even complain about going to work.

But even when I draw blood, I'm still in Aconitum Hall. I'm still standing in my new royal bedroom. My new royal life. I throw myself down on the bed and scream into the pillows.

I'm still royally fucked.

CHAPTER 19

Nathan doesn't come to see me until two a.m. It's okay, though, because I'm still up, still furious, and I have the empty plate my burger was served on.

"Hey!" he shouts when the plate hits the wall beside the door as he opens it. He's forced to briefly retreat to avoid shards of airborne china, but he doesn't give up, even when I hurl my glass at him. That, he merely side-steps while closing the door behind him. "Bailey," he says, annoyingly reasonable. "Calm down."

The two words guaranteed to make me fly even further off the handle. I grab the bundled silverware I never used and hurl it at him. "Fuck you!"

This time, I manage to hit him, but napkin-wrapped cutlery doesn't inflict the devastating kind of damage I want to. It doesn't inflict any damage at all, other than making him look momentarily silly as he tries to swat it away.

"I'm sorry, I chose my words poorly." The way he says it makes it seem like *he's* the one who's been put in a shitty situation and *I'm* somehow making things worse.

"Fuck you!" I scream at him again. "Poor choice of words? The poor choice was banishing my sister and ruining my parents!"

It's late. My head is pounding. My body is trembling from renewed adrenaline, and I decide that maybe sometimes, like now, for instance, violence actually is the answer. I run at him.

He doesn't move. He stands there and lets me collide with him, actually stops me from falling even as I punch wildly at him. I'm not as tough as I assumed I was; I'm not strong enough to actually hurt him or affect him in any way. But I try, abandoning my ineffectual punches for somewhat effectual slaps. He takes every one of them, even the hard blows to his face that make my palms sting.

"I hate you!" I scream at him, looking for any flicker of emotion on his face. But there isn't any, and a disappointment I couldn't have anticipated sucks all the strength out of me. I fall to the floor like a marionette with cut strings, and I finally let myself cry.

After a long moment, Nathan speaks. "Your father, your brother-in-laws, they plotted against me. Not just to remove me from power, but to do it permanently. To kill me."

"That's not true." I shake my head. My father isn't capable of plotting anyone's murder.

But Ashton might be.

I think about how cold Ashton was at dinner, how entitled. But is that an indication of murderous tendencies? If so, the man standing in front of me right now, watching me sob on the floor is probably also capable of it. But if he is, why didn't he sentence all those traitors to death? It was his right, by the law of the pack. They broke their oaths, and that's a worse crime than treason.

"We have ample evidence of the conspiracy," Nathan says. "And considering your father's part in it, I've been extremely lenient with him."

"But not with my sisters." I look up at Nathan, who'll be my mate in less than a week. "How can you do this to me and think I would ever want to be with you?"

That seems to move something in him because he can't answer me.

"Leave," I whisper. "Please."

He hesitates.

"Go!" I scream it at him with the last of my strength, and it dies out on angry, wracking sobs that feel like they'll break my ribs.

He makes no attempt to comfort me or even help me up. "If that's your wish."

I lay down, exhausted, and press my cheek to the cool wood floor. I watch his shoes as he goes to the door, and somehow rally myself to croak, "Don't take my sisters away. Please. Please. I'm begging you."

His steps slow, and he turns back. A flicker of hope sparks in me, and I can't let it go out, if he's actually going to listen. I push myself up on arms as limp as spaghetti and entreat again, "Please. Don't take them away from me."

I must be the most pathetic thing on the planet, because he actually comes back. He stands over me, and I can't look up because the perspective makes him seem so impossibly giant, and I hate feeling small.

"I can't reverse the banishment."

I inhale sharply, my lungs shuddering.

"But I can limit its parameters. I can allow them to return to the pack. But they would have to choose to leave their mates." He pauses. "And their mates would have to agree."

"You can't order them? By royal decree or something?" What's the use of being king if he can't make the rules he wants to make? A part of me thinks I should point that out; challenge him with an accusation of weakness. At the same time, I know it won't put him on the defensive the way it might another man.

Another maddening silence instead of an answer. All he does is offer his hand to me.

Sniffling, I take it, and he pulls me to my feet, then off them, lifting me up to cradle me against his chest. I let him carry me up the stairs and hate, hate, hate that unexplained pull between us. After what he's done to my family, to me…

My anger comes back as he sits me on the edge of the bed, and I glare up at him. "You lied to me."

He tilts his head in question and turns on the bedside lamp. "I said I would nullify your mating pact. I have."

"You said you thought I would be a good queen for you. That I would be a good mate." I can't believe I fell for that. How could he possibly have known? "You knew all along that I was going to be an insurance policy."

Wordlessly, he goes to my bathroom. I hear water run in the sink and he returns with the sleeves of his crisp white shirt rolled up his thick forearms, holding a washcloth. He hands it to me. "For your face."

The washcloth is cold and when I touch it to my skin, I feel immediately better. Physically, that is. I'm still emotionally miserable.

He sits beside me on the bed with a tired sigh. "I could have just as easily sent you away with your parents as your sisters were banished with their mates. You wanted out of your mating pact. I needed an assurance that your father won't make further moves against me."

"That makes me an insurance policy," I point out. "Or a hostage."

"Or a queen," he argues. "Didn't they teach you history in school? Kings and queens and noblemen?"

"Of course, they did."

"And those royal marriages? What were they based on?" He waits for a response I don't make before going on. "Political advantage. If a king marries his daughter to the ruler of a neighboring country, will he then attack that country? Put his daughter in danger?"

"Maybe." I don't want to give him the satisfaction of being even partially right, but now that my unsustainable level of rage is dropping, he's beginning to make sense. "But that doesn't change the fact that you told me it was a choice. You made me promise to become your mate, when you were planning to force me into this, anyway."

"No." His gentle denial sucks the air from the room. "That's why I asked you to make the choice, Bailey."

I meet his eyes and see a pain there that he couldn't possibly be faking. He wants me to believe him. It wounds him that I don't.

"I never lied to you when I said I thought you would be a good queen. You make difficult choices and follow them through. You survived on your own after you invoked the Right of Accord—something I thought only I had done. And I never lied when I said I thought you'd make a good mate for me." He tentatively touches my cheek. "I've known you are mine since the moment I laid eyes on you at the ball. Since the moment I touched you. I can't explain it—"

"You feel it, too," I whisper. His eyes widen in startled

surprise and even though that's enough affirmation for me, I add, "The...pull."

He nods slowly.

"What is it?" I ask, my voice barely squeaking out.

"I don't know." The fact that he doesn't is unsettling. "I've never heard of such a thing happening before. I wondered at first if it had something to do with the Right of Accord, if it's meant to keep us with our own kind. But what I do know is that I dream of you, Bailey. You haunt me. And I hate to admit it but if you had chosen to leave the pack instead of accept my offer... I might not have let you go."

Whatever the strange attraction is, it swells between us now. I see the hunger in him, the desperation I know too well, that I couldn't bury under my layers of anger and sorrow. It claws its way up through me, energizing me with raw need, and I feel it building in him, too, echoing what I feel and projecting it back a thousand fold.

I hate him. But I don't. I never want to see him again. But I don't want him to leave. And when he grabs me and kisses me so hard, I have to hold onto him to stay afloat, I realize that this has never been a choice for either of us.

He pulls me roughly into his lap and grips the hair at the nape of my neck, baring my throat to him. "You're mine," he groans against my hot skin.

"Yours," I whisper back, and I know to the depths of my soul that it's the truth.

CHAPTER 20

Maybe it's not a good idea to sleep with the man who just turned my entire world upside down. But ignoring the almost painful need that binds us is a growing agony, and the closeness of his body is a welcome distraction. It's not like things could get better by not doing it, and for some reason, Nathan's hands on me feel righter than my anger does.

His heated kisses reach the collar of my t-shirt, so I lean away to take it off. He pulls the lace cups of my bra down and buries his face against my breasts, and I arch my back, trusting that he can hold me up with the single hand splayed across my lower back. Gripping my thighs around his waist helps steady me, but it maddens me at the same time. I physically ache to feel his skin on mine, to touch as much of him as I can with as much of myself as I can, and my jeans are not helping.

"I couldn't get you out of my mind," Nathan murmurs. "All of the things I wanted to do to you…"

"Do you still want to do them?" I gasp as his teeth close over my nipple and I can't help myself. I grab the front of his shirt and give it a hard jerk, popping some of the buttons. He lifts his head and captures my gaze with his steely, intense one, and it's as though he can stop time at will.

Before I know what's happening, he lifts me off his lap and deposits me on the bed, kneeling between my legs. I scramble to unzip my jeans and shimmy them down my legs as he tears himself free of his shirt. He tosses it aside and helps me undress the rest of the way, his knuckles dragging against my flesh in his hurry to get my panties off.

I'm naked in front of him again, and it's just as thrilling at the first time. Less humiliating, too, unless a thrall decides to burst in.

When I think about the purpose of that interruption, I feel a little sick. I force it out of my mind; there's no reason I can't have this diversion. Besides, he's going to be my mate. I'm not doing anything wrong.

Even if I were, it wouldn't matter. Because the moment Nathan slides down my body, hooks his arms under my knees and spreads my legs, I would let him do so many very wrong things to me. I squirm, overwhelmed by the anticipation building as he presses his mouth to my inner thigh.

"I need this," he groans. "I need to taste you."

I can barely speak, but I whisper urgently, "do it."

He covers me with his mouth and parts my labia with his tongue. My hips buck involuntarily at the shocking wet against my own slickness and he grasps my hips in his big hands, pinning me to the mattress easily. I don't bother to test against him; I know I'm helpless and I love it. I thread my fingers through his dark silk of his hair and tighten my grip, holding on as he makes gentle circles around my clit with his tongue.

My skin is electrified, sparks jumping from everything that touches me. His mouth, the stubble on his jaw, the duvet beneath me and even the air around us, everything hums with sensation, overwhelming me, writhing and snapping inside me until I shout my release with my sweat-slick thighs clamped around Nathan's head. I'm so drunk on pleasure that when he rolls over and pulls me on top of him, the room spins. Or maybe it's just the agility with which he's able to pull me up with my knees on the bed and his head between them.

I shout in panicked overstimulation, but he holds me against his face, pushing his tongue deep into my pussy. My body shudders as I ride his tongue, insensate with the desire that climbs higher with every one of Nathan's groans. He licks deep, tongue curling and uncurling inside me, coaxing more of my wetness out until we're both sticky and panting. I pull at my nipples, my hips moving to the rhythm of his tongue inside me, his nose bumping my clit in firm passes. This time, when I break, I can't make a sound. My mouth falls open and nothing but the rattle of my stuttering breath issues as I buck and twist.

He sits up and growls, "get on your hands and knees," but I can't get my bearings fast enough, so he pushes me into position. I hear his belt buckle and zipper and it's all so startlingly like the dream I had about him that I'm momentarily afraid I'll wake up.

But I can't be dreaming the way it feels when the tip of his cock brushes me. I can't just be imagining how he stretches me as he thrusts deep and stays there. My imagination isn't this good.

He bites down on my shoulder, and I cry out, but he

doesn't relent, holding me there with his teeth as he slams into my body again and again, each slap of his hips against my ass punctuated with a low, wordless vocalization. An intoxicating mix of pleasure and pain and even some fear drives my own whimpers. He's so much bigger than me, so much stronger than me, and more powerful in so many ways. But when I clench down on him, when I push back to meet him, he sounds like the helpless one.

I moan in dismay as he pulls out. Is it over, this soon? "Don't stop!"

"I'm not." He wraps me in his arms and drags me from the bed with him, boosting me up to wrap my legs around his waist as he stands. I cling to his shoulders and yelp in surprise when his cock spears into me again, and I'm held aloft while he lifts me up and down, driving his length deeper, harder.

He's so hard and so big, I feel like I'm being bashed apart. I want more, I want it rougher, I want to fragment into the shards I see behind my eyelids as I come again, screaming. He drops into wing-backed chair in front of the fireplace, never pulling out of me. His hips surge up once, twice, and he grabs me, pulls me tighter to him and gives over to his own release with a roar. I feel him flooding my cunt with deep, jerking pulses, and it breaks new shivers out over my hypersensitive body. I dip my fingers down and rub my clit, undulating on his lap, milking every last drop from him with sharp squeezes of my inner muscles. The thick, wet sound of his cum leaking out with every thrust pushes me over the edge again, and it takes a moment for my head to clear.

I don't realize I've tipped backward until he catches me with a gentle, "Careful."

"Sorry," I croak, my throat dry from shouting. "I'm sorry."

He chuckles weakly. His softening cock slides from my body. My head begins to clear, and I realize how worn out I am, not just physically, but mentally and emotionally. He tucks my head against his shoulder and smooths a palm down my hair. "It's never been like that before."

"Like what?" I yawn.

He goes still and says, uncertainly, "Didn't you feel it?"

"Hmm?"

There's something I'm not getting, and it seems like it's making him uncomfortable. "The need. The hunger I felt for you, it was all-consuming. Violent, almost."

"I know. And I did feel that." I'll probably feel it tomorrow, too, whenever I try to do anything that involves my adductors. "I just didn't have anything to compare it to."

He gently pushes me away, so we're sitting face to face. "I think I'm misunderstanding something… are you—"

"Well, not anymore." I can't help my small giggle. "I was a virgin twenty minutes ago but not anymore."

His expression falls in utter dismay. "Why didn't you tell me?"

I take his face in my hands and kiss him. I don't know how I can feel this tenderness toward him, after everything that happened earlier tonight, but I do. "Because it didn't matter."

He opens his mouth to protest, but I kiss him into silence and he doesn't argue. Despite the sweat covering us both and the fast thrum of his pulse in his throat, he has enough stamina to carry me to the bed and pull back the covers. It's as soft as I would expect a princess's bed in a tower to be, and I give a relaxed sigh as he lies down beside me.

"You're all right?" he asks, far too concerned about the non-issue of my virginity.

"With what just happened?" I clarify. "Yes. With what happened in the throne room tonight? No. But we'll talk about that when I'm not made out of overcooked pasta."

He reaches over me to turn off the illuminated bedside lamp, then settles back on his own pillow. There's still a restless energy about him, though, and it makes it difficult for me to fully surrender to sleep.

He rolls over to spoon up behind me and his lips brush my ear as he whispers, "Bailey...did you mean it when you said you hate me?"

"No." I don't have to hesitate to think about the answer. I don't hate anyone. Not my father, for conspiring to kill Nathan; I understand the urge. Not Ashton: nothing he does affects me, now. Certainly, I don't hate Nathan. Right now, he's the most stable thing in my life. That's entirely his fault.

But he's all I've got.

CHAPTER 21

I wake to an unfamiliar voice.

"Your Majesties, a letter from the council."

I can barely open my eyes, convinced I've only been asleep for a few minutes, but the sunlight that assaults me through the windows says otherwise. I mumble something, try to push myself up, but I'm too exhausted and my muscles are too sore to expend any real effort.

The blankets rustle as Nathan gets out of bed and I watch through the reluctant, narrow opening of my eyelids as he walks across the bedroom, totally nude, like there isn't another person with us. He takes a scarlet envelope from the thrall's silver tray and waves the man away.

I momentarily duck my head under the covers when Nathan turns back, a strange mix of horny and bashful forcing a giggle up my throat that I subdue when I emerge and see the frown on his face.

He's standing by the bed, reading, a crease between his dark eyebrows growing deeper as his eyes flick across the page, and I have to sit up. Carefully. With the top sheet wrapped around me. Because in the light of day, without emotional turmoil and long delayed gratification between us, Nathan feels like the stranger that he is to me.

"What is it?" I ask.

He folds the letter up and tucks it back into its envelope. "Ashton has issued a challenge to our mating pact through the council."

"Is that…" I can't imagine that after being found guilty of treason, Ashton would have any standing to ask anything of the pack. "He can't do that."

Nathan tosses the envelope aside. "He can."

"Pack law isn't the same as the laws of the human world," I say, as if a king needs to be informed of such a thing. "There aren't appeals."

"It seems we aren't the only ones interested in archaic loopholes." Nathan's unbothered tone puts me at ease. If he's not worried, I'm not.

Until he says softly, "damn," and rips the envelope in half.

"What? What's wrong?" I rise up on my knees. "Is it like a trial by combat or something? Are you going to fight each other?"

Nathan scoffs. "He'd never be so foolish. He wouldn't survive."

Having felt the full force of Nathan's strength last night, I agree. "Then what is it?"

"It's a hearing before the council in he'll have to prove that he still has a claim over you and that the pact can't be invalidated." He pauses. "You'll have to testify."

Is that all? "Okay."

Cautiously, Nathan asks, "You'll testify for…"

It takes me a moment to understand what he's asking. When I do, I roll my eyes. "For our side, duh."

A small smile touches his mouth. "*Our* side?"

I gesture around the room. "Considering what happened here last night, I don't think it's unreasonable for me to use the word. That...thing that happens when we're near each other, the compulsion we feel? It doesn't seem like it's giving us much of a choice."

He sits on the side of the bed and his shoulders sag. I don't like the look of that, especially when he won't look at *me*. "Bailey...the council will be the ones making the choice now. And I'm not sure we should mention whatever this is when we have no idea what it is or why it's happening to us."

"So...it's not natural?"

He turns and gives me a close-lipped smile of reassurance. "To me, it feels very natural."

My pulse centers at the base of my throat. "He's not going to win, right?"

"I have enough experience to know that one should never say never." He motions me over and I shift awkwardly across the bed on my knees. I sit beside him, and he takes my hand. "I have enemies on the council. And he has allies. You may wish to prepare yourself for the worst."

My brain lights up with hope. "I know someone on the council."

"Who?"

"Well, he's not on the council yet. Ryan Hunter. He's shortlisted."

Nathan thinks for a moment, then nods in recognition. "He's going to be appointed to Wray's seat. It was decided before I banished him. How do you know Hunter?"

"We're like, best friends. All through school." So, at least one vote is secure. But more importantly, my friend has just earned a powerful place in the pack. "Does he know it yet?"

"I was meant to make the announcement at my afternoon audience, but it's been canceled." Nathan's thoughtful gaze settles on me. "It's better to let other conspirators stew for a day or two. Men make mistakes when panicked. I'm sure a few more traitors will out themselves. Sudden international trips, obsequious gifts, that sort of nonsense."

The nonchalance with which he describes his manipulation is another chilling reminder that I have no idea who Nathan Frost is. I know what he feels like, what he smells like, I know what my own wet pussy tastes like smeared across his mouth. But I don't know *him*.

"What if you told your friend about his promotion to the council?" Nathan asks, an idea more than a question. "Over a casual luncheon, here in the residence?"

"I—"

"Call him," Nathan says, rising from the bed. The contours of his muscles as he moves lazily toward the stairs make my body thrum with need. "Two o'clock should give you plenty of time to prepare for a friendly visit. I'll have a thrall from the events office visit you."

"Where are you going to be?" I ask, feeling a little silly and clingy about the question.

"I'll see you soon," is the only answer I get. I don't even have his phone number. Worse, he turns back and says, "If you can think of any other useful connections, let my secretary know. In the meantime, stay in the private residence."

And then he leaves me alone, wondering if I'll ever be able to describe other people as "useful" the way he does.

I hope not.

————

Ryan and Hannah are as confused by my invitation as I am. They accept it, of course, and come to the private residence, where way too much food has been prepared in the formal dining room.

"I feel like we're trespassing," Hannah whispers, her arms tucked into her sides as if she means to make herself as small as possible to keep from touching anything.

Meanwhile, Ryan is deeply troubled. "Tell me again what happened?"

I had to explain it to them over the phone, more than once, but I can understand why it's too surreal for them to fully grasp. Once more, I recount our late-night kidnapping, the banishment of the traitors involved, and the dissolution of my mating pact to Ashton.

"So, in conclusion, I'm queen now. Or, I will be, in a couple of days. But only if Ashton's challenge doesn't work in the council. Which was kind of why I called you."

"I'm not on the council," Ryan reminds me. "I'm only shortlisted for a vacant seat."

"And a seat is now vacant, and the council has given it to you." It does feel good to break the exciting news, but it feels selfish that I'm asking him for a favor at the same time.

"Are you kidding?" he asks, an uncertain smile growing across his face. "You're kidding. This is a prank."

"Yeah, it's a prank. She somehow got everyone in the palace to put all this together and go along with it. Including the King." Hannah makes a Gallic shrug and turns to me. "Are you okay? Are you like...a prisoner here?"

No sense in sugar coating it. "I'm pretty sure I am. He said to stay in the private residence."

"He might be anticipating some kind of retaliation." Ryan falls into deep thought. "Listen to him on this."

"Listen to him about everything. He's the king," Hannah admonishes him, and makes a cut-it-out motion across her neck while pointing at the ceiling.

I haven't given any thought to the fact that Nathan might have ears all over the palace, and that even this private meeting could be surveilled. Maybe the reason he didn't want to be here is because he thinks our tongues will be looser if he's not around.

I can't trust him at all. He's going to be my mate and we're somehow connected by forces we didn't know could even exist, and I can't trust him.

"I say all of this as a friend, of course." Ryan gets it, to my great relief. "I would never imply that you should disobey an order from the pack leader, but I know how you are."

"Nathan will make sure I'm protected." That part, I fully trust. If anything, his possessiveness is a huge red flag that I'm purposely ignoring. "He's very attentive when it comes to my safety."

Hannah nods slowly. "Of course, he is. Oh, but allow me to express my sympathy over your family's involvement in the conspiracy against your future mate. That must be devastating. I mean, finding out that your family is full of traitors but also, finding yourself completely isolated from them."

"Isolated" is the key word that stands out. Nathan *has* isolated me from my family. "He did what had to be done. They're traitors."

What I'm really saying, and what I'm sure Hannah and

Ryan are picking up on, judging by the stilted conversation between us, is *I know that what Nathan is doing is extremely fucked up but I'm not taking my family's side.*

"You could bring that up during your testimony. It would look very good for His Majesty's rightful claim." Ryan says, and I translate it to, *"If you want Nathan to win, say this."*

I reassure him with, "I'll do anything I can to fight Ashton. He doesn't have the right to dispute my future mate's claim."

That's not code for anything. It's just what I truly believe.

"Remember back in the day, when we did all that research on pack law?" Hannah asks. Of course, we do. It's how I learned about the Right of Accord. She goes on, "Maybe it would behoove you to brush up on challenges like this. We could help you."

"No, we can't," Ryan says quickly. "I'm a member of the council now. I've offered a little too much friendly advice already."

"Fine," Hannah says. "But my friendly advice? Get thee to the library."

"I can't leave," I remind her. "But a thrall could."

"I'm sure the king has resources available here," Ryan reminds us. "It's not just a pretty house. He works here."

"Then let's eat, so you can get to work," Hanna suggests. At a look from Ryan, she protests, "What? I'm not passing up food fit for a queen."

We avoid the topic of the challenge, talking about normal friend stuff only while we eat, but it's never off my mind. Neither is my inability to trust that my future mate won't be keeping an obsessive eye on me. Am I ever going to be able to have an honest conversation with my friends again? Can I ever be assured of my privacy?

The more I consider the situation, the more I realize that no matter the outcome of the challenge, the conspiracies and machinations are far from over.

CHAPTER 22

After Ryan and Hannah leave, I snoop through the residence and find a study. As one would expect, the king's bookshelves are filled with volumes on pack law, including the intimidating twenty-volume pack charter.

Research is way less fun when you're not doing it with two equally motivated individuals. And when your entire future hangs by a thread. But what it lacks in fun, it makes up for in not getting any results. It's dark out by the time I give up.

I glance out the window of the study and spot the moon. We're two days from Lupercalia. Two days from knowing what my life is going to be like.

By ten o'clock, Nathan still hasn't returned to the residence.

"Amanda?" I ask through the intercom in my sitting room. "Has the King left word of when he'll be back?"

There's a click and Amanda answers, "His Majesty isn't planning to return tonight. Do you have a message you'd like me to pass along to his secretary?"

He's not coming home. "Do you know where he's gone?"

Click. "By pack law, His Majesty is forbidden contact with you until after the council issues a decision on the challenge. Would you like me to pass a message along?" she asks again.

"No. Thank you, Amanda."

In all the reading I've done, I haven't uncovered that clause. It must be buried somewhere much deeper; in a subsection I haven't reached. One of the purposes of having such complicated laws, I assume, is to prevent pack members from knowing enough to question the council or pack leader. Why Nathan didn't just tell me about this ban on contact, I have no clue.

But I do know how to use it to my advantage.

Nathan invoked the Right of Accord because he knew about the Right of Accord. It's not totally absurd to assume he knows more than Ashton does about pack law.

I can either take a chance that Ashton doesn't know about this no-contact rule, just like he didn't know about the Right of Accord, or I can take a chance that the council, which might also be riddled with traitors, will decide in Nathan's—and my—favor.

It's not a hard decision to make.

But I have no idea how to get in touch with Ashton, or even how to leave the house. I don't have anything of my own. No money, no identification, no phone. Even my clothes aren't my own. They're just things Amanda went shopping for.

I hit the intercom again. "Amanda, all of my things are at my old house. I only need a few hours to collect them. Could someone take me there?"

Click. "I'm afraid His Majesty has commanded that you stay in the residence."

"I know but..." It's a last-ditch effort before I try to sneak out a window or something. "Could you contact his secretary and ask him if it would be okay? There are things there that I need."

"We can have them retrieved and delivered to you here."

I am really starting to hate Amanda's intercom voice. I snap, "Could you just ask him, please?"

I storm away from the intercom and pace, trying to calm my nerves. This *will* work. And, it will give me a chance to rub Ashton's loss in his face.

To my surprise, Amanda comes back with an answer within ten minutes, stopping by in person to deliver it.

"His Majesty was not able, under the rules of the challenge, to give you permission." Before my heart can sink too far, she continues, "Doing so would constitute contact. But so would denying you permission. You are, however, the highest-ranking member of this household in the king's absence, and as such you have the ability to make whatever requests or commands you wish."

"I want a car," I shoot back immediately. "I want a car, and I want the guards at my parents' home to leave. I don't want to see them and I don't want them watching me while I'm there. I'm going to be very emotional and I deserve my privacy."

"Yes, Your Majesty."

It's so weird being called that, considering my position isn't permanent yet. But I'm not going to turn down the advantages it affords me.

Twenty minutes later, I'm speeding through my old neighborhood in a car the roars like a lion and scares the shit out of me every time I touch the gas pedal. I pull up to the gates and find them padlocked shut. Luckily, the code for the pedestrian gate hasn't been changed, and I can walk the rest of the way up the drive.

If I intended to actually move my stuff out, the long walk would be a problem.

My first step is to walk the perimeter of the property. I pause every now and then as if I'm saying a tearful goodbye to a tree or a rosebush, but I'm actually looking for new security equipment or thrall guards hiding out. The only cameras I find are the ones my parents installed, and I know all their blind spots.

The security code to the back door is still the same, and I slip into the quiet, empty house with a tentative, "Hello? Hudson? Anybody?"

No one answers. In fact, our cheesecake dessert course from the night we were taken is drying out on the kitchen counter. It's like the entire house shut down the second we left.

Except for the lights. Someone turned all of those off. Turning them on feels dangerous, like I'm giving away my position, but I remember that I'm in charge. Nathan granted me ownership of all my parents' assets. I have a right to be here.

Someone has already been inside, cataloguing our belongings. Barcode labels are affixed to every item in the living room, every family photo on the way up the stairs, probably so the contents will be fully accounted for, and my parents can't sneak back and get something.

My room is untouched, thankfully; I'm not sure I could handle someone putting a price on my diary or my child-hood stuffed animals. I decide that I really am going to keep this stuff. When the challenge is over, I'll use my queenly powers to decree that the pack can't have *my* assets.

The asset I'm most grateful to find is my cell phone. It's been plugged into its charger the whole time I've been away. I find Ashton's number—I have it, but I've never used it—and I send him a text. *We need to talk. There's been a terrible mistake. Come to my parents' house. Hurry, I don't know how long I'll be alone.*

I sit on my bed and wait.

The phone rings.

"Are you safe?" is the first thing Ashton says.

"Right now, I am." It's not a lie. I'm safe right now. "Hurry."

"I'm on the way." He sounds too heroic to be worried about me, for real.

"There are security cameras around the driveway," I warn him. "Enter by the pedestrian gate and stick to the perimeter." It will take him past every camera on the property. "Meet me out at the pool house." Where he'll have to walk through a brightly lit patio area and be seen from numerous angles.

"Be careful," he warns me. "Don't put yourself in any danger."

"I won't," I promise. "Hurry."

I don't know where Ashton has been staying, but it must be close by. By the time I put on warmer clothes and throw a few things into a backpack to take back to Aconitum Hall, I barely beat him to our rendezvous spot. I just manage to hit record on my phone's camera and slip it into my pocket before he opens the door.

Ashton greets me with, "There's a private flight out of Bishop that leaves in an hour. We need to be on it. The

Colemans will help us this time, but they're afraid of Frost and what he'll do if he finds out."

Poor Colemans. Because Nathan *will* find out.

"Is this all you're taking?" Ashton reaches for my bag, and I pull it away, hoisting the straps over my shoulders.

"I'm not going anywhere with you," I tell him, feeling a mean thrill. "I'm staying with Nathan."

Ashton frowns in confusion. "You said you made a mistake—"

"I said there's been a mistake. And there has. By being here, with me, you've broken pack law that prohibits you from having any contact with me until after the challenge has been decided."

Ashton blanches. He's speechless.

"You should have just accepted your punishment. And you should have accepted that you will never, ever beat me." I can't help my laugh of relief. "It's over. It's all over."

Maybe "beat me" was the wrong choice of words. Because in a flash, Ashton's demeanor goes from knight in shining armor to violent beast. The slap he deals me comes too fast to dodge, connecting with my cheek with a crack that I'm not sure isn't the sound of my skull fracturing.

I didn't count on him being strong. I don't know why; he's a full-grown werewolf. He hits me again, more of a punch this time, and my miscalculation suddenly occurs to me in a sick, red haze. Maybe if he can't have me, he won't let anyone have me.

He's in too deep now, and he has a private plane ready for escape.

He might kill me.

I stagger backward and throw my arm out to brace myself against a metal shelving rack of pool chemicals and equipment. It's the only way I can stay up.

But he doesn't hit me again.

"I can't beat you?" he chuckles, and the sound is animal, furious. "I can't beat you? My father owns half the council. And the other half? They hate Frost. You're going home with me on Lupercalia, whether you like it or not."

"And I'm his mate, whether you like it or not," I shoot back, not knowing when to leave well enough alone and not caring. I just want to wound him. "He's already had me. Every time you fuck me, you'll be getting his leftovers."

Ashton stalks forward and grabs my face, crushing my mouth. My teeth cut into my cheeks, and I taste blood.

But I still can't help myself. Maybe it would be better if he kills me now. My sisters are gone. Nathan can be just as much a possessive douchebag as Ashton is. And I don't doubt that the council might still rule in Ashton's favor, just to spite the usurper king.

But like hell I'm going to let Ashton think he won.

I spit in his face.

He releases me and I shove him away hard, laughing at him. "You're so pathetic. Even if you win this challenge, Nathan is the king. He can keep seeing me. I'll make sure you always wonder if our children are yours, or his."

Ashton stares at me as if he's never seen me before. And he hasn't. This is the first time he's ever seen who I really am. What I'm really capable of.

He might be the first person who's ever seen the real me, at all.

"You will never own me," I tell him, wiping blood from my mouth, onto the sleeve of my white sweater so I can use it as evidence later. "I am Nathan Frost's mate, no matter what the council decides."

I move toward the door, braced for Ashton to grab me.

He doesn't stop me from leaving the pool house, but I give the covered pool a wide berth, afraid he might push me in. I don't go inside the house; I'll probably never go into it again.

I slide behind the wheel of the car, my hands shaking, and remember the phone in my back pocket. It's still recording. I manage to hit stop and take a few deep breaths before I start the ignition.

I have more than enough evidence that Ashton has broken pack law.

CHAPTER 23

Lupercalia. The challenge is here.

I'm taken from Aconitum Hall to the ceremony grounds in a chauffeured car. I sit by myself, across from two unsmiling, armed royal thralls. I get the feeling that they're protecting a piece of disputed property. I'm not the future queen tonight.

Not that I wasn't pampered like royalty. Before I left there were manicures and waxes, a makeup artist, a hairstylist, all of them sent to prepare me for my mating ceremony. There had also been a tailor, who nipped and tucked an off-the-rack suit for my testimony before the council; black pencil trousers and a single breasted jacket over a light blue silk chemise, all of it making me look much older than I am. My hair is in a careful twist, knotted at the nape of my neck, and it will, the stylist assured me, look as good down as up.

Because after my testimony, I'll be taken straight to the ceremonial chambers and prepared for whoever wins the challenge.

Unfortunately, the robe for my mating right is the one

made for me five years ago, with the pink silk and delicate embroidery chosen for me by my mother and Ashton's mother. I hope that doesn't somehow cause bad luck.

You don't need luck. You have evidence, I remind myself. The cell phone is tucked in my jacket pocket. I haven't let it out of my sight since last night. It's going to save me from Ashton.

We arrive at the ceremonial grounds, and I catch my reflection in the car window under the landscape lighting. The makeup artist did too good a job concealing my bruised cheek and split lip. I wipe some of it away with the inside of my jacket while the guards stare at me in confusion.

The council meets in chambers built on the foundation of the first great hall erected by our ancestors when they settled in the area. Those foundations are visible through the tempered glass floor of the entryway, and I'm careful not to look down into the exposed pit as I stride, head held high, toward the council chambers. I try to remember the polished, professional-looking woman I saw in the mirror at Aconitum Hall. She looks nothing like the scared child I feel like inside.

All night, I went over and over my circumstances. If the council decides in favor of Nathan, I become queen. I also enter into what seems like the second-most potentially manipulative, controlling mating pact of all time. If they decide in Ashton's favor, I'll enter into what will be the *most* manipulative, controlling mating pact of all time, now with added violence. And, I'll be mated to a man who's been convicted of treason and who's apparently living on the kindness of other traitors.

And some of them are on the council.

They can't ignore this evidence, I tell myself. *Get through your testimony. Deal with the Nathan problem later.*

They called me to testify at nine-thirty, and I wait awkwardly in front of the chamber doors until nine-thirty on the dot. The council guard opens them to admit me. I suck in a nervous breath, my confidence destroyed.

I've only seen the council chambers in my school text-books, usually depicted from the gallery, which is up so much higher than I expected. The council's seat, a semi-circular desk big enough for twenty-five, which runs around half the huge, round room, is much taller than it looks in photos. I feel like all twenty-five council members are glaring at me in judgment from on high as I walk down the aisle, through the rows of spectators. There's a small platform to stand on, with a rail that reminds me of the docks in old courthouses. I can't help but turn and survey the room when I'm finally standing in my place; I need a friendly face. I spot Ryan first, in his council chair, but it's not as though he can wave at me.

Then I see Nathan.

He sits on one side of the room, at a desk crowded with people I assume are his lawyers. Directly across sits Ashton and his legal team. I'm trapped between them.

It's a running theme.

After not seeing Nathan for over twenty-four hours, the need I always feel when I'm around him rears its inconvenient head. His gaze locks on mine and I swear he shudders. Every muscle in my body locks with tension to prevent the same thing from happening to me. I need to appear cool and level-headed. I can't let them think I'm afraid.

Something in his expression changes and I realize he's noticed the dark purple bruise across my cheek, which has set some of the assembled crowd murmuring. He's angry, and I worry for a moment that he'll order someone at Aconitum Hall executed in revenge or something like that. *Just chill out until I can present the evidence,* I silently will him.

It's too bad the bond between us doesn't involve telepathy.

A member of Nathan's counsel approaches me. "His Majesty respectfully submits the testimony of one Bailey Dixon, referred to within Mr. Daniels's filing as the 'disputed.'"

I can't help that my jaw drops in outrage, but I hurry to correct it.

The man serving as head of the council isn't anyone I know. He's a hunched over, just-past-middle-aged man with pasty pale skin and an unfortunate, slicked down side part that exacerbates how thin his gray hair is. He doesn't seem thrilled to be here.

I'm sure that's a great sign.

The council leader nods to Nathan's barrister. "Testimony is accepted."

The barrister, a young, handsome man with a post-vacation tan and perfect white teeth smiles reassuringly at me. "Ms. Dixon, when did you learn that your father had signed a mating pact promising you to Mr. Daniels?"

"About a month before I was to take part in the transformation ritual for the first time," I answer.

"Speak up!" the council leader barks.

I repeat myself, louder, and add, "That would have been January of 2017. Maybe December of 2016."

"And you invoked the Right of Accord in February of 2017, is that correct?" the barrister asks.

"I did."

"And did your choice to seek out this archaic law and invoke it have anything to do with that mating pact between yourself and Mr. Daniels?"

"I didn't—" I almost say that I didn't seek out the law, that I found it. I'm supposed to tell the truth here. But is omission really dishonesty? I decide it's not. "I didn't want to be Mr. Daniels's mate."

"And why is that?" The barrister nods and paces in front of me, glancing occasionally at Nathan. It's hard to keep my attention focused to one place, so I decide to address the council and not try to guess at what silent communication is happening between Nathan and the barrister.

"At first, it was that I just didn't know him very well. At all, really," I say, quickly adding, "And after I returned to the pack, it became apparent that he doesn't know me, either. Our personalities are not compatible."

"Many couples don't think they're compatible," the barrister says, drawing my attention back to him. I'm not sure if he's arguing with me and I'm not sure why he would, but he asks, "What, specifically, makes you believe you couldn't be a suitable mate for Mr. Daniels."

"He's violent," I blurt, to an echo of murmurs from the assembly behind me.

"Is that what happened to your face?" the barrister asks.

"It is." I turn and deliver my condemnation directly at Ashton. "Last night, Ashton Daniels visited me, in person, after issuing his challenge, in violation of pack law as it pertains to matters of disputed mating pacts."

One of Ashton's legal team stands; he's a boring-looking near-clone of the guy who's been questioning me. I really can't tell werewolves in suits apart, I guess.

"Councilman Renner," Ashton's barrister begins, "This is a wild and baseless claim. Without supporting evidence—"

"I have supporting evidence." I reach into my jacket pocket and produce my phone. "Audio of not only the meeting, but the assault."

"Audio?" Ashton's barrister scoffs. "Councilman, it's impossible to positively identify—"

"If you check the surveillance video footage from my parents' former home, you'll see his arrival. The time-stamps on my recording and the security recordings should leave no doubt." And while I know I should shut up and let the legal experts handle things, I can't help but editorialize a little. "Mr. Daniels is a traitor to his king and pack leader. He broke the terms of this challenge and he assaulted me. He isn't a worthy mate for any woman in this pack. Certainly not for me."

"Thank you!" Nathan's barrister says, openly nonplussed. He takes the phone from me with a look that entreats me to stop talking, so I do.

"Let's hear this audio recording," says Councilman Renner.

Someone from Nathan's side runs off, presumably to somehow get the security video here. I didn't think of that. The delay might mean there will be no decision tonight. I'll have a full year before I have to worry about the mating pact to either of them if the council decides to wait.

The barrister turns up the volume on the phone and the room is a silent as the grave while the recording plays. My jeans pocket muffled the sound somewhat, but it's unmistakably Ashton, promising to break pack law by sweeping me away on a private jet, aided and abetted by Councilman Coleman. From his council chair, Coleman signals his innocence with a smirk and a shake of his head.

When I say that I slept with Nathan…that's unmistakable, too. I don't sound so much like the type of person who'd be a great queen. That's part of the equation I didn't consider before. The council isn't just deciding on who deserves the marriage pact. They're deciding if I should be queen.

What have I done?

When the recording finishes, Ashton's barrister says, "That did paint a vivid picture for us. My client has a small detail he'd like to add, however. Councilman Renner, if I may?"

Renner rolls his eyes and motions for the barrister to carry on.

"*'We need to talk. There's been a terrible mistake. Come to my parents' house. Hurry, I don't know how long I'll be alone,'*" Ashton's representation reads. "That's the text message my client received from Miss Dixon last night, urging him to break a pack law that, if the audio recording can be believed, was known to her and not to Mr. Daniels."

Council members quietly talk amongst themselves at this. I glance over at Nathan. He looks hopeless and furious.

Furious with *me*.

"It seems to me that Miss Dixon entrapped Mr. Daniels, with the intent to interfere in this proceeding," Ashton's barrister finishes.

"I believe we've heard all we need from Miss Dixon," Councilman Renner says, condemning me with a glare for wasting his time. It's the night of the full moon and no doubt all the council members are ready for the Lupercalia celebration forming at the ceremonial grounds and the transformation ritual that will follow. The sooner they get this trial over with, the sooner the party begins.

They rush me out and, though everything in me screams not to, I catch Nathan's eye and I mouth, "I'm sorry."

Two female guards wait outside the chamber doors to lead me away. We'll go to the ceremonial chamber.

And I have no idea which man will join me.

CHAPTER 24

The chamber is as cold and dark as I imagine. My arms ache. I've been waiting, chained, for what feels like hours, but through the grate overhead, I can tell the moon isn't directly above us yet.

This isn't how Tara said it would go. She'd mentioned a ceremony, other people being here with us.

I'm all alone, in a cell that smells of earth and is oppressive in its chill humidity. The acolytes did anoint me, that part was true, but they didn't wait for my mate to arrive. Now, with my back to the door, chained to a damp wooden post, there's no way for me to tell who will come in. And if I change my mind…

It's too late to change my mind.

I stifle a sob of fear. I can do this. I gave my testimony. Sure, I messed up by playing that recording and by entrapping Ashton. I thought I was doing the right thing but apparently, I wasn't. Whatever happens, whoever comes through the door, I'll face the consequences of my actions and I'll do it without becoming a sniveling crybaby.

I really want to cry, though.

In the center chamber, an acolyte begins to chant. My heart races. I think I feel a flicker of the familiar pull, but I can't be sure it isn't just nerves. I squeeze my eyes shut tighter and tighter as my mate approaches. The door screeches on its hinges and he enters.

My knees go weak with relief, and I sob aloud. It's Nathan. I feel him. It's undeniable.

The heat from his body penetrates my thin silk robe as he presses close. "I told you to stay in the residence."

"I'm sorry," I whisper, my brain fizzing and popping with endorphins.

He grips the top of the expensive ceremonial robe and rips it all the way down the back. He moves away and I know what comes next.

I just don't expect it quite so quickly. The lash snaps across my flesh and it feels like a knife. I gasp at the pain.

"You will never defy me that way again." Another agonizing slice of the whip.

"Never!" Tears leak from the corners of my eyes, either from pain or relief, I can't tell.

"You will never endanger yourself that way again." There's a note of real fear in his command, and it surges through the tie between us, just before the next whistle and snap of the whip.

"I promise," I shout, and I stumble sideways, losing my balance. The chains keep me from falling, but the manacles cut into my wrists, and I yelp as my arms jerk in their sockets.

Nathan is with me in an instant, lifting me onto my feet and crushing me between his body and the post. His lips brush over my ear as he whispers, "We almost lost each other."

The connection between us is too strong. I need him,

gasp for him like oxygen, want him so bad I'm willing to do whatever it takes to have him.

You do have him. You're about to become his mate. And he will be yours.

Is that where Nathan's possessiveness springs from? The primal tie binding us?

"How many more?" I whimper. I'll take twenty more, a hundred more, a thousand lashes if that's what it takes to own him completely.

"No more," he rasps, his lips finding my neck. "At least, tonight."

Maybe he's joking. Maybe he's not. But I'm willing to do all manner of filthy deeds with him to celebrate my freedom from Ashton.

"It's time," Nathan groans. Overhead, the full moon has reached its apex in the sky. I smell the blood on his breath; he's consumed the ceremonial flesh that initiates the transformation. He's ready, and so am I.

He growls with pleasure, his mouth changing shape against my throat. Needle-sharp fangs graze me, and I question the safety of this part of the ritual. Only for a second, though. He's my mate. He'll never let anything harm me, not even himself.

The coarse hair on his chest and arms becomes the silky fur of his werewolf form. I can't help myself and push back on him, savoring the new sensation. He can't speak, not as a wolf, but he communicates his reaction just fine by wrapping his elongated arms around me and lifting me off my feet. I scramble to grab at the post and settle for holding my chains for support; he jerks my legs apart and steps between them.

There isn't going to be any foreplay tonight. This is just base, carnal fucking. The fact that the acolytes stand just outside makes it all the more wicked; Nathan and I are far beyond caring who hears us. I'm out of control, desperate for him, willing to take anything he gives me, and more.

Do it, I beg silently. *Take me. Make me yours.*

"Yes," I moan when I feel the tip of him touch me. Then I realize with a shock that the transformation doesn't overlook a single body part; his cock is larger than before, at least double its girth. I open my mouth to ask him to wait, but the words don't make it out and probably wouldn't have made a difference, anyway; he rams his entire length into me and I scream. White hot starbursts of torture explode through every nerve in my body.

I thought I wanted it rough and wild, but as he pummels my body with relentless thrusts, stretching my cunt painfully wide, I regret my own desire. I want nothing more than for it to be over. If I even survive it.

He roars and a scalding burst deep in my pelvis makes me sigh in relief and sag in the chains. It's over. He's finished.

The acolytes enter, but Nathan doesn't let me go or make any move to cover me. He doesn't even pull out; if anything, he grinds deeper as the thralls unfasten my chains. Nathan snarls at them and they leave quickly, slamming the door behind them.

That punishingly hot gush in my cunt grows startling cold and prickly, and Nathan withdraws only long enough to turn me in his arms. I'm face-to-face with my monster husband, who watches me through his feral, contorted features.

I throw my arms around him and kiss the side of his muzzle, ignoring the tickle of his sparse hair. The fluid leaking from my pussy leaves heightened sensation in its wake. Nathan's cock, still brutally hard and impossibly large, brushes my thigh. Cum still leaks from his tip, and the wet trail his touch leaves behind ignites my nerve endings.

Outside the door, the acolytes begin a chant. It grows in volume as Nathan boosts me up and thrusts into me once more.

Now, it's pleasure that makes me scream, a pleasure like I've never felt before. It's unreal; I lose track of where I am, what's happening—I might even lose consciousness for a moment. His cock never stops pumping out copious amounts of cum, and it never stops igniting higher and higher degrees of intensity. My thighs are slick to my knees and the fluid splashes onto my clit with every stroke of him. I fumble my hand between us and reach down to feel how substantially he's spread me. When I pull my fingers back, I lift them to my mouth. Holding his gaze, I smear his cum over my tongue, and he growls what sounds like a warning, nipping at my hand.

The chanting in the main chamber rises in volume, but it can't cover the noises I'm making. I'm lost in a world of nothing but want and desperation and fulfillment all blended together, and I'm hungry for more of it.

"Harder!" I shout, slapping his chest. He pushes me against the packed earth of the cell and drives into me faster, his breath coming in distorted huffs. His claws dig into my hips as he jerks me back and forth. The welts on my bare back scrape into the dirt and I push harder into the pain.

I want to feel everything.

Nathan holds my gaze as he pounds into me over and over, his pace quickening with the tempo of the acolytes' chant. In his blood-red eyes, I see the depth of his claim over me, the finality of this moment. We can never go back now. We've joined here, in the ceremonial chamber, on Lupercalia, beneath the extra blessing of the full moon. We're as joined in our lives as our bodies are right now.

"I'm yours," I whisper, and I arch up, seized by ecstasy so powerful I'm not sure I'll survive it. I twist and scream in his grasp, lost to an orgasm that goes on and on as my cunt gushes around him.

The acolytes' chant reaches a peak, and the air in the chamber crackles with pure power. Nathan drives deep and hard one last time, his teeth closing over my shoulder. Unlike our first night, he breaks the skin; I feel warm blood trickle down my breast, the roughness of his tongue as he licks it away. My head falls against his and I surrender all of my weight to him.

Gently, he pulls out and sets my feet on the floor, but I can't stand. I'm drenched and worn out and ready for twenty-four hours of uninterrupted sleep.

When I can't walk without staggering, Nathan lifts me in his arms. He's still in his werewolf form; there's no sense in shifting back before morning. It's strange, being held by him when he's so much larger than usual and so monstrous. He's terrifying this way, and it thrills me to know that I'm safe with him, werewolf or not.

Nathan is my mate. Nothing can separate us now. My tired brain knows vaguely that tomorrow I won't be so psyched about that. Tonight, though, just like Tara promised me it would, it felt *right*.

"The moon," I whisper dreamily as I stare up at it through the grate overhead. It's so much brighter than I've ever seen it before. Exhausted as I am, a new, powerful energy calls to me. It's now or never. I still have to enter the pack officially.

I have to transform.

CHAPTER 25

Nathan carries me down the path, to the ritual grounds. The other members of the pack have already transformed; I hear their calls from the dark woods.

I twirl some of his fur in my fingers, my head cradled in the dip of his shoulder. "I didn't expect it to be like that. I don't know what I expected it to be like, but not that."

He makes a noise like the snorting of a bull and his claws tighten around me.

I slap his chest. "Control yourself. I've still got to transform. I wonder what I'll look like."

My hair is blonde, and I've seen blonde werewolves that turn out white or gold. People with darker or ginger hair take on varying shades of brown or black or even the deep silver of Nathan's fur. And I'm interested to see how my face ends up. Just like with people, every werewolf looks different. I reach up to touch Nathan's muzzle, and his lip pulls back to bare his teeth in warning.

I'm not worried he's going to bite me or eat me. I'm more worried that he won't make it to the ritual grounds without throwing me down in the grass and fucking me again.

"When I'm in my werewolf form, I'm going to snarl at *you* like that," I warn him.

Thrall acolytes wait for us at the top of the hill, and Nathan sets me on my feet at the perimeter of the circle. He hooks a massive claw under the shoulder of my torn robe and peels it down, then removes the other, severed half of the garment. He takes my hand and leads me to the monolith depicting Lycaon.

It's been half a decade, but I know every word of this ritual, which I once dreaded. The Hierophant steps forward. He's tall and thin, with dark skin and eyes, and his head bears a regal crown. He's the same man I looked in the eye on that night five years ago, to whom I cited the Right of Accord.

He doesn't begin the ritual right away; maybe to give me a second chance to back out, this time forever.

I drop to my knees before him and bow my head.

"And so it was that Lycaon roasted the flesh of his own child, Nyctimus, and served it unto Zeus, in a test of the God's omniscience." The Hierophant turns to an acolyte, who hands him a bowl. The scent of the blood inside makes my mouth water and the moonlight makes my skin feel impossibly tight. The creature inside me, the thing I'm meant to be, grows desperate to escape.

"For his trickery, Zeus cursed Lycaon to become as an animal, and in revenge on Nyctimus' behalf, slew the wolf pups of Lycaon's issue thereafter. All except one." The Hierophant dips his fingers into the bowl and brings them up dripping with human blood. He paints a stripe down the center of my face. "Beast and man in one, Lycaon the Younger roamed the Earth, visiting each coast, every kingdom, leaving behind new werewolves, new myths. Gifting generations with the powers of beast and man. Do you accept his gift?"

"With my whole heart." I've heard these words in my head for years now, wondering what about my life would be different if I'd just said them.

Another acolyte steps forward with a bowl bearing a heart. It's all I can do not to jump at him and consume the entire organ before the ritual is finished.

"Do you reject the punishment of Zeus, who cast his favor upon humankind and destroyed the children of Lycaon?" the Hierophant intones.

"With all the wrath my soul can bear." I'm trembling, not from the cold of the night, which is chased off by the heat of the ceremonial fire, but the way the moonlight has become a solid thing that coats my skin and writhes into my body.

"Then consume the flesh of man and take your place beside Lycaon in the Pantheon of Arcadia." The Hierophant reaches for the heart, but Nathan growls low in his chest and steps forward to take it.

It's Nathan who raises the heart to my lips. It's Nathan who looks me in the eyes as I bite into the tough meat and tear away a chunk of it, blood dripping down my chin. And Nathan is the last thing I see before my vision flashes with the lightning that struck down Lycaon's progeny.

I've wondered before if it hurts; anyone who has been through the transformation has assured me that it doesn't, but I've never believed them. And I find that it *is* unbelievable, yet true. My body doesn't fight against the transformation; it welcomes it. When my arms elongate, when my face changes shape, it's none of the agony I've seen portrayed in human films. It's soul deep elation.

When my vision clears, the sights dazzle me. All color has been stripped from the world, which is repainted in shades of blue from the near black of the night sky to the cool, silvery white snow that glitters on the ground like millions of tiny flashbulbs. It might as well be full daylight; I can see every needle on the spruces, every branch on every tree, all of it shivering and whispering with its own voice, urging me to run. A motion near the tree line, too far for human eyes to see in the dark, captures my attention and there, highlighted in swirling gold, is a small rabbit. The yellow aura around it drifts sparkles this way and that, enticing me to run after it.

Nathan's claws grip my arm before I can run, and when I look at him, he doesn't look any different than the monster he was before I transformed. But he's the most beautiful thing I've ever seen.

I try to speak, but what comes out is a silly little yip; Nathan's mouth draws back in a lupine smile, and he tosses his head, pointing with his muzzle toward the rabbit. Then he releases me and swats me on my behind.

I run, hard and fast, covering so much ground but giving up hardly any energy. When I feel I should tire, a surge of the moon's light reinvigorates me. I chase the bunny into the forest, following its blazing aura deeper and deeper through the ancient trees. Nathan is on my heels, and knowing he's running with me makes me wish I could laugh. The equivalent in my werewolf body seems to be a series of high, chattering barks, and I let them free as I lunge over fallen tree trunks and bank off stones on the increasingly rocky ground.

There's a steady, crashing roar somewhere, and the smell of water. I abandon the pursuit of my prey and follow the scent and volume of the sound. My feet find a cold, trickling stream, and I lope up it, the current becoming stronger and deeper until I reach the shallow basin beneath a half-moon cliff. Water cascades over the lip of the rock shelf that juts out far overhead, into the pool below.

There are other wolves here, drinking the water, lounging on the frozen, muddy banks. I hear the growls and grunts of mating not far off; in my human form, I would be mortified. The beast I am now shivers with joy. I want Nathan to take me again, to roll with me on the pockets of snow sheltered by the trees. I want to see the stars over his shoulder. There are so many more stars in the night sky than I've ever been able to see before.

A wide, flat rock just barely surfaces the freezing water, and I wade over to it. Nathan is near; I feel him moments before he emerges from the trees, half the rabbit clutched in his jaws. He splashes through the stream and nudges my muzzle with the portion of the animal that he's saved for me. I take it from him with my teeth. I sit cross-legged on the rock and savor the warm, wet meat and the crunch of the animal's bones between my teeth. I devour it in seconds and toss the skin aside.

Nathan puts his arm around me and draws me close to him. I nuzzle his neck, breathe in the scent of the forest that clings to him. This is right. The problems that plague our other nature still exist, but they're impossible to focus on now. When I look human again, when my mind isn't consumed by the joy and beauty of the natural world, and my preternatural part in it, I'll have so many challenges to face. A family in exile. A pack full of traitors. A mate I can't trust.

A throne I'm not ready for.

But tonight, under the light of the moon that's become

as much a part of me as my heart or my brain, everything is perfect.

Deep in the forest, someone begins a far-off call. The howl rings through the crisp air, and all the wolves around us stop, poised to listen. It's Nathan who answers, his voice mournful and deep as he pays tribute to the night sky.

The others join in, becoming a symphony of worship all around me.

This is my pack. I'm a part of them now. A part of a world beyond mortal comprehension. I toss my head back.

And I howl.

CHAPTER 26

Two days after my first transformation, I'm still ravenous. At first, I was exhausted. I didn't mourn the fact that my mating ceremony reception didn't happen; I would have slept through it, anyway. I spent twenty-four hours sleeping, waking up only to pee and scarf down whatever the thralls left in my bedroom, regardless of its temperature. When one's body has completely transformed into a totally different creature and back again, even rubbery, cold eggs are delicious.

"Maybe I got a parasite from that rabbit," I muse aloud. I finally woke up enough to come down to breakfast with my mate, who watches with amusement as I demolish plate after plate of pancakes, ham, bacon, fried potatoes, and more apple juice than my body should be capable of holding.

"A parasite wouldn't affect you like this so soon." He chuckles to himself. "From the rabbit or from me."

It takes me a minute—and another spoonful of oatmeal —to get what he's talking about. "I wouldn't refer to a baby as a parasite. But maybe we should have discussed this before we had all this unprotected sex."

"What is there to discuss?" He frowns and cuts another bite from his extremely rare steak.

"The timing, for one," I say cautiously. "I know that we're going to have kids. I just don't know when you were planning to start actually trying."

"We've given it two tries already," he reminds me. "The sooner we have an heir, the better. You're, what? Twenty-two? Ideally, we have over a hundred possible children, if you become pregnant every year."

I actually snort apple juice up my nose. I cover it with my napkin and gasp, "A hundred?"

"I would settle for eighty," he says, as if that answer is somehow going to make me feel better.

I might faint.

He grins at me. "I'm joking, Bailey."

"Don't do that," I admonish him, sheepish that I actually fell for it. "I have no idea what kind of a person you are. I thought you were serious, and I was going to have to throw myself out a window."

"The windows on these floors don't open," Nathan laments.

I can't stand even a momentary silence. "So, how many kids do you want?"

"I never gave any thought to a total number. At the moment, I'm more focused on that first heir. And of course, we'll need backups."

"You're talking about your children." His cavalier attitude doesn't sit well with me. "But it sounds like you're thinking of them as a means to an end."

"I'm thinking practically." He drums his fingers on the

tabletop. "I get the sense that you're going to be more emotional on these topics."

Is he kidding? "A person is supposed to be emotional about their kids."

"I'm sure I will be. People tend to have great affection for their offspring, and it would be strange for me to be immune to that." He considers for a moment. "You're not equally emotional about me, are you?"

It's like he's making sure I'm not getting attached, and it causes a huge pit to open up in my stomach, one that can't be filled with food. I might as well tell him exactly how I feel about him, since he's basically invited me to. "I have some feelings about you. But as I said, I don't know you. From our interactions so far, it's obvious that you can be a kind person. But you can also be arrogant, possessive, and you callously disregard people when they aren't useful to you."

He nods slowly. "I suppose that's a fair assessment."

"And closed off," I add. "As I said before, I don't know you. I'm married to you, and I don't know your middle name—"

"Richard."

"—or how old you are—"

"Forty-three."

"That's not the point." I take a breath to quell my rising exasperation. "Those are superficial details that people learn within weeks of meeting each other. They know them before they end up fucking in a dirt hole and sharing a raw rabbit together."

He smiles. "You're very charming."

The connection that binds us flares up in me. I ignore it. "Stop that."

"Would you like to hear my assessment of you?" he asks. "I think it's only fair."

"Fire away." I'm less confident than my answer suggests. What if he says I'm a brat and he can't stand to be near me?

"You're funny. I don't think it's intentional. You aren't 'on.' You're smart, but you're reckless, hence your stunt before the council. How's your face, by the way?"

I reach up to touch the bruise from where Ashton hit me. It's fading fast, owing to my transformation, but it's still tender. "It's fine."

"You're a bad liar." He winks. "I would suggest practicing that."

"How do I practice lying?" That sounds awful.

"You don't have to be malicious. Make up something outrageous and try it out on a thrall. Tell them you've performed in *Cirque* in Las Vegas, it doesn't matter. But you need to be able to lie convincingly to be queen." He leans forward slightly. "A trick I use is to simply believe that what I'm saying is the truth."

Well, that's an alarming thing to hear from one's mate. "I'll keep that in mind."

He understands my double meaning, I can tell from his amused expression. "How many pancakes is that now?"

Probably fifteen. It's a good time to practice that wild lie. "Just two."

He beams with pride. "You'll be a professional in no time."

"You know, I lied to get Ashton over to the house," I say. "And he believed me."

All the friendliness drains out of the room. Nathan's face turns to stone. "And look how well that turned out."

"I'm here, aren't I?" Sure, my plan ended up backfiring

when it was pointed out to the council that it was technically entrapment, but Nathan had gotten the votes he needed to keep me.

"After you left the chamber, do you know what Ashton's barrister argued?" Nathan pauses for an answer he knows I can't give; we have haven't spoken since my transformation. "They argued that there was no way to prove that Ashton acted in ignorance of the law, but the fact that he was willing to endanger his claim out of fear for your well-being was proof that he valued you more."

That's absurd. I have a purple stripe on my cheek that says otherwise. "There's a recording of him hitting me."

"There's a muffled recording of the inside of your pocket during a struggle. There's no proof at all that he hit you, and he has no history of violence within the pack. They claimed that I beat you, here in the residence." Nathan's disgust is evident in his tone, in the way he clenches his jaw for a moment in silence. "It was your friend on the council who spoke up. He testified to seeing you after I left, and that you had no mark and didn't mention any violence."

If Ryan hadn't gotten that council seat... "How close was the vote?" I ask softly, suddenly not hungry anymore.

"Thirteen to twelve. I almost lost you."

It astonishes me that Nathan seems wholly uninterested in me as a human being but devoted to me as a mate. I would feel objectified, or like I'm property, if he didn't feel so genuinely consumed by our unexplained tie when we we're together. There's something between us, and while I wouldn't call it love, it's something powerful enough that I know he truly cares.

I refuse to dwell on how toxic an excuse that is.

"You didn't lose me, though," I say, so chipper I annoy myself. "And all that strife is in the past."

"There will be new strife any day now." It sounds like a joke, but I know he's serious.

"I assume the council's decision hasn't made you more friends?" It's a little—okay, a lot—scary to become queen of a pack that's not psyched about its king.

"Your assumption is correct." He sips his coffee and motions to a nearby thrall to top off his cup.

"Be honest," I begin, though I wouldn't know the difference if he wasn't. "Are we in danger?"

"You're never in danger, as long as I'm around." He thanks the thrall and reaches for the small porcelain creamer. "And that's not a lie."

It isn't a straight answer, either. "You can tell me things. I promise, I won't go rogue again. Any political action I take, I'll run it past you first."

A smile slants across his beautiful mouth. "Now, who's being dishonest?"

He gulps down his coffee with a grimace, then pushes back his chair. "I have a busy day. The allies we have must be kept happy, those who oppose us must be courted or bribed."

That sounds like royal business. "Don't you need me for that?"

"The thralls may refer to you as Your Majesty, but you're not queen in an official capacity," he explains gently. "I promise, after your coronation, you'll be more involved in the running of the pack. I chose you as my queen because I see your potential. Not just for the twenty children you'll bear me."

"Not funny," I remind him, and I don't crack a smile at all. He can stop making those jokes at any time.

"All right, message received." He leans down to kiss my forehead. "But I would like you to pay attention to your cycle. Let my secretary know your fertile days, so I'll be sure not to travel over them."

He's going to do a bunch of traveling and not take me? His mate? That's going to cause an argument in the future.

"Of course, we don't have to confine our meetings to those days." He heads toward the door, stopping to add, "I did enjoy having breakfast with you. We must do this again."

"We could make a regular thing of it," I say sarcastically. In what world wouldn't a married couple have breakfast together?

But he doesn't seem to interpret it as sarcasm, so much as a good idea. "I like it. I'll have my secretary note it."

His secretary sounds like a third party in our relationship. That will be fun.

"Wait, Nathan," I call to him just as he exits, and to my relief he comes back. I feel silly and shy about asking, but, "I need your number."

"Amanda has the number for my secretary," he reminds me with a bemused frown.

"Right, but if I needed to text you or call you..." I trail off, perplexed at why I have to explain to my own husband why I want his cell number.

"Why would you need to call or text?" he asks. "Amanda has my secretary's number."

I open my mouth, but I get what's happening. For some reason, my mate doesn't want me to contact him.

"Right," I say, pretending I'm having a ditzy moment. "I'll just get in touch through Amanda. And your secretary."

He gives me a smile, says, "I'll see you soon," and leaves.

The last time he said that I didn't know where he was for two days. I have a feeling that I'm not going to get to know Nathan Frost any better.

CHAPTER 27

When I was a little girl, I sometimes wondered what life was like for Cinderella after she married the prince and her wicked stepmother was punished. The story ended after all the exciting parts; did that mean nothing ever happened to her again? It's starting to feel like that was the case.

Aconitum Hall has no shortage of diversions. Televisions in nearly every room, a glorious, multi-room pool in the basement, a library with more books than we had at the academy, and of course, internet access.

Werewolves are feudal, but not completely stone aged.

There are only so many episodes of syndicated television I can watch, though, and only so many social media sites I can scroll before I'm intensely bored in a too-quiet house. I call Hannah, and she answers on the first ring.

"Is everything okay? You never call me," she says in lieu of hello.

"Sorry, I know." I can count on one hand the number of times Hannah and I have spoken on the phone since I returned. "I didn't mean to alarm you, I just wanted to make sure you dropped everything to talk to me."

She laughs. "I have to drop everything for you, Your Majesty."

"Not Your Majesty yet." I'm glad she can't see my eye roll. I'm annoyed at myself for being annoyed by Nathan's earlier remark. "But you should drop everything and come over. I'm super bored."

"You're in a castle and you're bored?" Hannah scoffs.

I drop back on my sofa and glare up at the beams overheard. "It's not like there's a Renaissance fair going on in here. It's so quiet and there's no one to talk to."

"What about Nathan? I assumed that after the mating ceremony, you two would be all..." Hannah makes a disgusting squish noise with her mouth.

"Ew, and no. I slept for like ever after the transformation. I only just saw him this morning for breakfast, and he took off right after." I don't tell her about the "soon" remark. It's not a great look to call up your friend and start bitching about your husband less than two days after the mating ritual.

"Well, I guess that's what happens when you marry royalty," Hannah says with a sigh. "But I can't come over today. Jo-jo's colicky and I don't have the energy to shower."

"I get it." I'm disappointed, but I get it. "You have to come visit soon, though, okay?"

"I'll visit soon," she promises, and we hang up, and I'm all alone again.

———

Nathan doesn't come home that night. At least, he doesn't come to see me. I'm still not sure where his bedroom is, and he never comes down to the sitting room or dining room. I end up falling asleep on the couch where I almost had sex with him weeks ago, only to be awoken by a thrall and sent off to my bedroom like a child.

Aconitum Hall is a prison. I'm not allowed to leave the residence still, for my own "protection." The thralls are the only people present and none of them are interested in me beyond making sure I'm behaving. I can't just keep Hannah on the phone with me until someone comes along to entertain me, but even in London I didn't spend this much time alone. I'm not used to the quiet, I'm not used to people not filling up my time, and I'm not used to not having any responsibilities. Maybe other people would love it, but it's definitely not for me.

I don't see my mate again until breakfast the next morning, and I can't take another whole day of nothing.

"What are your plans for the afternoon?" I ask, digging my fingernails into my palm beneath the table to stop myself from asking where the hell he's been. "Maybe we could... do something."

"Do something?" He frowns like I've asked him if he'd like to eat a bug.

"Yeah, like...hang out or..." I should have thought of something before suggesting anything at all. But what does one "do" with one's much older mate, when one doesn't really know that mate at all? "I just thought, you know. To get to know each other."

"Why do we need to get to know each other?"

The question is like a slap in the face. I don't need Nathan to fall in love with me, but I don't want him to be a stranger forever.

"Because we're mates. And we're going to rule this pack together. And I'm starting to think that maybe you're not as 'intrigued' by me as you claimed." That makes me sound super vain. I added, "And I'm bored."

"The thralls will bring you anything you desire," he tells me, as if nobody has mentioned it yet.

"I know they will. That's the answer I got any time I tried to talk to any of them. I'm lonely. I don't have many friends and you won't let me leave the residence."

"For your own good."

"I can't even walk around the whole house 'for my own good'?" I'm raising my voice, something Mother always chided me for. *"It's unattractive, Bailey."* I take a deep breath. "I feel like I'm just killing time here. I have no purpose. I used to have a job, back in London."

"You'll have a job here." Nathan spreads his hands. "You're about to be crowned queen next week."

"But right now, I'm alone. And I'm unhappy. And I don't think it's too much to ask that my mate spend time a little time with me, when he's engineered it so that nobody else can."

He sighs deeply and tosses his napkin on the table. For a moment, I'm afraid he'll leave the room and tell me to call his secretary. Instead, he says, "Bailey, I recognize that this is a difficult transition. But you've come into great power. And power is lonely."

My lip quivers under the strain of my disappointment. I look down at my plate and silently order myself not to cry.

"I promise, I'll make time for us, just the two of us, when I return from London."

My head snaps up. "You're going to London?"

"For business unrelated to the pack," he says with a

nod. "I'll be back in time for your fertile days. Thank you, by the way, for sending the information so expediently."

"Thank my period tracker app," I snap back. "You're going to just leave me here and run off to London? I know people there, I could see them—"

"No, Bailey." He doesn't even give me a reason. "When I return, we'll spend every moment together, I promise."

"For five days. While you try to get me pregnant." I scoff. "Un-fucking-believable."

He watches me in silence. I have no idea what he's thinking, but it's probably for the best. Judging from his expression, it isn't complimentary. When he speaks, it's to change the subject. "I've sent an offer to your sisters. They may return as prisoners of the crown and stay here, with you, at Aconitum Hall."

I much prefer my sisters to Nathan, so I'm happy to let his bullshit trip go for the moment. "What did they say?"

"No word yet. But as soon as my office has an answer, they'll inform you."

"Can't you just order that they come back?" I ask, though I know it's a selfish wish. Would I really want to tear them away from their mates? I got the impression that they actually like theirs.

All Nathan says is, "My office will let you know what your sisters decide." His phone chimes and he pushes his chair back. "My car is here. I'll see you on Saturday."

"Nathan, wait," I call after him.

He stops, and the tie between us surges. How can I be so helplessly attracted to someone who is such a dick?

I struggle to keep the tremor out of my voice when I ask, "Were you going to tell me that you were going to London, or were you going to just leave me wondering when I would see you again?"

"I didn't realize you wished to be kept apprised of my schedule." He sounds sincerely apologetic, while at the same time missing the point entirely. "I'll be sure that Amanda receives a copy on Monday mornings. She can go over it with you—"

"Amanda is a supercilious peon who talks like a customer service robot and looks like a Laura Linney impersonator," I snap. Fuck it, I'm queen. I'm going to act like one. "I'll be hiring a secretary of my own."

Nathan blinks at me in shock. "I—I suppose that's all right. I can have Amanda compile a list of suitable thralls—"

"Not a thrall. I'm going to hire someone within the pack. I'm sure we can afford it." I stress the *"we"* as a shot at his finances, another thing about him that I'm not sure of. Aconitum Hall comes with the title; maybe if he weren't king, we'd be living somewhere less grand. Of course, no one in the pack is impoverished. Even my parents, who've lost all their assets, have probably already secured loans and a guest house from their remaining allies.

My chiding works; Nathan says, coolly, "You needn't worry about our ledgers."

"I'll remember that when I'm all alone the rest of the week, shopping online," I warn him.

"Whatever it takes to fill your time," he says with a fake, gracious smile. I sit back and survey all the wasted food that we couldn't have eaten on our own. My appetite is slowly returning to normal, but I grab one of the heavily frosted Danishes and chew angrily as I contemplate my next steps.

CHAPTER 28

"Good morning, Your Majesty." Hannah glides into my sitting room with baby Jo on her hip. They're wearing matching pantsuits, compliments of Hannah's new boss.

I spent thousands of dollars on them.

"Good morning, gal Friday," I giggle back. "Wait, is that what gal Friday means? My dad always used that phrase, but he's like, a hundred and thirty."

"Yeah, my dad is actually cool, so... I wouldn't know." Hannah sits Jo in the playpen I bought to keep in the residence, with the toys I bought to go with it. "What are you going to spend your husband's money on today?"

"I don't know. How does one buy international real estate?" I tap my lips. I don't want a vacation home in Negril, but maybe somewhere less sunny. "I'm sure Nathan would love a cozy little cottage in Siberia. That's a place, right?"

"As your secretary, I must advise you to hire a tutor." Hannah sighs. "And as your friend, who wants to keep her new, very high-paying job, I must advise you to not piss your mate off too much."

"I don't think I can make him mad." Well, there's one thing that will make him mad, but I'm not interested in putting my own safety at risk. But I am curious, "Hey, what happened to Ashton?"

"From what I heard, he ran off to Quebec." Hannah hesitates. "Ryan said it's all but an admission of guilt."

"It doesn't matter if he admits guilt or not. Nathan says he's guilty." I shrug.

Hannah tilts her head. "Your face looks a lot better."

"I think the transformation sped healing up. Is that how it works?"

Hannah nods. "Yeah, if I get a papercut or something, it's healed in an hour, tops." She looks away and clears her throat. "Listen, I didn't know how to say it before, but... what the hell. I think what you did? Trying to trap Ashton? That was really brave. And you're a stupid bitch because you could have gotten really hurt."

"I know. I had to take the chance, though." I give her a tight, closed-lip smile. "I guess I endangered the proceedings more than I helped. But hey, everything came out okay in the end. Okayish."

"Better than the worst-case scenario." Hannah sits down beside me. "When does the second-worst case scenario come back?"

"Today." I wish I haven't been counting down the days until his return, but here I am. I know it will be today, though, because according to the calendar, my soil is ripe for sowing. "Maybe in an hour, maybe at ten tonight. I have no idea."

"Still no contact?"

"None whatsoever. And I refuse to contact him through his secretary. Now that I have a secretary, I'm going to contact his secretary through my secretary. And

I'm going to get a cellphone *he* can't call. Fuck it, he wouldn't even care!"

"Whoa!" Hannah holds up her hands. "What's all this about?"

"It's the stupid thing..." How to explain the odd connection Nathan and I have to my best friend, the asexual. "Have you ever heard of anyone having a mystical attraction to someone else?"

"Isn't that what they write songs about?" Hannah snorts. "Love at first sight?"

"No, it's not love. I think I hate him." Even though I promised him that I didn't. And when I look back on that night, on his arms around me, him asking me if I really hated him, like he couldn't stand the thought, my stomach aches. "But it did happen at first sight. The very first time Nathan and I saw each other, something happened. And he's never heard of something like it happening, either."

As she listens, Hannah's expression goes from skeptical to concerned. "So, you think it's something that doesn't happen to everyone else?"

"If it did happen to everyone, wouldn't we have heard of it?" I gesture at her. "Wouldn't it have happened to you?"

"Maybe not," she says with a shrug. "You didn't tell anyone about it? Not Vivianne or your sisters?"

"Yeah, I don't know where you got the idea that my mother would be open to frank conversations like that. And I didn't get a chance to talk about it with Tara and Clare before Nathan had them hauled off into exile." If they did feel the same pull toward their mates as Nathan and I felt for each other, I doubted they would leave their husbands behind to come be prisoners in their sister's house.

"They might know something. I definitely don't feel that for Ryan." She presses her lips together but she can't hold in her laugh. "And I know he doesn't feel it for me."

I lean my head back and sink into the corner of the couch. The baby makes a noise and I look over. The kid's adorable red curls look just like her mom's, with huge dark eyes and golden-brown skin. I wonder what my babies will look like.

"Is it weird, having a baby?" I muse.

Hannah hesitates at the sudden turn in conversation, so I explain, "Nathan wants to get me pregnant right away. It's why he's coming back today. It's the first fertile day in my cycle."

"Yikes." Hannah raises her eyebrows. "I remember keeping track of all that for in vitro but...you guys just mated like a week ago."

"Turns out, he can't wait to have an heir." I look back to the baby. "How would you feel if Ryan didn't love her?"

"Do you think Nathan isn't going to love your kids?" Hannah touches my knee to get my attention. "Bailey?"

I blink back tears when I look at her.

"Bailey, I'm worried about you."

I shake my head and force a smile I know she won't fall for. "A lot has been happening. I'm a little overwhelmed."

"That's totally understandable." She makes an apologetic side-to-side bob of her head. "And it's not going to get better. You're gonna be queen. It'll be nonstop stress. So, if you need to get rid of me and get a real assistant—"

"Shut up. You're already more competent than my head-of-household." I look over my shoulder, because Amanda could literally be blending into the wallpaper, and I wouldn't notice. "If I told you that I wanted a cheeseburger and to be left alone, what would you do?"

"I'd tell you to stop being so rude and get your own damn cheeseburger."

I drop my chin and give her a sidelong look.

"Oh, if I was your employee?" It only takes her a second to think. "I'd get you the cheeseburger and leave you alone."

"You're hired." Hannah looks down at her phone. "Ooh, I'm vibrating. And... it's your husband's secretary. His car has just pulled up to the gate."

I hate the elation I feel knowing that. The bond startles to life and I know that it's just going to get more intense the closer he is to me. Does it get stronger during periods of absence?

"He probably won't come see me right away." I stand and go to the window; from my tower, I can see the private drive near the exterior entrance to the residence. I'll get a glimpse of Nathan before he comes inside, and maybe that will prepare me to interact with him later.

Or maybe the tie will make me super horny and miserable until he bothers to come around and mount me.

A sleek black sedan pulls to a stop on the white gravel shoulder of the paved drive. The back door opens, and Nathan gets out.

So does someone else.

"Hannah!" I call, waving my hand frantically. "Hannah, do you know who this person is?"

As Hannah crosses the room, I rattle off details, just in case she misses her. "Red hair, big boobs, kissing my fucking husband?"

"What?" Hannah picks up the pace and gets to the window just in time to see Nathan and the mystery woman before they stop sucking face.

It doesn't matter, I tell myself. *It doesn't matter because you don't care about him, and he doesn't care about you.* And yet, I still want to claw his face off.

"Oh my god..." Hannah drags the word out. "Bailey...that's her. That's Amber Rogers."

The name rings a bell as the woman Nathan is rumored to be romantically involved in. Not so much a rumor now.

"I've heard of her," I say woodenly.

"Yeah, because she's the former queen of this pack." Hannah gasps as Nathan kisses Amber's hand and helps her back into the car, which drives off again.

"He took her to London." I step back from the window with a bitter laugh. "I've been logging six hours a day on TikTok in this musty old dungeon and he took her to London."

Hannah watches me pace; she's not great at providing unrealistic comfort in terrible situations. "Did you really want to spend all that time with the guy? You hate him."

"That's what headphones are for! I'd put them on noise cancelling mode and at least I'd be able to get out of the damn house. I haven't even seen the sky in like—"

The door to the sitting room opens and Nathan strides in; he must have bolted up the stairs to get here so fast, and he's not wearing the navy jacket he had on in the driveway. He's pretty close to not having a shirt on; he's working the buttons and doesn't notice Hannah and me standing there.

"Bailey?" He calls, and only then does he catch sight of us. He motions to Hannah. "Take the baby and give us the room, please?"

"Uh. Your Majesty, I—" Hannah gets caught somewhere between a curtsey and a scramble. She collects up Jo and their diaper bag and hurries out, pausing just long enough to say, "I'll be in my office."

Nathan pulls his shirt and undershirt over his head, nodding toward me. "Get undressed."

"What?" After I saw him sucking on some random woman's tongue? Not some random woman. The former queen, who still thinks she belongs on the throne.

The former queen who apparently wants my mate.

CHAPTER 29

"Stop!"

My shout alarms Nathan, but he does, at least, stop taking his clothes off.

"What the hell do you think you're doing?" I demand.

"It's the twenty-third." He gives me a moment to realize my error, which I obviously don't, and then goes on, "My secretary said—"

"Who the fuck was that?" I jab my index finger toward the window, but Nathan's gaze falls on the playpen and he looks over his shoulder, in the direction Hannah has just gone.

"I assumed she was someone you knew—"

"Not Hannah!" I press my fingers into my temples. "The woman you were kissing outside!"

He doesn't react the way a man who's been caught cheating on his wife should react. That is, with any remorse at all. He blinks. "You saw that?"

"Yes, I saw!" I pace furiously in front of the fireplace. I wish he gave me a wedding ring, so I could throw it into the flames. "Who is she?"

"Amber Rogers." He doesn't try to deny it at all.

"The former queen?" I hate the way my voice accelerates upward with my anger.

"The deposed queen, yes." Nathan still doesn't seem to grasp that he's done anything wrong. That he's hurt me in any way.

But has he? When I think about what I saw in the driveway, I can't tell if my feelings are hurt, or just my pride.

"Did she go to London with you?" I ask, folding my arms over my chest.

He nods. "She did. I don't understand—"

"You don't understand why I, your *wife*, would be angry that you took another woman on a trip I asked you to take me on?" I'm not sure my mate is even from Earth, if he can't grasp why I'm pissed about that. "I've been going out of my mind with boredom here! I could have seen my friends, I could have—"

"Your mortal friends?" Nathan raised an eyebrow.

"Yes, my mortal friends! From when I lived in London! The place where you just went and took another woman!" I can't believe he thinks he hasn't done anything wrong. "And not just any woman, one that wants to be queen of this pack! The thing I want to be!"

"And you're going to be," he says calmly. "Amber was upset that I married you. I took her on a holiday to apologize."

"You—" I feel like I'm going to be sick. It's the same out-of-control, barfy feeling I got around Ashton.

"I'm sorry that you're disappointed," Nathan goes on. "But I could hardly take my wife and my mistress on a trip together. And frankly, I have more in common with Amber than I have with you."

"So, you went on a honeymoon with your girlfriend instead of your wife," I whisper.

"If that's the way you wish to see it."

"The way I…" I can't look at him. I turn away and focus on the seam between the ceiling and the wall, blinking back tears. *You're not the one in the wrong here. You're the one who's been wronged.* "Have you ever been around other people before?"

He sputters the beginning of a non-answer.

I talk over him. "Do you have any idea how someone with a functioning sense of empathy works? I'm not asking you to love me. I'm not asking for some great romance. But I'm asking you to not publicly bone down with a woman who literally wants to take my place!"

"Amber doesn't want to take your place," he begins.

"Stop saying her name!" I've never screamed so hard at another person in my life. I think I'm going to burst a blood vessel in my eye.

"*She* doesn't want to take your place," he says patiently. "She was queen, she was deposed, and she has no desire to return to the position."

"Bullshit. She couldn't return to the position and that's why you're with me, not her!" He couldn't have mated the woman he truly wants to be with because she's a traitor to the pack.

"I don't want her to be my mate," he says, maddeningly even-tempered. "She tried to give this pack to New York."

"And people accuse you of wanting to give Toronto to Greater London, but you're still running around with a traitor? Do you have any idea how that looks?"

"I'm sorry, is this a political argument, or a relationship argument?" How can he look so tough and imperious without a shirt on? I'm fully dressed, I should be the invulnerable one here, but I feel so small as he continues to speak. "If my relationship outside of our marriage hurts you, I'm sorry for that."

"But you're not willing to break it off, are you?" I hate the tremor in my voice.

He slowly shakes his head. "I'm not."

"I'll be publicly humiliated," I point out.

"They'll think ill of me for it," Nathan reassures me. "You'll put on a daring gown and go to parties, pretending you don't care, and they'll admire you."

"But that's not what I want." How can I explain to someone who clearly doesn't have feelings that mine are hurt.

He has feelings. Just not for you.

"Why would you do this?" I ask helplessly. "I don't understand. The same people who think you're here as a traitor, they think she's a traitor, too. You're not endearing yourself to any of them with these rumors—"

"So, you knew about my affair before you agreed to be my mate." He states it like it's a point he's won.

"I heard rumors," I reiterate. "That's all. You never had the decency to tell me, yourself. And let's not start talking about what I agreed to. I was in a position where I could choose to be your mate, or the mate of a violent man at his lowest, most dangerous point." My heart crushes in my chest. "You used me against him to make a point, and then you almost lost me to him, anyway. You didn't care what would happen to me."

"That's not true!" For the first time in the entire conversation, Nathan raises his voice. "I didn't want to see you with him. I knew you'd be miserable, and I knew you didn't deserve it. I knew he didn't deserve you."

"But you do?" I scoff. "If you're so fucking deserving, if you value me so much more, why did you take your girlfriend on a trip days after our mating ceremony? Why don't you ever talk to me, or spend any time getting to know me?"

"Why would we need to get to know each other?"

It's the verbal equivalent of a slap to the face.

"I'm twenty years older than you. Perhaps that doesn't seem like much, considering the length of our lives, but I assure you, we likely have nothing in common." He sighs and refastens his belt-buckle. "Bailey, you're intelligent. You'll be a good queen. You'll raise our children with an understanding of what's truly best for them because you know what it means to make a leader of oneself when no one around you thinks you're capable. But that's all you need to be."

His opinion of me, that he thinks I've made a leader of myself against all odds, is strangely flattering. But I don't want to be flattered. "It's all you need me to be. Maybe I need more."

"Then take a lover. Not now, of course. Wait a few years—"

I yelp in offense.

"So that you've proved your loyalty to me, that's all I ask." I have no idea why he thinks that will placate me. "And then romantically, you may do as you like."

"It's not about romance, okay?" I can only imagine that he's so in love with himself that he can't believe I'm not. "I'm not asking you to be in love with me. I'm asking you not to make me look like a fool."

We stand there in silence both of us unwilling to bend, while the stupid connection between us grows more urgent, begging us to given in.

"End it with her," I plead in a whisper.

His denial is a hoarse, "No."

"Do you love her?" I'm prepared for the answer to hurt because, as much as I dislike Nathan, he's my mate. I want him to at least care about my feelings. It's such a small thing to ask of him.

Nathan laughs at my question. "That's incredibly naive of you."

"Why naive?" I demand, my stomach turning over at the way he dodged the question.

"One needn't be in love with one's mistress." It's still not an answer, and he won't look me in the eye. "Any more than one needs to be in love with one's own wife."

I say absolutely nothing, while he casts his gaze around the sitting room. "If that's all, we should go upstairs."

If that's all? I do my best to push down my shock, my hurt, and the loneliness of the past week in the prison of my tower. And I say, "No."

The attraction between us is a physical ache. His broad chest and strong arms look so good to me. I want to be trapped underneath him, my nails raking down his arms, legs locked around his waist.

Mystical bond or not, I value myself too much to compromise my principles.

Nathan cocks his head, almost as if he's amused. "Are you cutting me off?"

"If that's how you want to perceive the situation." I can't stand the sight of him. I won't be able to stand myself if I give in now and give up any more ground in the fight.

"You're angry—"

"You're right. I am angry. I've asked you to do something important for me, you refused, so I'm refusing something that's important to you." *There. How do you like it?*

He smirks. "You're expected to produce heirs to the throne."

I cluck my tongue in mock sympathy. "And you were so looking forward to having those heirs." I go to the intercom and call Hannah. "Hey, you can come back. My *mate* is just leaving."

Nathan shakes his head, still smirking, still not understanding that I'm going to win and he's going to lose. He picks up his shirt and swiftly unbuttons it and turns it right side out. "To be clear, you're asking me to break things off with Amber—"

I tut in admonishment at the mention of her name.

"You're asking me to break things off with my mistress, and if I do not, you won't let me fuck you?"

Damn his choice of phrase. The obscene word jolts through our connection and I want to squeeze my thighs together. My willpower is steel, though. "I'm asking you to choose your queen and your heirs over your vanity. We all have to make sacrifices, Nathan."

He nods, never dropping that smug expression that tells me he doesn't take me seriously, he will never take me seriously, that I don't matter at all. He says, "I'll see you at breakfast," pulls his shirt on and strides toward the door, which he opens onto a very startled Hannah. She steps back as he stalks past her without a word, then she looks to me, bewildered, for an explanation.

How do I explain that I just won an argument but lost everything?

CHAPTER 30

Nathan doesn't see me at breakfast. He doesn't see me for another whole week. I thought for sure that his panic about needing an heir would drive him to my bed before my fertility window closed, but he's as stubborn as I am.

We'll be a hundred before we have any kids.

Meanwhile, I've started to doubt my course of action. Though Aconitum Hall is a castle, it's way too small when one is aware of one's mate on a microscopic, metaphysical level. Nathan is never far from my thoughts; our connection becomes more and more insistent the longer we stay near-but-apart, and I'm not the only one feeling it. I can smell his arousal every night as I lie in my bed, and I know he's doing the same thing I'm doing with my hand beneath the covers. Worse, he knows I'm doing it, and somehow that makes it even hotter.

I hate that I think about my cheating husband as hot.

"Hey, are you with us?" Hannah asks one afternoon, snapping her fingers in my face.

I swat her hand away. "Yes, sorry. I got distracted. It's

not like I have something super important that's stressing me out."

We're in the ballroom, which is absolutely swarming with thralls setting up tables and hanging heavy swooshes of shantung bunting as they prepare for my coronation reception. It's all in my chosen colors of gray-blue and gold, from the tablecloths to the napkins, to the new carpet I had installed everywhere but the dance floor.

Since Nathan doesn't seem pissed off by me spending excessive amounts of money or withholding sex, ruining Aconitum Hall is the next attempt on my list.

"As I was saying," Hannah repeats, gesturing across the room to Amanda, who's deep in conversation with a thrall from the king's office, "The guest list is getting a lot shorter. Your mate won't tell us why, but my inside info is that a new sect of traitors has been discovered."

"Which traitors? The ones who support Victor's sons' claims, or the ones who support my husband's girlfriend's claim?" I can't help but feel a little panicky at the reality of that last one. If I lose my position, I have nothing. Well, nothing, except my parents' assets. But no family, no power, and how could I show my face if I'm deposed and suddenly nobody—

I hit the big red stop button on the carousel of spiraling anxiety that's filling my head with demonic calliope music so I can concentrate on Amber's answer.

"The former. From the same plot your family was involved in." She lowers her voice. "The council voted this morning and found them guilty."

"So, is Amanda getting that updated guest list for the coronation?" We'd had several iterations so far, all of them handed down like a decree from my husband's office.

"Yes. And I will remove the names we discussed," Hannah promises.

Nathan's mistress had magically reappeared on every guest list we removed her from. "Keep checking, right up until like, ten minutes before the ceremony."

"She's not getting in," Hannah vows. "I say that as a best friend, not an employee."

I take her hand in mine and squeeze it. "I would not be able to get through this without you."

"I know." She scrolls her smart pencil down the tablet cradled in her arm. "Did you get an answer from his office about adding your sisters to the guest list?"

"It was a hard no." My parents will be in attendance, though they won't be given a place of honor or any recognition. They're basically there to be poor and shamed in front of the rest of the pack. But my sisters? Their absence —and Nathan's explanation for it—stings. "He said they're traitors and it's in my best interest to distance myself, lest others think I'm a traitor, as well."

Hannah's expression goes tight. "He's not suggesting that you…"

"Maybe? I don't know?" I'm pretty sure he's just in a pissy mood because I won't have sex with him, but I don't need everyone in the ballroom to overhear that. "It's probably just a shitty thing to say because he can."

Hannah's face softens. "I'm so sorry. I know you didn't want this life."

"No, no, no," I wag my index finger at nothing in particular. "I didn't want Ashton and the shitty life I would have with him. I can put up with an awful mate in exchange for being queen and living in a castle."

"That's very romantic of you," she says wryly.

I lower my voice to shoot back, "you of all people should understand what a marriage of convenience is."

"Yours isn't a marriage of convenience," she corrects me quietly, barely moving her lips. "It's a dick measuring contest."

"He wins," I say at normal volume, and Hannah barks a surprise laugh.

But now I'm thinking of Nathan's dick, and I swear I feel a hot flash creeping on.

I clear my throat, square my shoulders, and say, "I'm getting my sisters back. He lost the right to worry about appearances when he decided to keep his mistress."

That is something the thralls should hear. There's no doubt in my mind that everyone working in the palace knows of their king's affair. I want as many people to know that I know about it as possible. The more people who think I'm okay with it, the less pathetic I appear.

"Fair," Hannah agrees. "But maybe wait until after your coronation? You might be able to just command their return."

"Tara and Clare would *love* that." As far as I'm aware, they haven't responded to Nathan's invitation to return, which probably means they want to stay with their traitor husbands.

"There have been ladies-in-waiting to other queens," Hannah reminds me. "You could bring the tradition back. They wouldn't be able to turn you down."

"I don't want them here if they don't want to be here." They probably hate me, already. "Besides, Nathan would just send them back if he disagreed."

Hannah sets her tablet down and puts her hands on her hips. "Are you kidding me? What is the point of being queen if you're going to be such a coward?"

"Every time I try to do something sneaky behind his back, it's just another opportunity for him to win," I remind her.

"That's not how a healthy partnership works." She pulls out one of the white, gilt accented chairs—I purchased hundreds of new ones for the occasion—and motions for me to sit, then she sits, herself. When she leans forward and initiates intense eye contact, I know she's going to hit me with something that's probably right, but that I don't want to hear. She says, "You and Nathan cannot rule this pack while you're constantly fighting. You guys don't have to be madly in love, but if you're fighting with each other, you won't see all the people fighting against you. And that's the reality of this pack right now, Bailey."

One night earlier this week, Ryan had come for pizza night and a political primer. Hannah, Ryan, and I all hunkered down around my coffee table in my private sitting room while Ryan drew complex diagrams to explain family alliances and how they'd been changing since I invoked the Right of Accord.

The main three factions are those who support Nathan and I, those who support the claim King Victor's sons are making, and those who feel that the former queen did nothing wrong. Which I can't get my head around, and not just because I'm biased against her for fucking my mate. Her actions cost Victor the throne; the only way anyone could support her would be if they were in favor of the Manhattan pack seizing Toronto.

What if that's why Nathan won't break things off with her? I hate being practical about anything, but this is politics. By not banishing her, maybe he's hoping to win some of her supporters to his side.

In which case, does that mean he's going to get rid of me and make her queen, if it becomes politically advantageous to do so?

"I've changed my mind about the guest list," I say, getting to my feet and heading toward Amanda. I make it to her side just in time to interrupt her conversation with the thrall from Nathan's office.

"Stay," I reassure the thrall, and she does, bowing her curly blonde head. That's the last time I address her; I just need her to report this, so Nathan knows about it. "It's about the guest list. Amber Rogers. She's invited, correct?"

"Um, yes, Your Majesty," Amanda says, producing a paper copy of the list from a folder under her arm. "Should I remove her ag—"

"No, of course not." I smile sweetly. "She may have been deposed, but my husband, in his wisdom, has shown her mercy. She should not only be present, but highly, highly visible. Put her at table three. That's at the foot of the dais, correct?"

Amanda nods and whips out her tablet. "Yes, it is, but there are—"

"Oh, are there people there that don't like her?" I feign a noise of disappointment. "Well, I'm sure they can all get along, for my sake. I'm sure it will be a difficult day for her. Table three is directly in front of His Majesty's and my seats?"

Hannah snorts a laugh.

"It is." Amanda gets the hint but is too well-trained to comment. "I'll be sure to update the list."

"Oh, and make sure she gets a new invitation. With a seating chart. Highlighted." I smile sweetly. "Make sure it comes directly from my office, will you, Hannah?"

"With pleasure, Your Majesty," Hannah says, making a note on her tablet, as well.

If Nathan wants his girlfriend at my coronation, I'll be sure to welcome her with open arms and give her a seat right against the glass, so she doesn't miss a moment of me stealing the throne. Maybe that will prove to him that I'm not playing around.

"Thanks, Amanda," I say, turning away and motioning for Hannah to follow me.

"What's next, Your Majesty," she asks with a note of pride in her voice.

Though it's not a plan she can exactly help me with, I tell her, "Next, I get my sisters back."

CHAPTER 31

That night, I wait until the residence is mostly silent, and I set off to find Nathan.

I have no idea where his bedroom is. I've never been there. Whenever I've asked anybody, they've been evasive about it. But I was wrong about Hannah not being able to help me in this; she finds out in about three minutes, just by playing ditzy to a guard.

I study her scribbled map and tuck it into a drawer with a deep breath before I leave my sitting room. Now that I know Nathan has a bit on the side, I'm not sure what I'll find when I arrive at his room. What if I barge in there and he's mid-coitus with his mistress?

Ugh, what if that's what I've been feeling every night, when it seems like his sexual energy is going to reach out grab me and pull me straight into his bed?

The door to Nathan's tower is hidden. No joke, it's a hidden panel in the wall of his study, and I have to admit, it's pretty thrilling to pull a candelabra on the wall and see a huge bookcase swing open to reveal a spiral staircase.

But it would be way more fun if I were in an old haunted house movie or something, instead of my life.

At least I'm dressed the part, in a long, silky, white nightgown.

I climb the stairs, my heart in my throat. He's in here, the tie between us gives that away. But he hasn't come to investigate why I'm here, and as I reach the top steps, I'm sure I'm going to find him with her. And I'm going to be wearing a thin silk chemise with spaghetti straps, like I've come here on a seduction mission.

It's really more of a teasing mission. I know he'll be able to see the dip of my navel where the fabric clings to it, the points of my nipples against the silk. But if he's already fucking someone, I'm not sure it'll be much of a tease.

I really hope he's not fucking her.

But he's just sitting in a chair in front of a crackling fire, having a glass of something dark. He raises it to me as if in toast. "You found me."

"Yes, despite your ridiculous, Captain Dracula bookshelf nonsense, I found you." I try to mask my relief at his otherwise empty room with snark.

"Dracula was a count. Not a captain," he corrects me. He gets to his feet, and I note his lack of clothing, apart from some black silk boxers.

If he approaches me, I'm going to fling myself against his body. I won't be able to help myself.

When he doesn't approach me, I'm disappointed.

"I need to talk to you."

"Is it about the *gracious* invitation a friend of mine received?" At least he seems amused by it, not furious. "She sends her regrets, by the way."

"Oh, gosh, I'm so disappointed," I say in my most

obnoxiously syrupy tone. "I hope it wasn't anything I *did…*"

"It's what I did," he says with a shrug, refilling his glass from a decanter on a side table.

The king's room couldn't be more different from the queen's. While I'm over there in a dollhouse built out of cupcakes, he's practically drowning in a pool of testosterone. The four poster bed is topped with finials of carved wooden antlers. Mounted deer heads look down on us from every wall, and a taxidermized cougar is caught mid-spring above the enormous mantle.

"And what did you do, *Gaston?*" I ask, gesturing to the black bear rug on the black-and-white checked marble floor.

Nathan chuckles. "I haven't had time to redecorate. King Victor's taste was… compensating for something."

"Uh-huh." I walk slowly across the room, avoiding the rug, to stand beside the second armchair in front of the fire. "What did you do?"

Nathan sighs deeply. "I told her not to come. That you didn't want her there and that, as queen, it was your right to remove her from the guest list."

"Because it is my right. And you should have done this from the beginning." If he thinks I'm going to thank him, or grovel because he's thrown me this one, tiny bone, he's delusional.

"Was that what you needed to speak to me about tonight, Bailey?" Nathan's voice around my name might as well be his arms around my body. "Or are you here for another reason?"

"Not the reason you're hoping for," I shut him down immediately. "You have to do a lot better than keeping your potentially traitorous deposed former royal side piece from coming to my party."

"You're very good at being queen, already," he quips.

"I've decided to bring my sisters to court."

"To...court?" He takes a sip from his glass, and I can almost hear his mind working. He swallows and says, "I haven't heard any mention of a court for a long time."

"That's very shortsighted of you." I say it as though it's a compliment. "You would think that with traitors everywhere, you'd want to have your allies as close as possible. And the people who aren't your allies, of course."

"Yes, I'm familiar with the adage about enemies and their proximities," he says dryly.

"Then you understand why I'm bringing my sisters to be my ladies-in-waiting." I pause so he can object, and when he doesn't, I go on. "Their husbands won't move against you if their wives are in your house, serving your queen, under constant scrutiny from your guard."

"They won't move against me from Newfoundland, either," he points out.

Newfoundland? Yikes.

"So, are you forbidding me?" I ask, crossing my arms over my chest. The motion draws his eyes to my cleavage. *Good.* I hope he suffers from the worst ball-ache in history tonight.

"I'm not forbidding you. I'm just not sure what currency you think you have to spend here." He sits back down, knees apart. "You're hardly in a position to demand things from me."

"You want me to have sex with you to buy this favor?" I wasn't entirely unprepared for that possibility when I got dressed to come here.

"Sexual bargaining is what you brought to this marriage. Not me," he reminds me.

"One night," I tell him. "This buys you one night."

"This is an awfully big favor for just one night."

"Then you'll have to make the most of it." I wonder if he'll wait for the full moon, if he'll take me out in the woods, under the starlight—

The attraction that binds us grows almost painful. I ignore it, he does, too, and we both end up just pretending we're not miserable not having sex with each other.

He considers a moment. "I hope you understand what you're offering me."

A chill runs up my spine; am I missing something important in this conversation?

"You may bring your sisters here. Say it's on my royal command. If there are any hard feelings about having to leave their mates, they can direct those complaints to me," he says.

"And in return, what do you want?" Since this is a negotiation, I'm open to pretty much anything. I want my sisters back that badly.

"One night. Just as you've said. But I will plan to make the most of it, per your suggestion." He leans back in his chair, the black silk boxers riding up his muscular thighs. "You may be quite shocked by what I ask of you."

"Maybe not." I will be. There's no doubt about it. No matter how much porn I may have furtively watched on my phone this week, I'm still easily shocked by things that are apparently normal for most of the mortal world. "But it's not going to be tonight."

"I wouldn't dream of asking such a thing. I don't expect payment until delivery." He motions that I should come closer. "I do, however, require a show of good faith."

"What—" I begin, but he just gets more comfortable in his chair and tugs down the waistband of his boxers. He's half-hard already.

"In your own time," he teases.

My face flames with indignation. I'm supposed to, what? Blow him as a thank you for listening to me?

But my mouth waters at the thought and before I know it, I'm on my knees on the awful bearskin rug, my hand circling Nathan's cock as best as it can.

"You're more ruthless than I imagined," Nathan praises me as I slowly stroke him. "I'm impressed."

His erection surges in my hand and I murmur, "I can see that."

Yay for me, my mate is aroused by the fact that I'm bartering sex.

I hold his gaze and lick my lips as I lower my mouth to the head of his cock. I let my breath drift over his tip as I say, "I've never done this before. You're the first."

He groans, his eyes locked on mine as I suck him between my lips and swirl my tongue around him.

What is it about men and wanting to be the first? Hannah once mused that it was probably because those men were bad at making women come, but that's not a logical argument when it comes to Nathan. He's more than capable of getting me off; I think he's just turned on by the fact that he's the only one who's had me.

Possessiveness isn't a turn-on, I remind myself. Sadly, it's the only way I can feel like he actually gives a damn about me. And if it weren't for our connection, he probably wouldn't give a damn at all.

I take as much of him into my mouth as I can without choking myself, and he grips the arm of the chair with a clawed hand. So, I'm doing something right. I close my eyes, so I don't imagine that hand on my body. So that I don't imagine peeling off my nightgown and climbing into his lap to ride him.

My pussy clenches at the thought and I begin to make all sorts of stupid excuses in my head about why it wouldn't hurt to fuck him, just this once, and go right back to hating him. *What do you care if he has someone else in his life? You're his mate. He belongs to you.*

But he doesn't really belong to me. I don't need him to, either. I just need him to prove that this isn't a wholly one-sided marriage.

You're really proving your point by blowing him.

I don't know a lot about giving blowjobs, but I know that after a while, he's not as in control of his body as he was when we started. His hand is in my hair, gripping it tightly. His hips lift in time to the bobbing of my head, and when I swirl my tongue around his shaft as I raise up, his breath hisses out of him. I follow all those cues and settle into a pattern that he clearly enjoys, and it's not long before his body jerks up and he bursts in my mouth with a strangled moan.

"Don't swallow." He somehow manages to sound calm and in control while his cock is still twitching in my mouth. He pulls out and sits forward, sweeping two fingers into my mouth full of cum. "Stand up."

I get to my feet, trembling, and he lifts up my nightgown. I'm bare underneath, and so aroused from what we just did that it takes hardly any pressure for him to plunge those fingers into my pussy. The difference in texture between my own wetness and the cum on his hand is stark; my knees go weak. It's not enough to just be penetrated. I want him to fuck me with those fingers, want to ride on his hand as I straddle his thigh. His thumb brushes over my clit and my body goes up in flame, but that's all he gives me.

He pulls his hand away with a wink and says, "Waste not. You can swallow now."

I somehow didn't realize I still held a mouthful of cum, and I grimace it down. "So, our agreement?"

He blinks for a moment like he doesn't remember what the point of this whole thing was, then says, "It will be the first item on my agenda in the morning. Will I see you at breakfast?"

I smile sweetly and shake my head. "I would honestly rather eat breakfast off an airport bathroom changing table."

A smile threatens the corners of his lips, but he doesn't say anything. I turn to leave and I'm at the top of the stairs when he stops me.

"Bailey."

His voice is so quiet, I almost don't hear him.

I turn and what I see stuns me. Nathan isn't "on." He's not walled-off or commanding, he's just a man, and he seems so vulnerable.

"Yes?" I squeak out uncertainly.

"You're not always going to be able to do this, you know." His voice is hoarse. "You're not always going to be able to get what you want by bartering sex."

I hold his gaze, nod, and say, "We'll see."

CHAPTER 32

For a man who assured me he won't be manipulated with sex, Nathan sure works fast. My sisters arrive from Newfoundland the morning before my coronation, less than twenty-four hours after Nathan and I made our deal.

Hannah pulls me away from a fitting for my coronation gown to head down to the empty throne room. There's already a secondary throne on the dais for me. Even though I'm not queen yet, I take it, anyway.

The majordomo is there, and he waits for Hannah to signal him before the guards open the doors and he announces, "Tara and Clare, formerly of the Toronto pack."

The "formerly" part of the sentence has to sting. So does, I imagine, the part where their last names have been stripped from them. Even from across the throne room, I see Tara flinch. But Clare holds her head up regally as they approach, and they both curtsey when they reach the dais, but I jump up and nearly tackle them.

"I'm so glad you're okay!" I don't care that tears roll down my face while I hug them.

Clare steps back and motions to her clothing. "I'm wearing overalls and an unraveling acrylic sweater from Value Village. Do I look okay?"

Tara, I note, is wearing a holey t-shirt under an unbuttoned flannel and ripped dockers. "They have us staying at two different motels. We're not allowed to talk to each other."

"Motels?" Does Nathan think he's going to be able to keep them in motels for a century?

"It's not permanent. We're going to be moved to trailers on pack land. With the other banished traitors," Clare grinds out.

"Well, for right now, I think you're going to stay here." I can't believe they would entertain the idea of going back. But they don't need to know that it's my choice, either way.

And yeah, that's shitty of me, but it was shitty of their husbands to get them banished in the first place.

"That's the impression I got," Tara says cheerfully. "I was hoping it wasn't too good to be true."

"As long as we fall in line with her mate, the king, I assume it isn't," Clare snarks.

I'm getting the sense that they're not real keen on Nathan. They can join my club.

But I don't want them to know there's friction between him and I. "Is that... like, are you mad at him about being here?"

"No," Tara says firmly, over the top of Clare's strident, "Yes!"

Tara sighs in frustration. "Maybe you can talk some sense into her, Bailey."

"Oh, I'm the one who needs to come to her senses?"

Clare scoffs. "You practically jumped into the car when you got the chance to abandon Josh."

This sounds like a kettle that's been brewing the entire way here. "Look, maybe we can talk about this after you've gotten to your rooms, and you've changed your clothes—"

"I didn't abandon Josh!" Tara shouts. "He abandoned me when he decided to get involved in an assassination plot!"

Thank you! I agree silently.

"I mean, are you going to blame this ladies-in-waiting thing on Bailey, just because the king is her mate?" Tara demands.

Shhh on that maybe, I plead silently.

"No," Clare says, icy and calm. "If she does support his choice, she's doing the right thing. We're supposed to be loyal to our mates."

"King and pack, then mates," I put in softly. They don't acknowledge it and that's probably for the best. I saw some epic fights when we were growing up and I still don't want any part of one.

"So you're saying you support Julien's choice to try to assassinate the king?" Tara asks, and I cast a glance around at all the thrall guards in the room.

"I'm going to have to ask you to think very, very carefully before you answer that," I warn. "I know that, of course, you would never advocate for the assassination of your king and pack leader, but I wouldn't want someone to misunderstand you."

"Why? Are they going to send me back to my mate where I belong." Clare won't be subdued by what she probably perceives as an obnoxious flex from a little sister who's been elevated way above her station.

My heart sinks. "Is that what you want?" Out of all of us, Clare is the one I would have counted on being the most psyched about this arrangement. I could see Tara surviving without luxury, but not Clare. Unless... "Do you love Julien?"

I know the question puts her on the spot, but it's important. If she doesn't want to be here because of some altruistic concept of tradition and loyalty, I don't feel terrible about making her stay. Those rules about what we should value as the females of the pack? Those are bullshit and I'm not going to respect her for clinging to them. But if she loves him... When she doesn't answer, I feel even worse.

"Just...take us to our cells. I'm tired of this whole day."

"Yeah, sure," I say, disheartened. "You both have the afternoon off. I know Amanda has some coronation related stuff to go over—"

"Amanda?" Clare makes a face, like she's decided to dislike the thrall based on name alone.

Hannah steps out from behind the dais and greets my sisters warmly. "Tara. Clare. It's been such a long time."

"Hannah?" Tara's defeated frown turns into a huge grin. "Oh my gosh, what are you doing here?"

"I'm your sister's personal assistant."

"But today, she's going to personally assist you two with getting established in the palace," I tell them.

"That's right," Amanda begins. "We've got wardrobes to choose, menu preferences, phones to set up, it's going to be a long day."

"And tomorrow is going to be longer," I remind them. "So, tonight there's spa time."

Clare warms to this a little. "Which spa."

"Well...we're not leaving." *Because of what your husband did,* I do not say.

"Royals get their massages and pedicures at their houses," Tara explains for me.

Clare makes a noise of unimpressed understanding. "All right. Let's get started."

I can't believe it's gone this badly, this quickly. Clare walks two steps ahead of Hannah, as if she knows where they're going. Damn, is my sister ever good at power plays. Tara hangs back, just for a second.

"Thank you," she whispers, and hugs me tight. "I don't know what's going on with Clare, but thank you for trusting me."

"Trusting you?" I ask, but Hannah calls back to ask if Tara is coming, and she scampers off. As I watch the three of them go, I realize what Tara meant. *"Thank you for not thinking I had anything to do with the plot".* She's happy to be with the pack again.

But Clare isn't, and she's really unhappy with Nathan. Did she want to see him dead, all along? Did she support the claim of Victor's heir? It doesn't matter now. I'm about to be queen. She's not going to do anything that would endanger my life.

Right?

I glance over to the head of Nathan's royal guard. I don't have my own security yet—it takes longer to vet the thralls and select them than it does to organize a lavish coronation—so in the meantime, Nathan has entrusted me to his personal retinue of bodyguards. I motion the man over. He looks more like a math teacher than a security expert, with curly salt-and-pepper hair to match his salt-and-pepper mustache. He never smiles, either. Not even when I try to crack a joke.

"Your Majesty," he intones, bowing stiffly.

"My sister, Clare... I'm going to need some extra eyes on her." I hate what I'm implying, so I just say it. "I need to know I can trust her."

"We have eyes and ears all over the house, ma'am." It's an assurance that he understands my request, and I'm grateful for it. I don't want to have to outright explain that I think my sister may be on her husband's side. That she might not be on mine.

I go back to my rooms, utterly dejected by the reception I got from my sisters. Not Tara, of course, but Clare's rejection stings enough to ruin my day. I'm staring down at my feet when I enter my sitting room, so when I glance up at spy Nathan standing at the window, I startle and yelp.

"What the fuck!" I press my hand to my chest to see if my pulse has restarted. "You can't just loom around in a house this old and probably haunted."

He sniffs. "I don't believe in ghosts."

"Humans, you can believe, ghosts are a step too far." I snort. "I hope you didn't come here thinking you were collecting on our agreement right now."

"Here? In the middle of the day?" He toes aside one of Jo's toys that escaped the playpen. "What a waste that would be."

"Then why are you here?" I hope it sounds as antagonistic as I feel.

"I was trying to discern which angle gave me away," he says, turning back to the window. "And where I should place new hedges."

"Oh, I have a few ideas where you could put them."

He barks a laugh as he faces me again. "I did leave that open, didn't I?"

"You sure did." I don't smile. I don't want him to feel

welcome in my personal space. And the way the air crackles between us, it's dangerous for my will power if he stays. "Is that all?"

"Until tonight," he confirms.

"What's tonight?" Nobody has told me about any pre-coronation social obligations.

"Oh, I'm collecting," he says, slipping his hands into his pockets and slouching a bit. "On our arrangement."

I roll my eyes. "Nathan, tomorrow is my coronation and—"

"You'll be so tired after, I'm sure," he says with mock sympathy. "Which is why tonight is better. And it works better for me."

"Why, do you have something going on tomorrow?" My stomach sours and I realize I don't want to know the answer. "Never mind. What time?"

"Come to me at nine," he decides after a pause. "I liked the white nightgown. Wear that."

"It's dirty. Someone got cum on it," I say dryly.

"Do you have it in red?" he asks, like I'm a freaking department store.

"I don't think I do."

"You will," he says with a lift of his eyebrows. He walks to the door, not stopping as he passes me. He doesn't look back as he leaves me with, "It's going to be a late night. Rest up."

CHAPTER 33

I enter Nathan's study a few minutes before nine. I don't want to be late to close our transaction. It might affect future negotiations. The secret door is open. The staircase winds up into darkness. I take a deep breath on the first step. Nathan is waiting for me. The closer I get, the stronger our connection becomes. I hold my breath as I climb, and by the time I reach the top, I'm lightheaded. I would be anyway.

Nathan stands in front of the fire in the white shirt and black trousers he was wearing during the day, but I notice that this time, he's not drinking anything. It strikes me as odd because he's almost always drinking some kind of alcohol. Its absence alerts me to its near constant presence, and for a moment, I'm concerned that he might be using it to cope with the stress of his position.

Well, he could make things at home a lot less stressful if he stopped being a cheating asshole who can only get his wife to fuck him as payment for favors.

He glances down at his watch before he takes it off. "Right on time."

"I wouldn't want to be accused of stalling." I glance over at the bed and note the absence of pillows and covers. A single black sheet is on the mattress, and thin black cord is draped across the headboard. I think I know what it's for.

He motions me over and makes me walk all the way to him, never trying to meet me by even a few steps. When I reach his side, he loops an arm around my waist and pulls me close. "I knew it would look even better in red."

I look down at my nightgown, which had been delivered to my rooms only an hour after Nathan had promised it. The silk hugs my body the same way as the white one does, but the deep, blood red makes it feel more sinful, more exhibitionistic. I've worn it specifically to turn him on, to get fucked in it, by his request.

I don't want to make eye contact with him, because I don't want him to see my hunger. I don't want to see that hunger reflected in his gaze. `Wanting him hurts. And I want him.

I lean into him, and he tilts my face up to kiss me, hard and desperate. He's been as miserable as I have, and in a passion-drunk moment, I can't remember why we denied ourselves. Tonight, we don't have to.

He lifts his head, fingers still cradling my chin. "Do you trust me?"

I laugh. "Of course, I don't."

A bitter smile touches his lips. "I mean, do you trust me not to harm you?"

I do. With all my heart and soul. "If there is one thing I will never doubt, it's your vow to keep me safe."

His throat moves with what looks like a painful swallow. His cocky smile is obviously forced. "Good," he says, giving my butt a playful swat. "Then you won't mind if I tie you up?"

I was right about the cords.

"Are you going to do painful stuff to me?" I ask doubtfully, images of paddles and handcuffs crowding out my desire.

He leans close to my ear and whispers, "Not that kind of pain."

Before I can ask what he means, he takes my hand and leads me toward the huge bed. There are implements laid out on a towel, but nothing in the whips and chains genre. They're bizarre items: a glass vial of milky blue liquid, a paintbrush, and a two-pronged pink thing about the size of my palm that I'm pretty sure is a sex toy.

"What's all this?" I whisper, a thrill of trepidation running through my pelvis.

"It's for...making the most of the night." He pats the mattress. "Go on. In the center."

"Should I take this off?" I gesture to my nightgown. He chuckles. "Fuck, no." I climb onto the bed as he instructed and lie down. There are padded cuffs linked to the cord running across the headboard. "Am I supposed to have a safe word for this?"

"A simple 'no more' will suffice," is his ominous answer. I know he won't hurt me. I know he won't violate me or do anything to cause me trauma. I know it because even though I despise him, the bond between us betrays how much he treasures me.

Unfortunately, that probably goes both ways.

While I'm preoccupied with the cuffs at the head of the bed, he locks something around my ankle. It's a rigid bar with an identical cuff on the opposite side. He takes my other, bare foot and lifts it to his mouth, sucking my big toe into his mouth. I gasp. He's had his mouth on my pussy before, but somehow, this feels more intimate. My hips arch up, and he lowers my foot to the bed.

"That reaction is exactly—" He pauses, then fastens the other cuff. "—why we need these."

"You don't want me to move?" I see my pulse in the silk over my chest. He slides my nightgown up, crawling over me until the fabric reaches my waist and his face is tantalizingly close to my mound. I want to arch up, but he's right; with the bar between my legs, my lower body is cumbersome and heavy.

"Understand now?" he asks, his breath teasing my already engorged clit peeking out from between my labia.

Trembling, I nod.

He moves away and adjusts the bar; my legs are forced open wide, and so is my most private part. I feel my wetness in the cool touch of the air; even the fire in the hearth can't match the heat of my body. I'm fueled by my need, already burning up.

Nathan gets off the bed and takes up the cuffs at the center of the headboard. He snaps his fingers at me in silent command to raise my arms, and I do so automatically. My reaction stuns me. I should be furious, to be ordered around like this. But obeying his wordless—and rude—command makes the connection between us throb.

It makes other things throb, too.

My arms are over my head, wrists bound together, and I instantly panic. I test the bonds and try to sit up, but Nathan is there in a moment, lying beside me, his body a protective cradle around mine. He turns my face to his and kisses me, tender this time instead of hungry.

"You trust me," he says, a statement of fact and not a question. The reminder soothes me, and I cease my struggling. The fear in me subsides, leaving only a strange exhilaration at being so helpless and exposed for him.

When I'm calm again, he leaves the bed, unbuttoning his sleeve cuffs. He removes his shirt and undershirt and tosses them both aside and picks up something from the bed. It's another towel. He unfolds it and moves to tuck it beneath my lower half.

"What—" I begin, not sure where any of this is going.

"You'll need it," he says. "You'll be very, very wet."

I gasp in what I think might be outrage but is definitely excitement. I believe him because I'm already achy and dripping.

He picks up the paintbrush; it has a rounded tip that ends in a slight point. "I made a mistake before," he says, almost apologetic. "I was so overcome with wanting you before, I didn't take my time."

I say nothing because I don't know what to say.

"It occurred to me that, in your inexperience, you might think you have to settle for instant gratification."

I scoff. "Someone thinks highly of himself."

"Someone is realistic," he corrects me, moving down to my feet again. "You can't pretend that you didn't come. The proof was smeared all over my face. I felt your cunt ripple around my tongue."

The words are like direct touches to my clit.

"I don't have anything against a quick, hard fuck that leaves us both satiated," he goes on. "But you deserve to experience the bliss of delayed release. The torture of teasing."

He strokes the paintbrush from my heel, over the ticklish arch of sole, and my foot flexes and spasms.

"Don't you want to know what that's like?" he asks as I

squirm. "Don't you want to know how I can make you beg? How I can make you writhe?"

Another stroke makes me giggle from the sensation, but it's not like a playful tickle.

"Don't you want to know how hard I can make you come?"

Another stroke, this time in reverse, swooping down around the ball where my ankle meets my foot.

"Yes," I say, though I'm not sure he's going to prove his hypothesis through tickling me. He drags the brush over the top of my foot and my toes wriggle helplessly. But I'm less sensitive now, not as a ticklish.

Until he moves to the other foot.

"You don't want to feel lop-sided, do you?" he playfully admonishes while I giggle and make a futile try to avoid the brush. This time, when he's finished with my foot, he moves further up my leg, just along my calf, to the bend of my knee. The featherlight touches are somehow the most overwhelming sensations I've ever experienced, and I realize with a pang of worry that it's going to be a lot more intense. He hasn't reached my pussy yet, and by the time he trails the brush up the inside of both thighs, I'm so grateful that the suspense is at an end. I crave direct contact, even if it is just the brush. But the moment the bristles reach my labia, he moves away.

I choke out a wordless sound of dismay, and he laughs. "Oh, Bailey. We've barely begun."

He lifts the vial of strangely opalescent fluid. "I'm sure you remember our mating."

It was the last time we had sex, and yes, I remember it. I remember it started off horribly, as he pummeled my body with the strength and size and brutal hardness of his werewolf form. And then, it had all changed.

"Did you know the process of werewolf mating? Beyond the simple mechanics. Did you know what it would feel like?"

I shake my head.

"There's a hormone we release during the full moon. It's especially strong at Lupercalia, because of it being a fertility festival. You remember when I came inside you, the first time?" He asks.

I eye the vial suspiciously. "Is that...magic werewolf cum?"

He laughs. "This? No. This is a synthetic derivation of that hormone. It produces the same aphrodisiac effect. The heightened sensation." He pops the top off the vial. "Thralls are so clever at blending silence with their magic," he muses, dipping the paintbrush into the fluid. A single drop hangs suspended at the point of the bristles. He smooths his palm over my silk-covered belly, then to the top of my mound. Parting my labia, he exposes my clitoris, and as I moan in relief at the touch, he slides the hood back, leaving the too-sensitive gland fully exposed. He dangles the brush directly over it, the drop of fluid poised to fall.

He continues, "They've managed to somehow make it even more potent."

And the drop falls.

CHAPTER 34

It's like being struck by lightning. But in a good way. My body convulses from that single drop. My lungs heave for breath, my empty cunt clutches down on a phantom intrusion that I welcome, and I scream, racing toward a climax that will burst me apart at the seams.

A climax that never comes.

I never come.

"What did you do?" I gasp, sweat rolling down my face as every nerve strains with the agony of need.

"I told you. It's more potent." He moves up my writhing body to cup one of my breasts. The touch, even through the silk nightgown, should be enough to bring me over the edge, but I'm stuck. He lifts my breast free and sucks my exposed nipple into his mouth, closing his tongue over it.

"Please," I whimper, overcome by the aching want that grows stronger by the second.

"The only thing they can't quite get right," he says, referring to the thralls that formulated the substance, "is how long it lasts."

"W-wha—"

"And there's such a long period of time before orgasm is even possible—"

"What?" I shout, tugging at the restraints.

"Don't worry. You'll come. Eventually." He opens the vial and dips his finger in, then circles my nipple. I scream in frustration as the fire from my core settles in the tightly drawn up flesh.

"I need—" I gasp, shifting to get away from him. I'm restrained too well; he frees my other breast and repeats the torture on that side, too. "Please, I need to come!"

"You will. Just not for a while." He puts the vial on the bedside table and strokes my damp hair back from my face. "In the meantime, you'll suffer sublime anticipation."

"Fuck you!" I shout, but what I mean is *"fuck me, please, fuck me, make me come, do whatever you want to me just so long as I get the release I so desperately need."*

He chuckles and picks up the pink toy. He presses a button, and it gives a low hum. "You've used one of these before, haven't you?" he asks. "A vibrator, I mean. Not this specific type."

"Of course, I have," I snap.

"I only wondered because you were...inexperienced." He lowers the toy to my throbbing clit, and I moan. The soft silicone nubs bracket my stiff flesh, the vibration more like slow pulses that reverberate through my entire pelvis. He balances the toy on my mound. "Hold still. Right there."

I open my mouth to question him, and he warns, "Not a single muscle. Otherwise, it won't stay."

What does it matter, if it won't give me the relief I so desperately need? Then again, the thought of losing the stimulation is somehow just as bad. I feel my body climbing toward its peak and I silently chant, *yes, yes, yes*. But the moment I reach the apex of pleasure, it escapes me.

"No!" I shout, biting my lip when what I want to do is pound the bed and thrash at the unfairness.

Nathan pulls a chair up beside the bed, near my head, and sits back in it, just watching me.

"Are you enjoying this?" I hiss at him.

"I am." He slowly unbuckles his belt, unfastens his fly. "I'm about to enjoy it even more."

I don't have to ask him what he means. He's hard, the flesh peeking from beneath his foreskin flushed red. He grips himself and strokes slowly, groaning.

Another climax teases me, and it's no less devastating to have it pulled away just because I know what to expect. A tear leaks from the corner of my eye. I've never been so close to orgasm, so painfully ready for it, only to linger at that point endlessly. It's maddening pleasure and blissful torture.

"You're so beautiful this helpless," he says, his sweeping gaze drinking in every inch of my trembling form. His fist pumps his length in an unhurried rhythm. "It reminds me of the last time we were together."

The last time, I was chained up in a dirt hole, I want to snap, but I can't. Another near-orgasm approaches and I reach out for it with the only part of me that can move, my voice.

Nathan closes his eyes and makes a low, hoarse sound as my scream rises in pitch. He leans his head back. "You're going to make me come."

At least one of us will, I think, then I worry what that means for the rest of the night. Will he still fuck me? Will he make sure I finish once he has?

Of course, he will.

He has to, doesn't he?

I focus on his hand moving on his cock, my head swimming against wave after wave of unrelieved lust. I don't know how many times I nearly make it, closer and closer every time, until finally there is no build-up, no climb to enjoy, just the acute pain of needing to let go, wanting to let go.

It still never comes.

"It's driving you mad, isn't it," he asks with a cruel smile.

"Make it stop!" I beg him.

"It will stop," he assures me. "In time. I would never do anything to permanently harm you."

"Fuck you!" I scream.

His breathing speeds up. So does his hand.

"Le me come!" I plead, knowing he has no control over the matter. I have to beg, anyway. "Please!"

"Be careful what you wish for." His voice is tight. He lets go of his erection and stands to take off his pants. "You've lost count of the number of times your relief has been denied."

"W-was I supposed to count?" I whimper, my mind barely rising above the maddening denial.

He shakes his head slowly and removes the cuffs from my legs, tossing the bar aside with a clatter.

"No. I'm merely saying that because…" he moves to kneel between my legs and strokes himself again. "When the potion releases you from its hold… every single climax you've been denied…you'll feel all off them, all at once."

Fear lances through me. I'll die. I know I will. The pleasure will be too keen. It will tear me apart.

"And that should be…" he murmurs, pressing the head of his cock against my opening, "right about now."

I open my mouth to ask him how he knows, but all that comes out is a howl that grows louder, shriller, as he thrusts deep and stays there, erupting inside me as every nerve in body ignites. He roars with his release as I scream through mine. I'm not sure if it's pleasure I feel; whatever it is, it robs me of my senses until all I hear is the rush of my blood, all I see are bursts of hot white light. My legs wind around Nathan's back, holding him to me, and he batters me again and again with his still hard cock, cursing and grunting.

"I don't want to stop fucking you," he groans.

"Don't!" I shout, jerking at the cuffs that still restrain my arms.

And he doesn't; he pounds into me until he's as sweat slick as I am, until his breath bellows out of him from exertion.

And the whole time, I plunge into the abyss, over and over again, recovering from one orgasm for only seconds before drowning in another. I rise up to meet his thrusts, swear at him and demand, "harder!" and "faster!" despite his guttural shouts. He must be in agony, his oversensitive flesh trapped in my sopping, squeezing cunt.

Good.

"Don't stop," I chant, over and over, because he deserves whatever torture he's feeling, after the way he tormented me. He never goes soft, and suddenly, with a grunt of surprise, he drives as deep as he can and his body shudders over me. The hot burst as he fills my pussy again triggers my last climax. I throw my head back and shriek, gripping the cord that restrains me, and my body flails against his.

When I come down, he slowly withdraws from me, an obscene gush following him.

"I told you that you'd need the towel," he chuckles, and leans up to unfasten my cuffs.

I weakly flip him off.

I lay there in a puddle until he moves the towel, dabbing me with a dry corner. I can't move to cover myself. I can't move to do anything.

He leaves the bed and returns with a thick duvet. He spreads it over me and slides beneath, pulling my limp body against his side.

I don't resist him. He's hot and I'm suddenly so cold.

"How long?" I whisper because my throat is impossibly dry. I would ask for water, but I don't want to sit up to drink it.

"Hmm?" Nathan is already nearly asleep.

"How long was...that?" It seems like the sun should be coming up any time now.

"An hour, maybe." He chuckles sleepily. "I said I'd make the most of the night. Not that I'd use up most of the night."

"I—"

"Shh," he orders. "You have a long day tomorrow."

———

"Good morning, Your Majesty."

My eyelids barely peel open before I remember where I am. Nearly naked, in the king's bed, barely covered by a corner of the duvet.

And my best friend is giving me a very judgmental look.

I scramble to sit up, holding the duvet to my chest.

"Funny meeting you here," she says with a wry lift of her eyebrow. She tosses me a robe; it matches the nightgown that I'm still kind-of wearing below my tits and above my waist.

I tug the spaghetti straps over my shoulders before I drop the duvet and pull the robe around me. "Mind your own business. That's an order as your queen, not your friend."

She smirks and says nothing. For the moment. I know she's never going to drop this.

"There's breakfast in your sitting room. Light stuff. I know how your stomach gets," she says, and hands me an envelope. "The king sends you this."

I look around; there's no sign of Nathan at all. I glance toward the bedside table and the vial of evil potion is no longer there.

At least, he cleaned up the sex stuff before Hannah came to wake me.

I slip my nail under the pretentious black wax seal and read the message inside.

Bailey—

I know that you hate me for my indiscretions. I know that you want what I am not willing to give you. But I do care about you. I believe that with you at my side, we will be the leaders this pack needs. We can surmount the coming challenges.

I wonder at that; are there new problems arising that I don't know about? Is the state of the pack far worse than I'm aware?

I read on.

I am proud to call you my mate. And today, I will be proud to see you become my queen. You are not my second choice. You were born for this.

-Nathan

My heart lodges in my throat. I try to clear it away.

"Is something wrong?" Hannah asks.

I blink to hold back tears that surprise me with their sudden presence, and I shake my head, so they won't be heard in my voice.

Hannah claps her hands together. "Then come on. It's time for you to become a queen."

CHAPTER 35

"Ready?"

I glance up from the mirror. Staring at myself isn't going to fix any of the myriad flaws I suddenly find with my appearance, which has been impeccably styled by a gaggle of strangers who brushed and blushed and zipped and tucked me into the regal woman in my reflection.

Clare stands at the door, looking more like a queen than I ever will. She wears a gown with a similar cut to mine, a faux-Tudor look with heavy brocade trumpet sleeves and a tight bodice with a low, square neck. My skirt is a little fuller than hers, and mine is white and gold where hers is pale yellow; when we walk out of my sitting room—currently a staging area for all the preparation that went into my look—we make a swishing sound.

"I'm nervous," I whisper, as if it's not a foregone conclusion.

Clare, always the more practical of my two sisters, advises, "Don't let them see it."

The lack of comfort is oddly comforting.

In the entry hall of the residence, we're joined by a

retinue of thrall guards, and Tara, who waits in an identical gown to Clare's. She beams the moment she sees me. "You look amazing!"

"Thanks." It's not my most pressing concern, but I put a hand to my wavy updo self-consciously, anyway. "I'm sweating. Do I have pit stains?"

"Not yet," Tara tries to reassure me.

Tries being the operative word. I give her a smile and take her hand, squeezing it lightly as we walk.

When we reach the hall outside the throne room, that's when the panic truly sets in.

Nearly every member of the pack will be present, whether they want to, or not. Hannah told me, straight from Ryan, that there are more members of the pack disgruntled by Nathan's handling of the assassination plot and the sentences he pronounced. But those people will be here today because they can't risk being seen as rebellious.

People like Ashton.

I don't know if I want to see him in the crowd. A part of me feels like it's awesome that he has to watch me become more powerful than him, after he spent so much time lording his power over me. Another part doesn't want him to lay eyes on me ever again. People like Ashton are dangerous, letting their resentment fester until it drives them to do truly abhorrent things.

I learned that from the mortal obsession with true crime documentaries.

Ashton already tried to kill my husband. What are the chances he'll stop now that he failed? He's lost everything, so there's no danger to him.

I stand outside the throne room doors and take a deep breath. There's actual fanfare, from real trumpets, and the huge doors open to admit me.

All thought of Ashton or anyone else, really, clear my mind entirely. I instantly focus on Nathan, seated on his throne, the crown of our pack leader shining silver against his dark hair. The King's crown is a simple, polished band with peaks that rise up in the shape of fangs; pack legend is that they're *actual* werewolf teeth. I suppose now that I'm about to be queen, I could find out.

I should make a list of all the weird things I've always wanted to know. Since life around Aconitum Hall seems like it's going to be pretty boring, maybe I can write a definitive history of the pack or something.

Nathan doesn't rise as I approach the hierophant and his acolytes waiting at the foot of the dais, but he watches my every step with a smile of pride that, though he tries to subdue it, I can notice even if nobody else might.

"You were born for this."

That's what he believes. That I am meant to be a queen and rule at his side. With every step I take toward the throne, I begin to believe it, too.

No one ever seriously sets their goal on becoming a queen. At least, nobody I've ever talked to. Sure, it's fun to pretend when you're a child, but as you grow in the pack it becomes clear that some families are destined for royalty, nobility, seats on the council, while others are valued members but not worthy of the upper strata of werewolf society. While my parents were wealthy, I never considered the possibility of even being mated to a council member.

I just wanted someone who wouldn't be annoying and who could make a lot of money. *You got one of your wishes, at least.* But being rich and being powerful were different. And I'm about to have nearly unlimited power. It's a prospect that should terrify me, but the closer I get to receiving it, the more I don't just want it. I feel like I deserve it.

With Tara and Clare helping to hold the train of my gown, I sink into a low curtsey to Nathan. He inclines his head to me in deference, and I rise, allowing the hierophant to take my hand and lead me up the dais to my throne. At the moment, it's set slightly further from Nathan's than it usually will be. There has to be room for the acolytes and the hierophant to encircle me during the ceremony.

For now, the acolytes peel off to retrieve the ceremonial objects necessary, while it's the hierophant's job to issue the proclamation, opening the coronation proceedings.

He looks particularly regal today, the deep yellow of his robe flattering against his dark complexion. He faces the huge assembly and intones, "Wolves of the Toronto pack, I present to you, Bailey Marie Dixon-Frost, come this day to be made queen, leader, and servant to the pack. Will all here pay homage and dedicate their loyalty to her?"

It's a ceremonial question. Nobody is going to say 'no,' I remember.

As expected, everyone answers, "She is granted our faith and our trust."

Except, it sounds like some people are using the wrong words. I turn toward the discordant group, who sound like they were saying something just slightly different. There are nine men standing at the side of the throne room, near the towering stained-glass windows that bear scenes of Lycaon ruling over Lycosura. All of them are dressed in an odd way that takes me a moment to place; they're wearing business attire, not appropriate for a coronation.

I glance over at Nathan, but he's focused on the crowd

directly in front of us. And security doesn't seem concerned with the presence of the strangers.

What is going on?

I don't have more time to wonder. The hierophant turns toward me and motions for an acolyte to come forward; the woman carries a censer that releases clouds of incense as she swings it. She walks around my throne seven long, mind-numbing, sinus-attacking times. By the time she's done, a haze drifts over the entire throne room.

The hierophant stands before me again. "Will you solemnly swear and promise to lead and protect the were-wolves of the Toronto and Greater London pack?"

What?!

A murmur ripples through the pack.

"I—" I look to Nathan, uncertain, and he nods almost imperceptibly. So, I say, "I solemnly promise."

I hear a man's voice speak, loud enough to cut through the general confusion, "This is an outrage."

I wonder if Nathan is going to stand up and demand silence or try to bring some order to the proceedings, but he doesn't acknowledge them at all, even when the hiero-phant casts a pointed look at him.

There's nothing to do but continue, so the man says, "Will you exercise the virtues of integrity, loyalty, faithful-ness, and mercy in all of your dealings with the Toronto and Greater London packs?"

Please, stop saying that. What is happening? Are they seriously making me the queen of both packs? I've never met anyone from Greater London. And Nathan isn't king there, he—

He did just take a trip, without me, to London.

"I so promise," I choke out.

"Will you exercise the virtues of integrity, loyalty, and

faithfulness to King Nathaniel Frost, leader of the Toronto and Great London packs?"

No, because I'm going to murder him. "I do so promise."

But my answer is nearly drowned out by the building anger and shock in the room. I know how this looks. Nathan must know how this looks to everyone assembled.

They think this is a takeover.

I turn pleading eyes toward Nathan as an acolyte approaches with my crown. Twenty minutes ago, the sight of it might have filled me with joy but now it might as well be a coiled viper instead of a tiara of silver and rubies. The Hierophant takes it and holds it above my head.

"With the blessing of Lycaon, first of our line, first of our kings, you rise Queen Bailey of Toronto and Greater London."

The crown settles on my head, surprisingly heavy, and an acolyte comes to either side of the throne to take my hands to help me rise. Nathan stands, also, and I go to his side. The throne room is practically in chaos, but he just looks triumphant.

I just helped him steal the pack.

My father wasn't a traitor. Ashton wasn't a traitor. Nathan really is trying to take Toronto for Greater London.

My mind is spinning, so I barely register the shout of, "Now!" from the angry crowd. I turn toward the source of the sound only to be met by a spray of something hot and wet across my face and chest.

I only realize the acolyte at my side is dead when she falls against me and to the floor.

CHAPTER 36

Blood.

It's *blood* on my hands, across the front of my gown. I cast my gaze to my sisters, first; Clare and Tara are both wide-eyed, but I see no obvious wounds on them.

The acolyte is on the ground, a throwing knife lodged in her spurting throat.

"Protect the queen!" someone shouts.

It's Nathan.

I throw my hand out to grab him. I need an anchor in the chaos. He would never let them hurt me, never let—

He grunts in pain and staggers back. More blood splashes across my gown and I scream.

Someone grabs me, and I'm torn from Nathan's side. The last thing I hear him say is, "Get the queen to safety!"

"What's going on?" Tara cries as the thrall guard drags us into the empty ball room.

I look back at the crowd as the doors close and fear claws up my throat.

"Take them to the residence," the head guard orders. "I

want shutters, spike strips, nobody leaves through the front gate."

I blink at him, thinking he's talking to me, but he's speaking into his wire. Someone grabs me by the arm and physically hauls me through the ballroom.

"Nathan!" He's still out there, and he's wounded.

The bodyguards overpower me. I can't go back to help if I wanted to, which, frankly, I don't because I'm the queen and that definitely paints a target on my back.

I'm the queen.

And there's a coup happening.

The riot seems to be confined to the ballroom; more security guards than I've ever seen rush through the halls. I'm glad the people manhandling me through the corridors know a different way into the residence, one that doesn't require backtracking past the throne room doors. They practically push us up the back stairs, where more guards waited at the top.

"Is everyone okay?" a thrall with a red cross on her shoulder asks, bowing her head briefly to defer to me. "Your Majesty, are you hurt?"

Am I? I didn't really get a chance to think about it. "No?"

The answer gives her a small pause.

"The king is still out there. And Hannah!" Oh my god, Hannah and Ryan. They were in the crowd. What happened to them?

"Let's get the queen and her ladies to the safe room," the thrall says to another with the same medic patch.

"There's a safe room?" It would have been nice to know about that, just in case anyone else tried to kill me.

I'm the queen.

People are going to try to kill me.

The safe room is located behind the bar in the formal sitting room. A section swings out to reveal a narrow door that can admit only one person at a time. A door as thick as a refrigerator.

This thing can probably withstand a direct meteor strike.

Despite being a place one goes in an emergency, the safe room is oddly luxurious. It's actually more like a safe suite, with couches and a kitchenette and a *stocked wine chiller.* I roll my eyes. People are trying to murder us, and my mate is worried about not having a nice dry white to go with whatever luxury survival MREs are stocked in the cabinets.

Tara and Clare drop onto the sofa and an armchair, respectively. Tara is shaking all over, and a medic rushes to her.

"Is she okay?"

Clare's eyes are hollow, her face frozen as she stares at the thralls who cluster around our sister. "She's in shock."

"Get her legs elevated," one medic says, piling cushions under Tara's feet. "And get a blanket!"

"I've got fluids," another medic says, rushing in from another room in our windowless safe quarters.

Which feel very, very unsafe.

Clare and I watch in horror as they wrap Tara in a blanket and start an IV. A blood pressure monitor appears from somewhere, and a pulse oximeter.

"Make room!" someone calls in a voice so loud and gruff, it makes Clare and I jump. Which I'm sure is also great for Tara, who's being given oxygen through a little bottle with a mask on it. The source of the voice backs into the room, carrying something with another person.

The something is Nathan.

They carry him past me, into an adjoining room, and I run after, my shoes smearing the spatters of his blood into gory footprints on the carpet. They took his jacket off him, and his white shirt is soaked with red. My heart is in my throat as I follow them into a bedroom, but when they put him down, he cries out in pain.

But he's so strong. Surely, he can handle…whatever is causing so much blood.

So much blood.

Medics push in and I stand aside, helpless, as they cut Nathan's shirt off and reveal a deep gash across his abdomen. At first, I don't recognize the bubble-gum pink spilling from the wound. Then, in a horrifying second, I do. It's his intestines. His insides are on the outside.

Nope. Can't handle that. I run from the room, puke rising up in my throat. As I tear toward the kitchenette sink, Clare calls out, "Bailey, are you alright?"

I'll be perfectly fine once I paint the sink a lovely shade of my breakfast.

"We're locked down, Your Majesty," someone says, and I wipe my mouth with the back of my hand, not trusting myself to lift my head out of the safe zone yet.

"Hannah, my friend, my assistant, she's still out there." I shoot pleading looks at all the guards. "I need to at least know that she's okay."

"We'll have a report once the situation is secure, Your Majesty," is all the head officer tells me.

I almost say, *"Go back! This is your job, go back and find my friend!"* but it's not their job. Their job is to protect *me*.

I rinse my mouth out and try to stand as regally as I can after tossing up my guts in front of my subjects. I turn to where the medics are still working on Tara, but with less urgency now. Clare is at her side; if our big sister couldn't fret over us, she'd be as freaked out as Tara.

So that left me to do...what? Just "be queen"? How does that work? *Do I make a radio address about this?*

That just reminds me of what started this whole mess in the first place. *Queen of Toronto and Greater London.* Why didn't Nathan tell me? It's obvious now that his romantic getaway to London wasn't just a regular serving of adultery. He went there to set this up.

I glare at the door, where my liar of a mate is screaming and dying. *You better live because I have some words for you.*

He falls silent.

My stomach roils again.

"He's sedated," someone calls from in the bedroom, and my knees weaken with relief. "He's still with us."

"Your Majesty," a thrall says, taking my arm. He gently guides me to a chair. "What do you need?"

I just stare at him.

"Can I get you a blanket, some juice, are you hungry—"

Somewhere in the room, a phone rings. It's not someone's cell. There's a red cordless landline on the wall near the entry. The thralls closest to it give me a look, as if wondering if they should proceed, and the head of security barges over and picks it up.

I drop my head to my hands and await the bad news.

To my surprise, after a brief, quiet conversation, he brings the phone to me. "Your administrator. From Greater London."

"My..." I get to my feet. "I'm the queen."

The man nods at me.

I take the receiver with shaking hands. How does a

queen answer the phone? Clearing my throat, I say, "This is Her Majesty."

"Your Majesty, it is an honor to speak to you on the day of your coronation. Your subjects in London are—"

The man has a grossly obsequious tone, only made worse by his upper crust accent. I can *hear* his bowtie. "Thank you, but we are in the middle of a violent attack at the moment."

"Yes, that was the purpose of my call," he says hastily, not interrupting his pack leader but not letting me shut him down. "Additional security forces have been dispatched and will arrive later this evening. We're also sending members of our council, who will be available for anything you may need."

"I—" It's a good thing I'm sitting down. "How do you know about this? It happened just a few minutes ago."

"From our delegates, of course," he says.

The men on the side of the room, who seemed so out of place...

Nathan kept all of this from me.

Well, now Nathan's probably going to die. I don't kid myself that being eviscerating is something easily fixed with first aid; they can't just stabilize him indefinitely while we wait for a hospital. And if he's unable to rule, that only leaves one other option.

I force a calm, impervious tone. "The king is severely injured and currently sedated as first aid is administered. I am currently ruling in his place. As you are currently my most direct contact with the world outside this bunker, I need you to coordinate with my head of security. You will take no orders from anyone on the Toronto council. I know the pack has their fingers in every pie, so I want the passports of all members of the Toronto pack revoked and their assets frozen, effective immediately. It's only a temporary measure, but I don't want anyone leaving until they're investigated. In fact, let's make sure no one leaves the city at all."

"Yes, ma'am," the man says automatically.

Since nobody in the room is arguing or making faces like I'm fucking anything up, I add, "If there are any Saint-Laurent wolves in either the Toronto or Greater London area, I want them detained. And if they resist capture… have the thralls use lethal force."

That makes the head of security's gray eyebrows go up.

"W-with respect, Your Majesty," the man on the phone says cautiously, "such an action might be seen as an act of war by the Saint-Laurent pack."

I look around the room, at my sister in an oxygen mask, my mate's blood on the floor. The blood on my dress, from the thrall that died beside me.

"Well," I say, swallowing back a sudden thickness in my throat. "I guess we're at war, then."

CHAPTER 37

It takes two hours to round up all of the traitors on the property. There's still no word from Hannah or Ryan, though that could be because I get shitty mobile signal in the safe room.

Tara's condition is improved greatly, though the medics continue to monitor her. Nathan, however…

Once he's stabilized, I sit by his bedside, just watching his labored breathing. They've got him on oxygen, too, and they've put a sterile barrier over his wound. They stitched up some gory slashes on his face. Now, all anyone can do is sit tight until the surgeon from Greater London can arrive.

"Your Majesty," the medic in charge of his care says softly, breaking my attention away from the rise and fall of Nathan's chest.

"Your Majesty," the thrall says again, "I would be remiss if I didn't ask again for you to permit a closer surgeon—"

"No. I told you, no one from the Toronto pack." I'm too tired to be regal and furious but I'm tired of being asked the question. "Honestly, you're all only here because I can't keep him alive myself."

The thrall's dark eyebrows draw together. He bows his head and steps back. "Yes, ma'am."

You just have to hang on a little while longer, Nathan, I urge him silently. *Just a little longer.*

The head of security, whose name, I have learned, is Charles, steps through the door. "Ma'am, a representative from the office of the mayor is here, as well as the chief of the Toronto Police Service."

"Why are they here? Are we under arrest?" I've never thought about the consequences of our pack operating alongside the human world, but there are more of them than there are of us. And we just had a whole lot of people die on the property; twenty-six, if the early reports can be believed.

"Not under arrest, no. The pack has a long, established relationship with the city. They tend to leave us to our devices, but this incident was too large to contain," he says.

"And do these humans know that we're werewolves?" Secrecy has always been so important.

"*These* humans do," Charles says. "They're here to ensure other humans do not."

"And I can leave the pod now?" I ask, gesturing to room around us.

"The residence is secure," Charles says. "You're clear to leave the safe room."

At least I won't be having this meeting through an intercom.

"Would you like to change," Clare asks hesitantly. "You're..."

I look down. I'm still wearing my uncomfortable coronation gown but at this point it's become a part of my body. And it's splashed with the blood of the thrall we lost.

Anger surges through me. I haven't been able to be angry, I realize. I've been powerless and worried, but now I'm just furious.

"No. I don't think I will." I turn to Charles. "I want to make an address to the pack. Do we have the ability to do that? To distribute it via email or something?"

Charles nods.

"Would you like me to draft a letter?" Clare offers.

"No." I shake my head. "I want to speak to them directly. Get me a camera, a webcam, I'll use my phone if I have to, but I'm going to make a make a video address."

"Yes, Your Majesty." Charles gestures to the door and I lead the way out.

The moment I cross the threshold of the safe room, I'm greeted by the sight of security thralls at every door and window. Two of them, one on each side.

"They're not going to stand over me while I sleep, right?" I ask. I don't know what time it is, but I wouldn't be able to tell from the windows; they're all locked down with thick metal shades.

"Not if Your Majesty objects," Charles tells me. "Your meeting is in His Majesty's study."

"Is my crown right?" I ask, reaching up to touch my head. I haven't taken it off yet. It's beginning to feel like armor.

Charles is caught off-guard by my question. He probably doesn't get asked *"am I pretty?"* too often by the king. "It looks fine to me, Your Majesty."

"Good. I want them to recognize that they're meeting a

queen. Not the king's wife." There's a difference, and I won't let anyone ignore it.

When we enter the study, two men are waiting. One of them is a balding caucasian with a ring of white hair still hanging on in a strip around his head. He's in full uniform, holding his hat nervously. The man next to him is broad shouldered, with brown skin and dark hair parted on the side. He's wearing a business suit and an expression of horror as he takes in my gore-splattered dress.

"Her Majesty, Queen Bailey, leader of the Toronto pack," Charles says, prompting both of the men to bow.

"Your Majesty," the police chief says nervously, and he's echoed by the guy from the mayor's office.

I turn to that guy. "You're not the mayor."

"I'm not, Your Majesty," he says, apologetic.

"The mayor of Toronto can't deign to meet with the queen of Toronto?" I ask, blinking placidly.

"With respect, Your Majesty," the police chief begins. "You're the queen of your people. Not ours."

"I don't know how respectful it is to challenge me," I say with serrated sweetness. "After all, you're only humans. I'll be the queen here long after the mayor's term ends. After you retire. After everyone in your generation is rotting in the ground."

"Your Majesty—" Charles says softly.

I hold up my hand to stop him. "It seems I'm standing in a room full of men who need to put me in my place. So, let me remind you what my place is. I am a queen. You are in my castle. And you are here to listen to me, not to advise me."

"Yes, Your Majesty," Charles says. The other two exchange stunned glances.

I know what they see. I'm young, I'm blonde, and I'm

wearing a tiara and a ball gown. I probably look like a pageant contestant to them, and they expect me to stumble over the interview portion.

But I've had several hours of unfettered growing up.

"Sit." It's not an invitation, and the two men scurry to obey.

I step behind Nathan's desk. It's the size of a fucking pool table and the chair isn't some regular desk chair with a swivel base, it's a high-backed, padded leather monstrosity with no arms. It really helps me get into the mindset of being powerful and in charge. I get why he has it, although I can't imagine him not walking through his entire life feeling powerful and in charge.

Maybe all of this stuff is just props.

I hope the scale of the furniture doesn't emphasize how small I feel.

"You'll forgive me for being curt and for not offering you gentlemen anything," I say, trying to do my best impersonation of what I think a female Nathan would sound like. "But there was an attack here today, on myself and my husband and loyal members of my court. Now, the king is clinging to life and I have a pack to run. So, please. Get to the point quickly and leave."

"Y-yes, Your Majesty," the police chief says. "Well. That's what we're here to talk to you about. We received some calls about the incident and need to brief you on how the city is explaining it. People have questions."

I turn to the mayor's aide. "What are you doing here?"

He looks uncertainly from the police chief to me. "I'm sorry?"

"The chief is here to brief me on how the city is explaining this disturbance to citizens. But the mayor isn't." I prop my elbows on the desktop and clap my hands together. "He sent an underling."

"The mayor isn't aware of the presence of werewolves in the city, Your Majesty," the man explains. "The mayor isn't even aware of the presence of an office of human-werewolf relations within the organization. We're off the books, entirely."

"Hmm." Is all I say. "Well, then, what do you both require of me?"

"Just know that the story we're telling the press is that a movie is being filmed here at Aconitum Hall, that everything is all right, and that the filmmakers apologize for upsetting the local community," The police chief says.

The man from the mayor's office adds, "Filming permits have been filed retroactively. Everything will look completely above board."

"Good." I sit there and they just stare at me.

Charles clears his throat. "It has been customary, in the past, for our treasury to…"

I glance between the two men seated in front of me. "Is this true?"

"The pack makes generous donations to certain programs—" the mayor's aide begins.

"I believe you're describing something called 'quid pro quo'," I cut him off. "You've come to me, representing the city government, and you're asking me to repay you for… breaking the law?"

"It's not breaking the law," the chief begins.

"It sounds like it is." I feign confusion. "Filing paperwork? Creating a false story? And then you ask for money as my husband is lying just rooms away, dying?"

The chief's ears turn red. "The city has ignored the

presence of werewolves, has cleaned up several werewolf-related incidents—"

"And the pack is grateful," I say, dismissing him with a wave of my hand. "But I do admire both of you for your bravery. You come here, to a castle full of monsters—and not just monsters, incredibly wealthy and powerfully connected monsters—to threaten me and solicit bribes."

They say nothing.

"Things are going to change in Toronto," I state firmly. "We will continue our relationship with the human world. And any charitable donations we make will be generous. But in the future, do not come to my home with your hand open, when mine are still bloody!"

I push the chair back and rise, and they quickly scramble to their feet.

"Show them out," I bark at the guards stationed by the door.

I hope I look regal and not terrified as I sweep from the room.

CHAPTER 38

My phone rings at six in the morning. I answer it, my pulse lodged in the hollow of my throat, choking me. The surgeons from Greater London arrived around midnight, and they were working on Nathan when I went to bed. I'm sure this is the call I've been sleeplessly waiting for.

"Bailey? Is this Bailey?"

"Hannah?" I have never been gladder to hear my best friend's voice. "You're okay? You're all okay?"

"We're fine, we got out!" There are tears in her voice and muffled sniffing as she says, "You're alive."

"Of course, I'm alive." I fumble to turn on the bedside lamp. "Do people not know that?"

"No one knows anything," Hannah tells me. "There hasn't been a peep out of Aconitum Hall. Nobody knows if the coup was successful."

"It wasn't," I state firmly. "I made a video addressing the pack last night. It's going to be distributed through the private network."

"You made it?" Hannah asks. "Does that mean that the king…"

"Honestly? I have no idea." I rub my forehead. "He wasn't dead when I went to bed last night, but they were operating on him. Greater London sent surgeons here to work on him. Since he's king over there, too."

"Did you have any idea that was going to happen?" Hannah asks.

"I hope you're not accusing me of anything," I snap. I cannot handle it if my best friend decides I'm somehow in on whatever stunt Nathan tried to pull.

I hear Hannah's hurt across the line. "Of course, I'm not. You just looked so surprised when they said, 'and Greater London.'"

"Sorry." My nerves are tighter than the security around here. "I'm so tired and everyone is…really mean to you when you're the queen."

"I'm sure almost getting murdered probably isn't a great stress reliever," she says, and I know she's not holding my suspicion against me. She says gently, "I'm always going to be on your side, okay?"

"I know." I push myself up from the bed and put on a robe before I head down the stairs. I refused to let thralls stand guard over me while I slept, but I know they'll be all over my sitting room. "But now, I need you to shift gears. I need my assistant."

"Can I come down there?" She asks doubtfully. "I heard the place is totally locked down."

"I'm the queen. I can do what I want," I tell her confidently, because I don't care what the rules are, I can't run the entire pack on my own. "But it's still super early."

"I'm up with Jo," she reminds me.

"Okay. Well, here's a job you can do from home." I nod to the thralls in the sitting room and note that when I go out the door, two of them follow me. I have my own little retinue. "I need my own office in this place. I'm sure there's room somewhere in the residence. I need a desk, a computer, I need—"

"You need everything," Hannah says. "I did notice that there aren't any spaces set aside for the queen to do anything but sit around and wait between royal engagements."

"And breed," I say wryly. Though, if Nathan doesn't survive, I might not have to worry about that. I press my hand to my abdomen. I've still got a few days before pregnancy is even a concern, but stress always messes with my period. I might not be able to tell until symptoms become obvious.

Even then, what would happen if Nathan dies and I *am* carrying his baby? Do I become queen regent? A baby can't rule the pack. *A baby can't rule two packs*, I revise.

"I don't know how long Nathan will be out of commission," I tell Hannah, then stop and turn to one of the thralls, mouthing, "Is the king dead?"

The thrall blanches but shakes her head.

I go back to my phone conversation. "I have no idea how long this situation is going to continue, but I do know that I need a political advisor. Ask Ryan if he wants the position."

"He can't retain his council seat and serve as your advisor," Hannah says.

I chew my lip. "Okay, well, ask him if he wants me to yank him off the council and bring him into my cabinet."

"Your cabinet now, huh?" Hannah snarks.

But she has no idea what it's like to be thrust into a situation like the one I'm in. "Yes. I need as many smart people around me as possible. And loyal ones. I know I can trust Ryan, and he's up on current pack politics."

The head of security is waiting for me in the study. While he bows, I tell Hannah, "Come to the rear door, I'll make sure you're cleared to enter at the gatehouse and the residence. But I've got to go."

"I'll see you around nine," she tells me. "With furniture ordered."

We hang up and I address Charles. "How is the king?"

"Alive, Your Majesty," Charles answers without hesitation. But he adds, "For now. You'll have to speak to his medical team."

"Bring someone to me, at once," I instruct. "Also, my assistant, Hannah Hunter, will be coming and she will be admitted to the residence."

"Yes, Your Majesty." He moves to leave, but pauses, his shoulders going rigid before he turns back. "I hesitate to ask this of Your Majesty, as it is a sensitive topic. But His Majesty's…friend."

"Amber?" My jaw tightens against the bile in my throat. "Has the king asked for her?"

"No, ma'am. The king has, as far as I'm aware, not regained consciousness yet." He clears his throat. "But she has been quite persistent in her requests to see His Majesty. She's become increasingly upset by our refusals."

"Hmm." I nod thoughtfully, but I already know my answer. And it's *hell* no. "Please advise Ms. Bennett to remember that her place is not at Aconitum Hall, and it never will be. Remind her that her place in the pack in tenuous, regardless of how much the king enjoys her company. And tell her, from me, that if she continues to attempt to gain access to the king, I'll be forced to view her with suspicion of treason. My husband might pass light sentences for that offense, but I will deal with her swiftly. Do you understand what I'm saying?"

"Yes, Your Majesty. You've made it perfectly clear," Charles replies.

"Good. See that she understands, as well. I think she forgot that she's no longer queen of this pack." Not that it would be so bad if she *was* queen again, even just for a few hours, so I could take a break. "Where have they taken the king?"

"His Majesty is still in the safe room, as are your sisters, Your Majesty," Charles informs me. Before I ask a follow up, he supplies, "Their rooms aren't in the residence, so I felt it best to keep them where they're secure."

He felt it best to keep an eye on them, I think. I hope they're at least comfortable.

When I go to the safe room, my sisters are decidedly *not* comfortable. They're still wearing their gowns from the coronation, and they're sleeping on the couches with thin emergency first aid blankets over them.

That's ridiculous. Nathan has a whole medical team to sit around and stare at him, so I decide to take care of my sisters, first.

Their mistresses haven't been trying to insert themselves into a pack-wide crisis. They get priority.

"Tara?" I whisper, giving her a little shake. She looks so much better now, even after having slept with a throw pillow twisting her head at a weird angle all night. "Wake up. Let's get you to my room. You can sleep in an actual bed."

I look to one of the thralls standing by. "My sisters need clothes from their rooms. Find someone whose job that is?"

"Right away, Your Majesty."

Tara laughs sleepily. "Wow. You got the hang of the job quick."

"I had to," I say quietly, moving to wake Clare. I barely touch her shoulder before she flails awake, and I have to dodge her sleep-drugged karate moves. "It's just me. Go up to my room, get some sleep in a bed."

She sits up and yawns, shaking her head the whole time. "Once I'm up, I'm up."

I almost argue that the bags under her eyes are telling a different story, but a medic steps out of the room where Nathan is being monitored.

"Your Majesty." The thrall has an English accent, thank god. I don't know why I trust the Greater London pack so much more than the Toronto pack. I don't know any of them and it's pretty clear that they're trying to take over Toronto, but nobody from Greater London tried to gut my husband yesterday, that I know of.

"Would you like to see His Majesty?" the thrall asks.

I nod and walk stiffly to the door. I don't know what to expect or how I'll feel when I see what's happening in the other room. I badly want to run away. I'm angry at Nathan for springing the Greater London crown on me. I'm angry that this was the result.

And I'm kind of angry that he didn't die for such a stupid stunt.

The room is full of beeping. It's basically a hospital room; when I was in here last night, I didn't notice exactly how like a hospital room it actually is. There are outlets on the walls for plugs I don't recognize, an IV pump dripping several bags of fluids into Nathan's arm, and a ventilator assists his breathing.

None of that seems good.

"It looks worse than it is, Your Majesty," the thrall doctor assures me. "He came through the surgery well. The bowel was exposed, but not injured, which was our main concern. But he had some signs of brain injury, so we elected to keep him sedated for now."

I don't know how thrall medicine works; I know our advanced healing and their magical skills play into it, but werewolves usually don't have to think much about our health. I've never been seen a by doctor for anything. What's happening to Nathan is terrifying.

"Is he going to live?" That's my main concern, and from where I'm standing, it doesn't seem too promising. Two black eyes have formed overnight, and there are bruised stripes down both sides of his nose. His abdomen is covered in gauze bandages, and he has a tube down his throat. This is not the jumping off point for optimum health.

"We're doing the best we can, Your Majesty," the doctor says.

I look at Nathan lying there, so helpless. I haven't been able to get his screaming out of my mind. He seems so strong and in control all of the time, but I guess having your guts ripped out would break anybody's composure. And now he's laying here, all alone, without any family or anyone who loves him.

Does he even have family? I don't know. I should figure that out and get in contact with them, so they know what's happening.

For a moment, I feel a pang of regret that I've barred his mistress from coming to visit. At least she *likes* the guy.

That pang passes quickly, though.

It doesn't matter how I feel about Nathan. He's my mate. And he's a person, if I'm forced to admit it. If I'm the only one here for him, I'm damn well going to be here for him.

I lean down and gently brush his hair back. I never

noticed that it has a little curl to it. He's usually so immaculately groomed. Because it feels like the right thing to do, I kiss his forehead. "I'm going to find out who did this to you," I whisper, and I hope he can hear me. Because I *am* going to find who did this.

And I'm going to make them suffer.

CHAPTER 39

Hannah arrives just in time for my video address to hit the inboxes of every member of the pack. She pulls it up on her laptop, and she, Tara, Clare, and I sit on my big bed, all squished together around the screen.

I'm not sure I even want to see it. I felt like a mess when I recorded it, and I didn't have a speech writer. But when the royal seal fades from the screen and I see myself, with my head held high and my hair messed up, my eye makeup smudged but my face a stone mask of anger, blood spattered across my gown but my spine stiff and straight, I don't recognize myself. The person on the screen doesn't look like a terrified and unqualified twenty-two-year-old who just barely survived a political uprising.

"This afternoon, I stood before the Toronto werewolf pack and pledged my life for the good of my subjects," the unrecognizable me on the screen says.

"Are you doing an English accent?" Tara whispers, and Clare shushes her.

"Some of my subjects took that as an invitation to take my life, the life of my husband, the lives of loyal werewolves and thralls." Me on the screen pauses, gazing steely and assured into the camera. "They succeeded in killing five of their fellow werewolves. twenty-seven thralls. Thralls who have served this pack loyally for nearly a millennium.

"The traitors tried to kill their pack leader, in what is the second attempt on his life in less than a month. They failed again. His Majesty is injured, but he is certain to recover. And they failed to harm me, queen of the Toronto and Greater London packs, in their cowardly attempt to seize the throne. While His Majesty, King Nathan, convalesces—"

"Whoa, ten dollar word," Tara whispers.

"—I will conduct a thorough investigation into this act of treason. Those responsible for orchestrating this horrific attack will be brought to swift judgment."

I'm proud of myself for not yelling that heads will roll, though that's the direction I'm leaning in. Now that the adrenaline and shock have faded a bit and the anger has had hours to simmer, I'm wondering if I can wield the ax myself.

I suppose precision and strength really only matter when you care if it's a clean death.

"I call upon my loyal subjects to relay any information they may have that will help in this investigation. Those involved in the plot are no longer members of this pack. They are traitors and apostates.

"These next few weeks may be dangerous. While I ask you for caution, I'm also asking you to be calm. If you are innocent of this horrible crime, you have nothing to fear."

Now that I hear that line, it's pretty chilling. I should have left it out. Which is exactly why I need an advisor.

"Stay strong. Stay vigilant. And stay faithful to the pack."

The screen fades back to the pack logo. For a long moment, nobody says anything, until Hannah breathes, "Wow. You really are a queen."

I don't flatter myself that she's talking about the content of the video. "It kinda just hit me, too," I admit.

Clare taps a finger against her lips in thought. "I wouldn't have included the word apostates," she muses. "You could be construed as a religious fanatic."

"Noted." I'm grateful for the critique. "I'll be careful to walk that back."

"Only if you can do so without making things worse," she warns.

Maybe Clare should be my advisor.

Hannah's phone beeps. She answers it and her eyes dart to me. "Thank you," is all she says before hanging up. She gives me a tight smile. "He's awake."

I don't know why I bolt from the bed as fast as I do. Something in me screams that it's imperative for me to see him, to speak to him, just in case he suddenly dies or goes into a coma or something.

My security crew practically has to jog to keep up with me, I'm walking so fast. I'm glad I followed Hannah's advice and got dressed, because my robe would have been flapping the whole time. The guards part as I barge into the sitting room and toward the safe room. I don't even have to slow down for them to get out of my way.

But when I hit the threshold of his room, I freeze.

I don't know what I expected. Maybe for him to be sitting up, bright-eyed and sarcastic. They said he was awake; did he fall back to sleep? He hasn't changed position from when I saw him last.

Our link crackles weakly, though, and compels me to his side, where I sit in the chair pulled up to his bedside. That's where I sat for hours watching him, hoping he wouldn't die and leave me to run the pack on my own. Now, I'm more concerned about Nathan my mate, not Nathan my business partner.

He peels one eye open, then squeezes it shut. His voice is a thick whisper. "You're okay."

A tear rolls down his temple, into his hair. It's enough to break me down completely. I take his hand and carefully lift it, holding it against my cheek. "I'm okay."

"I saw…" He takes a long pause, wincing when he breathes in. "There was blood on you."

"It wasn't mine," I promise. "Not even a scratch."

"I tried to get to you." His eyes are red and watery as they fix on mine. "It happened too quick."

"I know." I can't help my glance at his bandaged abdomen. "Do you remember anything? Do you remember who did that?" I tuck his hand back at his side.

He shakes his head, a small, careful movement. "I'm not sure what happened. I was surrounded by thralls, and suddenly they were dragging me over the dais, toward the back hall. But nothing else, until I woke up."

I wonder if his memories will recover. I hope not; he doesn't need to remember screaming in agony as his intestines were being kept in his body by a thrall's bare hands.

"They won't tell me much about the injury, but that I've been injured," he chuckles bleakly. "Did you see it?"

"It's bad," is all I can say.

"Oh, I can tell," he replies with a bitter chuckle, then grimaces. "I was looking for specifics."

Will telling him traumatize him or something? I hesitate, until he softly commands, "Bailey. Tell me."

I take a deep breath and decide to start top down. "They think you have a brain injury. You're awake and talking, so I guess that's a good sign?" He makes a thoughtful noise as he listens. "You have seven stitches on your forehead and thirteen down your left cheek. It was basically slashed open."

He groans and I can't tell if it's from pain or vanity. "Is it going to look horrible?"

"It's probably going to look better than your gut," I say.

"I don't have a gut!"

Relief washes over me. He's with it enough to be obsessed with his looks. He'll be fine.

"You almost didn't have guts. They were on the outside of you," I tell him. "Worry about that."

"It's occupying quite a bit of my thought, actually," he says. "Perhaps you could convince them to give me more pain medication? Can't they cast a spell or something?"

"I'll ask your doctor," I say. But before they give him anything that might knock him out, he needs to know that I've been running things while he's been unconscious. "Listen… without you, I didn't know what to do. So, I did the best I could to lead the pack."

"I know you did." He chuckles weakly. "I'm always right."

"Why don't you wait until you're back in the big chair and you've seen what I've been up to before you start believing in me," I joke.

"No." He's not joking. "I've believed in you since the moment I laid eyes on you."

Then why are you with someone else? my pride cries out. I

silence it. Nathan is politically savvy; he could have had Amber as his queen if he wanted to, but he didn't. He chose me. And maybe it's just because of some weird link that's out of our control but the end result is the same. I'm Nathan's queen.

For just a second, I consider asking if he wants to see Amber. But I know Nathan. He's probably already asked his damn secretary for her.

Nathan's eyelids grow heavy and for a moment I'm afraid it might mean something dire, until he lets out a soft snore and startles himself awake.

I giggle. I can't help it. "I never realize you snored, before?"

"Usually, I'm not stitched together like Frankenstein." He casts a sly look my way. "And you're usually exhausted by the time I'm asleep."

I dip my head, face flaming. "Wow. Still horny, even with dental floss holding your intestines in."

"I'm a fast healer. Stay limber."

"Okay, you can barely stay awake to harass me, so I'm going to go." I move to stand, and he summons the strength to reach for my hand.

"Just stay a moment longer," he whispers sleepily.

I sit back down. "Sure. What should I…"

"Just be here." He drifts off, and the snoring starts again.

CHAPTER 40

Though werewolves heal fast, Nathan's wounds are so severe that even aided by thrall magic, he's still confined to his bed two weeks later. I get updates on his condition multiple times a day, from an entire team of thrall doctors and physical therapists.

With every positive health milestone he achieves, the more I allow myself to be angry with him. He had to know that by announcing us king and queen of both Toronto and Greater London he would create an uproar. I had to scramble to organize an emergency council meeting, to force them all to swear fealty again.

At least, those council members who aren't currently in our dungeons.

Not that I could trust any of them, even when they trembled on their knees in front of me. People are scared of me, so my video address at least did something. But there's no way people just *happened* to come to the coronation armed, no way they just *happened* to have those weapons concealed well enough that security didn't detect them.

The riot was planned, and my every waking thought that isn't about how I can't wait for Nathan to be fully recovered so I can kill him with my bare hands for his little stunt is spent consumed with uncovering the traitors.

At first, information is slow to trickle in. No one wants to turn in another member of the pack to aid a queen and king they already hate. But security tapes and anonymous tips have gotten us far. After the full moon ceremony, which Nathan can't attend and which my guards advise I shouldn't go to out of concern for my safety, tongues are looser.

"The moon often brings moments of clarity," Clare explains to me one morning in my office. "A lot of people probably just realized how deep the shit they're in really can be."

I'm listening, but I'm also staring out the window. The ballistic shutters have been opened once more. It's so nice to see sunlight streaming in again. Hannah picked out a large, rectangular room that was apparently once a more intimate ballroom in the residence. The high ceilings and tall windows make the space airy and cheerful, as does the pale shade of cherry blossom pink on the walls. I have a desk just as big as Nathan's, with just as many people running around and doing things for me as he ever did.

But I long for the outdoors like I never have before. The trees are still bare, but with the increased sunshine there's a promise of spring.

I hope Nathan will be able to transform in April. It would be nice to run when everything is starting to feel new and—

No. *Fuck* Nathan. I might never speak to him again. I'm exhausted all the time, bouncing between the crisis in Toronto and the running of the pack in London. The time difference makes me cranky and irritable and I wouldn't even remember to eat half the time, if not for Tara reminding me.

"You might consider amnesty for those who can offer helpful information," Hannah suggests, again, pulling my attention from the window.

"Why would I do that?" I'm tired of her constantly pushing amnesty. "I thought I made it clear that I'm not interested in bargaining with these traitors. I want them gone."

"I know," she says patiently. "I just assumed—"

"I'm starting to wonder why you're so hot on the idea that you keep bringing it up when I've already said I'm not interested in being merciful to these people," I snap. "Is there some reason you'd need immunity from judgement?"

Hannah's expression falls and I immediately regret my words.

"Of course not," she says, barely a whisper. "Of course, I would never—"

"I know. I'm sorry. I know." I drop my head in my hands.

Tara says quietly from her cozy spot on one of the window seats, "Maybe it's time to take a break, Bailey?"

"Yeah, if you're going to start condemning us, maybe you could use a nap," Clare states more bluntly.

There's a knock at the door. I wave my hand to the thrall guard standing by it to indicate he should open it.

Charles, head of security, walks in. Although, he won't be head of security for long. I've moved him onto the task force investigating the riot. In the meantime, he's running double duty, trying to select and train his replacement from the current pool of senior security officers. That's why it's not all that alarming to me when he enters with a grim expression.

"Charles," I acknowledge him as he bows in front of my desk.

"Your Majesty," he replies, and drops a manila folder in front of me. "There's something you need to see."

I lift the cover. There are photos inside, grainy, black-and-white shots blurred by movement. I look up. "Is this from the destroyed camera?"

During the riot, someone—or several someones—had the forethought to destroy the security cameras. They largely failed; so far, only the contents of two cameras can't be retrieved. Charles nods, indicating that the number has dropped to one.

"I've flagged the one that's of the most interest to our investigation," he says as I turn my attention back to the folder.

There's a small blue tag attached to one print-out, and I slide it from the stack. Someone has circled an area in red marker. I focus on the image and the world around me stops.

There's me, half-out of the red circle, being pulled away by thralls. There are guards, clustered around two clashing figures. One is unmistakably Nathan; his jacket is half-off, like he was doffing it for the fight. There's a dark stripe across his midsection, and two thralls are bearing the other man backward. He has an enormous dagger raised high above his head.

"*Now!*" echoes in my mind. Bile rises in my throat.

"That's..." I press a hand to my chest. "Hannah, come look at this. Tell me what I'm seeing."

She hurries over, while Clare and Tara exchange glances and watchfully wait.

Charles doesn't make me wait for Hannah's confirmation. "It's Ashton Daniels. We believe he struck the near-fatal blow to the king."

"Never say that outside these walls," I warn him. I don't want anyone to know how bad off Nathan really was that night.

"Yes, Your Majesty."

"Nathan was injured. But he was never in danger of death." Even though I want to kill him, I don't want anyone else to think they can.

"Yes, Your Majesty," Charles repeats again.

"This is photographic evidence that Ashton tried to kill the king," Hannah says, her brows pulling together as she stares at the picture. "There's no coming back from this. You've got him."

"Good," Clare says sharply. "She can banish him, and he'll get the sentence he deserves."

"That's not the sentence he deserves." I don't elaborate. "Thank you, Charles. I'm going to take these to the king, myself."

"Would you like me to accompany you?" Charles offers.

I shake my head. "I'll do it right now. I haven't checked in with him yet today. But you can walk with me to the door."

Charles follows behind me—the thralls always linger a step behind—as I leave the room.

"What about us?" Tara calls after me. "Do you want any of us to go with you? For moral support or something?"

"Thanks, I've got this." I head for Nathan's study. He's moved back into his own bedroom, and the safe room is restocked and shut up again. I hope I never have to go in there again.

The door to the study is closed, and two thralls are stationed outside, both of them slightly overlapping the posts with their shoulders. *That's odd.*

"Let me pass," I order.

"His Majesty asked to not be disturbed," one of them says hesitantly.

"And I say let me pass. Who's standing in front of you right now?" I demand, crossing my arms and almost smashing the folder in the process. "Do you think he'll find out you disobeyed his orders before I punish you for disobeying mine?"

They step aside and let me pass.

The bookshelf that covers the secret entrance is closed, so I pull the candlestick and the staircase passageway scrapes open dramatically. Nathan calls down, "I told you not to let anyone disturb us."

Us?

Suspicion weaponizes the adrenaline in my body and I take off like a shot. I'm at the top of the stairs before the "us" in question can hide from me. The "us" I know I'm going to find rolling around under all those stupid fucking dead animal heads up there.

Every one of my suspicions was correct.

There's my husband, who's supposed to be convalescing from a serious injury, sitting propped up in his bed in a navy-blue velvet dressing gown, with a half-naked red-head beside him, scrambling for cover.

"Darling," Nathan says, as if he's greeting his mate and not the being of pure wrath that I've become. "Have you met Amber?"

CHAPTER 41

Have I met Amber? *Have I met Amber?*

"I don't know. Does she have a scar from me cutting her face up with a broken bottle?" I snap. Then, I remember Nathan's scar, which is still pink and fresh and bumpy as it heals. I know he's self-conscious about it. I really hope my remark stings him to the core, but I hate that I feel that way.

"Your Majesty," Amber says, keeping her eyes downcast as she hurries to collect a blouse from within the bedding.

I ignore her. She isn't even in the room, as far as I'm concerned. I choose to keep being furious with Nathan. "I have been working my ass off trying to run not just the Toronto pack, but Greater London, with no help or advice from you. Because I thought you were still recovering."

"I am still recovering," he protests, gesturing to the bed he's lounging in.

The nerve of him. "No, you're fucking your mistress!"

"We weren't," Amber quietly interrupts.

"What?" I demand. How dare she speak to me, when I

haven't addressed her. How dare she assume I want her input in this at all.

"We weren't having sex." Her eyes are downcast, and she's focused on buttoning her blouse.

I snap, "Look at me when you're speaking."

To my shock, she does, and says, "Yes, Your Majesty."

It's not sarcasm, not that I can tell. I point to the door. "Get out."

"Yes, Your Majesty—"

"Don't leave," Nathan barks sharply. "Bailey, you have no right—"

"You have no right to say a fucking word right now!" I jab a finger toward the stairs. "Get your sleazy piece of traitor ass out of here, before I banish you from this pack permanently, as you should have been years ago!"

She curtsies, grabs a skirt and some shoes from the floor, and hurries out.

"She wasn't lying," Nathan says, raking a hand through his hair. A raven lock flops over his forehead in defiance of his attempt to clear it away; he hasn't had a haircut in a month and it only makes him more maddeningly attractive. "I was just cleared to have sex this morning, anyway."

"And you didn't waste any time," I shoot back.

"I wasn't going to have sex with her," he lies, like a fucking liar.

"Right. She was just here, in your bed, with her clothes pretty much off, but you weren't going to sleep with her." As much as I hate it, knowing that Nathan and I *can* have sex now makes me *want* to have sex with Nathan. Even though I've just caught him with another woman in his bed.

This connection thing between us is ridiculous. It

doesn't have any common sense and it can't be reasoned with.

"I don't have sex with her at all," he says, spreading his hands. "At least, not intercourse. I was just looking for a blowjob."

"Ugh!" I can't imagine a way for him to be any more disgusting than he already is. "Do you think that's supposed to make me feel better?"

"It would make me feel better," he says with a shrug. "You know I'm not going to have any children outside of our marriage."

"Right, the fact that you make me look like a fool in front of the entire pack, that's just a side note." I pinch the bridge of my nose. "I didn't come here to fight or to hear about your non-penetrative sex life. I came to show you this."

I move to stand at the side of his bed and drop the folder in his lap, then think better of it and cover his hand with mine when he reaches for it. "Wait. You should be warned about what's in there."

He raises an eyebrow.

"It's pictures. From a security camera in the throne room. You're in them. And so is the person who directly attacked you."

His expression hardens, and he slips the folder from beneath our hands. "Who is it?"

"It's Ashton." Saying it out loud makes me even more angry than I was before. "You should have banished him. You should have—"

"Will what I should have done undo this?" Nathan snaps, gesturing to the scar on his face. "Will it undo the pain I endured?"

I say nothing.

He flips through the photographs, barely lingering on the flagged one. "These are all from the same camera. What about the others?"

"Security already checked those. I put together a task force to investigate and they recovered most of the footage the day after the riot. All of the cameras were damaged but there were a couple that took extra time. We're still waiting on the final hard drive," I explain.

"All of the footage should be backed up on the servers," Nathan muses with a puzzled expression.

"They didn't get a chance to sync before they were disconnected." At least, that's what the security forces told me.

Nathan closes the folder and looks up. "You organized a task force."

"Yes."

"And you've been doing this investigation on your own?"

"I have."

He looks impressed. "I'm sorry I haven't been more help."

If he were sorry about that, he would be working and not scrounging for blowjobs from his mistress. "You will be. Once you're fully recovered."

"I think if I'm cleared for sex, I'm cleared for work." He pushes himself up straighter on the pillows and cautiously moves his legs to put his feet on the floor. "Could you hand me my cane?"

It's the first time I've noticed the cane tucked between the nightstand and the bed. Hammered black metal, topped with a swooping silver grip that ends in a carved wolf's head. It's regal, and extremely extra, perfect for Nathan.

He uses the cane for balance as he rises, unsteady, and I'm shocked to realize that this is the first time I've seen him upright in over a month. He's nowhere near as a powerful and strong as I remember, and a familiar fear slashes through my heart. It's the terror I felt when I thought he would die. It's what I felt when I saw his insides spilling out and heard his screams while the medics worked on him.

I'm not sure I'll ever forget that torturously specific fear.

"You don't have to—" I begin, swallowing back sudden tears.

"No, no, I promised myself that today I would try to return to at least some semblance of normality." He takes a few steps and pauses, his expression crumpling. "Oh, Bailey. Are you crying?"

I swipe at my cheeks and lie, "No."

He sits back down with a groan of pain he can't wholly suppress, and pats the bed beside him.

"Not until you change the sheets," I snap. Like hell I'm going to let him comfort me in the bed his side piece was rolling around in.

He sighs in annoyance, but his voice is gentle when he says, "I put so much on you, unfairly."

"No shit?" I cross my arms. "You didn't even tell me you were suddenly king of Greater London. You just spring that on me. A whole different pack to run."

"And then I was appallingly rude, getting all these stab wounds," he jokes.

"It's not funny." Gross thing I just witnessed aside, my miserableness exhausts me, and I sit on the bed beside him. "I was never in a position to be a queen. I wasn't in a position to manage a Tim Hortons, for fuck's sake."

He chuckles at that, but I know he's not making fun of me. For reasons I can't fathom, our arguments seem to endear me to him even more.

"The only reason I was able to keep things from falling apart without you was because I had to," I say.

"You had to, and you found a way." He puts an arm around me, and I'm acutely aware that I'm close to his injured side.

I stiffen and lean slightly away. "Careful, I don't want to hurt you."

"You're not going to," he assures me. Then he pauses and asks, "Do you want to see it?"

"I got a pretty good look at it when they brought you into the safe room," I say, shaking my head.

"I know you did." He undoes the belt of his robe and shrugs out of one sleeve. "But it's not that bad anymore. You need to see that I'm actually all right."

Well, just decide what I need, then, I gripe to myself, but he does have a point. How can I trust that Nathan is truly going to be okay if all I'm imagining under his clothes is a big pile of bloody macaroni hanging out of his side?

He's naked under the dressing gown, and I note that he's lost some muscle definition. Obviously, he hasn't been working out, but the quickness with which his body has atrophied startles me. It's only been a few weeks and he's already wasting away?

"See?" he says, leaning a little so I can get a full view of the scar that rips from mid-ribcage and across his abdomen in a diagonal slash to his opposite hip. He really was gutted.

"I didn't realize how long the cut was." I reach out as if to touch it and quickly pull my fingers back. Why the hell would I want to touch a gross, red scar still dotted with glints of metal staples? But it intrigues me, the idea that somehow he could recover from something that looked so fatal.

He touches the end of the scar, near his hip. There are bubbled pink pinpricks bracketing the wound, where some of the staples have already been removed. "It's grotesque, I know." With a grim chuckle, he says, "We can leave the lights off."

"You don't think I'm a very good person, do you?" I ask, reaching up to cup his slashed cheek. "You don't think I can overlook superficial stuff like scars?"

"I don't think that," he explains. "I fear it."

"You're afraid that I won't be attracted to you?" That's a weird fear to have, considering how little it matters for werewolves to be attracted to their mates. Procreation doesn't have to be an enjoyable, passionate thing; all we have to do is breed to keep our numbers up.

"I'm afraid that you'll think I'm weak," he admits. "I'm afraid that this has just proven I can't protect you."

"All this has proven is that you can take a major beating and survive." How could I possibly doubt his ability to protect me, when he could have fled the throne room without me, but made sure I was taken to safety, instead?

"Besides," I add, to lighten the mood. "It would take a lot more than an interesting scar to make you unattractive."

And, because he's such an egotistical piece of crap, he replies, "Oh, I know."

"I never doubted the power of your vanity," I say.

He takes my hand and kisses my palm. "I promise, I'll return to work. Tomorrow. Even if I'm stuck in my sickbed, you can bring what you need to me."

"Okay. I'll do that." Because I am super overwhelmed.

"And since you interrupted me," Nathan goes on, "Maybe you'd like to…"

I squint at him, not understanding. Until I do, and I shoot to my feet in disgust. "You have got to be kidding me."

"I have to know if it still works," he protests.

"Your hands weren't injured," I snap, and stalk to the stairs, not stopping when he calls, "Bailey, I was just joking!"

I wonder if it's possible for them to put him in a medically induced coma, for his own safety. Because I'm not sure how long I'll be able to put up with his nonsense.

CHAPTER 42

I don't help Nathan find out "if it still works" that night, but a nagging voice in my head tells me that if I don't, Amber will.

I'm not sure if believe him when he says they don't go all the way. His reasoning makes sense; birth control isn't a guarantee with werewolves. Plus, as king, he definitely wouldn't want to endanger the future claims of our heirs.

And if he did, and he got the former queen pregnant…

As Henry the VIII as it is, I have to get pregnant before she does.

So, I send Nathan a message the next morning stating that if he can walk from his bed to mine, we can find out "if it still works."

During the day, the only thing I'm focused on, though, is actual work. While Nathan might think he's going to dive back into running both packs, there are too many things I've started that I need to finish. Namely, an integrated council between the packs. I know that people in Toronto, maybe even people in the Greater London pack won't like it, but keeping the two packs operating separately won't work. Toronto will continue to plot against us and Greater London, and Greater London will very likely continue to plot against Toronto. I take phone call after phone call, draft letters, get briefed on background checks and new evidence in the investigation into the riot, until well after dinner time. I have to eat at my desk. By the time I practically crawl up the stairs to my bedroom, I've actually forgotten about my promise to Nathan.

So, it's a surprise to find him lounging, comfortably nude, on my bed. He raises an eyebrow at my shocked expression and makes sarcastic little jazz-hands. "Ta-da!"

I'm so tired, I don't even try to say something clever back. But I do laugh.

"You didn't think I could do it," he accuses with a smug grin.

"I will never again underestimate the lengths you will go to for pussy." I shake my head and take a seat in the armchair by the fire, bending down to unzip my ankle boots. When I first came to Aconitum Hall, I had comforted myself with thoughts of sitting in this chair and reading a book on cozy winter nights with a cup of tea. Though, I should have imagined sitting there and scrolling TikTok with a can of pop, if I was being honest with myself. In any case, the only thing I've had time to use the damn sitting area for is to take my shoes off.

"Come on, quit dawdling," he says, and I think he's joking. He better be joking. "I've been waiting quite a long while for this."

"You've been waiting less than twelve hours for this." I toe off my socks and stand to remove my slacks. He watches my every move as I step out of them and begin to unbutton my blouse.

"I've been waiting far longer than that." His tongue

wets his bottom lip like he's been starving for me. "The spirit was more than willing but the flesh was otherwise occupied."

"It looks fine now." I drop my gaze pointedly to his erection, which bobs against his stomach as he watches me.

I drop my blouse on the floor and give him a minute to take in my red satin bra and panties. I put them on in the morning with the intent to wow him tonight, and it seems to do the trick; he takes his cock in his hand and strokes himself slowly.

I've gotten used to our powerful connection, and I've been able to ignore it over the past few weeks when I've needed to. Now, it's too insistent to ignore. I squeeze my thighs together and my feet shift, restless. I reach behind me to unhook my bra, and he stops me.

"Leave it on," he says. "And the panties."

I go to the bed and slide up next to him. It feels so good to touch, to have our bodies pressed skin to skin again. It's like a cold bottle of water after a hard workout; it's refreshing, even if the person giving it to me is someone I can barely tolerate.

"Okay, I have to admit, I've missed this," I breathe against his shoulder, mesmerized by the sight of his big hand still slowly pumping his cock.

"I know you have. I could feel you."

"I'm sure you could." The only stress relief and self-care I have time for anymore is masturbation. And I've been under a lot of stress.

"I wondered if you'd taken a lover." It's a question disguised as a statement.

No, because I'm not unfaithful like you are. I'm not going to bring that up now. The last thing I want to think about

—the last thing I want *him* to think about—is that other woman. "I haven't had time to interview potential candidates."

"You did audition one," he says. "I noticed it was missing from my nightstand drawer."

I don't want to think about why he went looking for it.

He reads my thoughts on my face. "Don't pout. It's only for you. In fact, I bought it with you in mind. I was going to bring it tonight, but I found it was already here."

To my embarrassment, he pulls the two-pronged vibrator from beneath one of the pillows. He turns it on and offers it to me. "Show me."

I hesitate.

"Go on. I want those panties dripping wet before I bury my face in them."

Those words flood deep through my groin. Other things flood there, too.

I lean back on the pillows to get comfortable, and he clucks his tongue, scolding me. "No, no. I can't see anything from this angle. Get on your hands and knees."

I rise up on my knees, uncertain how to proceed or how it could possibly make his view better, and he adds, "Face away from me. Legs further apart, please."

Why is it so fucking hot when he bosses me around like this? When he tells me what to do in daily life, I want to smack his stupid, handsome face. But right now, all I want is to perform every task he gives me to his utmost satisfaction.

Well, and *my* satisfaction.

With my ass in the air, my panty-covered crotch centimeters from his face, I slip the vibrator beneath my waistband and position the prongs on either side of my clit, just as he used it on me before. Except now, after some experimenting on my own, I know exactly what settings I like. I nudge the button and find the speed and pulse that will fulfill his request.

"You thought of me," he says, reaching out to stroke a finger up and down the silky fabric between my legs. "When you got yourself off."

I did think of him, and I'm pissed off that he guessed it, but there's no point in lying. "I did. I remembered how good you feel inside me."

"Did you finger yourself while you imagined my cock in you?" His slow stroking separates my labia and gently nudges my panties between them. If he wants me good and soaked, he's going to get his wish; his touch and his words quicken the pulse in my clit. The vibe buzzes away and I push back on his hand.

Two fingers slip past the panties and into my cunt, and he hooks them down, pushing hard on my g-spot. I let out a moan so primal, I startle myself.

"Did you make yourself come like this?" He asks, grinding those fingers into my sensitive flesh. I feel the pressure and sensation deep in my pelvis as my clit is worked from both sides, internally by his hand, externally by the vibrator.

"Did you get this wet?" He asks, then says, "Listen. Do you hear yourself?"

I do hear it, the wet squish of my cunt around his fingers. I pump my hips and the tempo of the obscene sound picks up.

"You're going to drench me when you come," he teases, but I'm long past any kind of embarrassment. My muscles lock up and I accelerate toward the apex of my pleasure with a long, shrill mewl of pure pleasure.

"That's it," he groans. "Just like that."

I shudder and writhe on his hand until he says, "Let me get a taste of you," and I'm not about to argue. I put one knee on each side of his head and rub the wet satin against his nose. He groans and reaches up to move the crotch of the panties aside and drives his tongue straight to the source.

He makes a noise of satisfaction as his tongue twists inside me, and his lips work against me like he's trying to drink every drop of the juice he pulls from me. I grind my hips against his face and he stops what he's doing to groan, "That's it. Ride my mouth."

He doesn't have to tell me twice. He turns his attention to my clit, circling and sucking while I rock my pelvis and babble things like, "right there," "oh yes," and most importantly, "don't stop."

I come so hard, my thighs shake.

And he doesn't stop. Not even to let me get my breath.

I try to twist away from him, and he grips my hips, holding me fast. His teeth graze my clit almost in warning, and my oversensitive nerves sizzle.

"Please," I gasp, grabbing his hair and tugging it. "I can't take anymore."

He releases me with one last, slow lick that makes me reconsider asking him to stop. But he pushes two fingers into me, and I feel emptier than ever. I need his cock.

I fall back on the bed beside him, breathing hard. "How do we…"

"I think you'll need to get on top." He sounds apologetic.

"I've never done that." *He knows*, I remind myself. "But I'm willing to try."

"You'll excel at it, I'm sure," he says, coaxing one of my

legs over his hips. I'm careful to avoid his scar, which, though quite healed, still looks tender.

"Go slow," he whispers, and his vulnerability is shockingly endearing. "I'm not sure—"

"If something hurts, tell me right away," I say, and I position him exactly where I want him to be. Slowly, just as he asked, I slide back onto his cock.

It's been too long. Far, far too long.

I sit up straight and let all of him in, and I somehow want more. I clench down on him, and he lets out a deep moan that makes me rock my hips and ripple around him.

His cock is painfully hard, and I'll feel the consequences of that in the morning, but I don't care. I take things slow at first, because I'm worried about hurting him, but he's impatient beneath me, trying to speed me along with small pumps of his hips.

I give him exactly what he wants, moving faster and faster on him, the ridge of his pubic bone and the roughness of his hair tormenting my already over-sensitive clit to the throes of another orgasm. I lean back, hips churning, and he drives up from the bed with a pained shout as he empties into me.

I keep him inside me until the last jerk, then slowly climb off. I'm shocked at the wetness between my thighs and the silky slip of his cum between them. I'd forgotten that aspect in my comparatively sterile imaginings.

"Thanks," he says sleepily. "I needed that."

"I wasn't doing you a favor," I point out. "I needed that, too."

More than I want to admit.

———

As usual, when I wake up, Nathan is gone. I rub my eyes and reach for my phone, and my jaw drops when I see the time. It's almost noon.

I call Hannah, and she answers on the first ring.

"Good morning, sleepy head," she says in a sly sing-song.

"Why didn't you wake me up?" I ask, yawning.

"Because His Majesty, your husband, said no one was to disturb you."

"Next time, don't listen to him." My face flames at the notion of the entire staff being aware that I need to recuperate after getting fucked senseless by my mate. "Is there coffee?"

"Breakfast is on the way," she promises. "Oh, and… I don't know if you want to hear it, but…"

"No, I'm not curious at all, now," I snark. I sit up and a lump digs into my thigh. I pull the vibrator from the bedding and take it with me to the bathroom to wash it. "I'm going to pee while we're talking, by the way. I'm very professional."

"You always are." She takes an audibly deep breath. "Nathan is going to arrest Ashton this afternoon."

"Good." That's all I need to say on the subject. "Tell His Majesty that no one is deciding Ashton's sentence without me. Not him, and not the council."

"I will draft a letter from *you* that says that, as I cannot speak to the King of this pack that way," Hannah reminds me. "Okay, I'll get back to work. You have coffee and breakfast on the way to your sitting room."

We hang up, and by the time I'm showered and dressed, the smell of bacon and pancakes is too powerful. I decide to dry my hair later, throw it up into a towel, and head downstairs.

In the sitting room, there aren't any security thralls. Nathan really didn't want me disturbed. My jaw tightens. The ego on the man, thinking I need some kind of recuperation time because he's just that good.

He did make me come until I lost consciousness, but that's beside the point.

A thrall is setting the small cafe table near the window with a plate and service for one.

"Good morning," I say, heading over to inspect the food on the trolley. I'm absolutely famished.

But something's off. The thrall doesn't reply to me. I see a drop of sweat roll down his neck. I sniff the air and immediately recognize the problem. "You're not a thrall."

The werewolf bares his teeth and lunges.

CHAPTER 43

Werewolves only change at the full moon. Only with the ceremony.

But this one changes in my sitting room.

There aren't any real weapons around me; I grab a fork from the breakfast table. The werewolf's jaws snap at my face as I dodge backward. He manages to grab me, opens his mouth to roar, and I jam the fork into his mouth, into his soft palate.

And then he bites down and my arm comes away.

I stagger backward, speechless with disbelief for just a second because it's disconcerting to see your hand detached from your body. But then the pain hits me and I'm not speechless anymore. Somehow, I manage to scream out, "guards!" Then, I can't stop screaming it, higher and shriller as I topple the table between us to buy me time. My blood sprays in an arc across the carpet; that's not something I can buy time for. I'm already dizzy, but I can't turn my back on him. I have to focus. I have to concentrate.

It's not even a nanosecond, but it feels like a lifetime

before the thralls enter. The first one through the door doesn't hesitate; she runs full speed toward the wolf, vaulting the couch to launch herself directly into his side. He staggers off his feet and she pins him. I see her draw her firearm and I shout, my voice much weaker than I feel, "Don't! We need him alive!"

The thralls that followed behind are quick to join her, but they're not fast enough to stop him throwing her at the fireplace. She strikes the stones and falls to the floor. The other thralls manage to overpower the werewolf twelve to one.

But only barely.

"Bailey!" I hear Nathan yelling from somewhere far off.

"Stay back, Your Majesty," someone closer to me shouts, and if they mean me, they don't have anything to worry about. The room keeps listing like a cruise ship in a storm and before I know it, the floor is the wall and I'm slamming into it.

My hearing is fuzzy, and I want to puke when they lift me up. Someone does something to my arm that *really* hurts, like a blood pressure cuff that never stops squeezing.

"Safe room, now! Go, go, get them out of here!" Charles's voice booms.

And that's about the time I drop out of consciousness.

———

One second, I don't exist. The next, I do.

I reach up to rub my eyes and find an IV and tubes in the back of my hand. So, I lift the other arm and punch myself in the eye with a wad of tightly packed gauze. Pain electrifies down to the bone, all the way to my shoulder, and someone gently cradles my forearm and positions it on a wedge pillow at my side.

"Careful," Nathan says. "You need to keep that elevated."

Pieces arrange slowly in my mind. We're in the safe room, but this time I'm the one in the bed. I don't have nearly as many machines, though. Just an IV pump. And I'm here because… "He bit my hand off."

"They weren't able to reattach it," Nathan tells me softly. "I'm so sorry."

It's probably the drugs—and the fact that I can still feel my hand there at the end of my arm—that make me shrug that off. Or maybe it's just that I'm so glad to be alive after what happened. "It could be worse."

"It could have been." His voice is raw with emotion.

"But it wasn't." I sigh happily. I'm in a great mood because of whatever is dripping through the IV. "How did that guy do that? We can't do that."

"I don't know. We're trying to find out."

"Just ask him." Is he the first one to figure out how to shift our forms without the rigamarole of the ceremony? That would be so convenient.

"We would have. If you hadn't killed him."

I killed him. I kill my assassin. "That's so cool."

Maybe I'll feel guilty about that later. Maybe people will write stories about me. I ponder a title for my myth out loud. "The queen who lost her hand stabbing a were-wolf in the throat from the inside of his mouth."

"Actually, he choked to death on your hand."

Oh. "That's so disappointing."

"Are you in terrible pain?" he asks. "I could get the doctor—"

"No." I'm in pain, but whatever they're giving me makes me not care. "Are you worried about me?"

"Of course, I'm worried about you." He sounds stunned by the question. The mattress dips and I open my eyes.

I didn't realize I hadn't already done that.

Nathan looks like hell. His hair is tousled, and his jaw is stubbly. And tired. His eyelids are as heavy as mine.

"Am I going to die?"

"No." He lets out a heavy, grateful exhale. "It sounds like you're not in any danger of that. You'll just have to heal."

"Nathan?"

"Yes?"

"He wasn't from this pack." I would have known. Security would have known.

Nathan doesn't answer right away.

"Tell me." I want to sound commanding but I just sound drunk. "Despite my diction, I assure you, I kinda know what's happening."

"'Kinda'?" Irritatingly, he does a good imitation of me. "He was from the Saint-Laurent pack."

Great. The pack that wanted to kill my mate wants to kill me now, too.

"Do you know who sent them?" My heart races. I hear the beeps increasing and reach for my chest with my good hand. There's and EKG sticker there, a little plastic tab I want to peel off.

Nathan brushes my hand away. "Leave it. They have to monitor you."

"No." I try to sit up. "I have to get back to work. It could be Ashton. It could be—"

"It could be your father," Nathan snaps. "Or your sisters!"

"No." They could never.

I fall back against the bed and wince as my bandaged stump jostles.

"I don't know what they could do," Nathan says, gentler now. "I have to investigate everyone."

"Maybe I wasn't the target," I whisper. I hope that's the case, if my own family sent the assassin. But it has Ashton written all over it. "You were in my room last night."

"Night before last, yes," he corrects me. "You were in surgery most of yesterday and you slept all night. But that is something I thought of. That the assassin might have been sent for me and simply took his opportunity."

"I think he knew what I was." That's not right. "I mean, I knew what he was. And he knew that I knew that he wasn't a thrall."

"So, he could have attacked you because he had to. He was already found out."

I lift my hand to make a finger gun at him and then remember I don't have fingers on that hand. Or a hand on that hand. So, I just wave it a little and say, "Bingo."

Nathan chuckles. "I think whatever they're giving you, I might like some, myself."

"You had plenty," I remind him. "And I didn't get any when I was sitting at the side of your bed, waiting for you to wake up."

"You..." He pauses.

I finish for him. "Waited by your bedside, yes. I did."

"Why?"

That's a good question. Why did I wait at the bedside of a man who used me as a pawn in his political subterfuge, who insists on casually cheating, who explicitly told me that he's not interested in getting to know me?

"You know why." The bond between us made it impossible for me to leave him.

He nods once and looks away. "It terrifies me."

"Me, too," I admit. "I don't know what it is."

He makes a thoughtful noise. I wonder if he knows, and he's just not telling me.

"I have to get back to work." Did I say that before? I can't remember and I'm pretty tired.

"No," Nathan states firmly. "And you're not going to be a part of the investigation into the assassin."

"Because you think I won't look into my sisters." I won't. I refuse to believe they would be involved. Their husbands, maybe, but never Tara or Clare personally. "Where are they?"

"They're currently being held under guard here in the house. They're not being deprived of anything, don't worry on that account," Nathan is quick to assure me. "But they are never out of sight, and they aren't going to be allowed to speak to you."

"Does that mean I'm not allowed to speak to them?" Not again. He can't take them away, again.

"For right now, yes it does." He sounds truly apologetic. "I know this hurts you. But it's for the best."

"It's not them," I say. "But clear them, first."

"As fast as we can, so they can be returned to you," Nathan promises.

I can't believe I'm willing to even let him investigate them at all, but I'm not in a position to argue. My eyes drift closed and in the back of my mind, a memory swims up. Nathan's voice in the hallway. I fight through the painkiller haze and mumble. "You tried to come help me."

"I did." He strokes my hair and I cringe inwardly at how greasy it must be. "I fought my own guards trying to reach you."

"It was the thing, wasn't it?" I wave a finger in the air. "Our thing."

"I suppose it was." His answer surprises me because it's not as straight forward as the simple *"yes"* I expected. "I'll leave you now. I wanted to be here so you wouldn't wake up all alone. But you need your rest."

"You still do, too," I remind him.

"I know." He gestures to the door. "I'll just be out there."

He leaves the room, and a thrall immediately enters. She's wearing a security uniform. And I've seen her before. Tall, muscular, East-Asian, and her dark hair is in a long French braid down her back.

"Who are you?" I slur.

"Li Xiao, Your Majesty. I've been assigned as your personal bodyguard." She doesn't meet my eyes but keeps hers straight ahead.

"I saw you." The pieces start to come together. "You rescued me."

I think I see a smile quirk the corner of her mouth. But everything is kind of quirked at the moment.

From the other room, Nathan calls, "Go to sleep and let her do her job, Bailey."

"Yes, Your Majesty," I reply, though I'm not sure he can hear me. I know he can't see the flip-off I'm giving him with my remaining hand.

He definitely can't see the one I'm giving him with my missing hand.

Li Xiao sees it, though, and this time, I can tell she's smiling.

CHAPTER 44

I don't let myself malinger. As soon as I can convince the doctors to get the IVs out of me and the pain meds lowered enough that I can walk without swaying, I'm back in my office.

Li Xiao doesn't like my office. I can tell on the first day, because she paces until it freaks me out.

"I know this is a weird thing to say, since I did just have my hand bitten off by a werewolf, but maybe you could dial the hypervigilance back a notch," I say, frowning down at my handwriting. It's horrible. The guy took off my right hand, also my dominant hand. I should have thought of that before attacking with the fork. Now, I have to try to learn how to write legibly with the left.

There's a knock on the door; it's Hannah, we can both tell from the pattern. I nod, and Li Xiao opens the door, hand on the taser at her hip just in case.

"What are you doing?" Hannah asks, nodding toward the paper on the desk.

"Practicing." I push the scribbles away and drop the pen.

"You could always just type," she reminds me.

Typing is its own frustration. "I have to relearn that, too. Good news, though!"

"Yeah?" Hannah asks.

I give her a sweet smile and bat my eyes. "I have an assistant who can take dictation."

"Brat." She sticks her tongue out at me, then goes back to all-business. "His Majesty the King wants you in the throne room. He said you would know what it's about."

My nerves immediately skyrocket. I do know what it's about.

I glance down at my outfit. I've been rocking sweatpants and tank tops exclusively. I'm not even wearing a bra because I can't hook it in the back.

Gosh, it would be really neat to have some ladies-in-waiting right now.

"We need to run by my room first. And I'm going to need a hand." I wave my arm at her.

Hannah rolls her eyes. "That's going to stop being funny soon."

"I'm the queen. You still have to laugh." I lean around her to ask, "Right, Xiao?"

"Ha ha, Your Majesty," my bodyguard responds in wry monotone.

"His Majesty suggested you might want to change, anyway," Hannah says. "He suggested something 'serious'."

Because what we're doing is serious. But I don't want to mention it in front of my bodyguard. Thralls are good at keeping secrets, but right now, I feel I'm justified in having a little paranoia.

Xiao follows behind Hannah and I as we head to my bedroom. I cradle my sore arm against my chest and let

Hannah get all the doors. We move quickly through my sitting room; I don't like to spend much time in there, after what happened.

The cleaners did an excellent job getting the blood out of the carpet, though.

Upstairs, Hannah and I head straight for my closet. "Xiao, can you hang back?"

"Certainly, Your Majesty," she says with a deferential nod. She stations herself at the top of the stairs and I close the door behind Hannah and me.

My wardrobe is just off the bathroom, separated by frosted glass doors. When they open, it triggers the lighting that illuminates every shelf, every rack, every bar bearing the mountains of clothes I've purchased with Nathan's money, in addition to what I brought with me from my parents' house.

The first time I brought her in here, Hannah almost had an asthma attack. Now, though, she's comfortable pawing through everything, which she does with ruthless efficiency as I sit on one of the square white leather cubes near my shoe rack. It's amazing how easily tired one can get when they're trying to recuperate from a traumatic amputation.

"It has to be something I can fit my bandages through," I remind Hannah as she pulls out a narrow-sleeved blazer. "We might have to get a little formal."

"What's this for, anyway?" she asks. "It might be easier to narrow down what not to wear."

"We're sentencing Ashton today."

Hannah stops flicking hangers across the bar. She turns slowly. "What are you sentencing him to?"

I shrug. "Death, probably. I hope."

At least, that's what I asked Nathan to do. He wasn't fully committed to that when we spoke about it last night.

"And… you're okay with that?" she asks cautiously.

I narrow my eyes. "Why wouldn't I be okay with that?"

She puts up her hands, defensive. "I'm not inserting myself into this or arguing either way. I just want to know what kind of support you'll need from me, if we have to watch one of our childhood acquaintances get executed."

"I'll need help opening the champagne," I quip.

"Bailey, be serious," Hannah urges. "This isn't something you would ever take lightly. I know you hate him, but this is life and death."

"I know." I rub my forehead, trying to ease the sudden tension there. "But I have much different views of life and death these days. I have no problem with someone else going to their death because they tried to steal my mate's life."

"Fair," Hannah agrees. Even though she and Ryan aren't remotely interested in each other beyond a platonic level, I know it would devastate her to lose him.

I get to my feet. "There must be something in my ceremonial clothes that will work."

Hannah beats me to that bar of gowns. "What about this funerary garb? They sent it over in case—"

I hold up my hand. "I know what they sent it in case of."

The gown is similar to my coronation gown, a Tudor-inspired style in black brocade, but without the train. The sleeves lace to the bodice separately, so I'll be able to put them on without tugging on my bandages too much. Tiny white pearls accentuate the flowers embroidered on the fabric; Aconitum flowers, or Wolf's Bane.

"How many people are we expecting?" I ask.

"His Majesty didn't say. But judging from the number of thralls and vans dispatched after lunch, I would say a decent number." Hannah pulls the hanger off the rack. "We don't have a lot of time. Are we really going this Anne Boleyn route?"

"I don't see why not," I say. "Heads are going to roll."

———

With a final check to make sure my stump is hidden by the bell of my sleeve, I step through the door behind the dais, followed by Xiao and Hannah. Nathan is already there, speaking to two of the men from Greater London that had been in attendance at the coronation riot.

One of them has an eyepatch that I'm pretty sure I would have noticed before, and I get a little sick to my stomach. All morning, I've thought about the revenge I want against Ashton for almost taking my mate's life. Now, I'm face with graphic proof that Nathan and I aren't the only ones who were impacted that day.

I knew that, of course. My nightmares often feature the shocked face of the dying acolyte as she lay at my feet. Ashton isn't the only person who participated in the riot. He's not the only person who hurt someone. He's just the one who got closest to the crown.

Nathan turns when I enter. It's unnerving, the way we can feel each other. He takes in my gown and looks down at his own outfit. He's dressed in all black, as well, black shirt, black trousers, black jacket and tie. It matches the black beard he's grown out to try to cover his scar. He can't totally disguise it, though; the angry red line slices from just beneath his eye down to his jaw.

"You're still leaning toward execution, then?" I whisper when he gets close enough to hear.

"You clearly are," he shoots back, gesturing to my dress. "Was that for any particular special occasion."

"They worked fast when they thought you would die," I joke.

My sense of humor has gotten *grim*.

"Let's take our places, shall we?" he offers me his hand, and I make a point to walk to his right side. It's kind of cute that he blushes when he says, "I forgot. I'm so sorry."

"It's all right. Although…it was a little difficult to get into this dress with just me and Hannah at the wheel." It's not the time to ask, but everything in me has to know. "Can my sisters come out of time out yet? I could really use the extra hands when I'm getting ready in the mornings and stuff like that."

"That joke is becoming tiresome," Nathan warns. "Tara is cleared to return."

But not Clare?

I'll have to ask him about her, later, because the sound of angry voices in the hall outside the throne room doors spikes my anxiety through the roof.

"It's just the thralls bringing in our guests," Nathan says, leading me to our thrones. "I'm not going to let anything happen to you."

But my throat is tight with fear. The last time we were in here, the last time we were among our subjects, they tried to kill us. I look behind me, to where my bodyguard stands behind the dais, constantly scanning the room.

"Xiao?" I call, and she snaps her attention to me. "Could you stand closer, please?"

She moves to my side of the dais, still behind me.

"No, I mean…" I tilt my head. "Like, closer. Like, right next to me?"

"Of course, Your Majesty." She climbs the dais and stands to the left of my throne, just slightly behind it.

Having seen the way she attacked a fully transformed werewolf, I feel a lot better with her right by my side.

Some people in file in from a side door; I recognize them as council members from our own pack once I see Ryan, but there are others mixed in who I don't know. I assume they're from Greater London.

"I want to meet those people I don't know before they leave today," I tell Nathan.

He nods and watches as they take their seats. Then he asks me, "Are you ready?"

I face the huge doors across the wide room from us and take a deep breath.

"No one is going to hurt you, Your Majesty," Xiao says, astonishing me. She never speaks unless I speak to her. I must really be a wreck, if she's breaking protocol to console me.

I exhale and lift my chin. "Let's do this."

CHAPTER 45

The throne room doors open and suddenly, all I see are images from the night my family and I had been forced, terrified, into vans and brought before the king.

I look over at Nathan. His expression is totally cold, just like it had been that night. For the first time since then, I'm afraid of him.

My lungs heave for breath, and I can't stop swallowing. I'm trembling. I'm going to cry.

A hand touches my shoulder, squeezes reassuringly. The contact is so brief that by the time I look up at Xiao, it's already over. She hasn't stopped scanning the crowd.

How did she know I needed that reassurance? That I wouldn't object to it? This isn't the first time she's been eerily tuned into me.

I'm unnerved and comforted all at once.

The room is arranged differently than it had been that awful night. There are more seats. Enough for at least a hundred people. They're in a semicircle but parted by a single aisle; the thralls escort the sometimes-resistant werewolves down the outside and fill them in to the middle. It's chillingly structured, almost rehearsed.

Is this something Nathan enjoys? I'm not opposed to ruling by fear, at least, not right now. But I've been where these people are sitting; I can't imagine delighting in tormenting people that way.

It's all couples in the seats in front of us. What does Nathan have planned?

The one person I don't see is Ashton.

When everyone is assembled, Nathan nods to the majordomo, who thumps his staff against the floor with a thundering bang. It stuns everyone into silence.

Nathan remains seated in his throne, unnervingly still as he speaks. "Every family in this room is a traitor."

There are a few gasps, which the majordomo silences immediately with his staff.

"Some of you participated in the riot at the coronation of your queen and pack leader. Some of you participated in the planning of it. Others have made the grave error of withholding information vital to the pack's safety, either before the treasonous attack or in its wake." Nathan motions to some guards, and they leave at the signal. He goes on, "Those of you who attended the coronation with weapons concealed on your persons, intending to harm your fellow pack members will be executed at the next full moon."

Someone screams. A woman in the front faints.

I feel like I might faint, too.

Guards move in on the two front rows and begin zip-tying the hands of the men who are now prisoners. But not the women.

I don't have a chance to wonder why.

"I am not unmerciful," Nathan calls, his voice carrying

over the growing hysteria. "The children of this pack cannot be made orphans. They must be cared for. The mates of the executed will inherit the assets formerly belonging to them and be spared execution themselves." He motions to remaining guards around the edges of the room. "Take them out."

All I can do is watch, unable to catch my breath, as the men are ripped away from their mates. Some of the men go stoically, some of the women cling. Some of the men are crying, the bravery of the attack long faded away in the face of the consequences. Maybe I should pity them, considering they've been sentenced to death, but they didn't pity me when they drew up plans for ours.

It seems to take forever to clear the throne room of the condemned and their spouses.

The remaining pack members are stunned silent. Waiting for the ax to fall.

The two guards Nathan sent away return, Ashton in tow. They don't take him to a seat but force him to his knees at the foot of the dais.

"This traitor," Nathan pronounces, "deserves special recognition for his treachery. Not only did he participate in the planning of a thwarted attempt on my life, but it was also his hand that sunk the blade into my side at the coronation. He attacked his king and his pack leader. And he did so in conjunction with the Saint-Laurent pack, who only two weeks ago made another attempt on the queen's life."

Did Ashton have anything to do with that? I interrupt Nathan's rehearsed tirade to stand and march down the steps, just out of Ashton's reach. He glares up at me with pure hatred in his eyes and I am certain he regrets the day he asked my father for that mating pact.

I whip back my sleeve to reveal the bandaged stump of my arm, ignoring the murmurs of shock and intrigue that result. I'm only concerned with Ashton. "Did you have anything to do with this?"

A smirk slants his mouth. "Believe it or not, more than just one person in this pack wants you dead."

My hand clenches to an unconscious fist. Unfortunately, it's the hand that's not there anymore and my brain still moves the tendons of my forearm, sending burning agony all the way up my neck. Somehow, I don't crumple or swear. I turn around and walk calmly back to my throne.

Whether Nathan plans to do it or not, I want Ashton dead. I feel no compunction about it. He tried to kill my husband, twice. He almost succeeded. He tried to trap me into an abusive, controlling marriage. And I don't believe for a moment that he had no hand—no pun intended this time—in planning the assassination attempt against me.

I'm not going to wait to find out. "Ashton Daniels, for the crime of treason, I sentence you to death by beheading at the next full moon."

"And for the grievous sin of laying your hands on your king and pack leader, I sentence you to Lycaon's banquet," Nathan adds. "Your flesh shall be served to the rest of the traitors assembled here, as Lycaon served the flesh of his son to Zeus."

What the fuck.

I've heard of that punishment before, but I thought it was a legend. A spooky story they told us to warn us not to cross our pack leader.

Judging from the deathly silence in the throne room, it's having the intended effect.

"You'll pay for this," Ashton warns. And why

shouldn't he have his say? He already faces the worst punishment any werewolf could receive. He has nothing to lose. "The Saint-Laurent pack will not let this—"

"Let the Saint-Laurent pack rescue you then," Nathan snaps. "If they'd like to send their men to die." He jerks his head, and the guards roughly pull Ashton to his feet to drag him off in the direction of the other prisoners.

"Those of you who wish to avoid Lycaon's Banquet have an option," Nathan tells them. "You may confess your misdeeds to the council—" He motions to the small group standing beneath the windows, who definitely weren't all council members a few weeks ago. "—and your sentence will be decided based on the quality of information you provide us about your co-conspirators. A full confession, and full cooperation, will spare you the shame of consuming your werewolf brother. And it may save your necks.

"In the meantime," he goes on, "The pack will continue to hold your passports, your bank accounts, your drivers' licenses, and the keys to your homes. The thralls stationed in your home will continue to report to me, and they are still authorized to use deadly force against hostile action."

That was my doing, while Nathan was still living hour-to-hour. I'm strangely proud that he didn't rescind my orders when he took the family business back.

"Spread the word of what happened here," Nathan concludes. "Those still faithful to the pack will be heartened to hear that they have been protected today."

He rises and turns to me, offering his arm. I stand and carefully maneuver my injured one through his, and we walk down the back of the dais together and out of the throne room.

When he releases me, I realize Nathan is trembling. I frown up at him in concern. "Are you all right?"

"I'm fine." He nods and dabs his sweating upper lip with a handkerchief from his jacket pocket. "If you'll excuse me?"

He walks away and I start after him. "You don't look fine."

"We'll talk later." He picks up speed and snaps for his guards, who fill in the space between us.

I stop and watch him walk away.

I'm baffled and hurt by Nathan's abandonment. What happened in the throne room was terrifying. We'd passed a sentence so horrible it had gone out of fashion in the middle ages. Nathan hadn't given me any indication that he was even considering that.

Maybe he's angry that you took over sentencing Ashton. It's certainly possible, but I had no idea Nathan's considerable ego was *that* fragile. I can't imagine anything that could penetrate it.

"Your Majesty?" Xiao prompts me gently.

I turn and force a polite smile. "Sorry. I'm going to go back to my office. Is Hannah—"

Xiao speaks into the communications device on her wrist. "Secretary to the queen to queen's office."

"That sounds like a chess move," I quip.

Xiao tilts her head. "Do you play chess?"

I look back at the throne room. What I did back there… did it make me a strong ruler or a paranoid tyrant?

"Not well," I respond.

CHAPTER 46

Tara comes to see me while I'm still changing out of my gown. She bursts into my dressing room and practically pushes Hannah down to get to me.

I hold my injured arm out of the way, so she won't accidentally bang into it when she collides with me and wraps me in a strong hug.

"What happened to you?" she cries against my hair.

How does she not know? It's the whole reason she was —and Clare still is—under lock and key. "Nobody told you what was going on?"

Tara steps back, shaking her head, eyes fixed on where my hand should be. "They said the king ordered further investigation of our husbands' plot. What happened to your hand?"

"An assassin bit it off," I say, more concerned with what was going on while I recovered. Especially since Tara goes pale, clearly receiving this information for the very first time. "You had no idea I was attacked?"

"No! And I don't understand...how did an assassin

bite your hand off?" She still can't take her eyes from my bandaged stump. "How could anyone possibly—"

"He was fully transformed at the time," Hannah puts in.

Tara frowns, even more confused than when she thought someone just gnawed my arm off with their regular teeth. "That's not possible."

"Apparently, it is. Which is just more trouble than we need heaped on top of this." I wonder why Tara and Clare weren't told any of this. "Didn't they question the two of you about it?"

"Is that why we were under house arrest?" Tara asks, and I think she might need to sit down before she passes out. "Did you think we had something to do with it?"

"No." The answer is automatic. "I know you didn't. But Nathan is protective. He wasn't going to take any chances."

"And given our husbands' history..." Tara does sink down to sit on one of the leather cubes. She clasps her hands together in her lap and it strikes me how fragile she truly is. She'd never planned on a life immersed in pack politics.

None of us were supposed to be here. Our father never even had council aspirations before I invoked the Right of Accord. I return, and within weeks, he's embroiled in assassination plots. Suddenly, I'm queen, and it affects everyone around me in a ripple effect of danger.

Tara's eyes are wet and pleading. "He knows, doesn't he? His Majesty knows that we didn't have anything to do with this?"

"He knows you don't have anything to do with it," I tell her. Because she wouldn't be here if he didn't believe in her innocence.

"And Clare?" Tara asks.

Hannah's gaze flicks to mine, and she supplies the answer. "Clare remains under house arrest, for now. Her Majesty receives daily briefings."

"They're treating her well?" I ask.

"They locked us in our apartments and wouldn't let us leave," she says with a nose scrunch of distaste. "But we weren't beaten or starved. We had clean towels."

"And were you permitted to speak to each other?"

"Our sitting rooms adjoin, so yes. We even had dinner together at night." She pauses. "Am I allowed to tell her what happened to you?"

"Do you believe she would relay the information to Julian somehow?" I counter.

"Never say never," Tara agrees grimly.

Hannah says, "You should tell her what happened yesterday."

"What happened yesterday?" Tara demands. "What else could possibly have happened?"

I feel her exasperation but multiplied ten-fold. "Hey, if all this is tiring to you, imagine how I feel," I remind her.

Hannah ignores me and focuses on the question at hand. "The attackers who carried out the physical violence at the coronation were all sentenced to death. And Ashton Daniels was sentenced to Lycaon's Banquet."

It takes Tara a moment to place the term. When she does, her eyes widen in horror. "I thought that was a myth. An exaggeration, at least."

"It's about to become reality," I say with a shrug.

"But it's horrifying." Tara's voice dies to a whisper. "Does the whole pack have to partake?"

"Only those who were directly involved in the planning or concealment of the riot plans," I reassure her. "But I'm sure we'll all be on hand to watch."

Tara shudders and presses a hand to her mouth but composes herself before she gags. "Bailey, how do you feel about this?"

"I feel like serious crimes deserve a serious punishment." I don't ever want to live through anything like the riot, ever again. If this deters the rest of the pack, I'll be able to sleep easier at night.

"But this is Ashton," she sputters in disbelief. "You've known him since you were children—"

"And he gutted my husband," I remind her tersely. "Ashton's pride will never allow him to stop coming for me, or Nathan. He's not going to quit trying to win. If I have to choose between his life or mine, I'll gladly remove his heart, myself."

Tara stares at me as though she's never seen me before. I don't blame her; ever since the riot, ever since I was attacked by the assassin, I don't recognize myself, either. But her disappointment and shock still sting me.

"I'll do what I can to get Clare released, too. Then, things can go back to normal," I say.

I'm not sure who I'm trying to fool with that last part.

———

I decide that Clare and Tara shouldn't have dinner together anymore while Clare is on house arrest. There must be a reason that Tara was cleared and she wasn't. I invite Tara to dine with Nathan and I. It's not an attempt to mend fences between the two of them. Nathan banished her husband and seized all their assets for the pack, leaving them cast out and penniless. That's not something I could expect her to forgive. But I want Nathan to know her, to see what she means to me, so that hopefully, no matter what her traitor spouse does, he won't punish her.

It's nearly seven when my phone chimes with a message from Hannah.

His Majesty regrets that he must cancel your dinner plans tonight.

Also, the bitch is here.

I toss my phone down in anger and storm from my office to his study.

There are raised voices inside as I approach. I hold my finger to my lips to warn the guards not to speak, and I linger just outside the door.

"You started out at ten, now where do you go from here?" Amber asks, sounding as exasperated with Nathan as I usually am.

But he sounds just as exasperated with her. "I didn't start at ten. I started at eight, perhaps—"

"You backed yourself into a corner today," she shoots back. "There is no punishment worse than Lycaon's Banquet. This is going to cause outrage in other packs. Nathan, you'll look like a tyrant!"

I shoulder past the guards and throw the door open. "I believe you're meant to address him as Your Majesty." I turn my glare at Nathan. "You need to get changed for dinner."

He sighs in exhausted irritation. "I sent a message to your assistant."

"I read it. And I don't accept it." My heart pounds as I realize that I can make the biggest scene I want, right here in front of his mistress, and he *will* choose her over me. I lost my temper and as a result, I'm going to lose face.

I'm going to be humiliated, and the anticipation of that already clouds my vision with tears.

I lash out with my embarrassment, hissing at Amber, "You failed at being queen once before. It's not your role, so keep your mouth shut on political matters when speaking to His Majesty."

"Bailey," he cautions.

"No!" I whirl back to him. "I am your mate, and I am your queen. She is the desperate climber who spreads her legs for you. I'm warning both of you, right now, that I will not lose my place here."

Way to voice your greatest fear to them while they stand there staring at you like you've completely lost control. And I have, I realize. I'm yelling because Nathan, one of the people I least like having dinner with, cancelled on dinner with me. I'm yelling because Amber, in addition to being my husband's mistress, gave voice to my anxiety when she called Nathan a tyrant. I saw that same thought expressed clearly on Tara's face earlier.

"You will release Clare from house arrest," I tell Nathan, the exhaustion of the day sapping me of my rage. "If you can't find out who sent the assassin for me, perhaps turn your attention to the one person in this room who stands to gain most from my death."

Amber gasps sharply at my accusation, but Nathan shrugs and replies calmly, "She's already been cleared."

"You investigated me?" Amber's shock is almost comical; she thought she was above suspicion, that much is plain.

Nathan doesn't answer her. "Bailey, as I said, I won't be coming to dinner. And the future, I would appreciate it if you would knock bef—"

"I would appreciate it if you'd stop vacillating between

respecting me and treating me like I'm the fucking furniture," I shout over him.

Amber moves toward the door. "I think it's time for me to leave."

"It's time for Bailey to leave," Nathan says, his jaw tight. "Amber, you and I have things we need to discuss."

I don't move.

Nathan looks up, then simply calls, "Guards?"

"Are you seriously going to have me dragged out of here?" I demand.

"Not if you leave." He's furious with me. *He* has the nerve to be furious with *me*.

I turn and go, head held high. It's bad enough the guards in the hall have heard my massive tantrum and my own mate calling to have me removed by security.

But as soon as I get back to my office, I slam the door and cry.

CHAPTER 47

I'm on the sofa in my office, my laptop on my chest, chin tucked down very attractively, I'm sure, when Nathan enters. He murmurs a dismissal to the guard at the door; Xiao hit her limit of work hours a while ago.

"What are you doing?" he asks softly.

"Watching a body language expert on YouTube." I close the lid and precariously move the laptop to the floor. I can't wait until my other arm isn't so sore that I can't use it to carry things. "Trying to learn how to catch liars."

Nathan is shirtless, wearing gray sweatpants, of all things. I assume that means he's fresh out of bed with his mistress. Or, he didn't get any and now he thinks those stupid gray sweatpants that are ridiculously flattering of the bulge region are going to tempt me.

That's not out of the question, as furious with him as I am.

He comes to the sofa and lifts up my feet, putting them in his lap when he sits. "Do you think human psychology works on werewolves?"

I raise an eyebrow. "I didn't say I was going to use it on you."

"You don't need to. I don't lie to you."

Yeah, it's so noble of you to carry on your affair openly. And to spring the crown of Greater London on me because you technically weren't lying.

"Do you think that I might be happier if you would?" I ask.

He shakes his head. "No. And I'm not saying that to make me feel better about having an affair. I think you'd be angrier if I lied to you."

"I know you're not trying to make yourself feel better," I say. "You can't feel better about something you don't feel bad about in the first place."

He looks away with a sad smile. "You might be surprised to learn how I feel about it."

"Surprise me, then." A flint of hope strikes against the steel in my heart.

It snuffs immediately when Nathan changes the subject. "It's four in the morning. Why are you still in here?"

"It's comfortable," I lie. He doesn't buy it, so I admit, "Because I'm afraid to be in my sitting room. I don't like to walk through there."

He makes a thoughtful noise. "I understand. It was difficult for me to be in the throne room today."

"It didn't show," I say, but then I remember the sweat on his brow as we left, the way he hurried to get away from me. I rise up on my useable elbow. "Was that why you took off so quickly after everything?"

"It is." He hangs his head. "I didn't want you to see me upset."

"So, I wouldn't see proof that you have emotions?" I

try to laugh it away as a joke. "Don't worry. I never suspected for a moment."

"Bailey..." he stops himself, then starts again. "I don't let people get close to me. It's nothing personal. It's not that I don't respect you or that I dislike you."

"You just don't give a shit about my feelings." I'm not going to let him get away with such a *"poor me"* answer. Even if his sadness is written on every chiseled feature. "It doesn't make me feel any better when you're aloof and cruel to me to know that you're that way with everyone. It still hurts. Your intent, how you treat other people, none of that lessens the hurt."

"You think I'm cruel to you?" His tone tells me that he doesn't want it to be true. But if he was that concerned about it, he could have altered his behavior at any point. Especially after I made it clear that he's hurt me.

"Yes. You are cruel to me. You're possessive and protective one minute, then the next you're treating some other woman like she's the queen of this pack. Going to her for advice, screwing around with her in your bed." My throat constricts and I sit up. "When I woke up from surgery, you were..." there isn't a better word for it. "Loving. You acted like you cared about me. But tonight, you acted like I was a petulant child—"

"You were quite...tantrummy."

"Yeah, I lost my temper," I admit. "I said hateful things and frankly, I misdirected my anger at Amber. She's not doing anything to hurt me. You are. And for someone that you claim not to care about. I'm worth less to you than someone you *don't care about.*" I emphasize those words so he'll hopefully understand how low, how depressed that can make a person. "You care about me in the moment.

You care about me when I'm in danger or when I'm hurt. You care about me when we're fucking."

"And you want me to care about you all the time." At least he gets it, even if it's strange that I had to explain the concept in the first place.

"Beyond just getting pissed off if someone tries to kill me? Yes. I think I would like you to care enough when a situation is making me unhappy." I don't want to mention the situation by name. "Maybe it's naive of me, but I thought you pursued me because you wanted to be with me. Not just in some symbolic way, or to breed. I thought you were interested in me. Do you realize how painful it is to hear your mate say they don't need to get to know you?"

He doesn't respond.

"When we thought you would die, I sat at your bedside for hours, hoping you would be okay. I cared about you. I *care* about you." Reality hits my brain painfully. "But you don't want me to. And you don't want to care about me."

"I ended things with Amber."

Maybe I took too many pain pills today. "Say again?"

"I ended things. It was clear tonight that you're far more troubled by her presence in my life than you first let on." A sad smile touches the corner of his mouth. "I don't want you to be lonely or sad. You don't deserve that. Your happiness matters to me, more than Amber mattered to me."

I've won. It feels hollow.

Maybe I can't trust him. Maybe he's just going to cover up his affair more cautiously. Since that's really all I wanted in the first place, I can be happy with that.

"I'm sorry for what I said before," he goes on. "About

not needing to know you. I might not need to. I'm not sure I truly know anyone. And certainly, no one knows me. But you're my mate. If not you, then who?"

"That makes sense to me," I say weakly. The connection we have makes its presence very known. It's such an opportune time; I don't want this conversation muddied with lust. "We can be a stronger team if we're not strangers who hate each other and occasionally fuck."

"You said you didn't hate me," he reminds me.

He's right. I don't hate him. I just wish I could. "There are moments when I want to. But no. I don't hate you."

"I don't hate you, either." He replies, though it's not something I was actually concerned about. I don't think I've ever given him a valid reason to hate me. He adds, "And I don't want to be cruel to you."

"Then don't be," I tell him, and I lean my head on his shoulder.

To my surprise, he rests his cheek against my forehead and inhales deeply.

His whole body goes rigid.

"What's wrong?" I ask, suddenly on full alert. "Is someone in here?"

I'm about to shout for the guards when Nathan grabs me and kisses the breath out of me. He pulls back, leaving me to reel in confusion for a moment before he kisses me again.

"What are you doing," I gasp, pushing him back with my hand against his chest. "Was this whole thing just you trying to get laid?"

"No," he says, shaking his head vehemently. But then he kisses me again.

"Stop it!" I jump to my feet and take a few steps back. "I'm serious, what the fuck are you doing?"

"You smell different," he says. "And you taste different."

I don't understand what he's getting at.

"Will you just…just trust me, all right?" He's flustered and confused, and I'm slightly concerned and turned on by the fact that he can remember how my mouth tastes just as well as I remember the taste of his. He reaches out and hooks his fingers into the waistband of my jeans, popping the button on my fly.

"Okay, I trust you, but this genuinely seems like you're trying to get into my pants. Because your hand is actually in my pants." And my panties; a gasp slips from me as he works his fingers over my slit, down to plunge into my vagina.

He withdraws his hand and sniffs his finger before sucking it clean, while I pretend to be disgusted.

I'm not disgusted. I'm confused and readying to pull my jeans off and tell him to finish what he started. Instead, I say, "Seriously, what are you doing?"

Somehow, the top half of his face remains stunned as the bottom half splits into a huge grin. "You're pregnant."

CHAPTER 48

I laugh in Nathan's face.

"I'm not joking." He laughs, but not in disbelief. He's overjoyed.

"Right." I'm not falling for it. "You can't possibly tell that from some pussy juice."

He arches an eyebrow. "I'm more than willing to check again."

I smack his shoulder. "Be serious!"

"I am being serious. Bailey, I know you inside and out, physically. You smell different, you taste different," he holds up his hands to indicate his helplessness. "I wouldn't joke about something I want so badly."

That's a good point. Nathan does want an heir. It doesn't seem like something he would joke about.

But I can't get my head around it. Not just the part where he can tell from the way I taste, but the fact that he noticed before I did. That he noticed something the thralls didn't even notice. "They did surgery on me, though. They must have tested me."

"It would have been too soon to tell," he reminds me.

"You were attacked the morning after the last time we had sex."

He's right. That would have been way too early.

Nathan pulls his phone from the pocket of his sweats and hits a button. I don't know who he's calling at four in the morning, but he's agitated and pacing in front of my desk.

I sit down on the sofa, tentatively putting my hand on my stomach. Pregnant? That can't be right. It takes a long time to get pregnant. Nathan and I haven't even had sex that many times.

But what had mother always warned? *It only takes once.*

What if I *am* pregnant?

"Rob," Nathan snaps into the phone. "It's urgent. We need a pregnancy test."

"It's not that urgent," I say with a roll of my eyes. "It can wait until morning."

Nathan frowns at me and says, "It *is* morning," and I'm not sure if he's responding to me or scolding whoever Rob is.

I think Rob might be his secretary.

"Why don't you just chill out a little," I suggest. "Let's go to bed, do a test in the morning, and see where we go from there. If I'm pregnant now, I'll still be pregnant in a few hours. Plus, it's not like we would announce it yet."

Nathan hangs up on Rob. Just hangs up, doesn't say goodbye or provide any clarification or further orders. He slips his phone back in his pocket. "Why wouldn't we announce it?"

"Because we're about to execute a bunch of people. One of those is going to be insanely gruesome." I'm not about to let our joyous news get muddled up in all that. "Do you really want our baby overshadowed by that?"

"Our baby," he says slowly, as if it only just occurred to him that a baby would be the end result of the potential pregnancy.

"Be patient," I advise him. "This isn't just about you. It's about us as family."

"And waiting to make the announcement after the executions might be a palate cleanser," he points out.

"You're forcing members of the pack to commit cannibalism. Nothing is going to make that palatable." When he doesn't have anything to say to that, I confess, "I eavesdropped on your conversation with Amber. And I hope I can say this without getting dumped, too, but... she's right."

Nathan comes back to the sofa and sits. This time, he sprawls out more, and I have to focus on the things he's saying and not get distracted by what those gray sweatpants are highlighting.

Unexplained, mystical attraction might seem hot in stories, but in real life it's super inconvenient.

"I didn't break things off with Amber because she offered her opinion. I broke things off with her because of how the relationship affected you," he reminds me. "Amber advised me on a great many issues with the pack."

Another reason it's good for her to be as gone as possible.

Nathan continues, "What you both must understand is that if I back down now, if I rescind their sentences, I look weak."

"Maybe not." I try to sit beside him without being directly in his lap, I don't get much choice, considering he's got one leg on the couch and one on the floor. It doesn't matter; the moment I sit, he pulls me closer, so I have to lay with my head on his chest and my back to his stomach. The position makes it difficult to concentrate. "What if you blamed it on me? Said that I have a weak constitution or something and I begged for mercy for those who would have to commit the actual act. I don't want mercy for Ashton, obviously. Cut his head off. But the rest of them—"

"There aren't many left," he notes. "Most of them became quite cooperative with our investigation when faced with the consequence."

"I can imagine they would, considering their choices. But what about people who genuinely don't know anything? They can't all be actually guilty, right?"

"Do you think I would mete out our pack's harshest punishment on a whim? Without concrete proof of guilt?" he's oddly defensive; the sentencing must have been more traumatic for him than I thought.

"No, I think you're too careful for that." There's no need for me to confess to my earlier misgivings about him. "But I think Amber was right. After this, there's nowhere else to go. There's no punishment that will top that one."

"Perhaps it will deter someone from doing worse, next time," Nathan says, though it sounds as if he doubts it.

"And if it doesn't? And they do something even worse?" I wave my truncated arm around a little. "Like trying to kill your wife again?"

"There's already a sentence for that," he reminds me. "But you have a point."

"Then, you'll cancel this whole gross thing?" I ask hopefully.

"No." He sighs deeply. "But I'll reduce the sentence for all but a few. It will be clear that I *can* be merciful, if I wish to be."

"And you won't look weak," I add.

"I know. I'm just repeating what Amber already proposed," he muses. "If you both think I'm wrong, then I must be."

Maybe I shouldn't be so glad that Amber is gone.

"Come on," Nathan says, gently nudging me to sit up. "Let's get you into bed."

Of course, if she were still around, Nathan wouldn't be carrying me up to my room.

———

The pack's medical center sends over a thrall first thing in the morning to draw my blood for a pregnancy test. First thing in the morning doesn't sound so bad, except I went to sleep about three hours before that.

Luckily, once they get the blood out of me, I can stumble back upstairs and into Nathan's warm, waiting embrace.

It's the second time in our entire relationship that Nathan has slept in a bed with me and still been there the next morning. Even more of a landmark, he slept in bed with me without us having sex.

I leave my robe on a chair and wriggle under the duvet, curl up against Nathan's side, and drift back to sleep.

When I wake up again, he's gone. But it's also almost noon and my phone is going berserk.

And it's Nathan.

"They're here with your results," he says, his voice a mix of anxious and thrilled all at once. "We're all in your office. We just need you."

"I'm on my way." I hop out of bed and find the fastest

clothes I can put on, a t-shirt and jeans. On my way downstairs, I'm struck by a lightning bolt of fear. Nathan is so excited. He wants this to be true so badly. What if it's not.

What if the whole change to my scent and taste thing is an indicator of a horrible disease?

What if Nathan is disappointed *and* I'm dying?

Every step is like I'm walking to the guillotine.

Xiao is waiting for me in the sitting room. She gives a quick bob of her head and a "Your Majesty" before she follows me out the door.

"Morning," I say, and make a mental note to apologize for my distracted greeting later. I don't want to be rude to the people who spend so much time serving us every day.

Nathan wasn't kidding when he'd said "we're *all*" waiting. Hannah is there with him, and Tara, as well as a thrall doctor I vaguely remember tending to me as I drifted in and out of consciousness after my amputation.

"Your Majesty," everyone but Nathan says as I enter the room.

And Nathan says, over the top of them, "She's here. What are the results?"

"Are you ready, Your Majesty?" the doctor asks me, clearly used to dealing with impatient mates.

"Yeah." I cast a glance to Hannah, the only other person in the room who's been through this part, at least, that I know of. "I think I am?"

I *think* I'm ready to hear the words that will change my life so completely, forever.

The doctor smiles. "Congratulations, Your Majesties. You're awaiting the arrival of your royal heir."

I'm off my feet and dizzy before I can register that Nathan has caught me up and swung me around. It's so out of character for him to let down his guard and show real emotion in front of his subjects that Hannah, Tara, and Xiao are visibly startled.

"This is so exciting," I babble once he sets me on my feet, though it's bizarre that I'm so amped up about something I've never seriously considered before. I didn't even know I wanted to be a mother. Then I remember the person missing from the room. "Oh my gosh, I have to go tell Clare."

Hannah and Tara share a look that I don't like.

"Not right now," Nathan says.

I put my hand on my hip. "Excuse me, she's my sister. I'm pregnant. This is the kind of news you share with your sister."

"You can't," Nathan repeats, and the crestfallen expression on his face chills me. "Because she's not here anymore."

"I don't..." I look at Hannah, and Tara.

Nathan's silver gaze swims with sorrow. "I'm so sorry. I hate that I have to tell you this. But there is evidence that your brother-in-law, Clare's husband, was a part of the assassination plot."

"We knew that already," I say with a hysterical burst of a laugh. "This is absurd. We knew that months ago—"

"The attack against you," he clarifies.

Then my whole world drops away when he adds, "And Clare may have helped."

CHAPTER 49

Despite Nathan's insistence to the contrary, I want to see Clare.

I have to see her.

Nathan tells me firmly that he's going with me, if only on the car ride. His presence is oddly touching, though I know it has more to do with protecting his pregnant mate than emotionally supporting me.

The pack's dungeons are located at the ceremonial grounds, beneath the council building. We pull up to the front doors and Nathan takes my hand. "You're sure you don't need me."

"I just need to see my sister alone," I tell him. Again.

It's not like she'd be thrilled to see him, anyway. He's the one who threw her in the dungeon.

The royal flags on the front of the car are enough to gain me immediate entrance to the building, and the first security thrall I meet inside takes me down to Clare's cell, no questions asked. I wonder if that's Nathan's doing, too.

The dungeon is exactly what the word invokes. Deep below the earth, with cold stone walls slick with mold and damp, it's probably the same foundation built by our ancestors. Pack history class taught us that during the full moon, some werewolves locked themselves in cages to prevent them from committing violence. That was before we learned to control it, before the ceremony that kept us safe and in control of our senses as we roam.

The only changes to the structure seem to be the metal bars and more hygienic plumbing. I note stainless steel toilets in the corners of the cells as we pass some of the empty ones. The ones that aren't empty, I don't glance into. I don't want to see the werewolves Nathan and I condemned.

They notice me, though. One man rushes at me, screaming, and a guard steps forward with a cattle prod that he deftly pushes through the bars. I close my eyes and take a deep breath, blocking out the furious shouts that follow me. The silence that suddenly falls is almost worse because I know it was purchased at the cost of injuring my pack mates.

They've put Clare at the end of the corridor, in a cell flanked by two guards. I dismiss them with a wave. "Leave us."

As they go, Clare doesn't react. She sits on her cot, staring at nothing. She looks like absolute hell, in limp pajamas they probably dragged her here in, and makeup still clinging to a face she hasn't been able to properly wash.

I wonder how long she's been down here. *I need to get her setting spray.*

The thought is so weird, considering what I'm here for.

She tried to kill me.

My own sister tried to kill me and I'm thinking of asking her for makeup advice like nothing has changed.

But she's my sister and I feel so much pity for her that I snap at the retreating guards, "Why doesn't she have any blankets?"

Clare still doesn't look at me, but she's the one who answers. "Because I tried to hang myself with them."

"What?" The very idea of it brings tears to my eyes.

She finally turns to me. "Bailey, I'm so sorry."

"Sorry doesn't reattach my hand," I whisper, and hold my arm up to show her.

She gasps softly.

"Did you know I survived?" I ask, keeping my tone as detached as possible. I don't want her to see how hurt I am. I'm the fucking queen. I should be angry. I should be imperious, and I shouldn't give a damn about someone who orchestrated an assassination attempt against me.

But she's my sister, and when she nods in reply, I can't sound quite so impartial with my follow-up question. "Did you know about the plan?"

Another nod, and a tear rolls down her cheek.

"Did Tara know?"

Clare shakes her head. The fact that she won't just say the words, that she won't own up to them verbally, builds a growing fury in me.

"Did you help?"

It takes her a long moment, but she nods.

"Tell me," I demand. "You owe me an explanation. Fucking speak! What did you do, specifically, to help your husband try to murder me?"

Her voice is barely a whisper. "I told him about the layout of the residence. I told him what your schedule is."

"Was I the only target?" That's what I can't figure out. I just became queen. I don't have much power.

"You were," she admits, looking down at her hands.

Yeah, you've got two of them. Must be fucking nice.

"Why?"

"Because there are forces at work greater than your husband's ambitions. And because with you gone, Amber Rogers could be queen again." The answer cuts so deep because I know in my heart that it's true.

It's confirmation that Nathan loved Amber. Loves her, maybe. It's confirmation that politics alone made me his mate.

He never wanted me.

I knew that, though. I knew he was attracted to me because of the weird bond we have. I knew he thought I was different, somehow, that I was like him because we both invoked the Right of Accord. But that's all there is.

He's never going to love me.

The thought almost brings me to my knees. I didn't realize I even hoped for him to love me.

And now, my sister, who's *supposed* to love me, who I *thought* loved me, has tried to have me killed.

"They're going to keep coming for you," Clare continues, "It's not your fault."

"Because of these ominous 'greater forces?'" I snap.

"Yes." She shrugs helplessly. "If you and Nathan never mated, you wouldn't be in danger."

"No shit?" I laugh in disbelief. "You were willing to kill me. Your own sister," I hope she feels as much disgust toward herself as I do.

"My allegiance is to the pack, first and foremost," she says. "And you know that you're not good for us. You were never prepared to rule. And your response to the riot, your anger in its wake—"

"They tried to kill me!" I shout. "Do you not understand what that means? I never wanted the throne. It's not something I ever thought I could aspire to. This happened to me. Others made this decision for me. Every part of my life has been decided ahead of time, and you were going to decide how much life I get to have?"

"You're a traitor to your pack, Bailey." Clare sounds tired of carrying the burden of that opinion. "You left. You thought you had the luxury of choice. You thought of yourself before you thought of the good of the pack and look at where it led!"

"You put the good of the pack over your sister's life," I snap back. "Look at where it led!"

"I would rather be in this hole than in your palace," she says. There's no anger in it. Just truth.

"Julian will be executed for this, you know," I tell her. As if the thought hasn't already crossed her mind.

"Your husband already sentenced him—"

"His Majesty, King Nathaniel of the Toronto pack," I correct her. "You're in no position to express familiarity."

She doesn't revise her statement. "And me. I've received my sentence."

My blood freezes in my veins, not just due to the chill and damp of the stones enclosing us. My sister is going to die. Yes, she tried to kill me. She chose a woman she doesn't even know over me, to replace me in my mate's bed. To put my mate's mistress on my throne.

It hurts far worse to learn that my own sister prefers Amber to me than it ever hurt coming from Nathan.

"He's going to have you executed?" I ask.

"I'm to be a guest of honor at Lycaon's Banquet," she says bitterly. "And then I'll be executed."

My stomach drops. "And Julian?"

"Julian has fled. He's under the protection of the Saint-Laurent pack."

My mind reels with all sorts of plans. I could aid her in escape. She could flee to Quebec. They could protect her. They—

They won't stop trying to steal our pack. They won't stop until we crush them.

I'll only be delaying the inevitable. We would have to inflict Lycaon's Banquet on the pack again. It will make Nathan and I look even more like blood-thirsty monsters.

"He left without you," I state flatly.

Another silent nod.

"I brought you out of exile," I remind her. "I brought you back so you could be with me and Tara. Your family. Your mate is a traitor to his pack and now he's betrayed you, as well."

Her head drops and her back shakes with silent sobs.

"I hope it was worth it." I turn and start to walk away, and Clare lurches from the cot to grab the bars of her cell.

"You are my sister!" she shouts after me. "You can't let him do this!"

I turn to face her, pushing all my emotions down so deep, even she, who has known me my entire life, won't see the storm of anguish raging in my heart. "No. I'm your enemy."

I turn away, my legs unsteady but my feet lead, growing heavier with every step as Clare calls my name until the heavy iron doors of the dungeon clang shut behind me.

CHAPTER 50

The full moon has arrived. She brings death with her.

The ceremonial grounds are somber; the pack hasn't seen an execution in centuries, let alone one of this scale. Every adult pack member is in attendance, gathered on stands erected around the open curve of the ceremonial building. Nathan struck down the condition that *every* member attend. He felt there was no reason for children to view the carnage of the proceedings.

The mates of the condemned are squeezed into a separate set of risers, a box constructed below the observation balcony. They have to watch. They need to see what their mates' treachery has wrought. And they've been positioned where the rest of the pack can see their anguish. Where everyone will watch them watching their mates die.

I spared our parents. They won't have to watch Clare die.

Nathan, Tara, and I are the only ones who look down from the mezzanine, though Tara's chair is behind and slightly to the right of mine. It keeps her from viewing the grounds She doesn't need to see our sister executed. She did nothing wrong, and she's as destroyed by Clare's betrayal as I am.

Nathan sits to my left, close enough that he can hold my remaining hand if I need the support. It's cold comfort, considering I'm about to watch my sister die. But at least, I know someone is on my side.

The monoliths to Fenrir and Lupa are covered with blood-red cloth, as if to hide our actions tonight from their gazes. But Lycaon's stone is wreathed in garlands of wolf's bane and anointed with blood. The pack is certain to feel his favor now.

I hope. Because at this point, Nathan and I need the gods on our side.

Acolytes move around the circle, swinging their censers and filling the night air with plumes of incense that carry our intentions to the moon, and to Lycaon in the spirit world. They're dressed in red robes and wearing black gas masks; the Wolf's Bane they burn will poison their human bodies.

The Hierophant is likewise masked, but wearing black robes embroidered with glimmering purple aconitum flowers. He asperges the circle with water flicked from a bundle of aconitum in his gloved hand.

A round scaffold stands over the pit where the ceremonial fire usually blazes. To compensate for the lack of light, shallow bowls of burning oil hang from posts around the perimeter of the huge circular platform.

The executions will take place before Lycaon's Banquet. The air is charged with fear and anticipation as the condemned are led into the circle. I expected cries of grief from the women in the stand below us, but there are none. I do note the way the heads of the condemned turn to seek out their mates; one man mouths something I believe is, "It'll be all right."

How terrible it must feel for one's last words to be a lie.

I think about Clare. I wonder if Julian lied to her in the same way.

If I start to feel sympathy for her now, I'll never survive the night.

There's shockingly little ceremony involved in the actual killing. Death is an unnatural thing to werewolves; we're so used to living for centuries, enjoying good health, and rarely falling victim to accidents. Maybe this ritual is so short because we don't want to confront the truth of what will happen before our eyes. We will see death take those we once counted as pack members.

Nathan gestures to the executioner, a hooded thrall whose face is also hidden by his gas mask. The hulking figure takes an impossibly huge sword, practically a guillotine's blade, from an acolyte as the first traitor is marched to the block. There are no final words. No moment of reflection. The thralls force the man to his knees, his head into the cradle of the block. They hold his arms clear, and the executioner brings down the blade. It's that simple. In one stroke, the deed is done, and the headsman whips the blood from his sword.

The first one stuns me. Someone's decapitated head rolling around, their blood spraying from their neck, quickly slowing to the chug of wine from the mouth of a spilled bottle, seems fake. It's incomprehensible. Heads don't come off.

The second one hammers home the reality, as one of the mates below us screams when the blade falls. That man's face stares up at us, his mouth still working in shock for a moment that feels like eternity.

By the third and fourth, I know that my lack of reaction to the scene is a sign of trouble to come. I should be horrified, unable to look.

What's become of me, that I'm willing to stay and see this horror, but do nothing to stop it.

The condemned men don't look so brave anymore as they wait. Some have tears in their eyes. Some shake. If I turn away from the scene, I will appear weak. The pack will think I don't have the courage to follow through with Nathan's orders. We're a unified force. *We* run the pack.

But I can't watch. I let my eyes lose their focus and concentrate on the flame of a lamp at the edge of my view, instead.

Fifteen men fall beneath the executioner's cleaver. Fifteen bodies are stacked in a cart the thralls pull away, with fifteen heads stacked on top.

Some members of the pack have gotten sick. Some have fainted. There are intermittent shouts and screams of grief.

You have to do this, I remind myself. *You can't let them take this pack from you. You can't let them hurt you, or Nathan, or your child. Never again.*

When the bodies have been cleared away and the scaffold mopped clean of blood, they bring out a long table and three sturdy chairs with manacles on the arms. Of the three prisoners marched into the circle, I recognize only one.

Clare holds her head high. She lays her hands willingly on the arms of the chairs and makes no move to resist as they clamp the metal bands around her wrists.

And she never looks away from me.

As thralls bring Ashton into the circle, the Hierophant addresses Lycaon's monolith, his words muffled by his respirator. "We honor you, Lycaon, with this traitor's flesh, consumed by those who would harm your children. Let them play the part of the treacherous Zeus, who struck you not with a curse, but a gift for generations. This sacrifice, we offer up to you."

"Blessed Lycaon," murmurs the crowd reverently, though reluctantly.

I thought I would be more concerned about Ashton. That I would revel in his death, in my final triumph over him. But now, all I see is the instrument of my sister's torture. I don't want her to have to defile herself breaking the pack's greatest taboo.

But I don't know what to do with all the hurt I'll carry forever, knowing that my own sister didn't care if I died. Knowing that she might do it again.

The executioner makes quick, anticlimactic work of Ashton's head. Then, the Hierophant moves forward with a dish and a knife. He slits Ashton's blood-soaked shirt up the back and carves a slab of flesh away; it steams in the chill air.

I thought I would enjoy watching Ashton butchered in front of my eyes.

I don't feel anything.

The Hierophant cuts a bite of the raw meat and skewers it with the tip of the knife. He puts it to Clare's mouth. Sick rises up my throat as she takes the bite, chews, and swallows.

"I'm going to throw up," I whimper, barely moving my lips.

"You're not," Nathan replies, equally stiff-faced. "You can do this. You're the queen of this pack and you deserve justice."

Destroying the Saint-Laurent pack, that would be

justice. Not having my sister ripped away from me. Not having to watch this horror.

"This isn't justice." I don't bother to hide my words now. "My family and my pack have been torn apart, and all due to the meddling of the Saint-Laurent pack."

"Are you proposing some kind of revenge?" he asks, still staring straight ahead.

"I propose we'll start with the Saint-Laurent pack," I say in a low voice, for Nathan's ears only. "They're a threat to us. They can submit or be destroyed. Then, we move on to Manhattan."

He turns his head, just a little, towards me, never taking his eyes off the gory spectacle below. "What do you mean?"

"I mean, we're going to create the strongest empire our kind have ever seen."

But I'll need help with that one. I seek out Amber's presence in the crowd. As much as I detest the thought of bringing her back into our lives, she'll be useful. She knows the Manhattan pack, has contacts there. And after tonight, she won't cross me ever again. And I can always discard her, after, if need be.

"Trust me," I whisper back to him. "Trust my instincts, and we can rule the world."

And Nathan reaches over to take my hand. "If you want the world, then you will have it."

I sit back, head held high, as Clare is marched to the block.

I raise my hand in signal to the executioner.

I feel nothing when the blade falls.

CHAPTER 51

My sister is dead.

I take a sip from my mug and stare across the kitchen.

It's after midnight. The last of the thralls that work down here have left for the night. No one is around.

No one except Xiao, who stands patiently by the door while I nurse my mug of tea in silence.

I'm sure she prefers the silence to the crying I sometimes do.

It's been a week since the full moon. Since I killed my sister.

The most difficult part of grieving Clare is the knowledge that she knew someone would kill me. She was willing to sacrifice my life for her mate's ambition. Or his revenge.

Would she have grieved me? Would she have felt this same guilt?

Xiao says something, but it's into the communication device on her wrist. She keeps her voice low, and I can't hear what's going on. It could be that Nathan is looking for me; he's been bossy and clingy since finding out about my pregnancy.

Of course, when I wanted him to give a damn about me, he was distant. Now, when all I need is space, he's constantly fussing over me.

"Your Majesty, Tara has returned. She'd like to see you," Xiao says quietly. "Should I say you've gone to bed?"

"No." I shake my head and chew my thumbnail. Tara went to inform our parents of Clare's death. I thought I should go, but Nathan outright forbid any contact.

"If your brother-in-law was a part of the assassination attempt against me and the attempt on your life, how do we know your father wasn't involved?" Nathan asked while we argued about it, and while the thought of my own parents attempting a hit job sounded absurd at the time, it's pretty unbelievable that Clare would have, either.

I get up from my chair and put the kettle on one of the gas burners in case Tara wants tea. She might not be stopping in for a chat, I remind myself. Maybe I shouldn't hand her a cup of boiling water until I know she's not going to throw it at me. We haven't spoken since the night of the executions, just before Nathan and I got into the royal limo. She pleaded for mercy I didn't grant.

I'm surprised she returned at all.

She enters the kitchen a short time later, in jeans and a hoodie from traveling. Something she wouldn't have been caught dead in unless she was exhausted.

"Tea?" I ask, gesturing to the stove.

She shakes her head. "I'm going to bed. I thought I would check in with you, first."

I frown, puzzled. "To see if you were allowed?"

"No, to tell you what's happening with our parents."

She's exasperated and tired and probably could have left the briefing until morning. The fact that she didn't suggests she has a lot to say to me.

And it's probably not going to be great to hear.

"How are Mother and Father?" I ask, taking the kettle off the burner before I sit down across the big, industrial island from her. "Where are they, for that matter?"

"They're in an apartment. A studio apartment. Living off money the Parks gave them." Tara fixes me with piercing gaze. "But it's unlikely any help will continue, now."

It doesn't take much to fill in the blanks. "People are afraid to have anything to do with traitors anymore."

Tara nods and I know she's somehow interpreted my words as a statement of regret.

They're not. "Good. That was the point. To deter people from committing treason."

"Have you ever considered that people might have had a good reason to go against the King?" she asks sharply.

"I can't see there ever being a good reason to kill your pack leader." I'm tempted to do it all the time, but I'm his mate and I have to deal with him on a daily basis. "This isn't a conversation we should have, though."

"Because you'll kill me?"

"Is that what you really think of me?" I ask, but just her asking the question tells me all I need to know. "You think I would just murder you for no reason?"

"I don't know what you'd do," she says flatly. "I didn't think Clare would try to kill you. I didn't realize that was the kind of relationship we all had."

"We don't have that relationship," I state firmly. "I don't believe Clare would have gone along with any of this if she hadn't been influenced by Julian. She knew I was going to be killed, Tara. Did she tell you about it?"

"No!" Tara's eyes go wide with fear.

"I'm not interrogating you," I reassure her. "I'm tired of passing sentences and uncovering plots. I don't ever want to see what I saw the other night, ever again."

"It must have been so hard for *you*," she snaps.

I almost snap back that it *was* harder for me, that I did her a mercy by not seating her with the rest of the pack, where she would have had no choice but watch. But lording my power over her won't help us in this moment. It won't repair our trust.

"Meanwhile," she goes on, "I'm the one who had to go to Mother and Father and tell them that the rumors they'd heard were true. That their daughter was dead. That their other daughter killed her."

"Did you happen to mention that Clare tried to kill me first?" *Are you really pulling a "she started it?"* I fold my arms over my chest. "That she was part of an assassination plot engineered by her mate?"

"I did. Because they deserve the whole truth." Her head droops, her shoulders sag. "You know, I never thought Mother liked us very much. We were never good enough—especially Clare. But if you'd heard her, the way she screamed…"

I don't want to think about it. I haven't had much time to process the fact that I'm currently a mother, myself, despite not having met my baby yet. But its presence has consumed me with thoughts of death, how vulnerable we all are, how protected my child is now, before it faces the world.

I don't want to imagine the depths of grief my mother

feels for Clare, because I don't want to imagine that it could happen to me.

"Why did you hold Clare responsible for this?" Tara asks. It's not the first time she's asked. She begged me, just before Nathan and I got into the car to go to the ceremonial grounds, to reconsider Clare's part in it. To see that it wasn't truly my sister behind the attack. She tries again, as if it will somehow change everything that's passed. "It was Julian who orchestrated all of it."

But even though Clare hadn't planned the assassination, she never thought to warn me. "You're right. It wasn't Clare who planned it. But she went along with it. She chose to side with her mate over her sister."

"Like you did."

The accusation crumples something inside me. I did allow Nathan to put Clare to death. Worse, I let him sentence her to Lycaon's Banquet. I never intervened. Maybe I could have saved her.

Maybe I didn't want to.

"You're right," I say, drawing myself up straight. "I did stand by Nathan's decision to execute Clare. Because that's what we're supposed to do, isn't it? We're supposed to obey our mates. It's been driven into our heads since we were little girls. So, if what Clare was doing was right, what I did was right, too. And you can't blame me for it."

"I can blame you for it all I want," Tara shoots back, and it's such a childish retort I almost laugh.

"How can you forgive her for trying to kill me?" I demand. "Yeah, she's your sister. But I'm your sister, too. Why is it okay for her and not for me?"

"Because she's the one who's actually dead, Bailey!" Tara shouts, standing so abruptly, her stool tips over.

From the corner of my eye, I see Xiao's hand move to

the taser at her hip. I gesture sharply to her to stand down, and she does, but slowly.

"She's the one who's dead," Tara repeats. "And you're the one who was too good for this life, and for this pack. You're the one who left. And now, you think you deserve some kind of understanding from me? Clare was there! She didn't blow off her whole life and run away on an adventure, then come back and suddenly start chopping people's heads off!"

"Stop it!" I shout at her. I hate that Tara's grief has changed the way she feels about me. Or maybe it hasn't; maybe it's just revealed her true feelings about me. It's unfair for me to demand that she forgive me, but my heart is a greedy, wounded thing in my chest. I want her to be on my side. I want to have something, at least, from before my life became a game of politics that I have to win or risk being murdered.

"Stop it," I repeat, softer. "She tried to have me killed, Tara. My fucking hand got bitten off."

"I see." Tara nods, her face twisted in a spiteful scowl. "It's different for you. It's always different for you. You don't have to conform to rules and tradition. You're special. And because you're so fucking special, I don't have a right to grieve our sister."

"I never said that—"

"Tell it to your mate, oh perfect wife," she spits, and turns to leave the room.

Xiao steps in front of her to prevent her leaving; no one just walks out on the queen.

"Let her go," I say, barely a whisper, and Xiao moves aside.

When Tara's gone, I repeat, "Let her go," and add, "back to our parents, for all I care. Back to her stupid mate."

"Your Majesty," Xiao begins, soft and hesitant. I make a noise of acknowledgment and she continues, "May I speak frankly?"

I nod, but I'm so tired, I'm not sure I'll even register what she has to say.

"Your sister might not understand the difference, but I do. Clare had a choice. She could have defied her mate. But you can't."

I understand that, and I'm trying to think of a nice way to tell her that I'm stupid, when she adds:

"Because of the binding."

That perks up my interest. "What are you talking about?"

"The binding," she says again, blinking her dark eyes in confusion. "The spell that's on you and His Majesty the King."

I stare at her blankly, but my brain works frantically inside my skull.

"You… didn't know about the binding?" she asks. "I thought you'd be able to feel it."

"Is it a weird connection that constantly makes me want to jump on his dick no matter what else is going on or how I'm feeling about him as a person at the time?" The words roll out on a numb tide of disbelief.

"That's the one," she confirms.

I get to my feet a little too quickly. It's that, I assume, and not the cluster bomb of totally bananas news I just got, that totally blacks the room out as I fall to the floor.

CHAPTER 52

Be nice, I implore silently as Nathan stares Xiao down across his desk. I sit beside him, close enough that I can feel how tense he is. It makes me want to give him a neck rub in sympathy. And sympathy for Nathan isn't my default.

"It's not a common spell." Xiao is in the middle of explaining *"everything"* as Nathan demanded. She's remarkably cool under pressure; Nathan isn't just the king of the pack, but he holds power over thralls, as well. But she delivers the facts like she's teaching a class. "Thralls use it sometimes when the spark is going out of a relationship or, in more unscrupulous cases, to trick someone into a relationship with them."

"And you practice this magic on werewolves? Without our permission?" Nathan growls.

"I've never heard of it before, but I've trained in defensive magic and combat, not love spells," she replies.

"Why didn't you mention this to us before?" I wonder aloud. "Why haven't any of the thralls mentioned it?"

"I can only speak for myself, but I thought you were aware of it." Xiao shrugs. "If I had known—"

"You couldn't have," I assure her quickly.

"The hierophant should have." Nathan's hand closes to a fist on the desktop. He reaches over and hits the intercom button. Rob, dragged from his sleep by his demanding royal boss, answers in what sounds like slow motion. Nathan barks back at him, "The hierophant. All his acolytes. I want them taken to council chambers at once—"

I reach over and slap my hand down on the button. "No. It can wait until morning."

Nathan's eyes narrow.

"Tell him," I insist. "And we don't need acolytes. The fewer people who know about this, the better."

With an exasperated exhalation, Nathan hits the button again. "Scratch that. Have the hierophant *summoned* to the council chambers first thing in the morning."

Good. We've had enough of black vans and midnight condemnations.

A thought occurs to me. "Is there any way to tell who put the binding on us?"

"I'm sure there is," Xiao answers. "But it would have to be someone far more acquainted with magic than I am."

"That's a good question for the hierophant," Nathan tells me, so I file it away in my brain and hope I remember.

Because it's so easy for something like, "who put a spell on me" to slip one's mind. I silence my internal critic.

Nathan turns back to Xiao. "Thank you, for your help in the matter. And for the excellent care that you've show the Queen."

"It's my honor, Your Majesties."

"You're relieved for the night. The queen and I will

retire." He gives me a raised eyebrow. "She's clearly very tired and not resting as much as she should."

Great. Now, I'm going to get bitched at for fainting.

"Yes, Your Majesty." Xiao stands and bows, then leaves the room. Nathan motions the thralls at the door to follow suit.

"You'll sleep in my room, tonight," he says, not really offering me a choice.

I don't mind sleeping with him. He's warm and good to snuggle and the connection between us, the *binding*, apparently, gives me all sorts of giddy, sexy feelings when I'm around him.

But I do like to challenge him, just to keep him aware that I'm not an employee. "What if I don't want to sleep with you?"

"Then I suppose you can go on staying up until all hours of the night, endangering yourself and our child," he says cheerfully, opening the secret passage bookcase to reveal the stairs that lead up to his room.

"I was going to stay with you, anyway," I tell him, and go up the stairs ahead of him.

Knowing that the connection Nathan and I feel for each other is a trick doesn't lessen its power. I can't take my eyes off him as he starts to undress.

I sit on the end of the bed and toe off my pumps. "I can't help but notice that you're lecturing me about getting enough rest, but you're still wearing the same clothes you wore to work today."

He doesn't look up from unbuttoning his shirt. "So are you."

"But I'm not scolding anyone." I lean back with my hand braced on the mattress.

"I can't believe they would do this," he mutters under

his breath, pulling his arms from his sleeves. The muscles of his big shoulders and broad back ripple as he tosses the shirt aside.

"It's fucked up," I agree, admiring the way his fore-arms flex as he unbuckles his belt. "But think about it… would we have ended up here if not for the binding? I mean, your personality is a real turn off. Basically, all that's keeping me here is the magic dick spell."

He stops pacing to face me. "You're accidentally making a good point. We wouldn't be together if not for the spell. You wouldn't be queen. You'd have two hands."

"You don't know that. I can be clumsy sometimes. It might have been inevitable." When he doesn't go along with my joke, I point out, "I wouldn't be pregnant with your child."

"You might have been. I'm magnetically attractive without the spell, and you're naturally very appealing." He chuckles, but then turns somber. "Bailey… your sister wouldn't be dead. Doesn't that make you angry?"

Apoplectically so, but my anger won't fix anything. "I'm angry that we've been manipulated. I'm angry that we've been used, and we have no idea why. But I have to look at the positives or I won't be able to get up in the mornings.

"I've lost everything. I'm not going to sacrifice the joy I still have." I shrug helplessly and rise, gesturing over my shoulder. "Get my zipper, please?"

He steps behind me and unzips my dress slowly, his big hands returning to my shoulders. "At least, we can rule out a few potential culprits. Ashton Daniels, for example."

"His whole family," I add. "They were fully dedicated

to gaining whatever advantages they thought I'd bring as their daughter-in-law."

"What about your parents?" He pushes the wide straps of my dress down my arms and brushes my ponytail aside to kiss the back of my neck. "Your mother was a social climber. Do you think she might have set her sights on—"

"I don't know when she would have had time. I got back into town on the night of the ball, and I was already…" Ugh, I hate to admit it, because I know he's going to be so proud of himself. "I was super into you literally the moment I laid eyes on you."

"You were?" There's that egotistical grin. I can't see it, facing away from him, but I hear it in his voice.

"Oh, you know I was." I roll my eyes. "You admitted feeling it that night, too."

He leans down to whisper against my ear, "Oh, I did."

The binding thrums between us, and he deftly pops the hooks fastening my bra. His hands slide under the dress, snaking around the front to splay over my belly. "I had the most intense dream of you riding me in my office chair—"

"Will you stop being a distraction? This is incredibly serious." I swat his hands down and he reluctantly takes them out of my dress. Facing him, I hold the fabric to my chest so as not to be a distraction, myself. "If we were already under the influence of the binding, it's something that either can be done very quickly or snuck into a person's food, or it happened to me in London. And since you very clearly know people in the Greater London pack, *King Nathaniel,* I would guess it happened to you there, too."

"But what could the purpose possibly be?" he wonders aloud. "You said they weren't aware of you."

"I said that they had no contact with me," I correct him.

"That doesn't mean they weren't aware of me. But I have no idea why they'd want us together."

His expression darkens as he stares off in thought. "I feel like I've been played with. I don't like it."

"We've both been played with." I pause, though. "Right? Both of us? This isn't something you're lying to me about?"

"I appreciate your faith in my acting skills, but no. You knew about the spell before I did." He gestures to my head. "Unless you forgot when you collapsed."

He goes to the bed and pulls back the covers while I step out of my dress and pop my earrings out with one hand. It's easier than getting them in that way, but I'm proud I figured them both out so quickly.

"I didn't collapse," I protest. "I fainted. Which is a completely normal thing for pregnant werewolves to do in the first trimester."

He makes a "hmm" noise that suggests he still doesn't believe me.

"The medic said so," I add. "You have to stop being so paranoid, okay? I'm young and I'm healthy and I'm going to be fine."

Unless I die or the baby dies or both of us die. I shut those thoughts down as best as I can; they'll still run on a constant loop in my mind but at least they'll just be background noise.

"I'll stop being paranoid when people stop trying to kill us," is all he says. He takes off his trousers and boxers and tosses them both aside before climbing naked beneath the duvet. "Now get over here. You're keeping me awake, looking like that."

I snort a laugh and shuck my bra and panties, though I'm not sure getting more naked is going to be less interesting to him. When I slide the band out of my hair and give it a shake to loosen my scalp, he audibly groans.

"The first thing I'm going to do in the morning is fuck your brains out," he declares as I get into the bed beside him. His strong arm catches me around my waist and draws me into the protective curve of his body.

I wriggle around to face him. It always stuns me how handsome he is close up. It seems unfair that a person would look fantastic from all angles and distances. "There's another thing we know for sure about the binding."

"Hmm?" He yawns and he even somehow looks hot doing that.

"Well, I'm already pregnant and we still want to go at it like squirrels." I giggle against his neck. "So, we know it's not about breeding."

CHAPTER 53

"It's about breeding."

I blink in horror at the Hierophant's words. The last thing I want a room of strangers thinking about is *that*. On the other hand, at least two people in the room saw it in progress at our mating ritual.

My face gets hot.

We're in the council chamber, but thankfully, there's no audience, and only two members of the council. They're both tall, dignified looking gentleman with transparent white hair and liver-spotted caucasian skin. They're on a subcommittee that handles thrall-werewolf relations, a thing I didn't realize existed. I just assumed we all got along like one big, happy symbiote.

The hierophant being here is surreal. I've never met him one-on-one, even now that I'm queen, and I've never seen him wearing just regular clothes and not his ceremonial garb. He wears glasses, too, with thick, red rims. They add an extra, wholly superfluous, air of authority to him.

"Pardon me?" Nathan asks, leaning slightly forward. We're all seated around a large, round table, as equals. It's fascinating to watch him in this dynamic, seeing him not in charge of anything.

"Whoever placed this binding on you and the queen meant for you to breed. That's the only purpose of it. It isn't a love spell—"

"No shit," I say, before I can stop myself.

The Hierophant isn't amused. He continues, "And it's not meant to alter your fates. The point of it is to make sure you that the two of you procreate."

"But we did procreate." I gesture at my stomach.

The Hierophant smiles slightly, and I remember that we haven't announced my pregnancy yet. "Congratulations are in order, then?"

"Yes. But we won't be making an official announcement until the next full moon. I would appreciate your discretion, gentlemen." Nathan is sure to meet the eyes of the other three around the table. I'm not sure there would be any consequences for disobeying him, but that means neither are they. Our secret is probably safe.

"My point was," I begin again, fully wanting to curl up and die in a hole rather than say this in front of these strange men, "it's not gone. It's still...doing its thing, if you get my drift."

The two council members shift uncomfortably. One clears his throat.

But the Hierophant is unbothered by the comment. "The effect might fade over the course of the pregnancy. It might not. This type of binding is an ancient magic. It's unrefined."

"Obsolete?" Nathan suggests.

The Hierophant spreads his hands. "It clearly still has some use."

"But we don't know who's using it—using *us*," I revise, "—or why. And that's my main concern."

"It's a great concern for all of us, Your Majesty," one of the near-identical councilmen says.

"Uh-huh." Nathan leans his chin on his hand, rubbing his index finger over his lower lip. "And is the spell put on us, specifically? Or could it have been put on me and it simply found Bailey and made her the target?"

"It could have been the other way around," I grumble. "Maybe they put the spell on me, and it got you."

"Why would they have put the spell on you?" Nathan asks, growing annoyed with me. "I'm the king of this pack, you were a runaway."

"Fine," I snap back. "Maybe they put the spell on you and I'm just so beautiful and interesting that the spell *chose* me!"

"It would have to be placed specifically on *both* of you," the Hierophant confirms, raising his voice over our spat. "And I assume whoever placed the spell on you would have had to have access to both of you within a fairly short time span."

"Then it had to be in London, right?" Suspicion confirmed. "When was the last time you were in London before you met me?"

"It had been over a year," Nathan says.

The Hierophant shook his head. "I doubt a spell so archaic could have remained uncompleted for that long and still been effective."

"That just leaves the ride home from the airport and a day in my parents' house," I point out. "Not a lot of time to do a spell."

But there had been stylists and thralls delivering dresses.

"I'm so dumb," I blurt. I glance between all four of the men around the table. "There were people in and out of the house that day. My mom had a stylist, my dad had someone dropping off his tailoring. I had my hair done…"

"Is there a reason you can think of that your parents might have wanted you mated to the King?" the other white-haired guy asks.

Nathan answers for me. "They wanted me dead. They counted on it, in fact. If they hadn't been caught, she'd be mated to Ashton Daniels."

"And my parents were social climbers, but I know for a fact they would never have picked me to be a queen," I explain. "If they were going to put any of their daughters on the throne, it would have been Clare."

There's a strange tinge of bitterness to my words that stings my heart. Was I jealous of Clare all those years? Sure, sometimes, when she glided through her teen years like a swan and I struggled through awkward phase after awkward phase. But I love her, and I haven't had a reason to envy her since I got back. I never wanted to envy her.

I blink back sudden tears, outraged that they'd dare make an appearance. I can't cry in front of these men, who already think I'm weak because I have a uterus.

"It would have had to have been someone in the house that day," Nathan agrees, ignoring the sudden change in my mood that I know he can sense. Everything in the connection between us is screaming out for him to hold me. I feel a little bad for him, knowing how strong that protective instinct is and how difficult it must be for him to fight it.

"Or, it could have been thralls in another pack working with thralls here," the Hierophant suggests gravely.

"She was in London," one of the councilmen reminds

us all. "And there's no denying that the King has connections there."

Nathan's expression turns to eerie stone. "I hope you aren't suggesting I had something to do with this."

"Of course not." The confidence in the man's answer is proof enough that he's telling the truth. "But it's not impossible for those connections to connect with others in this pack."

"That's a good point," I say quietly, hoping it will disperse some of the sudden tension.

Nathan nods slowly, but there's still an air of warning about him. "How many Greater London representatives are on your subcommittee?"

"None at present," the other council member answers. "We're still awaiting some final reassignments."

"Good." Nathan drums his fingers on the table. "Keep them off. And keep everything we've spoken about here off the record, and completely secret. If news of the binding leaks, I'll know who leaked it."

"Should we proceed with an investigation?" the other councilman asks.

Nathan shakes his head. "No. The queen and I will discuss how to handle this, for now. Hierophant, I would also ask you to treat this with the utmost secrecy."

"You may rely upon me," the man replies in his deep, serious voice.

"If you can do so without giving anything away, try to find out more about this binding spell," Nathan tells the Hierophant. "If it's ever been used on royals before, what the results were. If there's ever been anything specific written regarding an ethical stance."

"You wish to know if working such magic breaks our pacts," the Hierophant states plainly.

Nathan nods. "I do."

"I must caution Your Majesties," the Hierophant says. "Thralls will not be dealt with in the same way you dealt with the werewolves who betrayed you. You're both very young. You don't remember what happened the last time our peoples disagreed."

Very young? Nathan is like, in his forties.

That's not the point, Bailey, I scold myself. "Are you talking about the Great Breach? That was like, a hundred years ago."

The Hierophant smiles with serene malice, like a shark in a great mood. "I remember it well."

Thralls live as long as we do? That's the first time I've heard of such a thing.

If the information takes Nathan by surprise, he doesn't show it. "Are you threatening me?"

"Not at all." The Hierophant sits more comfortably in his chair. "I'm being diplomatic. If something even half as complicated as the Great Breach occurs, even I won't be able to control the thralls."

So, the Hierophant must have some kind of leadership power over the thralls, as well as religious influence over us. That's interesting and probably something I needed to know way before now.

"I'll keep that in mind," Nathan says. He taps my knee under the table to indicate we're leaving. When he pushes his chair back, I do, too, and I stand awkwardly aside while the men all shake hands.

I'm queen of the pack, but I'm still just an incubator standing nearby for them to venerate. I don't stick around to acknowledge their bows, slipping my arm through Nathan's as we leave them.

I wait until we're in the car to ask him, "So, if you don't

want them to investigate this, what's your plan?"

"I'm not sure yet," he admits, reaching absently for my hand. "But I know where we'll start."

I squeeze his fingers. "Great, where do we start?"

"London," he replies. "We're going to London."

CHAPTER 54

The pack has a private plane, a sleek, elegant jet that can whisk us to London within the hour. I barely have time to pack anything. Nathan suggests we leave immediately and just buy what we need when we arrive, but the thought of leaving without even a toothbrush makes me panic, so he relents, and we go back to Aconitum Hall so I can put together a bug-out bag.

I don't even have time to brief Hannah or Tara on the situation before we're off to the airport.

"So, tell me where I can sit on this plane that you haven't fucked your mistress?" I say as we climb the airstairs.

Coming up behind me, he makes a noise like he's thinking really hard. "You might be able to swap seats with the flight attendant."

I resist the temptation to shove him down the stairs.

"I'm joking," he says as I reach the top and turn to glare at him. He drops a kiss on my forehead. "I promise."

I'm not sure I believe him.

When we enter, he has to duck down. "I've never even been on this jet."

"Haven't you been king for a while now?" I definitely don't believe that he's never been on here. "You just went to England like two months ago. Remember? On our honeymoon that I didn't go on?"

"That was personal business. I flew charter. I would never misappropriate pack funds."

Now, I believe him. Nathan is a dick in a lot of ways, but he's not a thief.

A flight attendant appears and offers to take our jackets, and I wander further into the jet. It's not as big as a commercial airplane, but it's so much more luxurious. The seats are like armchairs and there's an honest-to-goodness couch across from an entertainment console with a flatscreen television.

"It's like a tiny living room," I say, more than a little charmed. Then I notice the royal seal on a door toward the back. "What's in there?"

"I assume it's the royal bedchamber." Nathan comes my way and there's not a lot of space to squeeze past him, so I just move to the door head of him and open it up. Sure enough, there's a cozy bed you have to squeeze by to get to the nicest airplane bathroom I've ever seen. It's still small, but it's not all beige and stainless steel. The whole interior of the jet is done up in sleek gray tones with dark wood accents, nary a bit of textured industrial plastic or drab dark blue upholstery anywhere.

Leaving from a private airstrip in a private plane is so much different than traveling commercial. There's no long wait to taxi or take off; no sooner than Nathan and I are buckled safely into our seats, we're whooshing down the runway and into the sky.

There's a meal for us on board, a nice touch considering Nathan whisked me off before I could even have lunch. The flight attendant folds a small table down from the wall between two seats and soon I'm scarfing down sushi and sashimi with approximately nine gallons of sparkling water.

"You know, I'm not supposed to be eating this," I say, lifting a slice of raw tuna with my chopsticks.

"Oh?"

"Yeah, it's on the no-no pregnancy list. But I'll bite your fucking hand off if you try to take this from me." I'm still not super great with my left hand, and my chopsticks fumble. I quickly duck my head to catch the fish with my mouth.

Nathan smiles and shakes his head. "I'm sure this one time won't endanger the baby's life."

"Good." I try again with the chopsticks, then give up entirely. "Look, do you mind if I just make this finger food?"

"Not at all." He motions to the sliced dragon roll on the plate between us. "Sushi can be eaten with the hands, anyway."

"Well, good. Because it was that or I just eat straight off the plate with my mouth like a dog." I pinch some pickled ginger between my fingers and pop it into my mouth.

"For what it's worth, I'm impressed at how quickly you're adapting to..." he gestures at my other arm. "Has the doctor discussed any options with you, regarding a prosthetic?"

"Not really. I still have some healing to do. And I'm not sure I want a prosthetic. Every now and then, I try to move my non-existent fingers and it's like someone zapped me with electricity. I'm not sure I want anything touching that general area." I take a sip from my water and add, "But I've got an idea about what I want."

"Oh?"

"I've been thinking about a hook."

Nathan bursts out with a shocked laugh.

"I'm not kidding." I'm not, but I do giggle. "A real piratey one, like Captain Hook."

"Why on earth would you do that?" The corners of his gray eyes crinkle with amusement.

"Because I think it would be a good test of the people I meet," I explain, because I have put some thought into it. "I say hello, they go to shake my hand, I offer the hook. I think I would be able to tell a lot about a person, depending on if they shook my hook."

His smile makes me feel happier than it should. Do I actually want him to enjoy my non-sexual company? That would be a strange thing to want from someone I don't even particularly like that much.

"I think that's diabolically brilliant, actually," he says, snagging a few slices of sea urchin from their bed of shaved ice. "I hope you don't mind my asking about your hand."

"No. It's not like it's a secret that I lost it." Well, I didn't lose it; I know exactly where I left it. "In your investigation... did you ever find out how the guy managed to." I wave my stump. "You know?"

Nathan takes a sip of sake. "Unfortunately, no. But a friend in London knows someone who might."

"The same guy who's checking out the binding?" I ask.

Nathan nods. "The very same."

"I'm surprised he hasn't figured it out yet. Greater London has so many resources." Considering our efforts to merge the two packs, it seems like they should be working on the investigation together, as well.

"Our expert isn't in Greater London." Nathan glances over his shoulder briefly. "Our visit to him will be an unofficial one. Completely off the record."

"So, we're going to get up to intrigue?" I'm not sure why it's so exciting to me. All the intrigue I've dealt with so far has sucked.

"People don't tend to announce it," he says, holding my gaze so I understand what he's saying.

I hold a finger to my lips. "Say no more."

After dinner, we sit on the little sofa and Nathan turns on the television. I curl up in the corner with a cashmere throw. "Don't ask for my preferences," I tell him as he selects a streaming service. "I'll be asleep."

"You'll be jetlagged," he warns. "We'll be arriving around three in the morning, and you'll be wide awake."

"You underestimate how tired pregnancy makes someone," I inform him with a yawn.

"Really?" He turns slightly, the tv momentarily forgotten. "Because you've been up most nights, lately."

"That's… different." And I wish he hadn't pointed out that difference. For just a few hours, my brain has been so overwhelmed with shiny new information that I've been able to keep my guilt and grief in the back of my mind. Now, icky feelings that would be easier to ignore become so insistent that ignoring is no longer an option.

"I know it is," he says softly. "You could talk to me about it, you know. I'm not a complete monster. Just a bit of a dick."

"Oh, a *bit?*" I snort a laugh. But he's trying to open up to me. "I don't think you're a monster. But I don't know how interested you are in what I'm going through. You once said you didn't need to get to know me."

"I did. That wasn't fair," he admits. "I kept you at arm's length at the beginning of all this. Partly because the binding terrifies me."

"Is there something you should be telling me about it that would terrify me, too?" I ask. "One of us isn't going to explode or something, right?"

"No, I don't foresee either of us exploding." He shakes his head. "I was afraid that I would grow to… like you. And this thing that we can't explain would change or go away and I would be left…"

"Liking someone who doesn't like you back?" I nudge his leg with my bare toes. "You know I don't like you, right?"

"I never would presume otherwise." He smiles to himself. "But yes. I didn't know what the binding was, but I knew it wasn't normal. And I didn't want to get hurt."

"Because you've been hurt before?" I imagine some long ago love, a broken heart that never healed, that maybe only the *right* person can heal.

Yes, fix Nathan. That's a healthy project, I chide myself.

"No." He shrugs. "Because I've never been hurt before."

"And why start now?" I finish for him.

He leans forward and I push myself up to meet him. My head swims and I offer up no resistance when his mouth covers mine. The kiss is slow and gentle, and our bodies fall into a perfect fit. For just a moment, it feels different to be with him. The binding doesn't fuel any urgency. I don't want to rip both our clothes off and get in his lap.

It feels… real.

He leans his forehead against mine and whispers, "There's no time like the present."

CHAPTER 55

It's surreal to be back in London. Though I've only been gone a few months, it seems like a totally foreign place to me, despite having been my home for five years.

Of course, the area we're in isn't exactly where I used to hang out. I hadn't exactly been working with 18th-century-palace money.

"Is it this deserted down here all the time?" I ask as we turn down a practically empty street.

Nathan looks up from his phone, which has been pinging like crazy ever since we landed. "Hmm?"

"The area… seems kinda… dead." Which is fitting because the buildings we pass look like mausoleums.

"I'm not sure. I've never been to the royal residence. I know it's fairly close to the human royal residence, though," he says. "Where did you stay, while you were here?"

"Not anywhere you'd be familiar with." I leave it at that, because we pull up to the curb of a not super impressive-looking house. In fact, it's a bit dingy, compared to the other facades on the street, but it's nearly four times as wide as the townhouses around it.

So, big and crumbly? I guess it stands to reason that the Greater London pack has much older properties, but I didn't realize before just how lucky we are to have Aconitum Hall.

I just hope it's not damp and gross-smelling inside.

Unlike the townhouses around us, there are no steps up to the door. It's flush with the sidewalk. A thrall answers when Nathan rings the bell, and we step into an unimpressive foyer with broken tile and wavy glass in the dull wooden door. On, through a dim hallway, we reach another door and through that…

"Holy shit," I breathe as we step into a cavernous hall. The ceiling is a riot of frescoes divided up into squares and circles, the windows are so tall I almost get dizzy. The floor is here is decidedly *not* cracked; it's a twisting pattern of ribbons in pink and black marble that convene in a medallion in the center of the floor, near the base of an arching staircase.

Nathan leans down to whisper in my ear, just as awed as I am, "Welcome home, us."

Some of the tall windows are actually double doors that open onto a terrace. I head over to look out, only to be startled by the sound of footsteps coming down the stairs.

"Your Majesties!" A slender woman with pale skin and gray-striped, black hair in a large, poofy twist hurries down the stairs. She looks old *and* she's a werewolf, so that means she's really, really old. When she reaches the bottom of the stairs, she curtsies. "My apologies. I meant to have everything ready to welcome you when you arrived."

"That's okay." I jerk my thumb over my shoulder. "Is that a yard out there? In London?"

"It's your private terraced garden, Your Majesty. Beyond the fence, it's St. James's park."

"Oh." I make an impressed face and pretend I know what that means.

"And you are?" Nathan asks her.

She smiles. "Harriet Gauthier. I'm the housekeeper here at Wyrding House."

"Wyrding? Like magic?" That's not exactly subtle.

She nods. "This house was built by a wealthy thrall in seventeen sixty-six. It's one of the finest examples of architecture from that period."

"I don't doubt it," Nathan says, surveying the ceiling. "But what about security?"

"They're on the grounds and throughout the house," Harriet replies. "Your uncle preferred discretion when it comes to the staff."

"My uncle and I differ on that point," Nathan states firmly. "I'd like to meet with the head of security first thing in the morning, after breakfast."

Nathan's uncle lived here? But Nathan has never been here?

"And what time would you like breakfast to be served?" Harriet asks, and it strikes me that she's probably not been to bed yet and will be up early.

"It can be a late breakfast," I answer before Nathan can. "Eleven, maybe?" When Nathan opens his mouth to argue, I play the pregnancy card. "I'm *so* tired. I'd just like to be able to sleep in. And it could do you some good."

He exhales loudly through his nose. "Fine. We'll sleep in. We've come all this way on urgent business, but we'll sleep in."

"Perhaps you'd like to go to your rooms?" Harriet suggests, gesturing to the stairs.

"Room," Nathan corrects her. "Until we have proper security, the queen isn't leaving my sight."

"Yes, we heard about the horrible incident." Harriet clucks her tongue and folds her hands over the stomach of her frumpy purple dress. The collar goes all the way up to her chin; she's definitely a relic of another time. "Well. What a blessing, that you weren't seriously harmed."

My whole hand came off but sure, I guess I wasn't seriously harmed. As Harriet leads us upstairs and to the king's "apartments," as she refers to them, the housekeeper gives us a brief rundown on the history of the place. I don't recognize any of the names she rattles off, but if Nathan is king, then certainly they must have been related to him, somehow. And I definitely don't know much about the various aesthetic periods of English history, so the differences between "Georgian" and "neoclassical" fly right over my head.

When I can get a word in edge-wise, I ask her, "How long have you been the housekeeper here?"

"I started working for His Majesty, King Archibald, in nineteen-fourteen," she states with some pride. "No gap in employment since."

"Pardon me if I'm committing a faux pas by asking," I begin cautiously, then remember I'm the fucking queen and I can ask anything I want. "But why are you a housekeeper, and not a thrall?"

Nathan surprises me by answering for her. "The Greater London pack has a different relationship with thralls than Toronto does. My uncle didn't trust them to run the royal household."

"All of the below-stairs service work is done by thralls," Harriet explains.

"And your uncle was King Archibald?" I clarify.

Nathan just nods tersely and changes the subject with a bored, "Harriet would you mind having coffee sent up to my parlor at eight?"

"Of course, Your Majesty," she answers. We arrive at a set of double doors that seem naked without guards standing outside of them. I kept my eyes peeled for security thralls while we walked, but they must be very good at hiding.

"Here we are," Harriet says, taking her huge keyring from her belt and slipping an ancient key into the lock. Nathan makes a "hmm" under his breath and she assures him, "There's a more modern deadbolt on the other side. And, on the bedroom itself."

"And you're the only one with keys?" he asks.

"Me, and the head of security, of course."

He "hmm"s again and goes into the room ahead of me. He sniffs the air, the mustiness of which I assume is unavoidable in a house this old. "Thank you, Harriet," he tells her, scanning the parlor. "That will be all for this evening."

"Yes, Your Majesties." She doesn't turn her back on us to get to the doors, but I note that Nathan doesn't turn his back, either.

That sends a chill up my spine. So does the way he moves to the windows, checking each one.

"I can't help but notice that you're a little jumpy," I say quietly, not sure how far away Harriet is and if she'll be able to hear us. That's one of the good things about having thralls for servants; they have human hearing.

"I need to be," he answers, turning away from the

window and heading through one of the doors across the room. He opens it, checks behind it, then closes it again. "People have been trying to kill us lately."

"But nobody from the Greater London pack." I refrain from adding, *"right?"* on the end. It's implied.

"That we know of," he confirms.

I'm not going to get drawn into the paranoia. I can't spend every moment that we're here scared that I'm going to get killed. "This is a nice house."

"It is," he says from another room. There's echo like tile is present, so I assume it's the bathroom.

I sit on an antique chaise and look up at the molded plaster seal on the ceiling. When I unfocus my eyes, the chandelier becomes a glittering mass of rainbows. The walls are covered in pale blue satin with a painted pattern of ivory vines. If the place wasn't so fancy, it might actually be calming.

With a groan, I push myself up. Between the plane and the car, I've spent way too long sitting. "So, your uncle was the king here for like, over a hundred years."

"He was," Nathan confirms, distracted.

"And you've never been here?"

"I have not." He steps out of the bathroom and turns the light off.

"You weren't the favorite nephew, huh?" Considering Nathan didn't even mention that his uncle had died, I assume there isn't a lot of love lost there.

I follow Nathan into the bedroom. It's also blue, but in two-tone striped wallpaper. The bed is blessedly modern; I was expecting something with a canopy or a crown with long curtains. It's just a regular bed, sleigh-style, in mahogany.

"That's what held up my coronation, actually," he says,

finally relaxing enough to sit down in a wing chair and take off his shoes. "He didn't want me to succeed him."

"So, you're the king of two packs who don't want you?" That doesn't sound great. "What the hell did I let you drag me into?"

He chuckles. "I'm the king of one pack that doesn't trust me. Greater London does want me. I'm more welcome here than in Toronto."

"But you're worried that people will kill us here?"

He rises and comes to me, hooking his arms around my waist. "Considering what happened to you, I will always be worried that someone is trying to kill you."

"Just me," I say with a laugh. "You, you think you'll be okay."

"No, I think that you being attacked again is my greatest fear." He runs one hand down my body, to my stomach. "I'm your mate. I'm supposed to protect you. I'm supposed to protect this child. And I wasn't able to."

Is that what's been bothering him so much this whole time? "Nathan, you weren't responsible for that. You were practically cut in half. What were you supposed to do?"

"I know it's an unreasonable fear," he admits. "But I felt like a failure."

I reach up and cup his cheek. "You're not a failure."

He doesn't comment on that. Instead, he kisses my forehead and steps back. "Go on. You're exhausted and it will be worse tomorrow. Get in bed."

I sit on the edge of the mattress and give it a little bounce test. "Ooh, I think this is new."

"I should hope so," Nathan says, unbuttoning his shirt. "Archie died in here."

I wonder if it's too late to get a hotel.

CHAPTER 56

The moment the morning sky lightens, my brain stops sleeping.

"Do you think my uncle did this to us?"

"Jeez!" I press my hand to my chest to stop my heart from leaving my body. "What the fuck, Nathan!"

"I couldn't sleep." He's lying flat on his back, staring up at the ceiling, barely blinking.

"I almost peed the bed!" Speaking of which…

I set my feet on the floor and head for the bathroom. When I come back, Nathan hasn't changed position at all.

"Are you having some kind of crisis?" I ask, sliding back in beside him.

"My uncle didn't trust thralls," he murmurs. "Why would he turn to them to do anything against me?"

"What if he didn't mean it like a bad thing?" I suggest, with the caveat, "If he did it at all."

Nathan sighs deeply.

I scoot up close and throw my arm over his chest. He still hasn't gotten a haircut, and a curl falls into his eyes. I would move it aside, but I'm lying on my only hand. "Maybe it was an accident."

"I don't think people accidentally put spells on other people," He observes placidly.

"I didn't think the thralls put spells on us at all, until just yesterday," I remind him. "Or whatever day it was. I really have been keeping strange hours."

He puts his hand on my forearm, near my elbow, clear of the *"don't touch my arm because it feels weird"* zone, and gives it a little squeeze. "You can go back to sleep."

"I'm up, now. Besides, how could I possibly relax with you lying next to me all creepy and tense?" I fit my head into the little crook in his shoulder where I fit perfectly. "Speaking of creepy, though, what about that housekeeper?"

"She is very old." Nathan laughs, and it's good to know I can break through his worry shell, even if for just a second. "Archibald was older. The bastard lived to six hundred, if you can believe that."

"And he was your uncle? Not your great-great uncle or something?" It seems like a pretty huge age gap between generations.

"I was a late-in-life baby," Nathan explains. "My parents were nearly two-hundred when I was born. Archie was the oldest son, my father was the youngest. I had cousins who lived and died long before I was even born."

"When you put it into that perspective, I guess our age gap isn't so bad." I sigh. "Here, I was worried about being so much younger than you. For people like Harriet and your parents, we're actually… sort of babies."

"My parents are dead," he says flatly. "I'm sorry. That was very blunt."

"No, it's okay." I lean up on my elbow to look down at

him. "Up until you mentioned them, I sort of thought you must have been created in a lab or something."

"Because I'm so beautiful?" He grins, and damn him, he is beautiful, with his stupid stormy eyes and his ridiculous jawline.

I roll my eyes. "Because you're like weaponized annoyance."

He reaches up to thread his fingers through my hair, then draws me down for a kiss. The binding sparks to awareness and without meaning to, I writhe my legs together.

"You don't seem so annoyed now," he whispers against my mouth, and kisses me again.

How can I be so consistently irritated by this man but not give a damn about his morning breath?

I push myself up. The strap of my nightgown slips off my shoulder and he uses the opportunity to wiggle his hand inside and cup my breast beneath the silk. He idly strokes my nipple with his thumb, wondering aloud, "Do you think it's really this spell that's making us want each other like this?"

My eyes close and I whimper. It's a miracle I can collect my thoughts with him touching me. "Maybe?"

"You said yourself, it doesn't make sense for it to continue. You're already pregnant." He sits up and lifts my breast free from my nightgown. His lips close over my tight, sensitive flesh and I moan. He releases me slowly, letting his bottom lip drag along my nipple until the last possible moment of contact. "But I still want you. You still want me."

"Physically," I quip.

"Hush," he chuckles, burying his face in my cleavage.

I'm fine with shutting up. The more we talk about the

binding, the more I feel it. I don't want to focus on it right now. I just want to feel Nathan.

I duck under the blankets and wriggle down the bed, settling between his legs. His erection is poking above the waistband of his boxers. I wet my lips and press them against the underside of the head.

He takes a long, hissing inhale and pushes the duvet back. I grin up at him. "You'll have to give me a hand here."

"I'm putting a perpetual moratorium on that joke," he scolds me, but grips himself so I can keep my balance with my hand beside his hip. I dip my head down and give him a long, slow, swirl of my tongue. When I lift my head, his hand follows me up. When I take him back in, his hand drops down. We move together that way in a lazy rhythm, him stroking himself while I tease and suck. The veins in his cock throb against my tongue and his hips strain up; I know it's time to stop.

I sit back and push his hand away before he can finish himself off. I don't think it would take more than a few strokes.

"Settle down," I say, pulling up my nightgown as I straddle his hips. "Try not to come the second you get inside me."

"How can you be so demeaning and sexy at the same time?" he huffs. "I'll have you know I have incredible control."

But that seems debatable, judging from the way he moans and clutches at my thighs as I sink onto his cock. I rise up until just the tip of him remains inside me, then I squeeze my internal muscles around him as I slowly take him all the way again.

With a hiss, he amends his previous statement. "I have okayish control."

I laugh and throw my head back, churning my hips in a steady, unhurried rhythm, impaled on his unyielding hardness. He matches my movements, content with the lazy, slow roll of our bodies meeting and parting. The air around us is like silk on our bare skin, the silence broken only by our rapid breathing and the thick, wet sound of his cock plunging and retreating.

"Touch yourself for me," Nathan whispers. "Let me watch you come on my cock."

I lean back a little, but I'm hampered by the need for balance. Nathan brings his knees up behind me, effectively providing me with a back rest to lean on. The position doesn't allow for deep penetration, but it does press the head of his cock firmly against my g-spot. I can move, just a little bit, just enough to rub that sensitive bundle of nerves over him as he flexes inside me.

I open my thighs as much as I can, to give him a better view of my body spread open around him, and bring my fingertips to mouth, wetting them before I bring them to my clit. Nathan's eyes widen at that, and a shaking breath leaves him as he watches, transfixed by the sight. I want to drop my head back, close my eyes, and focus only on the pleasure building in my pelvis. But watching him watching me is such a turn on, I can't tear my gaze away.

A high, mewling sound pulls from my throat as I climb higher, and his attention moves from my furiously working fingers to make eye contact. It's far more intimate than anything we've done. Far more personal and connected and I'm not sure how I feel about it, but it's too late. I'm so close to coming that I can't stop. With a gasp that turns into a shuddering moan, I lose myself, both in the ecstasy of my release and the hunger in Nathan's eyes.

He curls up from the bed and grabs my ass to steady me, gaze still locked on mine, and with a few, shallow thrusts, follows me over the edge into his own climax. He breathes heavily through every pulse and burst, cum leaking out around the tight seal of our bodies' connection and smearing into the places where our skin meets. He keeps going, keeps moving for as long as he can stand to before he slides from me.

My heart clenches. There was something so personal about what just happened. Nathan staring deep into my eyes as he reached the apex of the pleasure he took in my body had made him strangely vulnerable. It touches something in me that I didn't realize I felt for him.

Trust.

Not just trust that he won't hurt me if he decides to tie me up in bed again, or trust that he can keep me safe from pack machinations. Trust that I can show him even my most intimate desires, trust that he revels in our passionate connection.

I might not like him, and we certainly don't get along. And maybe our hearts will never belong to each other in the way of a truly great romance, but we have these moments of private defenselessness in which the only thing protecting us is that mutual trust.

What if that's the binding, my thoughts torment me. *What if the spell is broken and you never feel this way again?* In this moment, that fear repulses me so much that I hope whatever the thralls did to us is never fixed.

CHAPTER 57

Our arrival in London hasn't gone unnoticed. I'm barely done with my oatmeal before my day is planned out for me. The biggest chunk of my time today will be taken up by a royal audience to receive members of the pack and introduce them to their new queen.

I don't have Hannah or Tara with me. Technically, Hannah's job isn't to be my stylist, but she does help me pick things out. And Tara knows all the flaws I'm self-conscious about, because they were put there by our mother. She's never going to let me go out in something that makes my hips look big or my neck look short.

Instead, I have a thrall who comes and tuts and frowns and tilts her head this way and that before finally giving up, I guess, and putting me in a mauve silk gown with an empire waist and a gauzy split overlay skirt. She gives me white elbow-length gloves that I have to politely explain will look goofy as heck on someone with no hand. In the end, she works a little magic with a curling iron so my hair falls in soft waves over my shoulders. But I'm on my own for makeup.

"Bailey?" Nathan calls from the parlor. "We're needed downstairs."

"I know." I try to keep my voice cheerful and bright, but my bottom lip trembles. I've gotten okay with left-handed shadow and contouring. Lip-liner and lipstick are trickier, but I put in a lot of practice.

It's eyeliner I'm afraid of.

Nathan steps through the open bathroom door and frowns at me. I know I look ridiculous, leaning over the sink in my formal gown, a liner brush poised millimeters from my face.

"Is everything all right?" he asks cautiously, and I burst into tears. He hurries to my side, pulling his crisply folded pocket square from the breast of his suit.

I wave it away and reach for the tissue box on the counter. "It's silly. And it's messing up my mascara."

"Is there anything I can do to help?" he offers.

I shake my head. "Hannah and Tara have been doing my eyeliner for me when I need it."

"Oh, because of your hand." He wiggles the fingers of his right hand. Noting the open pot of gel liner on the counter, he picks it up. "It's just paint, is it?"

"Yeah..." I'm not sure I like where this heading, because it seems like it's heading for Nathan trying to put my eyeliner on me. "But it's not really as simple as it sounds."

He leans in close to my face. "I think I could reasonably trace your eyelid for you. None of that pointy business at the corners. I'm a passable painter."

"You paint?" I have seen zero indication of a hobby in the months we've been together.

"When I have time to relax, which I haven't had much of lately". He takes the brush from my fingers and tilts my chin up in his hand. "I found I had a taste for watercolor when I was in school, and I never gave it up. Don't tell anyone. Now, don't move."

I close my eyes and hold very still, hoping for the best. *I remembered to bring makeup wipes, right?*

The silence of the bathroom makes me focus on Nathan's steady breathing as he concentrates. The rustle of his clothing and the tap of the brush in the product give me goosebumps. But it's not his closeness that makes my heart squeeze up tight; it's his kindness. It's his willingness to meet my vulnerable moment with intimacy.

"There," he says, leaning away. "Is that right?"

I open my eyes and face the mirror and shockingly, he did a passable job. He wasn't kidding about just tracing my upper lid, but he did vary the thickness of the line toward the outer corner. It's a bit Disney princess-y, but I can wear it.

"Yes, thanks." I blink back fresh tears because there's no reason to ruin the eyeliner. "Watercolors, huh?"

"Landscapes. Birds. Owls, mostly." He shrugs. "I can show you sometime, if you'd like."

"I think I would."

"Oh. I was supposed to bring you these." He reaches into his jacket and produces the damn opera gloves. Just as I begin to protest, he shakes one out; the hand is missing, the end sewn up. "The thrall who was here before just finished them."

I take them from him. Putting the handless one on is easier than the other, since I need an assist from my mouth. I'm wearing lipstick and I don't want to get it on the fabric.

Nathan steps in to help without a word. "When you need me, ask. I'm here for you."

Will wonders never cease?

————

"The Marquess Dubois and his wife, Lady Hargrave," a werewolf in some kind of military dress tells Nathan and me. There's a majordomo announcing guests properly as they arrive, but we're stationed in the receiving room where there's no need for anyone to shout at us. Wyrding House doesn't have a throne room, due to a spat that goes back to the Medieval period and an arrangement with the human English monarchy meant to soothe their threatened egos.

Or, so Harriet has led us to understand.

The Marquess and his wife bow and curtsey to us, and I have to ask, "I've never met a Marquess before. Is that a pack title or one you acquired in the human world?"

The moment I ask it, I sense a shift in the interaction. The man draws himself up a little straighter, and his mate's smile becomes tight.

"I'm sorry, have I committed a faux pas?" I ask, and the woman, a short, beige-complected sprite, shakes her bobbed curls emphatically.

Because who is going to tell a queen she's done something wrong?

"It's a title connected to my family's land," Dubois informs me, his boiled-chicken face still bearing the faintest traces of contempt that he can't conceal. "Granted by the human king Charles the second, but still prized as a unique bond between werewolf and human nobility."

"How impressive." I hope I don't sound sarcastic.

"Thank you for coming," Nathan says smoothly. "Your support means so much to me."

They move on and I give Nathan an awkward, apologetic wince.

"Daniel Rayner," the werewolf beside Nathan says, but Nathan has already recognized the man and is striding across the room to him.

"Dan! It's been ages." Nathan is so pleased to see the gentleman that he throws his arms around him in an aggressively friendly hug. Daniel returns it, slapping Nathan on the back heartily.

"Too long," Daniel agrees. "Far too long."

Nathan turns and gestures to me to come join them. "And this is my mate, Bailey."

"Nathan Frost, mated," Daniel says, a brilliant smile flashing across his light-brown face as he reaches for my hand. He bends to brush a kiss over my knuckles and yeah, maybe I swoon a little bit. His stubbly jaw is nearly as sharp and square as Nathan's, his dark eyes as warm as Nathan's are cold. Those warm eyes rake over me in a way that would probably get any other man escorted off the property, but Nathan just gives him a warning nudge with his elbow.

"Keep your filthy thoughts off my wife," Nathan warns with a nervous laugh.

"You needed to speak to me about something?" Dan says, lowering his voice a little. "Is now a good time or are you still 'receiving'?"

"Now is fine." Nathan calls over to the werewolf who's been making introductions, "Give us ten minutes."

We go to an almost claustrophobically small sitting room, seemingly designed for court intrigue, and Nathan lays it out plainly.

"The thralls did something to Bailey and me. They worked magic against us without our knowledge."

I question the wisdom of his bluntness, but Nathan isn't a fool. He must trust this Dan very much.

"Do you have proof for me to take to the council?" Daniel asks.

Nathan shakes his head. "I have no proof. That's the issue."

"Ah." Daniel slips his hands into the pockets of his trousers. "You know I stopped associating with that crowd a long time ago."

What crowd? Thralls? I'm in over my head.

"I can't go to a thrall with this. We don't know who worked the magic or why. You know they're more loyal to their own kind than they are to us," Nathan says. "And you know I never believed you stopped associating with magicians."

Magicians? That completely blows my mind.

"I'm sorry," I break in. "Are there magic users who aren't thralls?"

"There are," Nathan confirms. "And I'm sure Daniel can think of someone who can help us."

"I can, if you promise you're not going to roar off in a car with the royal flags on the front and draw attention to yourself." Daniel sighs in resignation. "You'll need to look and act the part. And not act like a dick, Nathan." To me, Daniel says, "Not you. I'm sure you're lovely."

"She can be," Nathan says. "What's this person's name? Where do we find them?"

"His name is Jonah, and he owns a club called The Underground. Definitely a different class of human down there than what you'll run into in St. James. You're going to need disguises."

"Can you arrange that?" Nathan asks.

"And a car," Daniel confirms with a nod. "I'll have it covered."

"I knew I could count on you," Nathan says, and claps Daniel on the back. To me, he says, "Daniel is one of my oldest, most loyal friends."

"And I still don't know a damn thing about him," Daniel adds.

That makes two of us. Although, at least now, I know about the watercolors.

"So, what do you say?" Nathan asks, almost giddy. "Would you like to go on an adventure?"

I'm not sure I have much of a choice.

CHAPTER 58

It's so late it's beginning to qualify as early when we leave Wyrding House, and we sneak out like grounded teenagers. We're definitely not dressed with a royal vibe; I've got on an impossibly short, super clingy long-sleeve mini-dress in an obnoxious lime and fluorescent yellow print, and Nathan is wearing gray track pants, a plain black tee shirt, and a black denim jacket with a gray hood.

"You look like an undercover cop," I whisper, leaning on him so I don't fall off my ridiculous Lucite heels. My ponytail is so high and tight I feel like my scalp is going to pop off, and I'm fairly certain I can feel the night air on my butt cheeks.

When I slide into the leather passenger seat of the waiting car, I whoop with shock at the cold.

"And you look like you belong on a sleazy reality dating show," he quips back. "At least one of us will fit in."

Nathan pulls away from the curb and doesn't turn the car's lights on until we're a few streets away from the square.

"Is this dangerous?" I ask, casting a glance over my shoulder. "Like, are we doing life-or-death stuff here?"

"I don't think so." It's not the super definite answer I wanted, but Nathan goes on, "Werewolves, as a rule, don't get tangled up with magicians. We don't need to; we have the thralls. But there's animosity between the thralls and outside magic users and that's what we need to worry about."

"Especially since we're looking for proof of something *they* did to us," I say, so Nathan knows I get what he's talking about.

"Exactly."

"So, you know the way to this place?" I ask, and he reaches over to the media console and hits a button.

"No, but Daniel does." Nathan presses the button for the GPS and he's right; it's taking us exactly where we need to go.

Where we need to go is a seedy looking building in Brixton with a logo that mimics the signs for the subway system, but in black and white. Fluorescent green letters in a spray paint font declare "The Underground" is the name of the club.

"This isn't exactly my type of place," Nathan says as we cross the street. We ditched the car on a different road, just to be safe, and took some questionable shortcuts to get here. "Is there a particular etiquette I should follow or…"

"Did you get the impression *I* was hanging out in a lot of dodgy bars?" I snap. "Keep your voice down and look less judgmental. Pretend you know what you're doing."

"I do know what we're doing," he says confidently. He holds my hand as we approach the bouncer at the door. He's a tall white dude with freckles on his bald head and a body that can only be described as *"truck-like"*. Nathan barely slows his step as he passes the guy, tossing, "I'm off to the see the wizard," over his shoulder and the bouncer doesn't bother to stop us. He turns his attention back to the sidewalk as we enter the club.

That's the secret password?

My shoes instantly stick to the floor.

"Oh, gross," I mutter, hanging onto Nathan's arm as we wind through the sweaty, strung-out party crowd. The music is loud, the lights are flashy, and artificial fog mingles with the obvious scent of a banned substance.

I've been in a place like this approximately once in my entire life. I didn't like it then, and that place was a lot less grimy.

"How will we know who we're looking for?" I raise my voice to be heard over the music, but I can barely hear myself.

"I think it will be fairly obvious." Nathan's jaw is tight as he nods toward the bar. There's a man holding court there in a group of women dressed not so differently from me, so I can't exactly judge them. But the guy is wearing a tropical print shirt, totally unbuttoned, and baggy khaki shorts. Atop his head is a party store wizard hat.

"That can't be," I say, shaking my head slowly. "That is not the super powerful magician."

Despite the fact that the guy is wearing sunglasses in a dark club, I can feel his gaze when it lands on us. He takes the glasses off and puts them in the pocket of his shirt before he motions the women away and approaches us. There's a ruddy tan on his caucasian skin that suggests a recent vacation, and his sun-touched brown hair is cut short and styled to look like he didn't style it at all.

My douche-o-meter can't handle the overload and explodes.

"Werewolves," he says, looking us up and down. "In my club."

"Dan sent us," Nathan says.

"Yeah, of course he did. Jonah." He sticks his hand out for Nathan to shake, then offers it to me before noticing mine is missing. He snatches the offer back quickly.

Hook, I think, giving Nathan a knowing look.

"So, you're the royals." Jonah tucks his thumbs through his belt loops. His pants are riding low enough to expose a cut of muscle plunging from his hip to beneath his waistband. "Guess that qualifies you for the VIP room."

It strikes me then that he doesn't sound English. As we follow him toward the back of the club, I say, "You have a west coast accent. Like, the west coast of North America."

"Good ear," he notes. "Vancouver, British Columbia."

"I'm from Ontario!" I declare excitedly, and way too loud. Some people we pass give me a withering look.

"Yeah, got that from the whole Toronto thing." He pushes a swinging black door open, revealing a room that's basically just a huge banquette in black velvet, surrounded by mirrors. He tells us, "Have a seat."

We slide onto the banquette, and he sits across from us, putting his feet up on the low, mirrored table in the center. "What can I do for you?"

"Discretion, foremost," Nathan says as an opener.

"You have my word as a magician," Jonah promises. "For all the good that will do you."

Though I know it will annoy Nathan, I can't wait around for them to posture their way into an agreement. "Someone put a spell on us. We need you to tell us what it is, what it's doing, who put it there. Dan thought you'd have some idea how to do that."

"Absolutely," Jonah says, and pulls a cigarette from his pocket and lights it, as if in punctuation.

Nathan and I look at each other. The relief we both feel is palpable.

"Fantastic," Nathan says, reaching into his pocket. "I assume there's payment involved—"

"Put your wallet away, King Friday." Jonah waves his hand. "I said I have an idea how to do that. I didn't say I would or even could."

"So, you know how to do it, you just can't do it?" I ask.

"Yeah, the thing with this spell is, I need to be able to see it. Physically. And I can't see it." Jonah gives us a *"What are you gonna do?"* shrug and takes another drag off his cigarette.

"Is there something you can do to make it visible?" Nathan asks. "A meditation or maybe we need to stand in a certain light?"

"I don't think that's how magic works," I say quietly.

"The spell you're under is meant to be as unnoticeable as possible. The fact that a thrall who isn't a magician saw it is pretty impressive; whoever it was must be sensitive to energies. But even with my training, all I can see is its presence and that it's a binding. The only way I could see it is if…" He makes a face that indicates we're definitely not going to like what we hear.

"Spit it out," Nathan snaps.

"I have to see the spell at work. And not just at work, I mean, performing its intended purpose. The energy needs to be raised way above the level it's at now. And the only way we could feasibly achieve that is if the two of you…" Jonah makes a circle with the fingers of one hand and penetrates it with the index finger of the other one.

"Oh, come on!" I object, not just to his lewd gesture,

but the very notion that I'm going to have sex with him watching me.

But Nathan says, "Go on."

"What?" I shriek.

Nathan pats my knee. "Let's just hear him out."

"It wouldn't have to be pervy," Jonah explains. "I'll be concentrating on a ritual, anyway. And it might help if I gave you both something to boost the libido. It could increase the visibility of the spell and make things less awkward."

"Because we'll be too horny to care that we're doing it right in front of a stranger?" I snort. "Not bloody likely."

Nathan turns to me with a grin. "You said 'bloody.' That's adorable."

"Don't patronize me!" I gesture toward Jonah. "And what if this guy magic roofies us or something."

"Oh, please, Your Majesty. Look around this club. Do you really think I have a hard time pulling? There's a girl over there in a latex bra, for god's sake." Jonah shakes his head. "Look, it's just an idea. Take it or leave it, but otherwise I genuinely can't help you."

Are we really entertaining this idea? The thought of this guy, this grubby club dude watching Nathan and I fucking is just about the grossest thing I've ever heard.

"Is that really our only option?" I ask, pressing my hand to my temple.

Jonah grimaces in confirmation and exhales a long plume of smoke from his nostrils. "Yup. I mean, you could always consult another magician. But it looks like you two went to a lot of trouble to get here tonight. What with the costumes and all."

Nathan turns to me. "You don't have to do this."

"You don't, either," I point out. "But right now, I think it's our only option."

With a sigh of resignation, Nathan tells Jonah, "All right. When do we do this?"

Jonah stubs his cigarette out directly on the glass tabletop. "Let's go."

CHAPTER 59

Jonah takes us to a back office that leads to another back office that opens up to a storage room with a very scary catwalk staircase up to the second floor. I'm pretty sure we're about to be murdered when Jonah ushers us up it and through a beaded curtain, into a room lit up with black light.

The floor is painted black, with sigils and symbols in glowing phosphorescent colors. There are beanbag chairs scattered around the perimeter of the room, and an impressively tall hookah in one corner. Shelves hold jars of herbs and dirt and murky liquids I want nothing to do with.

"So, where do we…" I look around. Clearly the bean bags are one disgusting option, judging from the very unflattering smears and spatters the black lights are revealing.

Jonah's teeth glow comically blue in the light. "Hey, that's up to you. Just not on the worktable."

He's talking about the huge workbench tucked into an

l-shaped corner. He opens a laptop and types something in.

"No spell books? Dusty scrolls?" Nathan quips.

"Magicians have been digitized since the nineties. Catch up, wolfman." While Jonah types, he gestures to a mini fridge. "Okay, King, the magic potion is in there."

"I'm sorry?" Nathan asks, unconvincing in his innocence.

Jonah chuckles humorlessly. "Yeah, you have no idea what I'm talking about. Dan doesn't come here specifically to procure it for you."

Nathan's eyes cut guiltily toward me before he goes to the mini fridge and pulls out a glass vial that looks very much like the synthesized magic werewolf cum that Nathan had back at Aconitum Hall.

"So that's where you got it," I say with a smirk.

"No, it's where he got a diluted form of it," Daniel says. "That shit right there? Pure hormone. You're gonna want to a grab a couple of those Red Bulls and throw two drops in apiece. Only two, I'm serious. Then chug them down."

"And what's going to happen?" I ask cautiously, moving to get the drinks from the refrigerator.

"Probably the best and most exhausting sex of your life," Daniel says, pulling out what appear to be welding goggles. He fits them onto his head and the lenses glow with swirling purple light.

"That's not an arcane GoPro, right?" I ask. I'm already uncomfortable with the situation. I don't need to be recorded and I certainly don't need the words "royal sex tape" linked to me.

Jonah adjusts the dials around the lenses. "They're

going to help me detect the signature of the magician or magicians who cast this."

Nathan carefully doses both the energy drinks, two drops per can, and swirls them around.

"Don't drink that yet," Jonah warns. "It works fast, and I still need to get a few things set up."

As Jonah putters, I hold the can without drinking it like an awkward teen at a party who doesn't want to look uncool but doesn't want to consume alcohol, either. "We're really going to do this?"

"Do you have a better plan?" Nathan asks. He reaches out and rubs my upper arm in reassurance. "Maybe think of it this way: we get to do something weird and kinky and then never see this guy again."

"If exhibitionism was my kink, I guess that would work for me," I grumble.

"I'm not entirely psyched for this stranger to see my O-face either," he admits. "It's just a sacrifice we're going to have to make."

I nod grimly. "Let's just hope the magic werewolf cum potion removes our inhibitions or something. Otherwise, I'm going to be dry as a desert with embarrassment."

Nathan's mouth quirks. "And I'm not likely to get it up."

"Okay,' Jonah says, clapping his hands. "We're all set. Knock those back in one go, if you can. Don't be shy about the burping."

I glare at Nathan and tip the can to my mouth.

The aphrodisiac kicks in almost immediately. One moment, we're just standing there, deeply uncomfortable from the carbonation. The next, we're ripping off each other's clothes—literally. There's no button left on

Nathan's jeans by the time I'm done, which is an impressive feat one-handed, if I do say so myself. The dress is stretchy enough to shrug out of, but I don't have to; Nathan grips the back of the neckline and tears it in half down to the waist. He jerks the front of my bra down and boosts me up to wrap my legs around him, sucking one of my nipples into his mouth as he drives me toward the wall.

"Okay, watch out for the—" Jonah shouts over our feral growls. My back collides with some shelves and things clatter and bang, but I wouldn't care if the room was on fire.

"Fine," Jonah sighs to himself. "I'll just clean that up later."

"Fuck me," I moan against Nathan's ear. "Please. I need it so bad."

He reaches between us and frees his erection. He shoves my panties aside with two rough fingers, briefly plunges them inside of me, then replaces them with his cock.

"Fuck, yes!" I scream, slapping my hand against his back as he pounds into me, grunting and cursing with every thrust. I'm hot all over, sweat pouring down my neck as that heat scorches through my veins. All at once, it switches to freezing cold, then back again, the sensations growing stronger and more intense with each new wave. I lean back to look into Nathan's eyes and they're glowing silver, illuminated with flashes of orange and blue. I realize with a strangled gasp that the colors are coming from us, from pulsing light that accompanies each beat of our hearts, drawing a map of our nerve endings.

"What's happening?" I whimper.

"I don't know." Nathan crushes my mouth with his and we tumble onto the beanbag chairs, the dubious cleanliness of them no longer a concern. He rams into me, his teeth sinking into my shoulder, my neck. I writhe beneath him, trying to get purchase to lift up and meet his battering thrusts. I climb higher and higher, the tension in my body wound to a near-breaking point and—

I don't break.

It's the stupid aphrodisiac. It's doing exactly what it did the night Nathan used it on me, but this time it's so much worse. My blood is burning and freezing and my skin is made of electricity and there's no escape.

"No!" I gasp against Nathan's cheek. "I'm so close!"

"Me, too," he groans into my ear. "I'm right there and I just can't—" He interrupts himself with a growl of frustration and drives his cock deeper, harder, faster, while I pant and plead, trapped at the same precipice. The serum is diabolical. My muscles cramp and strain and every time the base of Nathan's shaft drags against my clit, I'm sure that will be the moment that I finally reach the summit I'm striving toward.

I scream in frustration, my fingers twisting in the fabric beside my head. There's a loud tear and a plume of foam beads bursts into the air.

"Really?" Jonah exclaims in annoyance. "Really?"

"Shut up!" Nathan shouts at him. "How long is this going to last?"

"An hour or two?" When I wail in despair, he says, "Chill, I'm kidding, it'll wear off in a minute. That's what the caffeine was for."

"Oh, thank god!" I lock my legs behind Nathan's back and arch up, shameless. I don't care if someone is watching us. I don't care if this weirdo magician guy thinks I'm the horniest, sluttiest werewolf who's ever lived. I need to come, so desperately that I wouldn't care if we had an audience of thousands.

Knowing that the effect will wear off somehow doesn't cut through our bodies' desperation to *try*. Every brutal thrust forces a shout of pain from my throat, but Nathan doesn't hold back. We roll from the half-empty chair and onto the painted cement floor. The rough surface scrapes my back raw as I rock under every deep, violent stroke of Nathan's cock.

What if it doesn't wear off? My brain torments me with panicked thoughts. *What if it's like this for hours? Days? What if never goes away?*

I bury my face against Nathan's neck, whimpering, tears gliding down my face.

"I'm…" Nathan begins in disbelief. "I think it's…"

I don't hear him. Every muscle in my body seizes up, then cramps. The precipice I teetered on gets higher and higher and I reach for the edge with my hand, wedging it between our bodies.

With a grunt of frustration, Nathan pulls out and I sink my nails into his shoulder to try and hold him back. He can't stop now. Not when the aphrodisiac's grip is finally releasing.

He flips me onto my stomach, apparently forgetting that I only have one arm to brace on. When he shoves into me from me behind, I topple forward, scraping my cheek on the floor and biting my lip. The taste of blood on my tongue drives me into even more of a frenzy, and I know that I can't take much more of this torment without tearing myself—and Nathan—physically apart.

Nathan reaches beneath me to find my clit, rubbing me hard and fast, his hips slapping against me. He loses all sense of rhythm, giving over to furious, animalistic fervor.

His teeth sink into the back of my neck as he lunges over me, driving deep one last time. He bellows with unrestrained pleasure and the sound, combined with the jerk of his cock inside me and the persistence of his fingers playing over my flesh, burst through the potion's effects. Wetness cascades down my thighs, spatters on the concrete beneath my knees as I howl in the grips of an orgasm that feels like ten stacked together.

I collapse, and Nathan follows me down. I don't care that he's crushed me, I don't care that I've squirted all over a stranger's floor, all I want is sleep.

"That… should give me enough to go on," Jonah says, as if in disbelief. "I'll invoice you for all the shit you broke."

————

Once I get to my feet and head to the bathroom to clean up, it takes me a while to work up the nerve to show my face again. I'm mortified to my bones about what we just did, despite how necessary it was, and I'm still picking little polystyrene balls out of my hair.

"Bailey?" Nathan asks through the bathroom door.

"I'm having trouble with my dress," I tell him. "Someone shredded it and I'm basically naked."

He opens the door and hands me his jacket. I pull it on and zip it up with some difficulty before I come out.

Jonah's little work room is *destroyed*. Beanbag filling covers the floor in drifts. Shelves half-hang from their brackets, contents scattered and smashed on the floor. Jonah and Nathan are ignoring it all, leaning over the laptop.

"That's it, right there," Jonah says, and he spins the

computer so I can see the screen, as well. Not that what I'm seeing makes a lot of sense to me; it's some kind of glowing sigil in orange against a grainy blue—

"Is that a picture of us having sex?" I shriek.

"It's a picture of the signature left by the magicians who bound you," Jonah says, turning the laptop back to face him. "You're welcome."

"He's not saving it for salacious purposes," Nathan reassures me. "It would be foolish for a human, no matter how adept they were at magic, to make an enemy of a werewolf."

That second part isn't directed at me.

"So, now what?" I ask. "What did it tell you?"

"Nothing, yet. This was step one in a process. I need to sit down, analyze what I'm seeing, refer to notes and arcane records, you know. All the bullshit wizards do and get zero thanks for," Jonah complains. "You know, ninety-nine percent of what I do, magic wise, is reading stuff dead guys wrote."

"You and every English major alive," I snort.

Nathan keeps us on topic. "You know how to reach us when you have the results. We'll stay in London until then. Tell Dan when you want us to return."

"No, no, don't come back here. I'll come to you," Jonah says, pausing to give Nathan a brief, pointed once-over. "You look like a cop."

I hold back an *"I told you so."*

CHAPTER 60

We stagger back into Wyrding House just before sun-up and strip out of our "disguises."

"I need to take like four showers and burn this dress," I say with a grimace, holding the garment up with two fingers. "I cannot believe how foul that room was."

"Blacklight is perhaps not the best choice of illumination there," Nathan agrees. "But you should consider getting some sleep before showering."

"I just shot-gunned a Red Bull two hours ago," I remind him. "I'm up."

He glances toward the bathroom. "What about a soak?"

There's a jacuzzi tub big enough for two in the bathroom, and just the suggestion of it is a siren call to my sore body. "You've convinced me."

A little while later, Nathan and I are immersed up to our necks in the ridiculously deep tub. We lean against opposite sides, his legs on either side of me, my feet on his shoulders.

"Do you think the spell will still work, now that we

know it's there?" I ask, wriggling my wrinkly toes against his cheek playfully.

He pushes my foot aside with only partially-feigned disgust. "Not if you insist on doing that."

I giggle, but it's mostly nerves. The fact that he won't give me a straight answer isn't reassuring. "Seriously, though. It's basically the only thing keeping us together."

"The baby might be a factor," he reminds me.

"Oh. Right." Sometimes, I forget it's there. "I can't really get my mind around the fact that it exists."

"You probably shouldn't have had the Red Bull," he muses aloud.

"I'm sure it'll be easier to remember all the rules when I can remember that I'm pregnant. Like, when my pants don't fit anymore, or I start puking everywhere." Mornings are becoming somewhat dicey, but a carbonated water usually clears things up.

"I can't stop thinking about it," he confesses. "That's not to say I'm already a much better parent than you are—"

I splash him.

He wipes water from his face with a laugh. "What I'm saying is, I'm constantly worried about the baby, and about you, and the reality that we're a royal couple in the middle of a dicey situation. We need to have things under control before we have an heir who's a potential target."

I hadn't thought about our situation like that. *What happened to Marie Antoinette's kids?*

We're not like them, though. We're not spending the pack's cash and plunging our kingdom into miserable poverty.

I'm actually not sure what we were trying to do.

I struggle to sit up a little, and tuck my feet on either

side of Nathan's thighs. "Look… we're in a perilous position, right?"

He nods. "I would say that's an accurate description."

"Maybe you could clue me in on what your intent was when you became king of both packs. And made me queen of them both?" As someone who grew up in the Toronto pack and who had heard rumblings of distrust toward other packs, including Greater London, I can't help but feel like a traitor.

Like my family.

"I didn't have any intentions at all," Nathan says with a shrug. "When my father died, I knew I would eventually inherit his brother's throne. I'm the only suitable heir."

I hold up my hand. "Stop. Back up. Explain 'suitable'."

He blinks in what appears to be shock.

"You didn't say you were the only heir. You said you were the only suitable one. That means there are others out there. And if there are other heirs out there, that means our reign is threatened."

"It isn't," he assures me. "Archie had one son, and he was badly injured in a skiing accident forty years ago. He's been in a nursing facility ever since."

"And nobody is going to take up his banner in order to oust us?" I need a definitive answer to this question, considering everything that's going on back in Toronto.

Nathan shakes his head. "No. When Archibald named me his heir, the council of Greater London unanimously accepted the change."

"Then our biggest issue is the Saint-Laurent pack?"

"The biggest issue is the Toronto pack," Nathan says grimly. "And then the Saint-Laurent pack."

"Why go back there, then?" If nobody in England

wants to murder us, surely, it's safer to stay here. "Why not stay in friendly territory?"

"Because in a coup, you never leave the seat of power." He pauses. "I'm not certain coming here was wise. As soon as we hear from Jonah, we'll be on the jet and back to Canada."

"Where people want to kill us." It seems unfair that they want to kill me. I got roped into this mostly against my will.

Mostly, because while I might not have wanted the crown, I definitely wanted Nathan. And I still do, against all reason and sanity.

"We'll up security measures," he promises. "And I'm having your bodyguard join us here. She's been vetted by my personal security forces. The thralls here at Wyrding House haven't."

"But your security forces are thralls. Xiao is a thrall," I remind him "And thralls might have put this spell on us."

"Xiao saved your life. And she's the one who told us about the binding. She's proved her loyalty." He pauses. "She could be useful to us, in that regard."

"I'm not a fan of reducing people to their usefulness." I suppose it's just part of being a leader, but I don't have to like it. "On the other hand, I suppose her telling us about the binding shows she's loyal to the pack, not loyal to thralls who might be plotting against us."

"And we have no proof yet that they are. That's where Xiao might be able to help us. If she's willing to be our eyes and ears—"

"Willing to snitch."

He ignores my correction. "—we might be able to discern exactly what kind of problem, and what scale, we're dealing with."

"But I don't have to trick her into revealing anything, right?" I'm not sure I could, anyway. "I don't like manipulating people and I don't want to be fake. Especially not to a person who saved my life."

"Then be direct with her. Ask her for her help outright. That way, there's no dishonesty between the two of you." The tub jets reach the end of their timer, and Nathan sighs deeply. "I think that's a sign that our bath is finished."

"Does it have to be?" I laugh tiredly. The caffeine is rapidly wearing off. "Can't we just sleep in here?"

"Only if you'd like to drown." He stands and steps out, water cascading over every muscle. He offers me his hand. "I'd prefer that you didn't, though."

I waggle my fingers at him. "I kinda need this free to get up."

"Oh, of course," he says sheepishly, waiting for me to push up and grip the edge of the tub for balance before slipping his arm beneath my hand-less one to steady me.

"Thanks," I say as I set my feet on the plush bathmat. Nathan gets a towel from the artful stack of them in a nearby basket and wraps it around his hips. The motion draws my eye not only to the sharply defined L-shaped ridges there, but also the pink, puckered scar that nearly bisects his abdomen. He catches me staring, so I divert my attention to his abs, trailing one finger down the deep vertical line to his belly button. "You're really bouncing back."

"I'm trying. Not getting to the gym as often as I should," he notes, grabbing another towel for me. "But thank you for noticing the effort."

"You're difficult to not notice." The binding flares to life and I actually feel a little light-headed. "Wow."

Nathan gently wraps my hair in one towel before

taking another to dry me. "Maybe that potion hasn't quite worn off."

So, he feels it, too.

And I have to know. I have to, because I need some kind of certainty. Some stability. "Nathan, I'm going to ask you something. I need you to promise you'll give me an honest answer. Straightforward. No jokes."

He tucks the towel around me, and I hold it with my truncated forearm across my chest, not meeting his eyes, but he agrees. "All right."

I take a deep breath. "This binding… if it ends, if it suddenly vanishes or the people who cast it on us take it back… how will you feel about me?"

He seems to struggle with the question. "You're the mother of my child—"

"I know I am," I stop him. "That's not what I asked."

With a long sigh, he admits. "I don't know."

I didn't realize how much the answer to the question might hurt me, until *that* was the answer I received. An ache blossoms in my chest, growing larger and larger.

Before that pain can push a sound of anguish from my throat, he continues, "Bailey, I've never been in love with anyone before. I'm not sure it's something I can do. But if I could… I think I would love you."

If that's all I can have, I suppose I'll take it.

CHAPTER 61

By teatime the next day, Xiao is in our private parlor, waiting for me. She's sitting on one of the sofas, but she stands the moment I enter, and bows deeply. "Your Majesty."

"I'm so glad to see you!" It takes everything in me not to run at her and hug her; we don't have that kind of relationship. But seeing her is a balm that soothes homesickness I didn't realize I felt.

"I've done a preliminary sweep of this wing, and some of the public areas I've been briefed on," she begins. "The garden is a concern to me, considering its proximity to the park—"

"I'm sure you're doing a great job," I interrupt her. "And I'll listen to whatever suggestions you give me with regards to security. You don't need to explain."

That seems to take her aback. "Yes, Your Majesty."

"I'm not scolding you," I hurry to assure her. "Please, sit down. Would you like tea?"

"I..." she hesitates.

I ring the bell, anyway. "I've got stuff I need to ask you about."

"All right." She sounds cautious, but she takes a seat. "The last time you asked me about anything, you ended up in England."

"That's true. But it was for the best." I pause as Harriet enters. "Tea for my guest and me?"

Harriet bows her head. "At once, Your Majesty."

Xiao watches Harriet closely, waits until the door latch clicks, and we hear the thump of her gait retreating down the hall before whispering, "Your Majesty… your servant is a werewolf."

"I know." I wave my hand to indicate it's not a big deal. "The former King had a thing about thralls. I mean, no offense."

"I'm not offended. I'm concerned," she says, then stops herself. "It's not my place."

"You're my bodyguard. It's your place if you think there's danger," I tell her.

Her brown eyes dart across the high ceiling as she considers her answer. Finally, she comes out with the diplomatic, "If the former king didn't trust his thralls, there's probably a reason."

"You don't think it was prejudice, maybe?" It seems like it would be on brand for a werewolf king. "Our kind are pretty snobby."

"You are, but the pacts made by our families, our allegiance to the packs we serve aren't something taken lightly. At least, in my experience." She opens her hands toward me. "Yours might vary."

"We don't have proof yet that thralls put the binding on us. But we do have someone trying to find that out." At the mention of families, though, a thought occurs to me.

"Hey, you being here, that isn't messing things up for you at home, right?"

Her brow wrinkles in a frown. "At home, Your Majesty?"

"Yeah, like, with your family. Do you have a husband? Kids?" I'm ashamed I never asked before. Talk about snobby.

"No kids. Husband will never really be a thing, ma'am." Her lips compress in a silent *"whelp,"* and I get the hint.

"Oh. Well, do you have pets? Parents? What I'm getting at is, the king just flew you all the way over here at a moment's notice. Are you okay with that?" As she opens her mouth, I hold up one finger. "The truth. Not some answer about how you're pledged to the safety of the pack or something."

"That *is* the truth," she says.

"I know, but sometimes people can be annoyed at the truth or feel that the truth is being unfairly truthy upon them." I shrug helplessly. "There's no rule that you can't have gripes about your job, right?"

Though it appears to pain her greatly, she admits, "No, there's no rule about that. But I don't have a reason to gripe, either. There isn't much for the queen's bodyguard to do if the queen isn't there to be guarded. I've been going a little stir-crazy for the past couple of days."

"Great! Glad we cleared that up." And I'm glad that I've cracked the Xiao communication code; I just have to relentlessly badger her into admitting she has thoughts and feelings. "How are Hannah and my sister?"

"Hannah's fine. Miffed that she didn't get to come to England, but realistic about the challenges childcare at home would present." Xiao delivers the update like a general rattling off troop movements. "The Lady Tara is… coping."

I don't know what I expected to hear. That Tara is doing great? That she can't wait for me to come back because I'm the best little sister in the whole world? I just executed Clare.

"Do you think she needs anything?" I ask. "Should I be sending mental health professionals to her or something?"

"I can't say, Your Majesty." Xiao leans forward, her elbows on her knees. "But I think she's been communicating with her mate. I thought you should know."

I should know, and I definitely should worry about it. But the thought of cutting her off from communication with Josh, another person I took from her…

No, I didn't take him from her. Nathan is the one who banished him, and before I was queen.

"Thanks. It is helpful for me to know that." I hate to suggest it, but, "I think we should monitor her mail. Find a way into her phone."

"We can make that happen," Xiao agrees easily.

I immediately regret my words. "Do you think that's bad? Like, invading her privacy. Does it seem like I don't trust her?"

"It's not my place to examine the actions of the queen," she reminds me. Then, reluctantly, adds, "But if I were in the Lady Tara's position? I would understand why those actions are necessary. It wouldn't bother me if I had nothing to hide."

I have a strong feeling that Tara's opinion will differ.

"That said," Xiao says, "She doesn't need to know it's happening."

That doesn't make me feel any better.

Harriet returns with the tea service, the wheels on the

wobbly cart squeaking. She silently lays everything out on the coffee table between Xiao and me.

"Thanks," I say when the housekeeper is finished. She trundles off with her rattly cart, and again we wait until we can no longer hear it before we resume our conversation.

I pour a cup of tea out for myself, pretty happy with how effortlessly I maneuver the pot one-handed, but Xiao turns over her cup and glances up at me apologetically. "I'm off caffeine. Too high strung as it is."

"Right. I should have asked. Do you want something else?"

She casually brushes the air with the back of her hand. "But if we could circle back to the presence of thralls in Wyrding House? Or the lack of them, I guess?"

"Yeah, it's kind of weird, isn't it?" I put a few lumps of sugar into my tea. I don't even like tea very much, but it seemed like a very English and queen thing to offer someone at the time. "I mean, you're totally right, there must be a reason the former king found thralls untrustworthy. The king and I were wondering if you might be able to find some insight into that?"

My miserable attempt to approach the subject tactfully sounds sleazy and manipulative to my own ears.

So, it's no wonder that Xiao is offended. "I'm not a spy, Your Majesty."

"I know," I say quickly, and babble on when I should just be apologizing for making the request in the first place. "I guess I meant from more of a security perspective. Nathan didn't know his uncle very well. We have no idea if he's paranoid or if there's actually something we need to be worried about."

"I'm sure the results of your investigation into the

binding spell will give you that information," she says tersely. It's jarring; I've never seen her approach anything like disagreement with me, ever. What you're asking me for is a completely different skill set. Frankly, I'm not good at talking to people and gaining their confidence."

"I don't know," I say. "I trust you. I would tell you anything."

She leans forward again with a deep sigh, her long braid falling over her shoulder. "Your Majesty… I feel like you may be misunderstanding my role in your retinue."

"Oh, no, I totally get it, you're not a spy." I really offended her, and I feel terrible. "I'm so sorry. I wasn't trying to imply that you were dishonest."

"That's not what I'm talking about." She gestures to the tea set between us. "It's this kind of thing. The friendliness. Your Majesty, I can't be an effective bodyguard and your friend at the same time."

"Oh." That kind of stings.

"It's not personal," she assures me. "I'm supposed to be on alert to all threats at all times. If I'm distracted by emotional or familiar bonds, I could make the wrong choices or misread important situations. It's not safe for me to be anything other than your employee."

"Right." I smack myself upside the head lightly, as if I already knew that and forgot it. But I didn't know it. I assumed Xiao would fall into my little group with Hannah and Tara.

Both of whom are loved ones I've made employees. I guess it's not a huge surprise that I don't understand the difference.

"My number one priority is to keep you safe," Xiao promises. "It might mean I miss out on a potentially awesome friendship, but this is what I've dedicated my life to, in service to the pack."

"And I really appreciate it." I slap my hand on my knee and stand, saying, "Well, I'll let you get back to work."

"I thought I'd do a quick sweep of the rest of the house," she says, all business. "You're staying in here, for now?"

"I am." I gesture over my shoulder toward the bedroom. "Nathan is taking a royal nap. If anything happened, he'd be awake in two seconds."

"He'd need to be awake a second before it happened," Xiao says, then blanches. "Sorry. Bad professional habit."

"It's okay," I assure her.

I walk her to the door and open it.

The tea cart is sitting at the end of the hall.

"I thought she left," Xiao whispers.

"You can take a whole trolley down the stairs," I whisper back.

Xiao holds a finger to her lips and motions for me to stay where I'm at. She creeps into the hall, scanning every centimeter of the walls and ceiling as she does. She stops between two of the large oil portraits and softly raps the dark wood wainscotting. With a gentle press of her fingertips, it springs open.

She hurries back my way. Disused gas lamps flank the doorway; they're shaped like lilies on long, ornate stems.

Xiao touches one. "It's warm." She gives it a tug and it turns downward. There's no scrape, no creak from the antique metal. She presses her ear to the bell of the lily for just a moment before pushing it back into its original position. "It's a listening device. An ear horn, right into your parlor."

"What?" I step back into the room and examine the wall, searching for the opening at the other end.

There's a vent near the ceiling.

Xiao spots it immediately when she enters the room again. Never taking her eyes off it, she pushes a button on her watch and speaks into it. "Orange team, I need you outside the royal chambers. We may have a problem."

CHAPTER 62

Nathan isn't as concerned about the discovery of the secret spyhole as I am—or as concerned as Xiao wants him to be. He's more focused on our meeting with Jonah, who's set to arrive any minute with the outcome of the tests he ran.

"Old houses like this have concealed passages all over, so that servants can move around unobtrusively," Nathan explains, like I've never heard of such a concept. "And my uncle imagined malice around every corner; it's likely he knew about the eavesdropping mechanism already. He may have had it installed for his own use."

We're headed downstairs to the receiving room. I thought somewhere cloak and dagger like a servant's entrance would be more fitting, but Nathan pointed out that we're less likely to be overheard by thralls if we meet in a part of the house they're not allowed.

When he said that, I exchanged a glance with Xiao. Though we didn't speak, I could tell she's of the same mind as I am regarding what the servants will or won't overhear. I plan to always conduct myself like I'm on live television, because I don't know who's watching.

I have a feeling she'll approve of this plan when I have a chance to share it with her.

"You know," I begin as Nathan and I descend the stairs into the great hall. "If your uncle was so freaked out about people watching him or spying on him, wouldn't he have gotten rid of the secret passages? I mean, since he knew about them?"

Nathan doesn't have an answer for that.

"That's what I thought." I lift my chin and stride ahead of him toward the receiving room doors.

I skid to a stop when I see Jonah is already inside. He's not dressed to meet royalty. He's barely dressed to go grocery shopping without getting arrested for public intoxication. Ripped jeans, a wrinkled, over-washed gray t-shirt with a long drip of what looks suspiciously like ketchup down the front, and sunglasses inexplicably on the back of his head all combine into an ensemble that answers any questions I might have had about his daytime life. And raised other questions I wish I didn't have.

"Nice place," he says, pointed to the frescoed ceiling. "Now, I feel like kind of a dick for not springing for a hotel room, at least."

"You weren't expecting company," Nathan says, gesturing at a group of chairs near one of the two fireplaces in the massive room. "Let's have a seat."

I take one of the wing chairs beside Nathan and Jonah drops into one across from us. He sits sideways and throws his legs over the arm, sneakers planted firmly on the cushion of the chair beside him. He pulls a joint from behind his ear and asks, "You cool?"

"Not that cool," Nathan says dryly.

"Fair enough." Jonah puts the joint back.

The less time spent with this guy is probably for the

better, so I cut to the chase. "What did you find out about the binding?"

"Well, first of all, you were right," he tells me. "It *was* a thrall spell."

"Xiao is the one who suggested that," I say, then wonder if that crossed the professional line.

"Then Xiao was correct." Jonah's eyes dart to Nathan's. "You've been under the binding the longest."

"How long?" Nathan asks.

Jonah shrugs. "Twenty-five years, give or take a few, looks like."

Twenty-five years? I wasn't even born then. "How long have I been under the spell?"

"About six years now? They're not exactly time stamped. These are rough estimates." Jonah looks between us. "Anything substantial happen to the two of you thirty and six years ago."

My stomach flips over.

Five years ago, I invoked the Right of Accord and left my pack.

Twenty-five-ish years before that, Nathan had done the same thing.

I expect to see those facts register on his face, but they don't. My thoughts are such a jumble, the only way I can express what's going through my mind is to whisper, "The Right of Accord."

He blanches.

Intrigued by the change in tone, Jonah sits up, giving us an interested incline of his head. "All right, you two. Spill the beans."

Nathan casts a questioning glance at me, but I can only shrug. I have no idea what the rules are about disclosing this information to a human magician. I wouldn't tell a random human on the street about it, but he knows about werewolves already. Not telling him won't keep our existence a secret.

Nathan apparently comes to the same conclusion. "The Right of Accord is a rarely invoked law among our kind. Before accepting a place in the pack and transforming at the full moon, a young werewolf can leave their family and spend five years in the human world."

"Rumspringa," Jonah says. "But for werewolves."

"I don't know what that is," Nathan says irritably. "I invoked the right twenty-five years ago. And Bailey is the only other werewolf I've ever heard of who's invoked it."

"Five years ago," I finish for him, though I'm sure Jonah already got there. "Invoking the Right of Accord is what put the binding on us?"

"Not necessarily." Jonah reaches into his back pocket. Xiao makes a move toward him as he does so, and he puts his hands out. "Easy. It's an iPhone, not an IED." He slowly retrieves the phone, shakes it a little, then turns back to us. He scrolls his finger across the screen. "Your kind is familiar with runes, right?"

"Of course," Nathan answers for both of us.

Personally, I slept through that class in school.

"The spell on the queen uses runes from Tyr's aett; you're familiar with Tyr?" Jonah pauses to check.

"The Norse god of war. He sacrificed his arm to trap Fenrir," Nathan says.

"That," I agree quietly.

"Well, Tyr's aett is all over her." Jonah points his finger at Nathan. "And you are bound with etheric chains."

Nathan shakes his head. "I'm unfamiliar with the term."

"I think I can get it from context." I lift up my stump

and gaze at it in horror. "Whatever this spell is, I'm representing Tyr. You're Fenrir."

The wolf, bound by the gods until the end of time itself.

"Someone wanted you chained up. Someone from your pack." Jonah confirms for Nathan. "And they used her to do it."

"That's absurd," Nathan scoffs. "We're already bound. The thralls control whether or not we change our forms. They could have simply denied me."

"Nathan and I didn't know each other. He's from a powerful family, but I'm not. And the spell they put on him, they did that before I was even born," I point out. "Nobody knew I was going to exist, so how did they figure this spell would work? Really effective divination?"

"I assume they weren't looking for you, specifically. As an individual, I mean," Jonah revises. "Chances are, they were waiting for someone else to come along and invoke the Right of Accord, or whatever. They enchanted the Right, not you."

"That's quite a gamble," Nathan notes. "No one had invoked the Right for centuries before I did."

"Then whoever did this was patient," Jonah says with a condescending nod. "Maybe they were working on it for a long, long time? Maybe since an agreement was put into place between your two species?"

"The agreement is that they somehow get magic from us, and we're fine with that as long as they use some of the magic to keep us from becoming mindless killers at the full moon," I tell Jonah, just as condescendingly. "They need us for their magic. And we need them to harness it for us."

"So, they're farmers. You're their livestock." Jonah shrugs.

Nathan is on his feet, with his hand around Jonah's throat before the human can react.

"Easy, big fella," Jonah rasps. He presses one hand against Nathan's chest and the hand glows searing orange. Nathan stumbles back, smacking at the scorched print on the front of his shirt. Jonah adjusts the stretched-out neck of his t-shirt. "Nobody's hurting the wizard, okay? I'm a third party. You're the one who involved me. You're the one who's paying me."

"We're paying him?" I didn't know about that part.

Nathan shoots me an irritated glance. "Of course, we are. Money is the only thing his kind values."

"That's where you're wrong." Jonah swings his legs off the other chair and sits correctly. "All any magic user wants is more magic. More power. Even your thralls." Jonah nods at Xiao. "Am I right?"

Her hand flexes at her side.

"I'm feeling unwelcome." He slaps his knees and stands. "And underappreciated. I think I'm going to go."

"Wait," I start forward, then realize that I'm a frickin' queen. The word should suffice.

To my astonishment, it does. He turns, blinking pointedly as he waits for me to speak.

"Is that all the information you have for us?" I ask.

"Yeah, that's about it." He snaps his fingers. "Oh, except for this: the spell is intended to make you two irresistible to each other. So you produce lots of little puppies. Make of that what you will."

My hand drops to my stomach.

"Thank you for having me. Really, lovely home you've

got here," Jonah says with an exaggerated bow. As he leaves the room, he calls, "You have my PayPal."

Nathan starts forward but I grip his arm. "Let him go."

Xiao steps up and addresses Nathan. "Your Majesty. The human said the spell came from thralls in this pack. I'm concerned about the queen's safety, and the safety of your heir."

"I'm concerned about that, myself." Nathan stands by my side and covers my hand with his where it rests on my belly. There's a desperation in his eyes I've never seen before. He swallows thickly and says, "Pack. As quickly as you can, but without drawing too much attention.

"Xiao," he says, turning to her. "Don't let the queen out of your sight."

"Not for a second, Your Majesty," she answers.

He looks back to me and gives me a tremulous smile I don't believe. "It's going to be all right. But we must leave. Now."

CHAPTER 63

We haven't been at Wyrding House long enough to completely unpack; Harriet offers to help but I don't like people going through my stuff. Plus, Nathan and I barely brought anything with us in the first place.

"I feel bad for Xiao," I say, taking one of my shirts from the wardrobe and folding it over my arm. It ends up in a sloppy bundle, but it gets the job done enough that I can stuff it into my bag. "She just got here and now we're turning right back around."

"I'm sure she prefers having you in a more secure location," is all Nathan says, moving far faster than I am.

"Do you think they're going to be breaking down the door any second?" I ask, trying to keep my tone light.

"I think the longer we stay here, the more likely that becomes a possibility." He zips his small, wheeled carry-on. "We have a pissed off magician who could sell us out to the highest bidder and a house teeming with traitorous thralls."

"Only the below-stairs servants," I say, mimicking Harriet's pompous delivery.

He shoots me an annoyed glance.

"I wasn't trying to be funny." I double check beneath the bed to make sure I'm not leaving anything behind; I have a strong feeling we're never, ever coming back here. "I don't think it's Jonah we need to worry about. Bet your uncle doesn't seem so needlessly paranoid, now."

"No, he does not," Nathan agrees.

There's a knock at the parlor door. Nathan and I both freeze, our eyes locked as we listen for what will happen next.

"I just received word that the king and queen are leaving?" It's Harriet, and she sounds distressed by our departure plans.

Plans that she already knows about.

I make a move toward the door. Maybe she's just old and confused?

Nathan holds up one finger in warning, stopping me in my tracks.

"Something came up in Toronto," Xiao lies smoothly. "The king and queen must return immediately."

"What a shame! But I do need His Majesty to sign off on some documentation. I hope he won't be in such a hurry to leave that I miss him." Harriet's tone is too wheedling, too deferential.

Something's wrong.

"I'm afraid they're leaving immediately. Anything needing his signature can be sent to his secretary in Toronto. I'm sure you have the contact info," Xiao states firmly. "In the mean—"

There's a crash and a thud that hits the other side of the bedroom wall, like something has been thrown. Like *someone* has been thrown.

Then, there's a roar.

Nathan rushes for the door and I try to stop him, but even with both hands, I wouldn't be able to hold him back. "Stay here!" he orders, charging into the parlor.

The hell I'm going to just stand there. I follow him, but my feet fuse to the floor in the doorway.

Harriet isn't Harriet. She's a fully transformed werewolf in the remnants of Harriet's prim housekeeper dress.

Even though she's elderly, her wolf form is still dangerously powerful; there's nothing frail about the corded muscle rippling under her gray fur. She bats the heavy sofa aside like a housefly and it splinters in midair from the force.

Then what happened to Xiao?

Nathan is helping my bodyguard to her feet, but I'm surprised she's not dead. I know her uniform is plated with a bunch of tactical armor, but I don't know how that kind of thing holds up against blunt force trauma. But the second she's upright, she pushes Nathan behind her, shouting, "Get the queen out!"

That's when Nathan sees me, standing there defenseless, and that alerts Harriet to my presence.

My first thought is, *I'm not losing another fucking hand.* My second is, *I'll probably die, though.*

Harriet charges at me at the same time Nathan does. He manages to insinuate himself between me and her, toppling me backward and tumbling me into the bedroom, where I should have stayed. Nathan shouts in pain. Blood splashes across the floor and I pray it's not his while knowing it mostly likely is.

"Her necklace!" Xiao shouts, leaping onto Harriet's broad back. A gold chain glints against the wolf's fur. Xiao's black-gloved fingers close on it, but it slips from her grasp. "Get her necklace!"

Harriet's teeth snap in Nathan's face. He pushes her muzzle away with one hand. The other grips the pendant on the chain.

Before my disbelieving eyes, Nathan transforms.

It's not neat and tidy, like on the ceremonial grounds. It's violent and instant, tearing the sleeves from his shirt as his arms lengthen and splitting the fabric down his back. With one mighty shove, he sends Harriet—and unfortunately, Xiao—across the parlor.

When Harriet lands, she's the old housekeeper again, unable to fight effectively as Xiao yanks her upright. Nathan raises his clawed hand, holding the pendant and chain.

I try to think back to the man who attacked me at Aconitum Hall. I can't remember if he had a necklace. I didn't get a chance to notice fine details while my arm was spurting blood.

"Why?" I ask, my voice barely a whisper, and probably unheard over the blowing bellows of Nathan's panting. I ask again, louder, "Why, Harriet? Why would you attack us?"

"Because you will destroy our kind!" she rages, fighting against Xiao's hold.

"How?" I demand.

"You shouldn't have invoked the right!" Harriet shrieks at us. "You've doomed us all!"

I can't make sense of what she's saying, but I know it's important. Just like I know that it's important to keep her alive for questioning. Nathan knows that, too.

But Nathan's not fully himself at the moment.

He goes straight for the old woman.

"Nathan, no!" I shout, grabbing a handful of his fur. It's

about as effective as trying to hold back a train with a refrigerator magnet.

Xiao pushes Harriet behind her, but she just delays Nathan; he shoves my bodyguard aside like a feather that's drifted annoyingly into his face.

Harriet's hand shoots out and grips the pendant, returning to werewolf form in an instant. If she gets it away from Nathan, he'll transform back, I realize. He can't let the necklace go.

Instead, he covers her massive hand with his other one, effectively trapping her in her own hold on the pendant. He swings her against the fireplace and the marble surround cracks.

Xiao pulls her gun from her hip, and I scream, "No!" because guns make me nervous, *and* I don't want her to shoot my husband accidentally.

I don't expect my cry to actually influence her, but she glances my way and holds her fire, though she keeps the barrel trained on the sparring werewolves.

Harriet falls from Nathan's grasp and he staggers back. He staggers back on a man's legs, in a man's ripped up clothes. Harriet stands up, still a werewolf.

Xiao gets a shot off; it hits Harriet in the shoulder, but it only momentarily slows her, and Nathan rushes back in like a jackass.

"Stay back and let her shoot!" I yell at him, but it's too late. He snatches the pendant from Harriet's grasp, and they trade forms, leaving Harriet an old woman in a tattered dress, helpless in the claws of a monster.

She laughs, blood burbling over her lips. "They'll kill you. And her. And they'll kill that abomination in her belly."

Ice crystalizes in my blood. *How does she know?*

Nathan's claws flash and I scream, "No!" but it's too late. They tear through the housekeeper's flesh like paper. Her legs hit the floor with a sickening thud. Her entrails follow a second later, smacking the floor wetly. Still holding the bisected top of her body, Nathan bites into her throat, pulling at spine and sinew until her head comes off. It, too, falls to the floor, rolling in an irregular tumble to rest beside her feet.

If ever there was a time for morning sickness, I think this would be it. But as much as I want to heave my guts out at the sight, I can't. Nathan is still a werewolf, Xiao is still human, and the scent of blood is in the air.

"Lower your weapon," I say, calm and firm despite the terror that grips me. "Xiao, put it down."

I'm pretty sure that if Nathan sees a human pointing a gun at him, he's not going to be reasoned with. Not in his current state.

I approach cautiously. I know he won't hurt me, not intentionally, but I'm afraid of what might happen if he doesn't realize it's me behind him. "Nathan, it's okay."

His huge body heaves with each breath he takes. He's all motion and chaos and violence, barely constrained into physical being. He turns his head slightly, one silver eye fixed on me.

"Put her down, Nathan," I implore him. "She's dead. And we have to leave."

He drops what's left of the body, crushed to pulp in his fist. I lay a gentle hand on his shoulder. "Give Xiao the necklace."

She takes a step forward and Nathan bares his teeth with a warning growl.

"Give her the necklace," I say again, firmer. "I can't

take it from you, or I'll change, too. We have to get out of here, and we can't do that if we look like this."

That gets through to him. He extends one gore-covered hand to Xiao, and she swiftly snaps the pendant from the chain. She slips it into one of the many pockets on her pants.

Nathan steps back from the body. He's covered in just about as much blood as Harriet's earthly remains are, and I frantically run my hand over his exposed chest and shoulders, looking for any sign of a wound.

"It's not mine." He grabs my trembling hand and lifts it to his lips. "It's not mine."

"Your Majesties," Xiao says, holstering the firearm once more. "It's time to leave."

CHAPTER 64

"Black moonstone."

Xiao drops the pendant, now enclosed in a plastic baggie, onto the table between Nathan and me.

He leans forward in his chair and reaches for the baggie, but I'm not taking any chances. I smack his hand away with an annoyed, "Don't touch it!"

I'm still shaking, even though we're on the plane and safely away from Wyrding House, I'm still terrified that yet another shoe is going to suddenly drop.

I made Xiao threaten the thrall pilots and leave a member of her trusted team in the cockpit as a reminder.

I am not going to die today.

Xiao gestures to the unremarkable looking cabochon in the pendant. "The assassin who took your hand had some in a bracelet. I think it's fair to assume that this is what they're using to change."

I shake my head. "Moonstone is a pretty common gem, isn't it? I've never heard of it doing… this."

"Maybe that's why we never heard of it," Nathan

muses. "If we knew, perhaps we wouldn't need the thralls and their rituals."

"There's thrall magic involved here," Xiao says, and she's so confident in her answer that I have no further questions. She does, though. "But why would thralls send a werewolf to kill another werewolf?"

"Are you suggesting the thralls should have simply killed us themselves?" Nathan asks. His tone is not friendly.

"I'm saying that it doesn't make sense for thralls to set up a spell like the one the human magician described, then immediately kill the targets of that spell." Xiao takes the pendant back. "I'll hang onto this for now."

"I think that's the safest option," I agree. I have no idea what would happen if Nathan or I went full werewolf in such an enclosed space.

"Don't show it to anyone else. And don't let it leave your person," Nathan instructs her.

"Yes, Your Majesty."

One question has been screaming in my brain since we left Wyrding House. "How did she know?"

Xiao and Nathan look at me, waiting for further explanation.

"That I'm pregnant?" I gesture to my stomach. "We've kept that secret."

"There weren't any secrets in that house." Xiao shakes her head. "King Archibald was right to be afraid."

"It appears so," Nathan agrees. He looks to me, his expression unreadable as he studies my face. "I think we'll retire."

She nods. "I'll have someone wake you before we land."

Nathan stands and offers me his hand, and I'm too

numb and tired to do anything but take it and follow him back to the bed.

I have to ignore the pile of bloody towels on the floor; he showered the second we hit cruising altitude.

It's the first moment we've had alone together since the fight. I turn to him and reach up to brush a dark curl from his forehead. He flinches slightly as my fingers graze a slash across his hairline.

"We should have gotten that stitched up," I murmur, and I wish I was tall enough to kiss his cheek without hopping.

"It's not bleeding. It should be fine," he says, holding his hair back to reveal two butterfly bandages carefully positioned on his skin. "Xiao is well-versed in combat medicine. I have a horrible feeling that will prove beneficial.

"I'm sure it will."

"And you?" He's already asked about potential injuries a hundred times, but it's like he's incapable of believing I'm okay.

"I'm fine," I reassure him. "Nathan, you're the one who got really hurt."

"I would argue that Harriet was the one who got *really* hurt." The corner of his mouth flickers.

"Oh my god, was that a joke?" I know I shouldn't laugh, but at least it breaks the tension a little, finally. "Not cool."

"Not cool was attempting to kill you." He holds me at arm's length, scanning from the top of my head down. "You're sure nothing aches? Nothing stings? Sometimes, in the heat of a fight—"

"Adrenaline will prevent you from feeling pain, I know." I gesture to his head; at first, he insisted that all the blood on him was Harriet's, but her first swipe at him caused the blood I saw splattering across the wall of the parlor.

In an instant, I'm back in the throne room. The smell of blood overwhelms my memory. Nathan's blood. Nathan's screams as they tried to save him in the safe room.

"Bailey?" Nathan asks softly.

I shove him back with my shoulder, almost knocking him off his feet. "Don't touch me!"

He steps back, hands up.

My wits return to me with crushing embarrassment. "I'm not there," I whisper to reassure myself. "I'm not there."

"Not where?" Nathan asks, taking a cautious step toward me.

"I'm not…" I blow out a shaky breath. "Sometimes, I have to remind myself that we're not back in that room. During the riot."

He nods thoughtfully. "You never told me what it was like. Just that you sat beside my bed."

I almost tell him that I don't want to talk about it. I don't like thinking about it, that's for sure. But somehow, when he cautiously takes my hand and leads me to the bed to sit down, it all comes pouring out. "The confusion was the worst. Maybe the second worst. I looked down and there was a dead thrall and blood all over me. And then you were just gone."

He squeezes my hand. "I'm here now."

I take a breath and nod to indicate I need just a moment. Just the smallest pause to collect the scattered pieces of those memories, which all seem to be not a big deal and a Very Big Deal to my emotions all at once. "I've never seen someone really get hurt before. Or die. And now I feel like I'm doing it all the time. And even though we're fine… today we might not have been."

"We've been fortunate," he says, putting an arm around my back.

"And that luck will run out. Eventually, it just will." Tears creep into my voice. "Death is all around us. And I'm supposed to be making this life and protecting it."

"It's protected." He puts his other hand on my stomach. "And you're protected. With my life."

"Which you've almost lost before." I shake my head. "This isn't something you can just… reassure away. I saw you. I saw your insides coming out and I heard you screaming. And that… it haunts me. I can still hear you."

"Hear this," he says, kissing the top of my head. "You're here, now. And I'm here. I'm not in pain. I'm not in danger. You're in this moment, and you're safe."

It's such a simple sentiment, but somehow, it grounds me. It doesn't remove those horrors from my mind. It's not a long-term solution. But it brings me back to my body. It brings me back to who I am and what's happening around me, clears the adrenaline from my system.

All that's left are tears.

Nathan holds me and soothes me while I cry my heart out into his chest. I'm sure I'm getting snot on his t-shirt, but it's not the grossest bodily fluid he touched today. He doesn't try to tell me that everything *will be* all right, but he tells me that it *is* all right, and that's enough. That gets me through, until the ache in my chest subsides and my eyes dry.

"I need a tissue," I say, lifting my head. "Sorry about your shirt."

He grimaces down at it, then pulls it over his head and tosses it onto the ruined towels as he passes the pile on his way to the bathroom. When he returns with a box of tissues, I note the jagged scar across his stomach, following the line from his ribs on the left to his hip on the right.

"Does it bother you?" he asks, offering me the box. "I can put on another shirt."

I shake my head and smile up at him. "Actually, I'm glad to see it. It reminds me that all that stuff? Didn't happen yesterday. And that you're still alive."

He gives me a lop-sided smile. "Did you ever think there would be a day that you were happy to say that?"

I snatch a tissue and blow my nose loudly. "Don't tease me. I'm in a weird place."

"I always find the best women in weird places." He sits beside me again.

I toss the tissue aside with a disgusted noise. "First of all, that's a terrible line. And second, are you really hitting on me when I look like this?" I know my eyes are all puffy, my face red and splotchy, and the snot show wasn't exactly elegant.

"You look like my mate," he says, and puts his arm around me again, this time with decidedly different intentions. "My mate, who is carrying my child. I can't help it if that makes me feel things."

"That's the binding," I remind him, suddenly miserable again.

"Hey," he says softly, hooking two fingers under my chin. He tips my face up and holds my gaze, those silver eyes trained on mine with an intensity that's almost uneasy. "I'm not good at sentimental words or expressing emotion. So, you'll have to forgive me if this doesn't sound like the romantic declaration you've always dreamed of. Agreed?"

"I guess?" I narrow my eyes in playful suspicion, but my heart slams against my ribs.

"No matter what anyone says about the spell… its work is over. It has no power over me. Because what I've come to feel for you is far, far stronger than the binding ever was."

An astonished, "oh," leaves me on a breathy whimper, but it's all I can manage to get out before he kisses me. And kisses me. And kisses me.

And he doesn't stop until I know, for certain, that he's meant every word.

CHAPTER 65

We summon council members to Aconitum Hall. The Council Chambers are at the ceremonial site, and the ceremonial site is where all the thralls are.

It astonishes me that for centuries, no one—except Nathan's uncle, apparently—had cause to suspect the thralls as a source of potential treachery. It astonishes me more that now, with proof, convincing some members of the council is still nearly impossible.

"We've overlooked a major threat," I try to explain to the ten men seated around the large table in the conference room. There are only ten of them because we executed the others, which makes addressing this group that much more tricky. I don't want them to think that they have to outwardly agree with me or I'll cut their heads off, but that's probably what's going to happen. "Thralls are a part of our lives every day. They're in our homes. They're in our school, our businesses. And they're content to do all of that and allow us to live in luxury and ease because they can harness our magical power?"

A murmur of understanding comes from somewhere at

the table, and I look to Ryan. He's been my friend since our first days in school *and* he was part of the little anarchist study group he, Hannah, and I formed ahead of the change and our potentially disastrous mating pacts. He knows this isn't the position I ever wanted to be in.

Across the table from him, a different council member objects. It's one of the men we met with before our trip to London. "We don't simply use the thralls for free labor. They have an important function in our lives. Before they learned to control our change, we were little more than wild beasts at the full moon."

"The queen knows her history," Nathan responds. Of everyone in the meeting, he seems the most relaxed. Almost unbothered entirely, considering he'd just been attacked by a werewolf, himself. He's largely let me take control of the meeting and I can't tell if that's because he trusts me to do a good job or if he thinks they're more likely to listen to someone who isn't an outsider.

And outsider who came in and threw the entire pack into chaos in less than five years of his reign.

"I do know our history," I agree. "I know that before the thralls perfected their spell, their job was to chain us, lock us in cells. The dungeon beneath the Council Chambers was built for that very purpose. No one wants a return to those days of secrecy and fear."

Especially now, when the idea of letting a thrall lock us up and keep us vulnerable is terrifying.

"If they can control whether or not we change, then that probably means they can make us change when it's not even the full moon," I point out. "Or give someone else the power."

Nathan grimaces and gestures to my stump. "Hence."

"Exactly." I hold up my arm to further the point. "This

wasn't done by a werewolf in its civilized form. The man who did this stood in my sitting room and transformed before my eyes. And just yesterday—" Two days ago, who can say when one is so jet-lagged? "—a werewolf from the Greater London pack attacked the King. Using this."

I motion to Xiao, who brings the pendant forward in a clear acrylic box. She places it on the table.

"Black moonstone," I explain. "When the King merely held this pendant, he changed."

One of the council members, a young East-Asian man who graduated school a few years ahead of me, motions with his hand and says, "It can't just be the moonstone. My mate is obsessed with crystals and stones. I'm actually concerned about the combined weight of them crashing through our subflooring."

A ripple of misogynistic chuckles goes around the table and I add the mental note that all those empty council seats should be filled by women.

"We have black moonstone in our house. Spheres, jewelry, trinkets… this has never happened to us," he finishes.

"Then it must be enchanted in some way," another council member puts in. "Who saw this spell at work?"

"I did. And my bodyguard, Xiao." I turn and thank her and indicate she can take the box away. I didn't even want to bring it into a room full of werewolves, but the prop has proved effective. "She can testify that black moonstone was found in a bracelet on the assassin who took my hand."

"Transforming with the stone was one of the more disturbing experiences of my life," Nathan adds. "It was unnatural and unpleasant. And it ruined one of my favorite shirts."

I can't help my small smile, so I cover it with a cough.

"Sartorial consequences aside, what does this mean for us?" Ryan asks. He's a big picture guy and that's going to be immensely helpful to us. Hannah already had him on the job, armed with a dossier of the classified information we got from Jonah. "In the interest of transparency, Her Majesty has named me to an investigative committee focused solely on this work of magic against us."

"It was an act of magic against the king and the queen," someone down the table corrects him.

"It's an act against all of us." Ryan pushes his chair back and stands, casting his gaze around the entire table. "As long as the thralls are experimenting on us in secret with their magic, all of us are at risk."

"The hierophant already advised that this spell had to do with breeding." The other white dude from our pre-London meeting speaks up. "Our king and queen were put under a binding spell. They were meant, specifically, to be paired."

"We know more about that spell, now," Nathan explains. "And we didn't rely on a thrall for the information."

"An independent human magician examined the spell and found that not only was it cast with thrall magic, it was cast on Nathan when he invoked the Right of Accord as a teenager," I say. "And the second half of the spell was cast when I invoked the right. Decades later."

"Must you phrase it that way?" Nathan mutters under his breath.

I shoot him a warning glance, entreating him to control his vanity, before I continue. "The magic is ancient. This suggests they've been working on this for a long, long time."

"But the hierophant said that the spell had to be cast on both of you at the same time," the other guy from our last meeting points out.

"And we're taking the word of a thrall? When we know they're working against us?"

My question makes everyone around the table uncomfortable. To doubt the hierophant, to question our most sacred ceremonial leader, is blasphemy.

"You have a thrall guarding you," he counters. "In this very room. You must not be that concerned."

"I trust Xiao. She saved my life when I was attacked by the assassin here in Aconitum Hall. She's proved trustworthy." The last thing I'm going to permit is widespread prejudice when we don't have any idea who's behind this plot. "Not all thralls are involved in this."

"We're more concerned that werewolves have tried to take our lives," Nathan says. "It suggests that werewolves know about whatever the thralls have planned for us. And maybe those interests clash."

"Are you suggesting these werewolves might be working against the thralls?" Ryan prompts. He can't reveal everything, but I appreciate that he can steer the conversation in the right direction. "That perhaps these assassination attempts have more to do with the spell that was cast on Your Majesties and not mere political maneuvering."

"It seems more likely," I agree, as if we didn't have this exact conversation the night before.

"What is the spell, exactly?" a previously silent council member asks. "What is it meant to do?"

"It was meant to ensure that the queen and I found each other and bred," Nathan states flatly.

My cheeks burn with embarrassment.

"Then it should be fairly easy to avoid completing the spell," the councilman states. "Don't breed."

Nathan and I exchange a glance, and he gives me a small nod.

"We didn't know about the spell prior to our mating ceremony." No need to mention the boning down we did before that night. "And the spell was successful."

"Congratulations, Your Majesties," someone says.

"We've not given the news to the rest of the pack. This is private information and if it leaks, we'll know how," Nathan warns.

There's a rumble of agreement around the room.

"Until we find out what the thralls want with our child, we need to keep it as protected as possible," I add. What I don't say is that we clearly need it protected from our own kind, and the fact that we don't know why consumes my every waking thought.

Which is okay, because it means my every waking thought *isn't* consumed by my complicated grief for Clare.

"From this point forward, our meetings will be held here," Nathan tells the council. "We won't be filling the vacant seats until this situation is resolved. You're all here because you were judged loyal and supportive to the crown. Do not prove us wrong."

My phone alarm goes off and I hurry to silence it. "Gentlemen, I have a meeting I need to attend."

I feel Nathan's gaze on me. He knows where I'm going and how much I dread it.

"I encourage all of you to cooperate with Councilman Hunter's investigation," I go on. "He is my voice, and the voice of the king, in this matter. Unless we explicitly announce otherwise."

That won't be an issue; I trust Ryan with our lives, as well as our authority.

"This meeting is dismissed," Nathan announces.

I stand by awkwardly as they all rise and bow to us and shake hands with each other before they depart the room. Shifting from one foot to the other, I want to shout, *"Just leave! You're making me late!"*

When they've all finally filed out, Nathan stands and comes to my side, putting his arm around me. "Will you be all right?"

"No." I tuck my head against his chest. "This is going to suck so bad."

"It will," he agrees. "But you can't put it off forever."

Reluctantly, I pull away from him and lift my face for a kiss.

"Do you want me to come with you?" he asks when our lips part.

I don't laugh outright at the suggestion, but it's definitely ridiculous. "No. I don't think your presence is welcome."

"I understand." He gives me one last kiss on the forehead.

I turn to Xiao. "Okay. Let's go. Let's get this over with."

"Yes, Your Majesty."

It's time to visit Tara.

CHAPTER 66

Tara is dressed all in black, seated on the sofa in the parlor adjoining her room and Clare's. That door is closed, draped with black bunting.

I sit in the chair perpendicular to the sofa and silently will my sister to look at me, to speak to me beyond the mumbled, "Your Majesty," I got when she curtseyed formally at my entrance, or the offer of a beverage, which I refused.

"How are you?" I ask finally.

"It's very lonely here," she says flatly. "It was different, with Clare. More like when we lived at home, before we were mated. We didn't see each other much when you were away."

"Because you were newly wed?"

She nods.

"I understand that," I try, hating myself for even attempting to link my experience with hers. "Getting caught up in your mate's life and drifting away from your own."

"It's a bit different for you. You're also caught up in

being queen." She finally makes eye contact with me. "Do you think that maybe you got too caught up in it? And that's why…"

She doesn't finish her sentence, probably owing to the wobble in her voice near the end.

We've been over this, and she still won't accept the truth. "I didn't sentence Clare to death."

"No. Your husband did. And not just death. Degradation. You forced her to take part in Lycaon's Banquet. You made her—" a retching noise deep in her throat stops Tara this time.

"She sided with the traitors who tried to kill me." I stop myself. "Tara, I trust you. If I tell you something… it can't leave this room."

"What loyalty do you deserve?" she demands.

I don't have an answer for that.

"And you don't trust me. I'm under constant surveillance." She lifts her chin. "Do you think I can't tell that my mail has been opened? Do you think I haven't found it unusual that a thrall guard takes my phone away at night?"

"Do you think I haven't found it unusual that were-wolves are trying to kill me?" I bite back. I take a deep breath to calm myself. "Tara, listen to me, please. What-ever you or Clare might have thought about your mates' motives, about our parents' motives… it goes far deeper than control of the pack. Something was done to Nathan and me. By the thralls."

Tara's back goes straight. "What do you mean?"

"Do you know about this already?" If she did, and she never told me…

She shakes her head. "Josh never really clued me in on

anything. I was seen and not heard and definitely not briefed on secret plots."

"I had to ask. Before Clare died—"

"Before you had her executed," Tara corrects me.

I ignore it. "She told me that the plan had moved on from executing Nathan to executing me so that I could be replaced by my mate's mistress."

"The pack doesn't trust her," Tara protests. "Clare had to have been mistaken."

"She was. Or lied to." Which makes me even more furious. Clare was willing to murder me over pack politics. Did she even have any idea what the true goal of my assassination was? Or was she just content to see me die for her husband's political ambitions. "The pack wanting us dead has nothing to do with who controls the throne. There's a spell on Nathan and me. A binding. It's ancient thrall magic that somehow endangers the pack."

Tara nods slowly, and I see her mind working behind her blank, grief-erased expression. "So, they were acting for the good of the pack, after all?"

"I suppose you could frame it like that," I say, a little alarmed that she came to that conclusion. "But since we don't know what it is those werewolves were trying to protect us from—"

"Guess you should have left some of them alive," she snaps.

I take a deep breath to calm my urge to respond in kind. "Tara, I'm pregnant."

She takes a breath that isn't audible, but which raises her whole chest.

"The spell the thralls did, they did because they want this baby," I go on. "For what purpose, I have no clue."

"How did you find this all out?" she asks, not commenting on the pregnancy announcement.

What did you think she would do? Whoop for joy? I'm still the sister that killed our sister. I'm still married to the man who separated Tara from her mate, from any hope of having a child of her own. Why would she congratulate me? Why would she be anything other than furious, at me and at the unfairness of the universe?

So, I answer her question. "When Nathan and I went to London, we met with a human magician."

Tara's eyes widen and she turns her head sharply toward me. "Such a thing exists?"

"I know. I had no idea, either," I say.

"They're not thralls?" She's just as bewildered by the information as I was. "Like, thralls that ran away from the pack or—"

"Just humans who use magic." Since I don't know the details of how that all works, and since that's not really the point of the conversation, I go on. "We needed someone outside of any pack, who could examine the spell objectively and tell us what we needed to know, without any investment in the outcome."

"What did he find?" The fact that Tara is talking to me now, not just looking for ways to snipe at me, feels like a cheap thing to be happy about. It doesn't mean anything other than that she's interested in this particular conversation.

But I'll take it. "I'm bound with runes from Tyr's aett." I don't have to explain what those are; Tara's always been a bit of a mythology nerd. "And Nathan is bound with etheric chains."

"Like Fenrir," she says, referencing the wolf held

captive by the gods. She glances down at my stump. "Wait. Nathan didn't—"

"No, Nathan isn't the one who bit off my hand," I say with a roll of my eyes. "Look, I love the guy, but I wouldn't stick around if he decided to start munching parts off me. Anyway—"

"You love him?"

What a weird question to ask. "Do I love who?"

"Nathan. You just said you love him."

I laugh out loud. "Okay, I must have misspoken. Because—"

Because there's no way I'm in love with him.

Because that would be depressing, because he doesn't love me back.

Because he doesn't think he can love anyone.

"I don't really care," Tara says, waving her hand. Her callousness stings, and I'm pretty sure it's designed to. "The spell has you marked with runes from Tyr's aett. You lost your hand. Nathan's side of the spell is symbolic of Gleipnir… chains that will hold him until—"

I know this part. "Until the end of the world."

"You paid attention in class," Tara says with a brief smile, the first I've seen from her in a long, long time.

"I paid attention around the dinner table," I correct her. "Back when you wouldn't shut up about it."

"See, aren't you glad I annoyed you with it?" As if realizing that she's gotten too friendly, she shuts down her smile. But she goes on, "If you trust me enough to tell me all this, do you trust me to do further research? Look into what the symbolism could mean?"

"That would be really helpful." Impulsively, I reach over and cover her hand with mine. She doesn't pull away, and tears spring to my eyes. "And I'm grateful for the offer. And grateful that you're still here."

"Well, where am I supposed to go? Back to Newfoundland?" She makes a noise. "It's so dry there. Does nothing for my hair."

I want to leave on a good note, so I decide it's time to go. "I have another appointment this afternoon but if you wanted to have dinner or…"

"I think I'll pass on dinner with the man who murdered my sister."

So much for leaving on a good note.

"Right. Well. I'll check in." I stand and go toward the door.

"Bailey."

I stop and turn back.

Tara is twisted in her seat, one arm on the back of the couch. "I don't like him. But I'm happy for you."

I snort. "Happy for me because I'm with someone you don't like?"

"Happy that you found love with your mate." She smiles sadly. "It wasn't that way for all of us. But I'm glad it's the way for you."

"Well, I'm not sure 'love' is the right word for what Nathan and I have. We're under a spell," I remind her. "But if you can feel happiness for me, that might mean that I'll get the love of my sister back, too."

She doesn't reassure me that she does still love me, or that our sisterly bond will somehow recover. But she does nod, casting her eyes down, a tear gliding over her cheek.

That gives me hope, and hope is really all I can ask for.

CHAPTER 67

Somehow, in all the ugliness of pack politics and multiple attempts on my life, I totally forgot about pre-natal care.

I'm just not sure how to get it, at first. Thralls are in charge of all of our medical care, and I don't know how much we want them to know. But Nathan and I decide that we can't take a chance with the baby's life.

As we wait in the exam room, looking at all the posters of werewolf fetal development and the plastic anatomical model of the baby's head in the birth canal—no thank you —I find the situation becoming more real by the second.

"Did you ever think you'd have kids?" I ask Nathan, who's looking over a pamphlet about the first trimester.

He lifts his eyebrows and folds the pamphlet before neatly tucking it into his inside jacket pocket. "I assumed I would. In a hypothetical, detached kind of way. There's so much pressure to find a mate and breed right away. That's never appealed to me."

"It's not so appealing to me, but here I am. In a paper gown." I laugh nervously. "Having a baby."

"Are you…" he frowns slightly, almost like he's embarrassed. "Is this something you don't want?"

That's a good question. Sometimes, I think about the fact that I'm going to be a mother and it's all baby snuggles and soft, fuzzy edges. Other times, it's just a dark voice in my head reminding me that I was raised by someone who made her daughters hate every part of themselves and I'm gripped with the debilitating fear of ruining my child.

"I'm a female werewolf," I say finally. "It's never been a question of what I want. That pressure that you felt to have children? It's ten times, no, it's a billion times worse for us. I've never considered whether I want to have children, because the rule of the pack dictates that I will, by default."

"True," he agrees. "I suppose it wasn't a choice for you. I just assumed all female werewolves want to bear progeny for the pack."

"Our laws are archaic," I grumble. "But since you asked about me, specifically? I'm fine with this."

"I should have asked before—"

"Maybe," I cut him off. "But if you had asked, I would have told you that I've honestly been a little afraid, ever since I learned about how babies are made, that I wouldn't be able to have one. My mother and father had been married for decades before they managed to conceive us. They had to wait until science made it possible."

"No thrall magic to help with that?" Nathan wonders.

"No dominion over life and death," I remind him.

"Right." He taps his fingers on his knee. "I wonder where the doctor is?"

There's a knock at the door and a muffled, "The doctor is here," before the door opens to admit a thrall who appears to be in her thirties, with reddish-brown hair held back in a low ponytail and big freckles on her pale skin.

I cross my ankles and nervously drum my heels on the hollow metal base of the exam table, waving with my fingers. "Hi."

"Your Majesty." The doctor curtseys to me, then to Nathan, and somehow pulls it off while balancing an open laptop on her arm. "Your Majesty. I'm Doctor Campbell. It's an honor to serve you both during this blessed time."

"Um, thanks," I say, still not used to this type of formality.

"Your wrist looks like it healed well," the doctor notes. "Any troubles with that, at all?"

I look down at my stump. I barely feel my phantom fingers anymore. "No. Just adapting."

"And are you still on pain medication for that?" Dr. Campbell asks, sitting on the wheeled stool and sliding the laptop on the counter.

"Nope." I shake my head.

"She's tough," Nathan says with a chuckle. "She barely needed anything at all."

"That's probably for the better, then," Doctor Campbell says, her fingers tapping across the keyboard. "All right. Do we know the first day of your last menstrual period?"

"No," I admit sheepishly. "I used to track it on an app because it's been irregular in the past. Lately, with so much happening in the pack—"

The doctor nods in sympathetic understanding. "We can estimate fetal age by other means."

"We do know when the baby was conceived," Nathan says. "We were only together once between my recovery and her injury, and we learned she was pregnant shortly after that."

I think back, quickly trying to remember those jumbled events, and realize he's right. "Yes, because I had my period while you were still convalescing. You're right."

"I know I'm right," he says smugly.

"So that would have been…" The doctor looks between the two of us.

"Six weeks?" I shrug. "Eight? To be honest, I lost track of a lot of time while I was recovering. And then there was that… other stuff."

"I'm sure. It's been a stressful time for you," she says, nodding, and I honestly want to throw my arms around her and hug her and cry because I can't remember anyone else, not even my friends or my sister, recognize that all of the turmoil has taken a toll on me.

The doctor tilts her head. "It's still very early. How did you know?"

"I could tell," Nathan answers while I try to figure out how to phrase, *"He tasted it in my pussy juice."* He's much more tactful about it. "She smelled different."

A smile touches the corner of the doctor's mouth. "A lot of males know first, if they're especially in-tune with their mates."

I'm not sure we can describe Nathan as being "in-tune" with me, but I smile back weakly, anyway.

The doctor runs me through a barrage of questions: am I experiencing morning sickness? have I noticed weight gain? what about swollen feet, dizziness, fainting?

Every time I answer, I wonder if it means something, if my answers will reveal that surprise, I'm not really pregnant at all.

I must not be the first person to worry about that in this office, because Dr. Campbell says, "Relax. This is just a thorough record of your symptoms. We're establishing a history for you and baby."

"Oh. Good." I feel a little silly. "I know it's weird, because we had the blood test and everything, but I still can't believe it's real. That there's really a baby in there."

"Well, we're going to have a look with the ultrasound today, so you'll have photographic evidence," the doctor says. She pushes a button on an intercom and says, "We're ready," and just a minute later, a nurse arrives with a knock at the door. There's brief, low conversation; Xiao is standing right outside, probably interrogating everyone who comes in.

The nurse does appear to be a little shaken when she enters, pushing the machine.

Doctor Campbell explains that a traditional ultrasound won't show anything yet, so I have to put my feet in the stirrups and let them get a look with a probe that looks like an electric toothbrush in its travel case.

"Dad, if you want to stand—" Dr. Campbell sheepishly corrects herself, "I'm so sorry. *Your Majesty*, if you'd like to stand on the other side of the exam table, you'll both be able to see."

"I quite like the sound of 'dad,' actually," Nathan says, and the mingled hope and pride on his face makes my heart squeeze.

"All right," the doctor says, "Relax, this will be cold."

She's right. The probe *is* cold, and I change my opinion of the travel toothbrush case to popsicle for the first few seconds it's in my vagina. The doctor taps some things on what appears to be a truly ancient keyboard, then turns the screen to face us.

"You're right," she says, gesturing to what appears to be a tiny circle with a blob stuck to it. "About six weeks."

"That's…" Nathan's voice is thick with emotion. "That's our baby?"

"That's your baby." She indicates the tiny blob of flickering light. "And that movement you're seeing indicates where its heart will be. It's already practicing being a heart."

A tear rolls from my eye to splash on the paper exam table cover. "It's real."

"It is real," Dr. Campbell confirms.

Nathan takes my hand and squeezes it.

I squeeze back.

"Let me get some measurements, then I'll print you a photo," she says, turning the screen away.

I look up at Nathan, and he gazes down at me with a tight, close-mouthed smile. His eyes shine with tears. He's barely holding it together.

And I love him.

It hits me so hard, I almost can't breathe. I definitely can't keep looking at him. Panic crawls up in my chest. I've never been in love before. And now, I'm in love with someone who's said, over and over again, that he doesn't think he'll ever be able to love.

What should be one of the happiest moments of my life —at least, as far as I've heard—has suddenly changed for the morose.

I'm mated to a man who can't love me. And I love him with my whole heart.

CHAPTER 68

Two days later, we have a secret meeting in the conference room at Aconitum Hall. Just Nathan, me, Hannah, and Ryan, and of course, Xiao, who stands by, guarding the door.

Hannah has us all set up, with a white board and different colored markers— "to stay organized!"—as well as notebooks, pens, highlighters, all types of stuff we don't need.

"You just wanted to take a trip to the office supply store," I accuse her.

"I can neither confirm nor deny," she answers, contentedly stroking a pack of gel pens.

"While the abundance of stationary is impressive," Nathan begins, "Let's start with what we know so far."

He turns to the white board and writes *"wwksf"* in the upper left corner.

All of us, even Xiao, make alarmed noises at the chaotic shape of the letters.

"How about someone with better handwriting?" Ryan suggests, tacking on a hasty, "no offense, Your Majesty."

"He doesn't get to take offense in here," I remind Ryan. "Remember, this is informal."

"Well, who has better handwriting?" Nathan demands, annoyed. He sits in the chair next to mine.

I just shrug. "Not me, that's for sure."

Hannah gets up, erases the nightmare scribbles, and sets about making three columns. She titles them, *"werewolves," "thralls,"* and *"unknown."*

"She was born for this," I whisper to Nathan.

Beneath the *"werewolves"* column, she neatly prints, *"Nathan and Bailey: Reproductive Spell."* Changing from her black marker to a red one, she makes a bullet point below it: *"Bailey = Tyr"* and *"Nathan = Fenrir"*

"We know enough about the spell that we understand the symbolism," she says, moving to the next column. She notes there that thralls cast the spell on us. Then, under *"unknown,"* she writes *"moonstone."*

"The thralls are behind the moonstone," I correct her.

She caps her marker pointedly. "Do we have a definite answer that the thralls are behind it, or do we just assume they are?"

"They're the only ones that use magic," Nathan points out.

"Humans use magic, too," Ryan reminds us. "That's how you found out about the spell in the first place."

"I've done some research on human-thrall relations," Hannah says, opening a binder on the table.

She made a *binder*. This entire plot is going to be solved by Staples.

"It's difficult to get information, but not impossible," she goes on. "Humans aren't discreet about anything when it comes to the internet. I found a few online forums for witches, wizards, those types. There's an overwhelming sentiment against thralls. They view the thrall-werewolf symbiote as exploitative."

"Wait… they're talking about us on the internet?" I don't like that at all. "People can see that."

"The percentage of humans actually interested in what they consider supernatural is quite low," Nathan says, unconcerned. "Anyone visiting these sites likely already believes in our existence or at least considers our existence probable. And anyone who stumbles across this material without looking for it will dismiss it as fantasy."

That only makes me feel marginally better.

"How do they find our relationship to thralls exploitative?" Ryan asks. "They use our magical energy and in return, we grant them protection and stability."

Hannah shakes her head. "They see it as exploitative of *us*."

I laugh out loud. "Really? Because we live in mansions served by thralls. Our businesses employ thralls. If anyone is getting the short end of the stick—"

Xiao coughs quietly.

Oh, shit. We've been talking about her people while she's in the room, like she's not there.

"Xiao?" I ask, wincing at the question. "What do you think?"

I expect her to say that it's not her place to weigh in, but instead, she says, "I don't think werewolves truly understand the arrangement between yourselves and thralls."

"Could you enlighten us?" Nathan suggests cautiously.

"It appears to me that werewolves believe you're the ones with the upper hand in this. That you somehow control the thralls, and the thralls desperately need you. But you need us more than we need you."

I've never heard her speak so plainly. My jaw drops.

For a moment, I'm afraid Nathan will get all egotistical and angry, but he doesn't. He just nods thoughtfully. "Without thralls, we can't control what we become at the full moon. Which is the most important function thralls perform, really."

"And if we take that away, what are you left with?" she asks.

"There are human magicians," Ryan points out. "Why do we keep forgetting this?"

"And do they have access to the millennia of magic texts and techniques thralls have acquired?" Xiao counters.

"We're getting ahead of ourselves," Hannah says, almost nervously. I wonder if she's uncomfortable talking about this because she doesn't want to think about what would happen if the thralls took that control away from us, or if she's worried something will happen to Xiao for speaking her mind with Nathan in the room.

I know Nathan as my mate.

Hannah and Ryan and Xiao know Nathan as the guy who just enacted the most brutal mass execution in pack history.

"Right, back to the moonstone," I say. "But Xiao, I appreciate your insight. Please, feel free to join in with anything you think might be helpful."

She nods.

"King Archibald didn't trust thralls," I go on. "So, what are the chances that he was aware that some were working magic on werewolves?"

"High, though he never mentioned it to me," Nathan says.

"I found listening devices all through Wyrding House,"

Xiao puts in. "They might not have been for thrall spying. He might have been spying on the thralls."

"And poor Harriet is clearly used them." I pause. "Poor Harriet was loyal to your uncle. For over a hundred years. She could have killed him or hurt him at any time, and she didn't."

Nathan nods, brow creased in thought. "And if he had been concerned about Harriet's loyalty, he wouldn't have kept her in the house."

"Harriet seemed to have a real issue with thralls, herself," I point out. "Snobby."

"And *poor* Harriet tried to kill you," Hannah reminds me. "After you learned that thralls put the spell on you."

"Your Majesties, she could have overhead any conversation you had about the binding while you were in the house," Xiao adds.

"So, you think she tried to kill us because of the spell the thralls put on us?" My pregnancy-fatigued brain struggles a little to keep up.

"In which case, why would the thralls give her the magic she would need to throw a wrench into *their* plans?" Nathan grimaces and curses under his breath.

"I'm going to write this..." Hannah says, uncapping a new marker and turning back to the whiteboard. "...in blue... so we know... it's unsubstantiated..."

When she turns back, the *"moonstone"* entry has a color-coded bullet point that reads: *"humans"*.

"Fantastic," Ryan exclaims. "This gives us a direction to move in."

He reaches across the table and grabs a notebook and pen. "Make fun of Hannah all you want, Bailey, but look. She brought paper."

"Paper can be destroyed," Nathan muses. "Good idea, Hannah."

She gives me a playful little smirk.

I laugh and gesture at the board. "Okay. Now, let's talk about this Tyr and Fenrir thing. I admit, I'm not the expert in mythology here, but they never boned down, that I can recall. What's the point of symbolically making them have a baby?"

"Good point." Hannah writes, *"Not literal symbolism"* as a bullet point under *"Nathan and Bailey reproductive spell"*. She uses blue, so we know it's not a definitive answer.

I love my best friend.

There's a knock at the door. Suddenly, any sense of ease we may have felt as we got lost in our brainstorming? It's gone.

Xiao unlatches her holster and moves to open the door. I'm fully expecting a werewolf to burst in and bite off my other hand, but it's just Tara, standing in the hall with a gym bag that looks like it's about to burst.

Her gaze flicks down to Xiao's hand on the gun and Tara says timidly, "Bailey said there was a meeting?"

I can't believe she actually came. When I told her before, she'd been almost hostile in her level of non-commitment.

"I didn't think you'd come," I blurt, unthinking.

"Do you want me to leave?" Her eyes narrow in a petty expression I recognize from so many moments in our childhood, and my heart nearly bursts. This tiny drop of bitchiness momentarily quenches my fearful thirst for reassurance that we'll be sisters again someday.

The catch here is, I didn't tell Nathan she might join us.

"Pardon me," he says. "I say this with the utmost

respect to you as my sister-in-law and as a member of this court but with your history—"

"You're talking about the weird spell they put on you," Tara interrupts him confidently. "I know more about Norse lore than you do, and I've been researching nonstop since eleven this morning. Do you want my input or not?"

Without looking to Nathan for confirmation, I say, "We do. Please, explain."

She opens her bag and removes a few tattered paperbacks. The spines are unreadable, they've been cracked in so many places. One is missing a cover. All of them have a forest of neon tabs jutting out from their sides.

I hear Hannah's audible gasp of delight and admiration. I'm surprised she doesn't ask for brand, style, and inventory number of the tabs.

"Our pack is so obsessed with the story of our origins, we ignore the story of our ending." She opens one of the books and it lays flat, pages perilously close to falling out. There's a woodcut illustration of Fenrir devouring Odin.

"Ragnarök." Tara braces her hands on the table on either side of the book. "It's not an end, so much as a renewal. But for the gods, it's very much an end."

"I don't like the sound of that," I say, dread piercing my heart. "You know, since they're using Nathan and I as avatars for gods in their little plan."

Tara's expression is grim as she looks each of us in the eye, one by one. "The thralls aren't planning to end the world. They're planning to end the gods.

"They're planning to end *us*."

CHAPTER 69

The thralls want to exterminate werewolves? "That doesn't make any sense. They need us—"

"Needed us." Tara stresses the past tense. "They have all the arcane knowledge they need now, except for one thing."

"Dominion over life and death." Nathan stands and paces the length of the room.

The earlier sense of proactive hope sucks from the room.

"They basically forced you two to breed," Hannah says. "Dominion over life."

"There's more." Tara steers us back toward her research. "After the gods fall and the earth is submerged in water, life begins again. Two humans survive Ragnarök: Lifthrasir and Lif."

"How do they survive the end of the world," I ask, silently tacking on *and who would want to?*

"They hide. They run away to the woods and hide until everything is over," Tara says with a shrug. "And when they come out, they repopulate the world."

"That would be dominion over death, wouldn't it?" Nathan suggests. "Rebuilding anew on top of that destruction?"

"Are the thralls acting out Ragnarök, then?" Hannah wonders aloud, tapping her lips with the capped end of her marker.

Tara holds up her hand and flips it back and forth slightly. "They're certainly using the symbolism. I think we can safely say that they're trying to start something new, without us knowing about it."

"How does all of this tie in with the Right of Accord?" Ryan asks. "If that's how the binding was put on you, what's the significance there?"

"Make that another thing your team investigates," Nathan says, then, to Tara, "And perhaps you can find some parallel between the Right of Accord and something the mythology?"

"Nothing off the top of my head, but I'll keep digging," she promises.

"What I don't understand is why they would want to get rid of us all, but kick that plan off by making another one of us." I add, "And wait patiently for potentially millennia for that to happen."

"What is it about this specific moment in history?" Nathan asks. "What is it about Bailey and me, in particular?"

Ryan scribbles those questions down, nodding. "This is good. We can definitely work with this. "And with Your Majesty's permission, I'd like to ask the Lady Tara to join our committee."

Nathan doesn't answer right away, and every breath that passes before he does just winds the tension in the room tighter.

She's come to help us, I plead silently, wishing telepathic arguments were part of the binding. *Don't reject her. She's the best ally we have.*

I can see these same thoughts turning over and over in Nathan's mind, but each one must be branded with "traitor!" on them. Finally, he says, "Your sister trusts you. That's enough for me."

It's not. He's going to be watching her like a hawk. But I give him a grateful smile, anyway.

"I have a feeling we'll walk away from this meeting with more questions than answers," Hannah says grimly.

Ryan is quick to reassure us. "Questions are good. Questions point us in the right direction."

"Eventually." Nathan adds that caveat. "A lot of those directions will point us straight to dead ends."

"We have to work fast," Ryan agrees. "We need to know, by the next full moon, what's been planned."

"And how us uncovering the plan has changed it," Tara adds. "Will thrall efforts ramp up now that they know we know?"

"Maybe we shouldn't have gone to the Hierophant," I say.

"That's in the past," Nathan replies. "There's nothing we can do to change it, so we have to look ahead."

"And at the moment, the thralls don't appear to be your biggest concern," Ryan points out. "It's werewolves who've tried to kill you."

"Werewolves working against thralls," Hannah reminds us all. "Whatever the thralls are trying to do to all of us, the most immediate threat to Bailey and Nathan—sorry, the queen and king—seems to be werewolves."

"The easiest time to strike will be the full moon," Xiao

says. "You'll all be in you werewolf forms. Accidents happen."

"Not to me," Nathan practically growls.

I wave my stump at him. "To me, though."

That shuts down his ego a bit.

"There's something else we need to talk about," Hannah says, casting a glance toward Xiao. "Something that should be for werewolf ears, only."

"I trust Xiao with my life," I say.

Hannah barely waits for me to finish. "We all do. But this isn't about feelings or civility. It's not even about trust. This is werewolf business. For us alone."

Xiao gives me a questioning look and I nod. Without another word, she opens the door and steps through it.

"She won't listen," I promise.

"The conference room is soundproofed, anyway," Nathan says, waving a hand. "What do you have to say, Hannah?"

Hannah takes a breath. "The full moon is coming up."

"Bailey and I won't change. We'll remain here, under guard, at Aconitum Hall," Nathan declares, and my heart sinks. I've gotten to be in my werewolf form once. Just one time. I was looking forward to transforming again.

But Nathan's right and I can pout about it later. We *will* be more vulnerable in a dark forest with potential traitors.

"That will keep the two of you safe, but what about the rest of the pack?" Hannah argues. "Two werewolves have failed in their attempts to kill you, the objects of the thralls' spells. The thralls know about it. So, who's to say that they'll even allow us to turn? We're interfering in something they thought they'd kept secret. They could easily poison us, trap us, do anything to us when we set foot on that ceremonial ground."

"If all of us stayed home, they'd get suspicious," Ryan says. "Maybe they'd believe we were against them."

"Aren't we?" I ask. "They're working magic on us against our will, without our knowledge or consent. They're working against all werewolves."

"That's what we theorize, yes," Ryan says. "But for now, let's operate under the assumption that werewolves are your greatest threat, because they are. The thrall plan is coming to fruition. That's why werewolves are getting desperate."

I place my hand over my stomach. "They're running out of time."

Ryan points his pen at me.

I lean my elbow on the table and drop my head into my hand. "You realize that if Nathan and I do run… we're helping the thralls. We're basically working against all of you. You all might be safer if they killed us."

"Never!" Nathan snarls. "I don't care if we have to put the necks of every man, woman, and child in this pack on the block, they will not have our child!"

"You wouldn't," I say, shaking my head slowly. "And I wouldn't let you."

"And we won't let you entertain thoughts of giving up or sacrificing yourself for the good of the pack," Tara snaps. "This is our pack. No thralls get to manipulate us and wipe us off the face of the earth. Turn your wrath toward them, Nathan!"

"That's why I wanted Xiao out of here," Hannah says calmly. "We need to be realistic. If there's no other way to save the pack, we might have to take drastic measures."

"Like?" I ask.

"Like putting them down." Hannah glances around the table. "Don't look at me like that. We're talking about a super-powered brand of human that could take over the entire world. Decide the fate of each and every creature on the planet, once they've reached their end goal, which seems to be eradicating us."

"They could kill anyone, at any time," Tara says. "They would have that power."

"Or they could keep them from dying," Ryan adds. "There's a *Twilight Zone* episode about that."

Once a nerd, always a nerd. But he has a great point.

"We know that werewolves want you dead," Ryan states firmly. "And we know that thralls need you alive.'

"And they need that baby," Tara adds.

"Exactly," Ryan continues. "So right now, your best bet for survival is to stay away from werewolves until we can shut down this thrall plot."

"How do we do that?" I ask. "Just turn out the lights, pretend we're not home? We're the king and the queen. We can't just quietly drop out of our lives."

Tara points to the book. "Make like Lifthrasir and Lif. Head into the woods."

We all stare at her.

"We find a secret location and send you there," she goes on. "We tell the pack that you've gone into hiding due to a credible threat from the Saint-Laurent pack. They've already tried to kill you."

"Probably for the same reason Harriet tried to kill you," Ryan adds. "I'll look further into the motives behind the Saint-Laurent plots."

"If we leave, we look like cowards," I say, not liking the idea of that at all.

"Maybe you will," Tara concedes. "Or maybe all these rich assholes with round-the-clock security and panic rooms will think it's totally reasonable."

"You don't have to cede the throne while you're away," Hannah goes on. "We just don't let anyone know where you are, you continue to preside over pack matters from there, and we make it clear that this is being done to protect the future of the pack by protecting your progeny. No one needs to know anything about the thralls or the spell or the fact that the two of you might be key to, you know. Ending our entire species?"

"One problem at a time," Nathan says wryly.

"What about the thralls?" I ask.

"As long as you're still a part of their plan, they can't kill you, right?" Hannah says, and I do hope that she's right. "We can use that. They continue to protect you while we continue to investigate in secret."

"And when we don't need them anymore..." Tara raises her eyebrows.

I can't do it. I can't face another mass execution. I can't have more blood on my metaphorical hands. No more deaths on my conscience.

Nathan, however, doesn't seem to have that same view. "They should pray that such a time never comes."

That's what I'm going to pray, too.

CHAPTER 70

We plan furiously, and fast. Xiao secures a location, a tiny cabin that's way off the grid in Manitoba. We'll be isolated from the world, but most importantly, from the pack; they don't know that our thralls have hideouts all over Canada.

Even though she only has to make a few calls, we decide not to chance letting anyone know that we're leaving. Yet again, we're bugging out. We're leaving our kingdom because our subjects want us dead.

It's almost midnight when Nathan and I go to my bedroom, and I start hauling out all my luggage.

"You don't have to pack tonight," he says gently.

I don't look at him. "I don't have to. But I'm going to."

"You'll tire yourself out. We'll have a long drive tomorrow."

I shake my head. "Then I can sleep on the drive."

Nathan comes to my side and puts his hand on my arm. "Bailey… don't do this to yourself."

"Don't do what?" I snap. "Take anything with me to

fucking Manitoba? Just resign myself to dying in the wilderness, ripped apart by polar bears?"

He doesn't get angry at my tone, which pisses me off more. I'm angry. Not at him, but at this whole situation, and situations can't fight. I want to fight someone. Why won't he cooperate?

What he does is gently stroke my hair back from my face and whisper, "This isn't a failure."

My heart crumples in on itself. How did he know that was my primary concern?

I turn to him, tears in my eyes. "You said that leaving the seat of power during a coup is basically giving up."

"As it turns out, this is much bigger than a coup." He sits on the bed, elbows on his knees, hands hanging. "This is something I'm completely unprepared for. I'm out of my depth here. It was one thing when we thought we were fighting a potential takeover from another pack. But we're at the center of a conflict between thralls and werewolves."

"And the only way our side can win is if we die." I can't handle any of this. "We were supposed to sit down with all of Hannah's office supplies and solve this tonight."

"I think your expectations might have been a bit high," Nathan says with a gentle sigh. "We will not die for the pack, or for any other werewolf. If we have to stay in hiding for the rest of our lives, we will. And we can. Because we have each other."

"I don't know if you've noticed, but we're not exactly a dream couple with a dream marriage." The words are bitter on my tongue. "We only just started getting along and not hating each other."

"I've never hated you," he says, sounding hurt by the

suggestion. "I've never resented you or felt burdened by you in any way."

"I guess I didn't hate you," I admit, though I'm tired of admitting it. "But we're strong together. I don't see why we have to run."

"We are strong," he agrees. "But we need to know when to retreat from a fight."

"The thralls put this spell on us." My voice quivers with fear. "And now we're going to their secret location."

"But the thralls haven't been trying to kill us. Our own kind has," he reminds me. As if I needed reminding of that fact. When I came back from my five years away, I expected some people might dislike me. I never anticipated murder attempts.

Being away from the pack, I can handle. I've done it before. It's the total isolation from civilization that frightens me. "No one will know where we are."

"Hannah, Ryan, Tara, Xiao." Nathan counts them off on his fingers. "Do you think they're going to abandon us?"

"No." I laugh softly. "They could probably get all of this cleared up by next weekend."

He smiles. "There she is."

I raise a questioning eyebrow.

"My mate." He bumps his fist lightly under my chin. "The woman who hasn't balked at a challenge yet."

I look away. "We don't have much time. You should go pack."

"You should rest," he argues.

I shake my head. "No. I'm not going to run off to the wilderness without a change of clothes. Multiple changes of clothes, actually. I doubt there's a washer and a dryer."

"I'll help you," he says, standing and retrieving my largest bag. "Just tell me what you need."

"I need you to go pack your own stuff," I say with a tired laugh.

"I don't have any flannel, so I doubt there's anything appropriate for me to bring along." He disappears into my closet with the bag and calls back, "How many evening gowns do you think you'll need when you're being ripped apart by polar bears? Or can we skip those?"

I laugh and cover my face with my hand, then get to my feet.

———

In the parking area behind the private entrance to the residence, I hug Tara, Ryan, and Hannah.

"I'm leaving you in charge of the royal office while I'm gone," Nathan tells Ryan.

Sputtering at his sudden, serious promotion, Ryan assures him, "I will do whatever is asked of me, Your Majesty."

"There will be times we can't communicate safely. During those times, I trust you to make decisions in my absence that will protect and sustain this pack." Nathan puts his hand out for Ryan to shake.

And instead, Ryan drops to one knee and kisses the royal ring.

"Oh my god," Hannah mutters in embarrassment.

But hey, it's not like Ryan is as used to be around Nathan as Hannah is. To Ryan, Nathan is still the king, not a friend's mate.

"I don't know if this is safe. You, pregnant, going out

into the wilderness. What if something goes wrong?" Hannah asks as I power down my phone and hand it over to her. We can't take any devices with us; they're too easy to track.

I've been trying not to think about that, but I can't think of a reasonable alternative. "What if I stay and someone bites off my other hand?"

"Good point," she says, tears shining in her eyes as she goes in for another hug.

"Everything is going to be fine," Tara reassures me. Before, it would have been Clare's job to make sure Tara and I hold it together, but now, Tara and I just have to lie to each other.

"It will be." It's going to have to be. "Xiao is going to bring letters back, when she does a supply drop. We'll be in touch. It just won't be as immediately in touch."

"We survived five years apart. A few months is nothing." She throws her arms around me one last time.

Well, I hope just the last time for now.

"Your Majesties?" Xiao prompts us as she shuts the trunk. "We should move."

"Right." We wanted to be out before sunup. "Okay, guys." I give them all a tight smile. "Don't fuck it up while we're gone."

"We'll do everything we can to get you back, safely, before the baby comes," Ryan promises.

"All you have to do is sit on your ass and worry about growing that baby," Hannah adds, and I laugh, but I have to look away before they see my tears.

Nathan and I slide into the backseat of the car—not our usual royal sedan, but a generic four-door family car that won't garner any attention on our way out of the city.

I think about Ashton's warning to me about the pack's control of the police and fear slices through my heart. What if they're waiting for us? What if they know our plan?

"We'll drive to Moosonee. There's a plane we can take around Hudson Bay. I can put it down right in the lake by the cabin; no track in or out," Xiao briefs us.

"You can fly a plane?" I'm impressed.

"A small one, yeah." Her eyes meet mine in the rearview mirror. "I've got you, Your Majesty."

I give her a close-mouthed smile and look away as she steers the car down the drive. The towers and gargoyles of Aconitum Hall watch us go, and I watch back, all the way to the gate.

Nathan squeezes my hand. "We'll be back."

Will we? We'll be far from home, under the protection of people who have worked with our enemies for millennia. People who put a spell on us, who are using us as tools to bring about a hopefully metaphorical apocalypse. We will rely on thralls for food, for safety, for shelter, all the things we thought we provided to them.

Every werewolf in the world has believed that simply being in our magical presence was enough payment for the class who serve us. We gave them access to our homes, our lives, our secrets.

Our power.

And in all of those years, we never thought to tap that power for ourselves. Because we were too vain and lazy, too blinded by our belief that our arrangement with the thralls was equally beneficial, while secretly believing we were in control.

"We'll be back," Nathan says again, and I wonder who he's trying to convince.

Because as we pull out of the gates, as the spires disappear from view, I say goodbye to Aconitum Hall in the hopes that we never return.

ABOUT THE AUTHOR

Abigail Barnette is the pseudonym of Jenny Trout, an author, blogger, and funny person. Jenny made the USA Today bestseller list with their debut novel, *Blood Ties Book One: The Turning*. Their American Vampire was named one of the top ten horror novels of 2011 by Booklist Magazine Online. As Abigail Barnette, Jenny writes award-winning erotic fiction, including the internationally bestselling The Boss series.

Jenny has been featured on television and radio, including HuffPost Live, Good Morning America, The Steve Harvey Show, and National Public Radio's Here & Now. Their work has earned mentions in The New York Times, Entertainment Weekly, Slate, Vulture, and Fangoria.

A longtime supporter of community theater, Jenny has appeared on stages across West Michigan as Annelle in Steel Magnolias, Julia in Two Gentlemen of Verona, Bea Bottom in Something Rotten, and Hunyak in Chicago, among many others, and has worked behind the scenes as everything from director to prop master. They are a proud Michigander, parent of two, and spouse to the only person alive capable of spending extended periods of time with her without wanting to kill them.

The story continues on the Radish serialized fiction app,
May 2023

Or in paperback and ebook, summer 2024

www.ingramcontent.com/pod-product-compliance
Lightning Source LLC
Chambersburg PA
CBHW062103290726

48975CB00001B/85